Praise for *Again to Carthage*

"*Carthage* is a worthy sequel, and could make a runner out of a couch potato. . . . *Carthage* becomes a training manual, a nutrition guide, a love story, and a celebration of friendship based on the shared experience of runners training to the very threshold of what the body can endure."

—*Chicago Sun-Times*

"The last three paragraphs . . . they're perfect. You might have seen them coming, but I still think you'll find yourself breaking into a smile."

—*Runner's World*

"The training and racing sequences will resonate with anyone who has pinned on a race number whether for the Olympics or the neighborhood fun run."

—*Galveston Daily News*

"The author conveys the raw emotions that come with hard workouts and racing in a way that resonates with people devoted to the sport."

—*Buffalo News*

"One of the best accounts in print of the physical and emotional torments athletes endure in their superhuman efforts."

—*St. Louis Post-Dispatch*

Praise for *Once a Runner*

"By far the most accurate fictional portrayal of the world of the serious runner . . . a marvelous description of the way it really is."
—*Sports Illustrated*

"Time has not taken a toll on this gem. . . . Runners will find inspirational passages everywhere that they will want to save."
—*Minneapolis Star Tribune*

"Don't let twenty years of pent-up anticipation and expectation ruin your run through this book. It's paced a little like a marathon—controlled start, strong finish. . . . Don't think you have to be a world-class athlete to connect with Quenton Cassidy and love this book. If you've ever trained and competed at your own highest level, you'll get this guy."
—*The Kansas City Star*

"A finely-crafted work of fiction."
—*St. Petersburg Times*

"Part training manual, part religious tract, part love story, and all about running, *Once a Runner* is so inspiring it could be banned as a performance-enhancing drug."
—Benjamin Cheever, author of *Strides: Running Through History with an Unlikely Athlete,* in *Runner's World*

"*Once a Runner*'s famed ability to convey the thrill of the sport leaves its mark."
—*St. Louis Post-Dispatch*

"Inspirational."
—*Chicago Sun-Times*

Also by John L. Parker, Jr.

Once a Runner

Runners & Other Dreamers

Marty Liquori's Guide for the Elite Runner
(with Marty Liquori)

Run Down Fired Up and Teed Off

And Then the Vulture Eats You
(editor)

Uncommon Heart
(with Anne Audain)

Heart Monitor Training for the Compleat Idiot

Again
to
Carthage

A Novel

John L. Parker, Jr.

Scribner
New York   London   Toronto   Sydney

SCRIBNER

A Division of Simon & Schuster, Inc.
1230 Avenue of the Americas
New York, NY 10020

First Scribner trade paperback edition October 2010

For information about special discounts for bulk purchases,
please contact Simon & Schuster Special Sales at
1-866-506-1949 or business@simonandschuster.com.

The Simon & Schuster Speakers Bureau can bring authors to your
live event. For more information or to book an event contact
the Simon & Schuster Speakers Bureau at 1-866-248-3049
or visit our website at www.simonspeakers.com.

Manufactured in the United States of America

1   3   5   7   9   10   8   6   4   2

Library of Congress Control Number: 2004106530

ISBN 978-1-4391-9248-1
ISBN 978-1-4391-9249-8 (ebook)

The author gratefully acknowledges permission from the following source
to reprint material in its control: Sony/ATV Music Publishing for
"Hallelujah," © 1985 Sony/ATV Music Publishing LLC. All rights
administered by Sony/ATV Music Publishing LLC, 8 Music Square West,
Nashville, TN 37203. All rights reserved. Used by permission.

This is for my brother, Jim,
owner of two Purple Hearts and one of red,
still beating, thank God, after all of that

In such a night
Stood Dido with a willow in her hand
Upon the wild sea banks and waft her love
To come again to Carthage.

—Shakespeare, *The Merchant of Venice*

You've crossed the finish line,
Won the race but lost your mind.
Was it worth it after all?

—Lazlo Bane, "Superman"

Again to Carthage

1

Newberry Redux

THE CABIN SAT back off the road in the dripping trees like a part of the forest itself, earthy brown and plain, with a skin of cedar shakes, organic but for its giveaway straight edges. In the gloomy afternoon downpour the familiar shape seemed the essence of refuge.

Could it possibly have been just a year? Yes, and some days.

The screened-in front porch wasn't latched and he had already retrieved the front door key from his shaving kit where it had been for more than a year. Cassidy backed in dragging two big canvas equipment bags, disturbing spiders at work, breathing in the familiar scents of raw lumber, mildew, and the pepper and loamy decay of Spanish moss and north Florida piney forest. The place was perpetually unfinished inside, with stacks of building materials lying around and wiring showing in bare stud walls. Bruce wasn't kidding; he hadn't been out in a long time.

He dropped his gear in the chaos of the so-called living room and just stood there with his eyes closed, the cascading scents of an earlier life making him dizzy with nostalgia.

As the rain deflected slightly off the steep sides of the A-frame, it occurred to him that this was the kind of day that seemed to happen in your life when Something Big had just ended. He flashed on a day from his central Florida childhood, the last day of the school year in junior high; he was waiting for a ride in the tropical downpour under the bus shelter in the empty parking lot. Everyone was gone and he could feel his aloneness settling over him like a damp shroud. There were parties going on somewhere, he thought. Ordinarily, a summer stretching out in front of him like a small infinity of freedom would have filled him with primal kid joy, but he was just plain morose.

His father was late, but it wasn't unusual in the days of one-car families for kids to spend a lot of time waiting for grown-ups. His occasional bouts of melancholia made no sense to him. He put his stupid decal-covered three-ring binder on the ground and lay on his back on the concrete bench, contemplating a wasp's nest buzzing electronically overhead. He had not made any teams and he wasn't one of the cool kids and most of the teachers couldn't remember his name. That didn't bother him, but what *really* got to him was the sudden revelation that this rainy nothing day was what all of life eventually came to, that everything sooner or later devolved to a point somewhere on the gray horizon where you're just some sad kid waiting alone in the rain.

Now, standing alone again in the cabin as a young man, he had experienced a number of such rainy End of Something days in his life. But because he was still young and little touched by death, these days often had to do with school years or athletic seasons.

Back before it all happened, during all those long days, nights, weeks, months, and years of training, he thought of the future as a kind of foggy diorama. If everything turned out the way it was supposed to, his later life would be some kind of stroll with a desirable female into the middle distance, a happy American epilogue befitting the narrative line, inspiring music crescendo-ing into the Warner Bros. logo, a glad coda for a three-act culture.

But he had always kept it nebulous in his head, and now that the time had come he found that the girl had actually married someone else and gone away and he had not Won the Big Race and he would not grace any cereal boxes. Also, he didn't know how to stroll and there was no music except for one eerily chipper Gilbert O'Sullivan ditty he could not turn off in his head, something about climbing a tower and launching yourself into the indifferent void. Standing there in the familiar musty half-light of a late-summer thunderstorm, he thought, It's just like the lady always said: no bugles, no drums.

The small television set was where he had left it in the oven, cord wrapped round and round. A bunch of books were still stacked next to the cot in the small bedroom in the back: *A Fan's Notes, The Bushwhacked Piano, Zen and the Art*. He had done a lot of reading out here as he lolled around between workouts, trying to coax his body back to life so he could go out and carefully brutalize it again.

Loll. That was the word for it. Time lolled away napping, thinking, daydreaming, waiting for his damaged corpuscles to rearrange themselves into a more perfect union.

He went to the plate-glass window at the front of the cabin and, sure enough, down in one corner were the faint dusty outlines of the words he had written in reverse mirror script on the foggy pane one lonely winter afternoon long ago: *Help. Imprisoned in February.*

I should unpack, he thought. I should make the bed, get this place organized, *something*. But there it was: no ambition. At all at all.

So, he did what he had done so many thousands of times before when his life was at loose ends and he didn't have a thought in his head: He pulled on his togs and blew out the front door and was hitting right at six-minute pace before the screen door had even finished double-slamming behind him.

His battered lemon-yellow 914 was still clicking in the cool rain as he splashed down the rutty red-clay drive that always reminded him of North Carolina. He turned at the blacktop and after a quick half mile veered off at the familiar trailhead and disappeared into the forest. He had felt so logy that he was surprised his legs loosened up quickly on the carpet of pine needles, and it wasn't long before he fell into a miler's tempo stride and began clipping miles off at not much slower than five-minute pace. It was much too fast for overdistance, he knew, but he wasn't training anymore. He was just running.

The trail went deep into the endless stand of blackjack pine and water oak and up by Otter Springs and then almost all the way down upon the Suwannee River, where in fact very few old folks stay. Four miles into the run at the bottom of a gentle rise he called Blackberry Hill he was startled to see his own ghostly footprints at the edge of the trail. He remembered the day he had made them long ago. It was rainy like this and he was skirting a big puddle, trying to keep his shoes dry as long as he could. Strange to think the evidence of his ephemeral passing would still be here hardened into the earth, partially hidden by encroaching weeds, like poor little Lucy's footprints on that plain in Africa, still there after three million years. Taking the hill with big strides, he thought, We never really know what will happen to the scratches we make in this thin dust.

Familiarity made the trail go by quickly and he blinked back from a daydream having to do with bill fishing in the Gulf Stream to realize he was almost finished. Good thing too, with the glistening woods now darkening before his eyes. Eight miles and he hadn't seen a living soul. He had seen a herd of deer, a probable wild turkey—at this distance he couldn't be sure—a red-tailed hawk, and several mullet evading predators or just jumping for joy.

He finished, as usual, going hard down the last perfectly straight row of Sidecar Doobey's pecan grove, the flat grass inviting speed and bringing on the old fantasy of being in the final straight of the Olympic 1500, straining to reach the leader, leaning for the tape and reminding himself over and over: go *through* the tape, go all the way through it, with nothing held back. Just like the old days when he would be out there with Mizner and the guys, running along the sidewalks of Kernsville in pretend slow motion as the half-miler Benny Vaughn did his mock-serious announcer, giving them all funny foreignized names to make them sound more glamorous, doing the play-by-play as they made agonistic faces and leaned histrionically toward the imaginary finish line. Benny had named him Quintus Cassadamius, the famous Greek miler. It struck him for the first time just now—and with a quick flare of pride—that a new generation of dreamy kids might now accord him his own name. In these mock race scenarios Bruce Denton had no glitzed-up fantasy name, a gold medal being about as glamorous as you could get in their little world. Cassidy wondered now if maybe a near miss was worth something too.

Funny, he thought, I was there in real life yet running down this lane I go back to the same old fantasy. We few who get to experience both eventually find out that the real thing and the fantasy can coexist in your head. He would love to tell the undergraduates about that. It was the kind of thing they would talk about for hours on training runs. Mize, Nubbins, Burr, Atkinson, Schiller. Old dour Hosford. They were mostly gone now, graduated or otherwise scattered. Off to wars, other schools, wives. Where oh where, he wondered, are my light-foot lads? What has become of *the old team*?

He jogged in from the highway using the long driveway as a cooldown and was glad he had left the porch light on, dark as it was getting. He toed off the muddy shoes and left them outside, fetching a dry towel from the bedroom but returning to the porch to continue dripping. It wouldn't do any good to shower yet, he would just start sweating again, so he plopped down in an aluminum lawn chair and watched the rainy night come on. He had been wet so long his fingertips were wrinkled. Steam rose from his skin.

He didn't know if it was bad yet. Bruce said it would get

very bad before it got better. That was just part of it. The big buildup and then the *really* big letdown. Worse than you could ever imagine.

Truth be told, though, at this moment he was feeling pretty darn good.

He was through with the Trial of Miles, the quest that had consumed him these past umpteen years. He was wet and hungry and, in a general epistemological sense, adrift. He was sitting on a borrowed porch at the end of the road at the end of the summer at the end of his athletic career, dripping salty rainwater in a perimeter around a cheap aluminum chair. And he was once again staring into the moist gloom of Marjorie's ancient piney flatwoods.

But twenty-seven miles away back in Kernsville catty-corner from the campus was a white-columned faux Southern mansion that housed the University City Bank, an establishment founded by Sidecar Doobey's old man with the obscene profits he made running rum on shrimp boats from Key West up the west coast of Florida to Apalachicola, thence to Tallahassee and Atlanta on the seafood trains, bonded booze disguised by a scant layer of ice and red snapper, but in actuality protected by a well-paid bridge of crooks stretching from Monroe County all the way to Washington, D.C.

That bank had been his last stop before heading out to Newberry that afternoon. It contained a safe-deposit box, number 1347, newly opened in the name of Quenton Cassidy and paid for a year in advance, the key now dangling from the fresh-air lever of the beat-up Porsche in the front yard. Box 1347 was in the lower left-hand corner of the far wall of the vault. It was the smallest size offered. The slide-out metal drawer held only one item: a flat oblong leather box.

In that box was an Olympic silver medal.

2

Breakfast Game

"FRIED GREEN TOMATOES . . ."

"Good one."

". . . with freshly ground red, black, and white pepper in the batter!"

"Very good one. Some of these Southern delicacies have grown on me and that's one of them. How about this one: generous hunks of freshly cut pineapple . . ."

"Oooooh . . ." Cassidy's salivary glands jumped.

". . . served on a bed of shaved ice!"

The midmorning sun was baking the steam out of the glistening landscape, but not unpleasantly so, as they made their way along the trail at an easy pace, playing the Breakfast Game, which meant they would soon be driving around looking for a Shoney's.

"Okay, here's one and this will probably do it for me: cheese grits—"

"No grits!"

"Yes, cheese grits, real ones not instant, with salt and pepper and a little melted butter on top, but here's the kicker: interspersed throughout are chunks of that thick brown-sugar-cured bacon."

"Hmmm. Bacon, you say?"

"Brown-sugar-cured and cooked not too long, just nice and firm."

Denton considered this.

"Okay, as long as you put in the bacon. The grits then become just a transport medium for the cured meat and the dairy product."

Such is the guiltless chitchat of rare-as-iridium beings with less than five percent body fat. They ran along in comfortable silence, lost in thoughts of buttery dishes. When they reached the bottom of Blackberry Hill the undergrowth closed in on the trail so that even going single file they both got a good chilly brushing with wet leaves from both sides.

"Ick. Trail's not gotten a lot of use lately," said Denton.

"Guess not," Cassidy agreed. "You look like you're in shape, but obviously not from running out here."

"Nope. Been sticking close to home working on the ol' thesis. Getting in some miles though. The heels have been better lately. I've been thinking about racing a little."

They ran along in silence for a while. Then Denton asked, "Cass, are you really sure you want to be out here?"

"What do you mean?"

"Staying out here at the A-frame, away from everything."

"Why not?"

"It's just maybe not such a good time to be alone."

Cassidy considered this. Denton had never told Cassidy a single important thing that had not sooner or later turned out to be true.

"There has been something of a letdown," Cassidy admitted. "I know you warned me, but I honestly didn't think it would be this bad. It's a weird feeling . . ."

"I know."

"Kind of empty, you know?"

"Yep. It can get pretty bad."

"I've had a few bad days, but I'm all right. I've survived blue funk before."

"Well, I've talked to a lot of guys and it's pretty typical no matter how you did, win lose or draw. The thing itself is so cathartic, so *final*, that hardly anyone in the Games will have thought much beyond it. I read that somewhere, but I didn't understand it until I went through it. Come to think of it, it's one of the reasons that every one of you is there on the starting line in the first place. It's the single-mindedness that got you there."

"We definitely know our way around deferred gratification," Cassidy said.

"It's your *life* you've been deferring, Cass. That comes crashing in on you. Maybe it hasn't really hit you yet, but it will. You're maybe still sort of in the slipstream of it all, the hoopla, the interviews, the boondoggle invitations, flying around, your relatives calling to say they saw you on TV . . ."

"I think I'm out of the slipstream already," said Cassidy glumly. "Maybe that's the hidden blessing of coming second. Anyway, that's one of the reasons I wanted to come back here. I wanted something familiar."

"Ah yes. It helps to have something to come back to, that's for sure," said Denton. "Well, you're welcome out here. You know that."

Another silent mile went by.

"Heard anything from Mize?" Denton said.

"He's doing flight training in Texas. Helicopters. Says he loves it. I sure hope the whole mess is over before he goes over there and does something stupid."

"I don't know if it's ever going to be over. What happened to the army track thing?"

"He decided against it. Thought it would be copping out. He doesn't think much of the war, but he's strange about these things. You know what he also considered?"

"What?"

"Being a medic."

Denton whistled.

"He's always been like that. He wasn't in ROTC to line up a deferment either. In his own weird way, Mize has always been a kind of true believer. In another age he would have been a Quaker or something. But no. No track dodge for him. I'm sure they offered it to him."

"And no medic. Helicopters."

"Helicopters. Little ones. With guns on them."

"Well, to change the subject only slightly, what did you decide about school?"

"I'm going to go. I can't think of anything better to do. There's no deferment, of course, and I don't have a family like you, so I have no idea what I'm going to do about that, but I haven't been called up for my physical yet, so I'm going to at least start it."

"Where?"

"I'm thinking of staying here. At first it was just my backup, but I think I've changed my mind. Duke and Vandy are better law schools, but right now I can't imagine picking up and going to some new place. I'm thinking of taking some time off and starting winter quarter. They're being incredibly nice to me at Tigert Hall for some reason. I'm apparently no longer considered just a pain-in-the-ass loudmouth from a nonrevenue sport."

"Public opinion's shifting. Even Cronkite has turned. McNamara'll go to his grave saying our so-called police action was the only way to stop global blah blah. He'll be the only one. But hey!"

· "Yeah?"

"Want some advice?"

"No."

"Go ahead and start school now. Take some time later if you need to, but start now."

"Okay."

"I'm serious."

"I know."

"It will make it easier."

"Okay."

"And remember what Jumbo Elliot used to tell the Villanova guys."

"What was that?"

"Live like a clock."

"Live like a clock."

"Right."

"Live like a clock."

"That's what I said."

"Okay, I give up. I find Jumbo opaque at best. Where did you get this anyway?"

"Liquori. What Jumbo meant was keep to your schedule. If your morning run was always at eight A.M., you go out and do a token run at eight A.M., even if you're tapering for a big race or on summer break. You're not really training, you're just keeping your body on the same routine. Eat at the same time, sleep at the same time. Live like a clock."

"Like Mussolini's widow."

"How's that?"

"After the war she'd go work in the fields from sunup to sundown. People would say, Why do you do that? She'd say, It's good hard work and when you do it all day you can sleep at night."

"I guess."

"So this is like I've just seen my spouse strung up upside down with his mistress by an angry mob after losing a world war? That what you're saying?"

"No, I'm saying live like a clock."

Cassidy gave him a sideways look.

"Think about this," Denton said. "A man with a hundred-dollar bill and a day to live might conceivably—under the right circumstances—have himself a wonderful time."

"Okay," Cassidy said dubiously.

"But a man with a hundred-dollar bill and a week to live might well be in serious trouble."

"Anyone with a week to live is undoubtedly in serious trouble, regardless of his finances," Cassidy said.

"Context, Cass," said Denton. "Context and chronology are everything. Timing, if you will."

"I don't like it when you start 'if you will'-ing," Cassidy said glumly.

"You've capitalized yourself mightily to this point," Denton said. "For years and years now, putting everything in, taking nothing out." He gestured at the trail in front of them, as if it represented all their trials and all their miles.

"But it's perfectly okay to live your life a little now, Quenton," he continued. "You've earned at least that much. No one will blame you, no one will fault you. Everything doesn't have to hurt, everything doesn't have to be a battle."

Cassidy snorted. "How would *you* possibly know—"

"I *know!*" Denton said, too loudly. They ran in silence for a while, Cassidy thinking to himself, Oh Jesus, what an addlepate I can be.

"I wish someone had been there to tell me," Denton said quietly.

"Mmmm?"

"To live like a clock."

"Okay, Bruce."

They ran quietly again. Finally, Cassidy said: "Bruce, I've been doing that very thing for *years* now . . ."

"Exactly!"

"I lived like a clock for nearly four years in college, through quitting school and racing Walton, through the buildup for the trials, and then right to the finals of the goddamn Olympic 1500 meters."

"Right."

"And you're telling me—"

"To keep doing it."

3

Hadley v. Baxendale

ASSIDY RECLINED UNCOMFORTABLY, twiddling his thumbs on top of his paper-bibbed chest, watching Dr. Clark Hodge squinting up at the X-rays. The orthodontist occasionally turned back to Cassidy and, by gently grasping the point of his chin, rotated his head this way and that, murmuring, "Hmmm!"

Cassidy tried not to glimpse the film, finding it just plain alarming to recognize the faint outlines of his own lips and jaw and the less familiar but denser mortality that was his skeletal self. It was more, really, than he wanted to know.

But Dr. Hodge could not have been more fascinated.

"Well, well!" he exclaimed, tossing the X-rays onto the tray that also held Cassidy's sunglasses and a disturbing plaster model of his upper and lower jaws. "No doubt about it. Definite class-two malocclusion, moderately severe. Unquestionable case for appliances and possible follow-up orthognathic surgery."

"And it will keep me out of the draft? This is definite?"

"Oh, it's definite, all right all right. Every practitioner in the country just got a Selective Service directive referencing possible prosecution for unwarranted treatment. They sounded serious."

"I've been sweating this out for months, trying to get into ROTC, the Guard, and it's nothing doing. The waiting lists are huge. But this sounds too good to be true."

"Oh, it's true, all right. Uncle Sam wants you, but"—he paused for dramatic effect—*"he does not want your overbite!"* he said happily. Leaving the room with the X-rays, he called back over his shoulder: "You have no idea how good this has been for business!"

Quenton Cassidy began law school nine days later with a mouth full of gleaming wire and a grateful heart.

He quickly found his mind surprisingly amenable to little mental gymnastics like the Rule against Perpetuities, joint and several liability, *res ipsa loquitur,* and constructive breach.

And on the news every night and in the headlines every morning, the collective national horror show marched on like a wave of zombies no one could stop. My Lai, the Tet Offensive, Fire Base Alpha, Hamburger Hill, the Cambodian Incursion, it just went on and on and when you didn't think it could get any worse, it got worse. And then it got worse again. It struck Cassidy that the black-and-white photographs and the blurry video were mostly of things burning: villages, helicopters, monks, babies. It went on and on and no one really seemed to know why.

Cassidy and most of his classmates had been by stages incredulous, angry, frightened, ashamed, stunned, and finally numb. They went to rallies, they signed petitions, they wrote letters to the editor, and they even—in a paroxysm of irrelevancy—occupied the office of university president Steven C. Prigman, who was on a quail-hunting trip in Alabama with the president of the state senate and was thus regrettably able to become enraged only after the fact. Orators from the panhandle railed in Tallahassee about campus radicals and outside agitators and the governor snarled to reporters about long hair and other grooming issues. Legislation was proposed, but stalled in committee.

Cassidy lived like a clock.

Or at least he tried to. He ran most days. Five miles, six miles, ten, it didn't matter. It was so much less than the hundred-plus miles a week he had done for years that it wasn't hard at all. He even found—surprise!—joy in it again. Psychologically it was much easier to just go out and run than to be constantly bending his body and mind to an ironbound training regimen, where every workout had a purpose and every mile led to some far-off goal. He just ran. He was no longer a fanatic. He found that if he missed a day no comet came to destroy the planet, and if he missed two or three days in a row, it did not indicate a major character flaw, destined to snowball into a lifetime of lethargy and decadence. It was just a missed day or two. It took him a while to get over the old fear and guilt that once defined him, the unthinking discipline he had inculcated in himself over many years. But once he was over it, life seemed gentler somehow, less combative. Though he wouldn't have described himself as happy, he was mostly content.

He tended his little garden in the faint receding limelight due an Olympic also-ran, enduring with grace the occasional honorary event or award or recognition someone or other felt necessary to bestow upon some poor slob who, after all, was but a tick of the clock away from actually becoming somebody.

Quenton Cassidy had once been a runner. Now he was something else.

4

Green Skin of Hill

Getting shot at was not nearly as glamorous as it sounded, but it certainly held your attention.

And parts of it were a helluva lot more fun than most guys would admit. That was the way Mizner saw it. It had a school's-out, don't-sweat-the-small-shit quality that made the rest of life seem almost sleepy, faded, less contrasty.

At least that was the way it was for aviators, and it seemed more or less the same for the ARPs, the elite aeroriflemen he mother-henned every day. Maybe the true land-bound grunts felt differently, he didn't know. He had little interaction with them, but he suspected they felt it too.

Mizner was far from being one of the heroin-laced warrior-poets, but he had come to believe that however fucked up it was in so many ways, war could be amazingly interesting and occasionally quite beautiful.

You'd soar dreamily over an endless green skin of hill, lovely and serene and remote somehow like an aquarium, mesmerizing to watch rolling below. Sometimes you'd go down to peek beneath the leaves and see things right out of "Kubla Khan": gorgeous waterfalls, magic temples, a wild tiger ogling you with ancient yellow eyes. They wanted to land, roll up their cuffs, put their feet in the water, have a picnic. It was nuts. Skeeter once got off a quick shot at a dark-haired soldier in a gray uniform sitting in the top of a tree. The "soldier" immediately leaped fifty feet to the top of another tree and disappeared into the canopy. I saw his *face*, Lieutenant, Skeeter said later, I could *describe* him to you.

But most of the time what you got down there was the smell. That familiar repulsive stew of fish-based feces, rotting vegetation, and aviation fuel that would fill you with both revulsion and ennui and would forever be the essence of Vietnam for a lot of people. Then sometimes the jungle would start spitting up little yellow gashes of death at you and you would never be more focused on anything else in your life as you would on what was down there in the leaves trying to kill you.

And the hardest thing to do was to look directly into the harsh light of kill-you hate coming right at your eyeballs. To look unflinchingly into that light though every instinct in your being told you to look *away*. Skeeter claimed the light was physically painful to look at.

"You have to look at it though, sir," Skeeter told him their first time out. "It's hard to do but you have to make yourself look right at it."

If you couldn't look at it you couldn't kill whatever was making it and then you were very likely to get killed yourself.

He had had the minigun for some time now and he had used it a little but Skeeter was the one who did most of the damage, sitting behind him there in the doorway with the monkey strap his only physical connection to the motherland, an M-60 hanging from a steel cable bouncing in his lap like a big phallic bird, a box of frags nearby and the different-colored smokes ready on the wire while Mizner did what he was supposed to do and had been expensively trained to do and actually *liked* to do, and that was to fly the thing.

The thing was the OH-6A Cayuse, the loach, the so-called light observation helicopter that had become the focal point of his entire existence, that had in fact saved his life many times now. If such a thing were possible Mizner had fallen flat in love with the tough little machine.

Traveling at altitude to and from their assigned kill boxes at a hundred knots, he would slump comfortably in his seat with his right leg cocked up outside the open door to pick up a little breeze, bracing the collective with his left leg and flying with his left hand as the aquarium passed safely far below. But when they really went down into it and the radio was crackling with three and four levels of carefully monotoned battle chatter, he would have his shit tightly wired together, zipped up, tight sphinctered, and serenely focused. He would yank an armpit full of collective and goose the cyclic all over hell and back, working the pedals like a tricycle, making the little bird do whatever circus tricks he had mastered and some that he just made up on the spot, necessity being, he often maintained, the motherfucker of invention.

Skeeter had also seemingly come to terms with this strange line of work that involved finding a few scattered human beings in a vast jungle and making them dead. But they had been shot down together—once three times in one day—and they had both been wounded and they both had friends who had died sitting in a seat full of their own blood. Neither of them slept worth a damn and Skeeter occasionally hung out with the heroin guys.

"Will I meet them again?" Skeeter had asked drunkenly one night in the so-called officers' club in Phu Loi. A door gunner was no officer but like most of the pilots Mizner carried an extra set of silver wings for him when they were loitering off their own base somewhere. "The people I killed," he said to Mizner's raised eyebrows. "Do you think I'll meet them all when I die?"

Mizner shrugged.

What will I say to them? he asked the pilot. The guy in the

spider trap under the rubber tree who tried to shoot us down at the Michelin plantation, the one with the little kid? The girl in the cart with the hidden AK, who smiled like an angel and then threw down. Put one in the door frame so close I got steel splinters in my cheek? Is death where you get together again? Is death a final rendezvous of killers and killed?

There there, said Mizner.

They were working a steep valley, way out of their usual range, where fuel was always on their minds. They were in the usual pink team, supporting some kind of dumb-ass LRRP insertion that had gone terribly wrong. White loach, red Cobra gunships, two blue Hueys with their aeroriflemen—flying grunts, ARPs. And another complete team not far away on scramble alert, which meant playing cards and waiting for an invitation.

The snakes loitered upstairs while Mize skimmed the trees on the valley floor. He hadn't seen a thing until something flashed by right under them.

His headphones crackled: "Hooches," said Skeeter. "Equipment and stuff."

Mizner reported the find to the snakes as he kicked right pedal and worked the collective and cyclic to bank hard right and get a ways off. That was something you learned to do, come in from different directions, different speeds. Lots of guys didn't do that and lots of guys were dead.

As they flashed over this time Mizner spotted some AKs, an SKS semiautomatic, and some other military equipment lying around. "Pegasus three one, Pegasus one nine. We got hooches, tracks, weapons," he said into his mike. He heard the *chee-chee,* Dulin keying the mike twice: affirmative.

Cobras don't talk, thought Mizner.

Then: muzzle flashes. A red smoke grenade went down and Skeeter's 60 started cranking behind him as he kicked right pedal again, letting Skeeter hose the area as they banked off.

"One nine *taking* fire. Put your rocks on the red smoke. We *didi* now."

Chee-chee, said the radio.

He continued banking the bird as Skeeter hammered away, then he turned again and started working his way up the side of the hill to get the hell out of the way of the gunships, which had already lined up for their rocket runs before Mizner had spoken. They could have done this whole familiar dance without saying a word.

"Pegasus three one in hot," said Dulin, the Cobra talking at last, and he was. The jungle danced with fire and light.

Up on the hillside the hot air was funky humid and the chopper blades were clawing away at it impotently as Mizner neared the military crest of the hill like a slow fat June bug. Then they went directly over an enemy gun position and were shot full of holes almost immediately.

Mizner saw a .51-caliber on a tripod and a guy behind it working it for all he was worth. There were three or four others, too, very intense-looking NVA regulars with AKs, all firing on full auto. They had obviously seen the helicopter coming from a long way off and were good and ready for them.

At nearly the same moment he saw the enemy soldiers Mizner heard a bunch of metallic pings and knew instantly that they were hit all over, probably including the fuel cells—which were supposed to be self-sealing except that when they got shot up like that they weren't self-anything. Just about every alarm and warning light in the cockpit was going off and the collective and cyclic sticks were jumping in his hands and even the pedals were fighting him as the cockpit filled with smoke. He hadn't even had time to say *Taking hits* . . . into the radio. He was working hard just to stay airborne.

They had almost no forward airspeed and the whirring blades were biting nothing solid, so they really were sitting ducks. Jeezus, he thought, what were the odds of flying blind right over a gun position like that?

His instincts were to stall the tail rotor, do a hammerhead turn, and roll back down the hill, building up speed and staying aloft long enough to find a soft spot to autorotate down into. He actually thought about it for a second, but saw immediately that it would have taken them right back over the same gun position and then back down into the valley where the snakes were making another run. He really didn't have any choice but to try to climb the hell out of there. He could hear Skeeter behind him leaning out of the door and pouring lead back behind them.

The actual crest was coming up beneath his bubble finally and he had the collective to his chin, pulling as much power as he could, but it was going to be close. If they only had some firm air they might be able to claw their way out of there, but this hot gas was useless, a helicopter pilot's nightmare. Though his main focus was the crest he was also scanning the jungle for places to crash, as well as glancing at the instrument panel and trying to gauge just how badly fucked up they really were. That was more a function of his training than anything else because he could tell from the noise and the lurching of the ship just how bad it was. His heart raced at the rare bleat of the chip detector over the other alarms because it indicated pieces of metal in the engine: The machine was eating itself.

At some point the master alarm went off, and they were technically not supposed to be in the air any longer.

Over the noise he heard Skeeter's grim, satisfied voice on the intercom: "Got you, sonuvabitch." His gunner had killed their gunner.

They both knew if they crashed within range of an operational enemy .51-caliber machine gun they might as well go ahead and die in the crash. For the moment at least there wasn't anyone firing anything serious at them. Skeeter kept pouring fire back behind them as they lurched noisily on toward the crest.

Mizner almost slumped in relief when they finally reached it, but then he made a mistake. It was excusable maybe, a matter of habit, not something you could train for, or perhaps even be aware of. As he barely cleared the top of the hill, he instinctively pushed the nose down, getting ready to descend the back side, and knew it was a mistake because the ground effect disappeared. They had barely stayed aloft on the cushion of air a craft gets from its own thrust waves bouncing back directly from the ground, and when he pointed the nose down, even that left them.

Despite the sudden drop, Mizner thought they had a chance, and he strained backward on the collective as if it might have a magical inch or two more to give. The top of the hill was bare, so at least they didn't have to worry about clearing any vegetation, and Mizner really thought they might slip over.

But then the right skid caught in the ground at the very top and it flipped the sick little bird up into the air like a shuttlecock and slammed it down on the far side of the hill, rotors tearing into earth and vegetation, destroying everything around, including the rotors themselves. Inside the loach it felt like a very dirty and dangerous carnival ride, but once the rotors were gone there was a quiet, peaceful second or two when Mizner thought it might be over with him still alive. His right triceps felt like he'd been stuck with a hot poker, but he was otherwise apparently unhurt. It had gone dark light dark light dark several times as they rolled, but then that stopped.

Then, ever so slowly, he felt the bird turning on its axis, becoming perpendicular to the fall line, and then it started again. Slowly at first but picking up speed as Mizner braced himself in the cockpit as best he could, swearing out loud as map cases and K-Bars and clipboards and ammo magazines slashed and stabbed them all the way down, eighty feet or more, dark light dark light dark light dark light dark light dark light, and finally very dark and very wet and he was drowning.

Mizner remembered that the valley on the other side had been rice paddies, but they weren't in cultivation, so they were supposedly dry. But then he also remembered the bomb craters everywhere, left from a long-ago B-52 shitstorm, most of them partially filled with dark, unholy water. He was drowning in an open septic tank.

Skeeter, meanwhile, was being held underwater by his own monkey strap. All the way down the hill he had been thinking, Well, at least we're out of range of the .51-cal. And we've got friends who surely saw what happened. We might make it after all.

But once everything was still and quiet in the dark water he couldn't for the life of him get to the goddamn buckle on his goddamn monkey strap. The straps were all different, not military issue at all. Everyone knew that even the helicopters themselves had never been designed to carry weapons and that everything about this fucked-up war was ad hoc. Each door gunner concocted his own getup and went down to the dink store to have it sewn together.

So Skeeter had made his so that the buckle was on the chest and easy to get to. The problem was, it slowly dawned on him, the buckle had worked its way up under his chicken plate and there was no way in hell he was going to be able to dig up under the tight armor to get to it. He was going to be drowned by his own safety strap.

Then he remembered his K-Bar, which he used mostly to clear jams in the machine gun. It was sharp as hell and if he could get to it he could cut himself out of there. As he was feeling around for it he was running down mental checklists. Did he have any broken bones? Was he bleeding badly anywhere? What weapons could he get his hands on?

The K-Bar was strapped to his leg where it was supposed to be and he yanked it out and started hacking at the monkey strap. He cut his own forearm once and the strap in three different places before it released him, and he was very close to breathing in a lungful of the noxious water when he stood up frantically through the doorway of the helicopter ready for a huge gulp of God's own air. But though he knew he was out of the water, he was still drowning. His helmet and visor were still full and he had to wait several more horrible seconds for them to drain.

Shit!

He was looking into the faces of three very surprised North Vietnamese soldiers. After one stop-motion frame of shock, they scrambled for their AKs, now casually slung on their shoulders.

Skeeter quickly went back under the murky water, ripping off his helmet and frantically feeling around for any kind of weapon as he heard the sodden plinks of bullets hitting metal and water all around. His 60 was pinned up under the helicopter and probably would have exploded had he fired it anyway. He felt around for the CAR-15 assault rifle but couldn't find it in the jumble. There also should have been an M79 grenade launcher, a .45 pistol, and a box of frags, but the only thing he could get his hands on were the frags.

He was almost on the verge of breathing water again by the time he got two in his hands and the pins out. Like Poseidon rising from the depths he stood up through the door again, taking in a huge breath and throwing both frags at the same time, in opposite directions across his body, before ducking under the murk again. He felt around, grabbed two more, pulled the pins, waited until he could stand it no more, surfaced and threw them, and then went down again. He did this until he couldn't do it anymore and he rose from the water one final time ready to face his own death. That's when he felt a friendly hand on his shoulder as he cleared the murk out of his eyes and saw his pilot's smiling face.

"I think you got them with the first two," Mizner said loudly, apparently suffering some kind of hearing loss. He was standing up through his own door, his unfired .38 in his hand, his right arm soaked in blood.

Two dead NVA soldiers lay at the edge of the crater, and there was a bloody trail leading into the brush where the other one had crawled off.

"Let's *didi*," said Skeeter.

Mizner helped sling the muddy 60 over Skeeter's shoulder and leaned over to pick up several of the heavy bands of little lead bottles. He weighed them carefully in one hand and tossed all but one back. The belts might save their lives; but they might also slow them down and get them killed. Ah, war choices to delight a Hobson, he thought. But his sphincter was still a pinprick and he wasn't fooling anybody; he was scared to death. The grunts were scared in the air, and the fliers were scared on the ground. It was all a matter of what you were used to. By rocking the fuselage back and forth they had at least been able to get the big gun loose, and Skeeter wanted that gun.

With the gunner in the lead they started humping the hell out of there. Mizner noticed that his crewman had picked up some of the ammunition belts he had left behind, and he had finally found the CAR-15.

Their Cobra had been over to check them out but had gone back over the hill. Normally they would have had their own pink team capping the situation, but the other guys were probably putting more ARPs in and must have been pretty busy. You could hear the firefight from all the way over the hill.

Well, there was no question who was in charge now. Mizner was the officer and college boy and Skeeter was a noncom who'd barely gotten his GED, but if they were going to get out alive, rank didn't mean squat. They didn't see anything around them but the usual green garbagy tangle of rot and life and stingy things that is Jungle; millions of buzzy furry sets of jaws frantic to get a hunk of your skin or to eat out your belly. In some clearings the sun would break through the high canopy and brighten them for a moment, and Mizner could almost convince himself he was on some kind of hike, maybe taking a picnic down to the Millhopper in Kernsville. He flashed on a spring day an eon ago in north Florida tubing down the Ichetucknee with his friends and it caused him such pain and remorse he had to willfully put it out of his mind.

They huffed wetly along the little trail that led from the

bomb crater, and soon had slogged enough klicks to feel removed from the crash scene and thus somewhat more optimistic about life and some kind of future. Surviving the night even seemed a possibility if they couldn't get a lift out. They needed to find a place to hole up in a little clump of anything that wouldn't give them a rash.

A Huey could have maybe picked them up in a clearing without getting shot up too badly, but Mizner could tell from the noise of the firefight that they had their hands full over there. Mizner also knew from the radio chatter before they went down that fuel was getting short and that they had called in more loaches and Cobras, as well as a whole bunch of ARPs. They must have stumbled on a tunnel complex, a hornet's nest of NVA.

Mizner knew it would bug the hell out of them, not being able to get over to provide cover, not being able to extract them right away. Then having to leave to get fuel and ammo. He could imagine their oh-so-bored pilot voices on the radio. "Pegasus three niner breaking off. We bingo ammo. Gonna cut a chogie on over to Delta Tango for fuel and rocks. Be back chop chop."

They would be discussing the downed bird too, probably breaching radio protocol. But nobody would say squat to a guy who came back from a day's work smelling of cordite. If some new guy ever did start up, he instantly got The Look. The Look said, *I've been killing assholes all day and I wouldn't mind doing you right now.*

Like most pilots, Mize was usually calm under pressure, but the sound of the firefight on the other side of the hill told him the enemy owned this place and he was an interloper. The idea of spending the night out here filled him with an empty-gut terror, the kind of fear that made a hole in your stomach and then filled it with nothing but the idea of your own demise. He finally got the little prick ten, the PRC-10 emergency radio, working, but he could only receive. Apparently no one could hear his polite requests for assistance. The little radio was drenched and beat to hell, so it was a wonder it worked at all.

As they stopped once more to catch their breath, Mizner knew he was getting too weak to go any farther. Skeeter saw what was happening and steered them into a dense little thicket of something that looked like mountain laurel. Mizner's knees buckled as he slung the bandoliers onto the ground. There was even a small depression, so they were almost defiladed. He slid down to rest with his back against a tree.

He sat and watched with dull eyes as Skeeter used his own shirt to bind up his arm. It was loss of blood more than real fatigue, the gunner knew. Normally the lieutenant could hump all day and into the night like a regular grunt, and the grunts knew it too. They had both gone out with the ARPs before just to see firsthand what they did. The soldiers were amazed at the pilot's stamina, and when Skeeter told them where it came from they started calling him the Runner. They didn't know or care much about his past; none of that shit mattered out here, but they knew he could hump their asses off and that impressed them.

Mizner knew there were trees out here with sap that could eat your skin and he could probably remember what the leaves were supposed to look like if he could conjure up a memory from survival school, but at this point he was so goddamned tired he really didn't care. The arm didn't feel that bad, but there was a lot of blood and he worried more about leaving a trail.

Skeeter finished with the dressing and smiled at him.

"I'm going to go see if I can find some water, sir," the gunner whispered as he inspected the bandage again. "It's not really that bad, sir. Lost a lot of blood, but it's through and through. Probably jus' a fragment." Skeeter was talking very low, with great sympathy.

He patted Mizner's good shoulder. "You been carryin' most of it so you sit and rest," he lied.

He stood up and gestured vaguely around the little clearing. "And sir, try to straighten this shit up. Hooch is a rat hole."

Mize smiled weakly and waved him off. He was asleep before

his hand dropped into his lap. When he heard what he thought was Skeeter coming back he also heard a metallic click that sounded both familiar and alarming. He opened his eyes and was shot right between them.

It was the most important event of his young life and he missed it.

The firefight on the other side of the hill went on all afternoon and into the twilight. Trying to get the reconnaissance guys out, some of their own ARPs had gotten pinned down, then another blue team of grunts trying to relieve them had been pinned down, and then a Huey putting in still more grunts had been shot down. Two other loaches had been knocked down in the valley trying to support their aerorifle platoons on the ground.

It was one giant deadly goat rodeo is what it was.

When there were enough resources to send a loach over, Skeeter set off a smoke marker but he was nowhere near a clearing and the place was still crawling with enemy. Somebody from two boxes over had reported more moving NVA regulars and *tanks*. The loaches loitered for a while and put down some fire, but when they tried to get down to them they got shot up so quickly they had to pull back out. Eventually they got low on fuel and left. Another one showed up for just a few minutes to see if they were still alive and then he left too.

By late afternoon Skeeter was having a hard time staying awake but he could hear enemy all around him. Finally just before dark some Cobras came over and killed a lot of them and sent a lot of the rest scattering. But some of them got dug in pretty well and now it was obvious to the rescuers that the downed fliers couldn't move. If they couldn't get them to a clearing, they'd have to wait until they could get enough grunts over to get them out. They weren't coming up on the emergency channel so no one knew what their situation was.

What it was, and the others overhead had no way of knowing this, was that Skeeter wouldn't leave his pilot. He hunkered down in the dark and he jabbed himself in the leg with the tip of his K-Bar to stay awake. They almost found him several times.

At first light the next morning he thought he would cry when he looked up to see the sky filled with lethal bees, looking for their own, looking for *him*.

When they found him and saw he still could not move they took turns dropping in overhead and taking out their frustration on the surrounding countryside. Each time they stopped, the enemy would fire back a few times to say, *Still here, asshole.* They put down smoke markers and had the snakes make rocket and guns runs. Still they fired back. Skeeter chuckled. Tough-assed little bastards, he thought.

It went all the way up to a colonel circling somewhere overhead in a C&C Huey, who got red-assed all over again. Then *he* talked to someone back at the base, and then they got good coordinates on where the downed fliers were. Then they rechecked the coordinates again all up and down the chain of command.

Then they called everyone out of there. Everyone.

It grew so quiet that Skeeter could hear Vietnamese chatter around him. Then a little FAC OV-10 prop plane flew in and went straight to work marking various places with his rockets. The NVA were shooting everything they had at him because they knew what it meant.

When the FAC flew away it was quiet for a few minutes before Skeeter could hear them coming from a long way off. The fast movers flashed overhead and several seconds later the whole jungle became an earthly hell of vertical dirt and vegetation that seemed to go on and on. Skeeter was certain he could not survive it himself, but he did.

A few minutes after that they came back and ran their belts dry, glittering brass cascading incongruently into the tropical tangle below, some of it landing, still hot, on Skeeter, who didn't panic like the grunts sometimes did, having swept enough of the stuff out of the back of his loach after a busy day.

Another loach buzzed in to do a battle-damage assessment, poking around a bit until he amazingly took some scattered fire. He fired back for a few minutes, but then he left too.

Skeeter was stupefied that anything could be living out there, much less still fighting. But then it was quiet for a while and because the enemy seemed preoccupied, he allowed himself to doze off.

Then Spooky came.

The grunts sometimes called it Puff the Magic Dragon. An old prop AC-130 transport plane rigged up as a flying gun platform, this one with four 7.62 miniguns, two 20mm Gatlings, and two 40mm Bofors antiaircraft guns. It was capable of pouring such murderous fire from the heavens that anyone who ever witnessed it, enemy or friend, never forgot it. At night the tracers would form a solid red laser line from heaven to earth, a lovely-to-watch arc that would wiggle around against the night sky like a neon garden hose when the gun moved around. And the red tracers were only every tenth round. What the neon hose did at its far end was something closer to civil engineering than to warfare. It remade the landscape. The grunts would look up in the sky and shake their heads at each other and say, *Spooky knows.*

This Spooky had already locked in the little sweet spot of friendly jungle in the middle of a huge doughnut of destruction. It then proceeded to kill every living thing for three kilometers around that spot. It circled for less than seven minutes, chopping, dicing, and mincing the earth and all its inhabitants and then straining the results through its exceedingly fine and murderous colander. Then Spooky left, satisfied as usual.

When the whole area was finally quiet and seemingly freshly harrowed for spring planting, the Hueys at long last put grunts on the ground and they went in and found Skeeter. Within a few hours it was all over the base.

There were two black-clad enemy soldiers a few feet away in the little clearing, both shot in the head. There were bodies and parts of bodies of twenty-two more at various distances in a circle around them and numerous bloody drag trails leading away into the jungle. All of the gunner's M60 belts were empty, and the CAR-15 magazines were used up.

Skeeter, a loaded .45 in his left hand, was sitting next to his pilot, gently touching his arm. The door gunner had been shot in both legs and through the right shoulder. He didn't look up at the grunts. He was talking quietly to Mizner. As the grunts told it, what he was saying, over and over was:

"Aw, jeez, I'm sorry, Lieutenant. I'm *so* sorry, sir."

5

Home We Brought You

EIGHT DAYS LATER the Runner lay in an oak box at the feet of a childhood friend on a hot little hill of faded brown grass in the middle of the coral peninsula the Spaniards named for flowers.

The faint traffic hum from Interstate 4 in the distance drifted across the parboiled landscape of scrub palmettos and spindly pines, indicating that humidity and rabid insects notwithstanding the Sunshine State was on the move.

The preacher was waiting.

Cassidy made a noise just to be sure he could. Then he pulled some cards from his inside jacket pocket and looked up at the small group.

"Robert Penn Warren wrote about how there is really no one quite like a friend of your youth. Someone who looks at you later on in life and sees you only as you were when you were young. I cannot truly comprehend that we are here today for the reason that we are, and I don't think I'll be able to understand it for a very long time. And the one person I would want to help me understand it is the one person who cannot. He was a friend of my youth and that is the way I will always think of him."

He took a deep breath and looked at the cards in his hand. From them he read about the time you won your town the race we chaired you through the marketplace and how nice it was to die young while your records were all still standing even if you weren't. How it was good to leave early while you could still remember how the people cheered for you. He had to stop a few times.

Then he put the cards back in his pocket and looked at the small gathering of mostly simple, kind American folks, women with clipped grocery coupons in their purses and men with work-roughened hands. And among them a sprinkling of very thin, intense-looking young men too, standing there with mostly dry eyes. Several of them had been to the Olympics and two of them had brought medals back.

"I want to tell you something about Jerry," Cassidy said. "I knew him about as well as it's possible to know anyone. It takes a while to finish a ten-mile run and you get to know someone pretty well when you run a few hundred of them together. One of the things I found out about him was that he was the kindest, most considerate person I ever knew. And the other thing I found out about him was that he was the toughest runner I ever knew."

There were some chuckles from the thin young men.

"We ran together and against each other since back in junior high school and, boy, he beat me and beat me and beat me." Cassidy shook his head. He looked up at them for a moment.

"It takes courage to do it, to be a runner. We all found that out a long time ago," he said. "Because it's about more than fatigue. It's about pain, and dealing with it for a long time. And it's about resolve."

He looked up to see the young men looking at him, some smiling a little.

"You can't really be much of a runner unless you have courage, and so I don't want you to worry about him, or what he went through. He wouldn't want you to, believe me. That's what

I really wanted to tell you. We ran ten thousand miles together and I can tell you that for certain."

Cassidy looked out across the hot palmetto wasteland that surrounded the little cemetery.

"He was braver than all of us," he said.

While they were preparing to lower the casket, a soldier walked over from the honor guard and stood in front of Cassidy. He looked different from the rest, who were obviously young enlisted men. This one was older, deeply tanned, with a chest full of ribbons and medals; the only one of which Cassidy recognized was a Purple Heart. There were three of them.

"Mr. Cassidy?" he said.

"Yes."

"The lieutenant wanted me to give this to you. I'm sorry to do it here but I'm leaving right away." He drew a wrinkled sealed envelope from his tunic, looked at it, and handed it to Cassidy. He stepped back, stiffened to attention, saluted, and turned to walk away. Then he paused and turned back with a little twist of a smile on his brown face.

"You were really right about him, sir."

Cassidy only then noticed the slight limp as the soldier walked to the parking lot to join the others in the olive-drab government sedan.

Cassidy walked quickly over to the car before they all got in, tapped the soldier on the shoulder.

"You were with him?" he asked.

The soldier turned and studied him closely. Cassidy saw that his eyes were glistening.

"Sir," the soldier said, "I never lost a pilot before."

He got into the backseat and the car pulled away.

There was more pain in those eyes than Cassidy could imagine in the world. It was three days before he could bring himself to read the letter and he never told anyone what was in it.

6

Daybreak in the Subtropics

IT WAS THAT crazy head-floating scent of frangipani, oleander, Spanish moss, Gulf Stream, and some kind of spicy bayonet plant that always reminded him of the aroma of drawn butter sitting beside a lobster tail.

It was a salty tropical fruit salad is what it was and it woke him to the first rays of sun over Lake Worth. He lay drowsily under a single mostly symbolic sheet watching the orange glow suffuse the stucco surfaces and arches of his bedroom, stretching deliciously and almost without movement in the rare absence of air-conditioning's false chill.

It was a Monday, which meant multiple calendar calls, frantic pink phone slips from the weekend, and general hit-the-ground-sprinting pandemonium of a litigation-oriented practice. But it was Roland's turn in the barrel, which meant that Cassidy's Monday morning belonged for once to Cassidy. That was something they did for each other, the alternating-Monday thing, and they often remarked to each other that it was possibly the only regularly scheduled event in their lives that made any real sense. The guy in the barrel would be addled with his own stuff anyway, so why not have one be addled for both. Might live longer, said Cassidy. Might sleep longer, said Roland.

The only thing that worried Cassidy was that he had a pretty good rapport with most of the trial judges and he knew very well that Roland would be in there somewhere in the bowels of the Palm Beach County Courthouse, waddling back and forth and occasionally wagging his finger, lecturing a circuit court judge on some incredibly inane point of civil procedure. Before they had begun the alternating-Monday routine, Cassidy had once wandered into such a scene.

There was Roland, huffing and puffing hugely back and forth in front of the bench, distractedly jingling change in his left pocket, holding a volume of the *Southern Reporter* with his right, an index finger hooked into the appropriate precedent but arguing from memory:

"If the court would but glance at *Pelczynski* v. *Town of Lantana*, volume 303 of the *Southern* second, page 326, argued in our state's highest court so ably by my own esteemed partner, it would find some most convincing obiter dicta to the effect that . . ." The Caesarean curls on his capacious Greco-Roman head were glistening.

"Mr. Menduni!" the judge shouted in exasperation. "This is a . . . *calendar call*, sir! I'll grant your motion, whatever it was, if you'll just tell us whether you're ready for trial or not!"

The young opposing attorney, who had never laid eyes on Roland before, watched in astonishment as Roland, mopping his brow, plopped himself down self-importantly in his chair with a look of satisfaction such that he seemed like nothing so much as a very large, very smug child.

"Yes, indeed, Your Honor," he said. "Ready and able, sir."

Cassidy knew that possibly the only thing that kept Roland from being held in contempt of court the moment he opened his eyes in the morning was that he was very nearly always, absent some extremely rare hurried misinterpretation, close to a hundred percent right. Right as rain, dead-on accurate, smack-down-the-middle right. And in the early days he had convincingly demonstrated that to several judges who, completely undone by his finger-wagging, huffy-puffy, know-it-all personality, had ruled against him out of sheer animus. Roland had dutifully taken the poor magistrates "up" and had each of them resoundingly reversed, all without charging his clients a red cent for the favor, just because Roland was Roland.

And of course Roland excelled in the calmer, more academic appellate world, where he treated the judges' panels with a modicum of respect, and where pedantic personalities—when accompanied by solid arguments—were accorded a more thoughtful hearing.

It was a good strategy, getting those reversals early on. No trial judge liked being spanked in an appellate court, where all the world could read of his disgrace at length and between hard covers. For all time.

Roland still exasperated some of them, but they now knew to pay the hell attention to the "stupendous fatty," as one of Cassidy's friends called him.

Cassidy strode smoothly across the bridge toward the southern end of Palm Beach as the sun was still clearing the low vegetation of the barrier island. He couldn't help thinking, It's almost decent for running.

Despite growing up not ten miles from here and having run thousands of miles back and forth across this very same so-called lake, he never liked running or competing in the heat. Even the scant few hundred miles up to Southeastern University had blessedly placed him in a kinder clime for his schooling and racing days.

Up ahead he saw another runner heading in the same direction and Cassidy automatically searched out a traffic gap and crossed over to the other side, but it was no use. In a few seconds he was even with the fellow, whom Cassidy thought he recognized from some local races as a fairly decent age grouper, a thirty-four- or thirty-five-minute 10K guy. So of course when Cassidy glanced ever so slightly over his left shoulder he saw that the fellow had increased his pace to keep up.

Cassidy dropped into miler gear for the rest of the bridge and then turned alone toward the deserted Everglades Club, where he hopped the fence and thus gained access to God's own Atlantic Ocean.

It was a stunning morning on the beach, perfectly clear with a light breeze coming off the Gulf Stream but the sun high enough now to warm any exposed skin. Cassidy scarcely needed it. Though shirtless, he was already glistening as he made his way along the hardened strip of sand at water's edge. The ocean itself was almost a Bahamian turquoise, the darkened twin reef lines clearly fingering their way down the coast fifty yards out parallel to the waterline.

Cassidy didn't think much of the concept of the "runner's high," but as he made his way down the crystal-sugar-white-blue-green-autumn-cool-salty-and-faintly-fishy weekday beach he had to admit that he felt pretty darned decent. Yessir, pretty darned decent right at this very moment, right here on the edge of the Atlantic, Planet Earth, Mind of God.

It didn't hurt that he was still in okay shape despite being a very former Olympian, that he perhaps overly relished such opportunities to play hooky from the real world, and that he still thought of himself as being in his twenties despite evidence to the contrary. If he had also been in love it would have just been too much.

He was exactly six foot two and if he was up any at all from his racing weight of 167 it was only by a few pounds, unnoticeable to civilians. The raggedy sun-streaked and teammate-chopped hair that had in school won him the sobriquet "Blond Brillo" was now more professionally trimmed and conditioned,

and though he had honestly come by some squint lines around
the eyes, the high cheekbones and the general—despite being
relatively fair complected—red-brown visage were much the
same as when he had been younger. In fact, he had had dif-
ficulty at times, particularly when not suited, convincing some
new client or other that he was in fact the real attorney and not
somebody's kid playing behind the desk.

After he had gone an estimated two miles or so, he stopped
and toed off his sockless running shoes, pulled a mask and snorkel from the small of his back, and tiptoed into the surprisingly
warm water. He loved the push-pull of the little waves washing in and out, brushing prickly coral sand and periwinkle frag-
ments back and forth across his ankles and excavating tickley
grooves under his arches and toes.

When he was deep enough he did a flat eyes-closed racing
dive into the salt sea, being careful not to dislodge the mask now
riding on his forehead, snorkel dangling every which way. He
porpoised underwater a long way out, then surfaced and swam
like a human the rest of the way to the inner reef line where he
turned over and kicked along, facing the sky while he removed
the mask, turned to spit in it, rinsed and then placed it properly
over his eyes and nose. He bit on the snorkel mouthpiece, blew
hard, upturned, and disappeared into the blue-green.

A witness would have thought him surely drowned.

Skin diving and running were surprisingly unalike, but Cassidy had spent much of his childhood underwater and he had
long ago taught himself the studied serenity necessary to stay
down a very long time.

When he finally did come up, he surfaced barely long enough
to spout a hard bullet of seawater straight up, then kicked leisurely along the reef line trying to keep his backside low in the
warm water and out of the chilly air, seeing what there was to
see there among the living coral. What there was to see was
a swirl of impossibly gorgeous life-forms unsuspected by most
land dwellers: beau gregories, queen angels, rock angels, ser-

geant majors, blue tangs, yellow tangs, top hats, Cuban hog snappers, porkfish, butterflyfish, squirrelfish, lookdowns, bar jacks, grunts and wrasses of various types, and even an occasional dinner-sized grouper or snapper. He knew them all on sight, and loved them all.

Now he was merely a happy spectator, but on those occasions when he hunted the edible ones, he did so as he imagined a Native American would: solemnly, filled with respect and something not quite sympathy. To his mind the worst outcome of any hunting foray would be to mortally wound an animal and have it slither off heartbreakingly sideways to escape. If it holed up somewhere that he might still get at it, as grouper often did, he would be up and down, up and down until he either retrieved the poor creature or exhausted himself beyond all good sense.

And because even now he was a hunter at heart his senses reacted instinctively to the merest flash of potential prey: the neon sideways V of a yellowtail snapper, the mottled hide of a sizable grouper, the distant wiggling feelers of the much-prized spiny bug.

On his way back to shore, it was many many pairs of just such feelers that caught his instantly rapt attention: a conga line of nose-to-bung lobsters so long it disappeared into the distant haze of the amazingly clear water. He had seen such things on Jacques Cousteau but, in all the years he had plied these waters, never in person.

Now here was a quandary.

Cassidy couldn't resist. He slipped off his nylon running shorts and wrapped them around his hand, swooshed down on the scattering line, grabbed three of the sharp-skinned creatures and wrung their tails off right in the water, then swam back and jogged home with them cradled against his side. He suffered a few inevitable cuts in his hand but the salt water would heal them quickly.

$\mathcal{L}$

The house was a 1940s-era whitewashed Spanish Mission style, built around a courtyard gone wild with flowers. The thing Cassidy liked best about it was a little screened-in breakfast nook right off the kitchen out from some French doors that were never closed.

That's where Harry Winkler was when Cassidy came in red from heat and exertion to toss the lobster tails into the already overflowing freezer. He then went to the sink to run cold water over his shaggy head. Winkler looked up from the sports section of the *Palm Beach Post*.

"You been fishing?"

"Unintentionally. Ran into a conga line. Ever seen one?"

"Not in real life. Really? How many?"

"Couldn't tell, but a *lot*. Didn't have a thing with me, of course. Wrapped my shorts around one hand for all the good it did. But they're definitely walking out there. Probably means the gray groupers are coming in too. Hell, it'll be time for the mullet run before you know it."

Deprived of seasons, they measured out the year by pelagic fish movements.

Cassidy plopped down at the little table with a huge glass of orange juice, a banana, his training calendar, and a much-abused composition book. He made a notation on the calendar and began writing in the composition book, peeling the banana with his teeth. The floral tangle all around the outside of the screen was abuzz. After a few minutes he looked up at his red-headed roommate.

"How'd the Cubs do?"

"Lost."

Cassidy went back to writing, stopped to study a huge bumblebee noisily casing out a blood-colored hibiscus bloom.

"Hey, Wink."

"Yeah?"

"Let me ask you something."

"Okay."

"You ever miss horsing around with the guys on the team, Keller and Andy Owens and those guys? Not the games and the hoopla and all, but just hanging around, listening to Mahoney philosophize, that kind of stuff?"

Winkler's all-American face clouded in thought. He had been on both the basketball and the track teams at Southeastern, and in track he'd excelled in several events, getting close to seven feet in the high jump and seventeen in the pole vault, running the sprint relays, long-jumping. In the postseason he'd competed in the decathlon and had been nationally ranked. But he made it to the Olympics in team handball, a little-known European indoor game that resembled an unholy cross of basketball and soccer, something he had picked up in the service. He could play anything.

"Yeah, I guess. Sure," he said. "Although I obviously get my quota of horseplay chaperoning my own idiots."

"I hadn't thought about that."

"But it *is* the trivial stuff you tend to remember. Like Boyd Welsh in the back of the plane coming back from somewhere talking about blowing up mailboxes when he was a kid. I don't remember much of it but he had us all in stitches. Said if there was a federal prison for juveniles he'd still be in it. Sloan heard us and came back and put the fear of God in us. We had just lost to Vandy, so you can imagine his state of mind. Come to think of it, that may have been the time we got back to campus and he made us go to the gym and have a practice session at midnight."

"Yeah, that's what I'm talking about, that kind of stuff."

"Well, you know, we do still get little doses of it, like in league basketball and the Sunday volleyball tournaments. And there's always little stunts like that mile relay you did against those guys." Winkler thought for a minute, then chuckled.

"What?"

"Well, I was thinking about golf, like in the locker room? It's kind of similar, you know? With the jokes, guys giving other guys shit about some shot or something. But it's different. I wondered about that until I finally figured out that it's kind of a watered-down version of the same thing. Except there's no exclusivity to it, anybody with the cash can join, anybody can rent a cart. That's what made the difference back then. In school everybody around you was all-conference, all-state, all-something. It was a pretty darned select group. It was something special to be a part of it, and you were always sort of aware of that."

Winkler was lost in thought for a moment, staring out at the humming tropical garden as Cassidy scribbled away. Winkler began chuckling again.

"Cass, who was that football writer guy?"

"Jenkins?"

"Naw, the other one . . ."

"Gent?"

"Yeah. He said a golf locker room was a kind of methadone for ex-jocks."

7

The Ferm

THE LAW FIRM was located in a restored old arcade called the Mews on Royal Poinciana Way. It had once contained apartments for snowbirds who were only partially filthy rich or who still hadn't figured out they had no chance to break in with Muffie and Brownie and Boopsie and the gang, the Palm Beach regulars.

Joe Kern's father had bought it for a song after the hurricanes of '26 and '28 killed so many people that no one except bootleggers and land scammers wanted to go to Florida anymore.

It was Joe's idea to move his law firm in. That was in the 1950s, when his little outfit had outgrown its rented space on Worth Avenue. The smart money said he was crazy, that their snooty clientele would never go to lawyers doing business out of a Mizneresque barrel-tile-roofed mall.

In fact, the snoots were charmed down to their Guccis, and the "Kern Ferm" prospered like the kumquat trees and Spanish bayonets in its lush courtyard.

Cassidy was charmed too, heading up the flagstone walkway to the reception area to get his messages. It was so unlawyerly to be able to pick tropical fruit outside your office door that Cassidy made a point every day of plucking a kumquat from one of the fragrant trees as he went by. He was sucking on one end of the sour little egg when he noticed that Joe Kern's blinds were open and the man himself, polo-shirted and tan, was hunched over his desk, half-glasses at half-mast, poring over a stack of depositions two feet high.

Cassidy smiled at the lovely Estelle and poked his head in. Joe looked up over his reading glasses from what appeared to be a three-hundred-page deposition and seemed entirely grateful to be dragged away from whatever chicanery it documented.

"Having fun yet?" Cassidy asked.

"Real property thing with Ronnie Sayles, an easement going back to the Conquistadors. It's holding up the whole Crossman estate. I don't know what he's up to but I know I'd like to kill him. Again."

"Join the club. Hey, guess what? The lobsters are walking."

"If you really want me to guess, you have to insert a pause," Joe said. "How do you know?"

"Saw them. Took a mask on my run this morning and swam over about a thousand of them in a conga line."

"Wow."

"I know. It's amazing to see."

"First time someone told me about that, I thought it was a joke," Joe said. "I'll call John and try to get out this weekend. Mullet should be running soon too. Oh, just so you know, Karl's apparently on the warpath again."

"What did I do now?"

"Beats me. I wish you guys could work this out, though."

Cassidy was fairly sure that he and Karl Farkus would not be able to work this out. Karl Farkus hated every membrane in Quenton Cassidy's body. Cassidy figured it was the price you sometimes had to pay for publicly humiliating a proud and stupid man.

Farkus's father, now departed, had been Joe Kern's first law partner. With a Florida cracker pedigree and a Yale education, Farkus senior bridged the two worlds so perfectly that the success of the firm was virtually assured the moment the two shook hands. The clients poured in. Fellow Yalie Earl E. T. Smith came in. Then they got old man MacArthur's insurance and corporate work. Farkus senior even brought in some of the *Kennedys'* local work. They were golden from the get-go, connected through Joe to Tallahassee and Atlanta, through Karl to New York and Boston, and through both to Miami and points south.

They started looking for a third partner right away, thinking they would hire a politically connected circuit judge off the bench if they could get one. The rumor was that it was going to be Curtis Chillingworth, a World War II hero and the best legal mind on the bench in south Florida. He had also been a fraternity brother of Joe Kern's at Southeastern. That was just before a character named Joe Peel hired some West Palm low-lifes to take Chillingworth and his wife Marjorie from their beach home in Manalapan out into the Gulf Stream in the middle of the night, drape them in chains, and toss them overboard. Joe Peel was a crooked city judge and Chillingworth was getting ready to lower the boom on him. Peel eventually got life at Raiford and the firm didn't get its circuit judge.

But those were the good old days, and though old man Farkus had been a legend in Palm Beach County legal annals, Farkus *fils* emerged from a weird and privileged Palm Beach upbringing to become merely a balding, sniveling, envious newt.

Several years before Cassidy and Menduni joined the firm, though, Joe Kern had suffered a minor but troubling stroke. Farkus senior was doddering by then and Karl was given credit for holding the firm together. He was considered golden forever after that.

"I wish I knew how all this got started with you guys," Joe said.

"You know how."

"You suppose?"

"No doubt in my mind," Cassidy said. "Big Stakes at Twin Lakes."

"Yeah? And whose big idea was that?" Joe took off his reading glasses, rocking his chair back.

"Oh, it was my fault for sure," Cassidy said. "I didn't start it, but it was definitely my fault."

"And all the publicity?"

"*Not* my fault. I have no idea how it got in the papers."

"Yeah?"

"Wiggins found out about it somehow. But, yeah, it was my fault the thing got started."

"Yeah?"

"Did you notice that from day one Karl never said my name? It was always *the runner*. It was never *Good morning, Quenton*. It was *How is the runner this morning?*"

"Yeah, I thought maybe it was just good-natured joshing."

"Good-natured? Karl?"

"Point taken."

"Then he bugged me for months to play him at tennis. I said, 'Look, I know you're good, you'll kill me. What's the point?' But he kept on so I went over to his house one Saturday morning and of course he killed me."

"He *is* pretty good. Playing at the Breakers since he was a kid."

"I know, I know. So I thought that would make him happy, that that would be the end of it. But right away he starts in again, saying we should come up with some kind of running challenge. Talking about how in high school the track coach would get him from tennis practice to come over and win the hundred in a dual meet or something."

"This I didn't know," Joe said.

"And it probably actually *happened* once, you know. But he's all the time saying, 'You know, Quenton, I wasn't *just* a distance runner, I was a *sprinter* . . .'"

"No . . ."

"Oh yeah. So at the Christmas party last year he saunters up and we've both had a few and he starts in. We need to find some sort of challenge that would level the playing field to make it interesting, he says. We could run a hundred, but that wouldn't be fair to *you*. But a distance race wouldn't be fair to *me*—you know, giving the devil his due. Then he says, 'But you know, I *have* done some 5Ks, Quenton.'"

"Yeah, that's Karl."

"Joe, I couldn't resist."

"I can see that."

"I said, Karl, I got it. We'll do a mile relay. You get three other guys, gotta be lawyers, gotta be from the county. No ringers. One lap each. Mile relay."

Joe arched his eyebrows.

"Karl's suspicious. He goes, 'Who do *you* get?' I say: 'Nobody.'"

With a thump Joe brought his chair upright, placed his elbows on the open deposition, smudging the right-hand onion-skin page. He was rubbing his face with his hands.

"Jeez," he said. "He didn't see this coming?"

"Joe, honest to God, he was all excited."

Joe Kern was still rubbing his eyes, motioning Cassidy out of his office.

"All right, all right," he said. "Go. Go now. Maybe we'll see you out there this weekend. We're cooking kingfish at my place Saturday night."

"Can I bring anything?"

"A blonde and your ukulele would be nice."

⟡

Cassidy and Roland were having bagels and coffee at Green's Pharmacy on County Road.

"You know, this was supposedly where Burt Reynolds met what'shername," Roland said.

"Dinah Shore, Roland. I was the one who told you."

"Oh, right."

"Joe's a bit older than them but he knows John Casey and some other guys from that era. In those days he was 'Buddy,' not Burt. Joe said you could dive up lobsters right out of Lake Worth back then."

"Uh-huh. I was walking by, heard you 'fessing up to Joe about the race," said Roland, trying to keep some lox from sliding off his bagel.

"He asked. I think he already knew most of it, but he wanted to hear it from me. I think Karl's starting to get on even his nerves."

"You think he's mad? About the race thing, I mean?"

"At me? Naw. He knows Karl."

"Well, one of you needs to be put out of your misery. Karl's never going to get over it."

"Yeah, I figured that."

"And did you also figure what would happen with the race? Did you know all along?"

"Not really, though after a few weeks I began to get a pretty good idea. Did you know they actually had tryouts?"

"You're kidding."

"Oh yeah. He insisted that they have time to train, and he actually got some coach from Lauderdale to help them. I began to think I'd made a serious miscalculation."

"How so?"

"Roland, you get four guys can run a sixty-second quarter mile each, I'm in trouble."

"You can't run a four-minute mile?"

"Hell no, not off the shelf. It's not that easy, Roland. It took mankind hundreds of years to do it, don't forget. It wasn't until May 5, 1954."

"May 6. But the Swedes came pretty close in the forties," Roland said, nibbling at his bagel.

"Yeah, but they gave up. Said it was physically impossible. Arne got within a second or so, though."

"Yes, but it was Gunder the Wonder who came closest."

"What? No way. Andersson was faster . . . wasn't he?"

"Not at all. Hägg clocked 4:01.3. Andersson was three-tenths slower," Roland said.

"Roland, the record before Bannister broke it was 4:01.4," said Cassidy.

"That is correct. Hägg's time was rounded upward by the IAAF when it was ratified. At the time they only recognized fifths of a second," Roland sniffed.

Cassidy looked over his fork at him with a gimlet eye.

"How the hell do you remember this kind of stuff?" he said finally.

"How can you not? I thought this was your event," Roland said.

"Okay, okay. Uncle," Cassidy said.

"I understand that a four-minute mile is a difficult undertaking, but you most certainly ran faster than that in your youth."

"Right. And the operative words there are *in my youth*."

"How fast were you figuring you'd have to go in Karl's little scenario?"

"Just enough to win, whatever it was. Karl's big mistake was insisting that they have time to train. Then he got that injury that delayed it another couple weeks. All that time I'm sneaking out, doing intervals, running the bike path. It was pretty much a crash program but I was going at it hard."

"And you really didn't know?"

"Well, after a while I started figuring it out. You know Jamie Pressley, the tennis player, at the Randolph firm? He was number two singles at Southeastern our senior year. Anyway, I knew him from the training table and we went through law school together too. He was one of the guys Karl recruited. He went to some of their practices."

"You had a spy!"

"Sort of. Jamie was training with them and saw what was going on, how slow they were going to be. He told them they were going to get creamed. Karl knew we knew each other, so he figured I'd sent Jamie in to psych them out. Jamie thought it was funny as hell."

"What did he say about their guys?"

"These are ex-jocks and in pretty good shape, but no real runners among them. Jamie told me he was about the fastest, and he could only turn about sixty-five seconds or so. Karl was much slower than that. That's when I knew."

"And they really didn't have a clue?"

"Well, it could have been closer, but one of my conditions was that after they announced their team, I got to select the order they ran in. I knew from Jamie that Karl was their slowest, so I made him run first leg."

"Why first? I would think you'd want him running anchor so you could . . . what was that you used to say, *smoke him!*"

"What I wanted was to put the thing out of reach as quickly as possible, so I made Karl run first. He runs a sixty-nine or seventy-second quarter and I ran a fifty-eight flat and that was pretty much all she wrote."

"Yeah?"

"Surely you can see this. They were nearly a hundred yards back before the first baton exchange. Naturally I slowed down a bit, and the next guy was faster than Karl, but he was running completely by himself. He made the rookie mistake of trying to close the gap right away, and of course he died completely. Same with the next guy. They just kept falling farther behind. I ran about a 4:10, which was pretty much all I had, and they were nowhere to be seen."

"Impressive. One athlete taking on four runners . . ." Roland said.

"*Guys,* Roland, they were four *guys,* not runners. Karl was clueless. Without a clue. Afterward he was asking me all kinds of questions about training, illegal substances, weird stuff like that. He didn't seem to understand that there've been lots of high schoolers under 4:10, for crying out loud."

"But how'd the *Post* get wind of it?"

"I didn't find that out until later. Wiggins told me . . ."

"Yeah?"

"Karl invited him out to watch."

8

Lucia

FRIDAY NIGHT AND Winkler was with his team at an away game, so when Cassidy got in from his run at near dark he decided dinner would be a bowl of chili at Deacon's on South Dixie Highway. He had worked late and for once passed on Friday-night happy hour.

He showered and pulled on some faded khaki Bermudas, a white T-shirt, and some flip-flops, and he was off, hotfooting it down a shadow-strewn sidewalk, enjoying the flower-scented tropical air and the nearly perfect solitude of the deserted neighborhood. Behind the hedges of hibiscus and ligustrum central air units whirred in the night, bluish flickers bounced around living room interiors, and the eastern seaboard of the U.S. of A. began easing its way into its nightly alpha-wave coma of detective shows and sitcoms.

There was something about clip-clopping along a south Florida sidewalk that always took him back to his childhood and he couldn't resist removing the rubber sandals and slipping them into his waistband at the small of his back, luxuriating in the familiar gritty traction of the warm concrete on the soles of his callused feet. You didn't see kids going barefoot much anymore—or walking anywhere for that matter—and he wouldn't have been surprised to hear that an adult walking a city street without footwear was in some way illegal.

Going shirtless in Palm Beach surely was. He went out on his nightly runs half wishing to be ticketed so he could give the town's attorney, Bill Eaton, a little lesson on Florida con law in the Fourth District.

Deacon's was busy, but not unpleasantly so, and the Deacon himself, skinny, unshaven, dour, and horn-rimmed, looking exactly like the former Washington Square beatnik he was, was holding court. He looked up and, spotting Cassidy coming in, immediately set a mug under a running beer tap. He reached under the counter for one of the big white bowls and held it up questioningly to Cassidy, who nodded yes.

Pete Dexter, a feature writer for the *Post,* was cozied in at the bar across from the Deacon. Cassidy plopped down, leaving a stool between them.

"Pete here's been on assignment again," said the Deacon, gesturing at the shaggy-headed writer.

"Pete," said Cassidy.

"Counselor."

"Don't tell me you been hiring out as a migrant worker again."

"Nope. Just got back from Orlando."

"Let me guess. You went on the jungle cruise?"

"Sort of. I was a highly sought-after recruit visiting a company HQ. They thought I was a hot prospect."

"Some kind of real estate scam? Time share?"

"No, better. This is a company called Dare to Be Great, Incorporated."

"Isn't that a Glenn W. Turner deal?"

"Yup."

"Some kind of cosmetics pyramid-sales thing where you make money by recruiting other people to come in?"

"Sort of. The cosmetics thing is called Koscot Interplanetary, which was started by the same guys. All their goop is supposedly made with mink oil, which is so wonderful they couldn't believe the minks were keeping it to themselves. That was set up as a pyramid deal and I'm told it was fairly legit. This new thing is some kind of an offshoot. They decided mixing up all that eyeliner was too much work, so now you just pay to join the organization so you can get the right to recruit other numbskulls. That's really it. There's no complicated products or services to worry about. They send you some motivational tapes and such to get you all fired up about it, but that's it."

"Wow. What did they say when they found out you worked for the paper?"

The writer took a long pull on his draft, set the mug down, and gave Cassidy a sheepish grin.

"They were, shall we say, taken aback for a moment. They asked me what I did at the paper, and I said that I loaded the trucks. They laughed their asses off, and said, 'Hey, son, you don't want to be doing *that* for the rest of your life.'"

"What'd you say?"

"I said, 'Heck no. One of these days I'm going to be *driving* one of those babies.'"

The chili was wonderful. Simmering in a Crock-Pot all day, it was the Deacon's personal secret recipe. ("Brown sugar and whole canned tomatoes," he had once whispered conspiratorially to Cassidy. "Keep it under your hat.") Topped with a handful of chopped raw onions and some grated cheddar, served with a couple of chunks of garlic bread, chased by more than one draft.

Cassidy ate with his usual postrun gusto while Dexter recounted anecdotes from his trip. Finally Cassidy pushed the empty bowl to the back of the bar, but slid the mug down to Deke's waiting hand.

"This state has *always* been a scut bucket for charlatans,"

Cassidy said. "Who invented reptile farms and underwater real estate?"

"And all those phony rocket launches and moon walks," the Deacon interjected.

"Damn straight. Shoot some eight-ball, Pete?"

"Like to, but I gotta get back and finish this story. It's running Sunday and I'm leaving in the morning for the Keys."

"You being recruited by some flimflam shrimping operation?"

"Naw. Executive editor wants to go bonefishing."

"Greg Favre is a bonefisherman?"

"Not from where I sit. I don't think he'd know a bonefish from a sardine. Said he wanted to see what all the hubbub was about. Steve Hull blurted out I was a fisherman."

"Did you tell Greg the hubbub is about catching inedible fish in extremely shallow water?"

"Tried to."

"Well."

"Just seemed to get him going," said Dexter, sliding carefully off his stool.

"Well, if either of you figures out the fascination, give me a jingle when you get back."

"You don't want to go?"

"No, sir."

"What a surprise."

"Got a brief due at the Fourth District Tuesday and if I didn't I'd lie about it."

"Gotcha. See you, Deke. See you, counselor."

"Take it easy, Pete. And hey . . ."

Dexter stopped his loose-limbed amble toward the door and looked back at Cassidy with a raised eyebrow.

"You're too good for this boig, see?" said Cassidy, doing a remotely recognizable Cagney. "You should be writin' novels or somethin'. Go talk to Exley out on Singer Island. He'll set you straight."

"Yeah, yeah . . ." Dexter said, aiming his flip-flops for the door.

Cassidy walked home feeling contented, slightly righteous over his long workday, his late and swift seven-miler (circling the Breakers twice), his abjuring the siren call of the Friday-night Greenhouse rabble, and even his losing game of eight-ball—to an out-of-work small-engine repair guy from Terre Haute who was so drunk the only thing he said that Cassidy could understand was: "Briggs and fuggin Stratton! Hah!" This right before undercutting the cue ball and sending it off the table and bouncing toward the PacMan game. He looked up at Cassidy through the smoke of the Marlboro dangling perilously from the corner of his skinny lip and gave him an outrageous wink, as if to say that a sporting gentleman like Cassidy could surely tell he had done it on purpose.

Cassidy scratched on the eight-ball on the next shot and knew immediately that this was not going to be a good pool night and that his big empty bed was looking ever so much like the better part of valor. So he headed home, this time wearing his flip-flops on his feet.

He had just propped himself up in bed with the first book on the stack, *The Fourth Floor* by Earl E. T. Smith, when the phone rang and Lucia Finch-Hatton inquired what he was doing.

"Not too much, what are *you* doing?"

"I asked first. Are you . . . *with* anyone?"

"You must think I enjoy a pretty exciting lifestyle over here on South Olive," he said.

"There's been talk."

"Well, let's see. I just got back from Deke's and was curling up in front of the fireplace with a good mystery," he said, "by myself. What are you doing?"

"I believe everything but the fireplace," she said. "I'm *roasting* over here." She didn't like air-conditioning, but her little apartment was on the Intracoastal so there was usually a breeze.

Cassidy mumbled something. He was never quite sure how to take Lucia, who had been a year ahead of him in law school and now clerked for one of the district appellate judges. He had always been attracted to her pretty, angular face and sinewy dancer's body, and she had met his interest with that hot-cold thing women do because they think it's beguiling or because they can't make up their minds.

"I was looking for you at the Greenhouse earlier," she said.

"Would have found me usually. But tonight I worked late. Brief due Tuesday out at your place."

"I'm impressed. I thought you were a true last-minute kind of guy."

"Thanks very much. Got a deposition up in Vero Monday, so this was as last-minute as I could get away with."

"Well, anyway. I saw some of your friends."

"I hope they were reasonably well behaved."

"Not really."

"Ah."

"And that place was just awful. So many people all jammed together in there. When I asked about you, your friends said to stick around, you'd be in sooner or later."

"I thought you hated that stuff."

"A girlfriend wanted to go. I told her I'd keep her company. And, as I say, I thought I might bump into you."

"Well, I'm flattered."

"No you're not."

"I can be flattered if I want."

She was silent for several moments. Then:

"So. Do you want to come over?"

So it was back into the Bermudas and flip-flops and—after some serious gargling and brushing and pit checking—it was only two blocks to her little duplex on Flagler, across from Lake Worth. There was no traffic at all and it was darker and stiller now that most of the televisions were off. But it was balmy and pleasant and he felt like the last guy awake in town, maybe the world. Central air-conditioning units ruled the night.

He saw her dimly through the jalousies and she opened the door before he could even smile. The apartment was dark save for some candles fluttering softly in the windowsills from the breeze off Lake Worth. He could see from the streetlight that she was wearing a flimsy nightgown and that was, really, all.

She was tall, tall, tall and though her breasts weren't large, they were perfectly and somehow aggressively shaped and he had long believed that they would be incredibly firm as he believed the rest of her was, and that had made him a great deal more interested, in theory at least, in the ballet, as well as in her person.

The usually primly professional "up" hair now hung nearly to her shoulders and some of it fell across her face as she reached for him, untucking his shirt and encountering goose-flesh. Her fingers felt surprisingly cool. Green eyes looked up at him through a curtain of hair, mock shyly now, really putting it on, tugging, making little noises with her tongue and lips.

Cassidy nuzzled into the hair curtain, remembering now a dozen little come-ons and semirejections over the years, going back to a Remedies class they'd had together with old man Hughes.

He was just about to say something about it when she got a really good handful of T-shirt and pulled him down to a surprisingly hungry mouth. She was a little drunk, of course, and Cassidy could only think, Christ, a clue would have been nice. An exchange of greeting cards. Something.

But later, on her little bed, as the graceful etchings of her hardened body arched and slipped sideways to find and interlock fleetingly with the wet fluted lines of his own, he thought,

It must be a tropical thing, this kind of night heat that keeps a reserved young appellate lawyer girl sleeping alone in her proper single bed, simmering in the juices of old glances and innuendoes until at last it all boils over in a phone call so late at night that only the air conditioners are awake.

9

The Island

THE TIDE WAS ON the flood so the little open fishermen had to battle their way out of the Jupiter Inlet.

Roland sat like some grand pasha on the big cooler in the back of Cassidy's boat, swathed in a huge terry-cloth robe, arms akimbo, his face hidden under an umbrella-sized sombrero, his generous schnoz glowing with zinc oxide though it was still dark. The sun hadn't thought about coming up yet.

Cassidy steered, standing barefoot at the center console, and when the twenty-two-foot craft crested a particularly large backsliding roller and they plunged down the other side, it sent a sheet of warmish seawater over them, eliciting a startled "Egad!" from the pasha.

"Sorry," said Cassidy over his shoulder.

"Is there no way to drive this contraption with more decorum?" He shook the water off his oversized hat brim.

"Not with this tide. We could have run down the Intracoastal and gone out Palm Beach, but that would have cost us some time. We'll be outside in a minute or two and it'll settle down."

Cassidy was always surprised when Roland wanted to go on these excursions. The crossings could be rough, and once in the Bahamas, the lifestyle was rigorous. Most of them slept right on their boats, a kind of waterborne camping trip, but Roland always checked into the Jack Tar Hotel on Grand Bahama Island and began making friends with room service.

He had no interest whatsoever in hunting fish with a spear and wouldn't touch a rod and reel under threat of physical punishment. But he was surprisingly agile in the water, and with the monster weight belt he wore to counter his natural buoyancy, he dove deep and stayed long. The first time he'd seen it, Cassidy was amazed.

"I'm not kidding you," Cassidy told Winkler. "He's like some great albino sea mammal. First dive he was down a minute and a half. And all he does is collect shells and take pictures. He's got this expensive plastic-encased rig, with lights and a battery pack. I told him if that's all he was going to do he should learn to tank dive. Know what he said?"

Winkler arched his orange eyebrows.

"He said, 'Bubbles scare fish,'" said Cassidy.

Winkler's eyes widened in admiration.

"And then he said that he already knew how to tank dive, that he'd been certified for years."

Winkler was a photographer too, and soon whenever he and Roland got together Cassidy couldn't get a word in edgewise for all the talk of f-stops and depth of field and such.

The Gulf Stream was as smooth as slate and this first crossing of the spring was as easy as any he'd ever made. The four little boats were able to run at more than twenty-five knots the whole way, and it was still early when Cassidy raised Indian Head Rocks on the hazy horizon. He picked up the microphone.

"Argus, Granfaloon."

"Granfaloon, Argus. Go ahead."

"Argus, I've got the rocks about five degrees off your port."

Cassidy adjusted course slightly and Bill Eaton's *Argus* and the other little boats fell in with him. Soon the water went from the deep purple of the Gulf Stream to deep turquoise as the bank began to rise from the depths. A school of dolphin appeared from nowhere and cavorted ahead of their bow wave, rolling and diving. If you looked carefully you could see purple sea fans and reefs and even swimming fish a hundred fifty feet below.

Cassidy stood at the wheel with his eyes closed for a moment, breathing in the flowery land-scented breeze of an island nation and thought, I was six years old the first time I smelled this and all these years later the feeling is still the same.

After they cleared customs and got Roland checked into his room, the boats went in different directions. Roland went on John Kern's boat along with some others who wanted to snorkel on shallow reefs. Two other boats wanted to go tank diving. Winkler left his boat, *Gator Bait,* tied up to the dock at the Jack Tar and came onto Cassidy's boat and they headed north in the general direction of Walkers Cay to dive for lobsters off the scattered coral heads in the middle of nowhere.

It was a day made of blues and greens with no clouds. The pale turquoise water was ten to fifteen feet deep in all directions, without a speck of land in sight. They had run for about forty minutes before they started to see the dark blobs under the water that indicated coral heads.

"You want to be dragg-*urr* or draggee?" Cassidy asked.

"I'll stay dry for a while longer," Winkler said. He was already at the wheel and had a cup of coffee going.

"Fine by me, I like it." Cassidy already had his mask and snorkel on, and once he had pulled on his flippers, he threw the knotted line out behind the boat and flipped backward into the sea, shivering from the mild shock of the coolish water. He had the usual sense of déjà vu in the moment when all the topside sounds muted away to the background and almost all auditory input imploded into the bubbly roar of his own exaggerated breathing.

He looked straight down on what they had thought was a coral head, but it turned out to be a tuft of purple sea fans with just a few tropicals flitting about, so Cassidy grabbed the rope and pointed straight ahead.

Winkler goosed the throttle a bit and Cassidy frantically signaled him to slow down as the rushing water nearly ripped his mask off. The draggee couldn't tolerate much more than three or four knots, a speed that seemed absurdly slow to the driver, but almost scary to the diver.

The bottom was mostly a plain desert of white coral sand, so anything with any color or pattern stood out. As Winkler steered toward likely looking splotches, Cassidy used his flippers and body angle to arc back and forth behind the boat, covering as much territory as he could, looking for hidden ledges and outcroppings as well as the more obvious coral heads. Occasionally he would drop off the line and dive down to take a closer look at something. Winkler would circle the boat around and pick him up again.

They were trolling over a nondescript stretch when Cassidy noticed the water deepening slightly and a few patches of fans and grass here and there. Then he passed over a faint line of discoloration and was pretty sure he saw a number of telltale black *V*s wiggling around. He dropped off the line and inverted himself in the water, kicking straight down the twenty feet to the bottom. When he reached the little ledge, he gripped it with both hands and peered over into the cool shadows underneath.

It was always a thrilling sight to him: dozens of pairs of eyeballs on little orange stalks ogled him as the edgy creatures tried to back up farther into the crevice, a forest of antennae waving around in rhythmic defense. Cassidy felt a Pavlovian twitching in his salivary glands: dinner!

"Whatcha got?" Winkler had pulled the boat around as Cassidy surfaced with a gasp.

"Nice little ledge, really loaded with bugs," Cassidy said, breathing hard. The snorkel hung loose as he treaded water. "Give me the hook and I'll take it down and plant it so we can anchor right on top of it. It's kind of hard to spot."

"You're not kidding," said Winkler, handing the lightweight pronged anchor over. "I can't see a thing."

Their method of scouting the bottom seemed like a lot of time and trouble to some people, but they had learned over the years that it was probably the most effective way to locate otherwise undetectable spots such as this ledge.

Winkler handed down the Hawaiian sling and got into his own gear as Cassidy made his first dive, descending on the far end of the ledge so as not to scatter the creatures, swimming against the tide and away from the ledge so that he could approach it horizontally, flat on the bottom, spear in front and ready. The sling was an underwater equivalent of a bow and arrow, the spear fitting through a hole drilled longways through a thick wooden tube and a loop of surgical tubing held fast by tightly wound cord.

There really wasn't much sport in it and Cassidy merely tried to work efficiently, dispatching the creatures as painlessly and with as little fuss as possible. He would pull back on the sling, aim carefully, and let go of the six-foot stainless-steel shaft. The point would skewer the lobster between the eyes and that was that. On the Florida side you had to catch them by hand, but in the Bahamas either a hook or an unattached spear was legal. Cassidy tried to get two or three on the spear at a time to save up-and-down time. Winkler worked more conventionally and methodically, taking one up at a time.

Soon they were back on the boat in the shade of the Bimini top, munching ham sandwiches, eyeing a cooler holding twenty-three bright orange spiny lobster tails. Winkler motioned at the cooler with his sandwich, a little smudge of mustard on his upper lip.

"If we can find a couple decent-sized groupers or snappers, we'll have dinner pretty much knocked. Not a bad morning."

"Well, Joe's boat is going for grouper. That's almost a sure thing. The tank divers will probably come back with something or other too. Roland will be in heaven."

"Yeah, well, he's going to have to trade us. What's he after this time?"

"Trumpet tritons and royal grammas."

"Empty seashells and snapshots of purple and gold inedibles. Something tells me we're in a good bargaining position."

The early-afternoon breeze was kicking up a little wind chop as they finished lunch and Cassidy looked over at Winkler, who thought Cassidy's eyes were looking decidedly bleary.

"You feel like driving this thing?" Cassidy said.

Winkler laughed. "I guess I'd better. You look like you might have about five good minutes left."

"If that."

Winkler cranked up the twin Mercurys as Cassidy hauled in the hook and stored it beneath the sleeping platform. Then he pulled the canopy up over the front of the boat for shade and plopped down on one of the triangular cushions, pulling a pair of flippers and a wad of towel under his head for a pillow.

The boat skipped along to a rhythmic and hypnotic beat on the wind chop like a child chanting itself to sleep, and it gave Cassidy a happy feeling to watch Winkler steering the boat casually and effortlessly, standing on one leg with his athlete's innate easy balance, the other leg cocked up on a cooler, his red hair blowing back in the breeze, a nautical Sundance Kid on steroids. The wake flowing in a straight line in back of the boat indicated someone good at the wheel.

In that beautiful opiate state between sun and sleep Cassidy could see through half-closed eyes the unadorned western horizon and in a quirky mind trick he could sense the entire fifty-mile stretch of deep purple Gulf Stream between the tiny wave-skipping boat and the limestone-and-coral Florida peninsula. He could sense as well the huge pelagic fish that moved through the stream deep and shallow and also all the manatees and sunfish and whales as well as all the German submarines and wooden sailing ships and blockade-runners that had plied it in years and centuries past, some bringing Tories, slaves, bricks; others taking guns, drugs, rum; and some dealing death and leaving burning American boys in oily life jackets within sight of straw-boatered dandies strolling the boardwalks at Daytona.

In his presleep state he had the sensation of being able to grasp it all at once, as if in a four-dimensional painting encompassing both time and space, his own place in it an inconsequential squiggle of comings and goings.

10

Rafting Up

C ASSIDY HAD NO idea where or who he was when he heard
Joe Kern ask Winkler, "What's his problem?"

"Two speeds," Winkler said, "full speed ahead and all
stop."

The boats were all rafted up a quarter mile off the Jack Tar
Hotel and the cooking was well under way. The distant noise of
children at play carried easily across the calm turquoise water
and the lowering sun was preparing for an outrageous show.
Winkler sat in the back of the boat minding a huge pot of seawater steaming on the Coleman stove. He was using a piece of
lobster antenna to clean the bungies out of the tails.

Joe Kern sat barefoot on the gunnel helping him, stopping
occasionally to take a sip of Heineken out of the icy green bottle
he kept close by in a gimbal.

"Almost seems like an insult to use their own antenna on
them that way, doesn't it? Don't suppose you have another one
of those around?" said Cassidy, yawning and stumbling out from
under the canopy.

"John," Joe called to his son two boats over, "toss us a greenie for the captain."

Cassidy took the beer gratefully as he sat beside Joe and watched the cleaning process. Parched, he drained half the bottle and made a little geck-geck-geck sound.

"Thirsty much?" said Joe.

"Didn't know I was that tired," Cassidy said incongruously. "How long was I out?" he asked Winkler.

"Well, dinner's almost ready if that tells you anything. The whole way back plus most of the cocktail hour, you've been gone. Henry wanted to wake you up and get you cleaning grouper, but I made him leave you alone. I loaned him your Rapala blade, by the way. He left his on his dad's boat. Speak of the devil."

Henry was crawling across the gunnel with a basket of freshly fried grouper fingers that he had been taking from one boat to the next. Very tan and slightly overweight, with his neatly trimmed goatee and crisp Panama hat, he looked very Continental and arty, a young and fit Henri Matisse, though in fact he worked for Jim Branch as a real estate appraiser.

"Which I would like back, by the way," Cassidy said, nimbly hot-fingering several steaming yellow chunks of fish, "with the point still on it if possible."

"Yeah, yeah. What do you think? I used peanut oil."

"Incredible. What's the breading?" Joe Kern asked O-mouthed, sucking air around the fish to keep from burning his tongue.

"The usual. Crunched-up Ritz crackers and lemon pepper, soaked in milk and eggs first. The secret is getting the oil hot enough. Good?"

"Henry, you are the maharaja of fried fish. Just leave us some to keep our strength up while we finish these bugs," Joe said.

"Yes, please," said Winkler, who was trying to eat with one hand, balancing a beer in his lap and tossing lobster tails into the boiling water with the other hand.

"So you guys did some good?" Cassidy said to Joe Kern.

"Mmm. We went out to the reef lines west of here and trolled some deep lures for grouper. Got a few decent-sized ones and a bunch of rock hinds. I think that's what he just cooked up, the little ones."

"Long as it wasn't kicking up out there, sounds like fun."

"Pretty flat most of the day. Then just a little wind chop. Darned pleasant, all in all."

"How big were the big ones?"

"One was about twenty. Couple in the teens. But we were hitting a hundred feet or so, so even the little ones were some work."

"You can have it. I'd rather dive to sixty feet in a current than crank up groupers all the dooh-dah day. Like trying to fish up umbrella stands."

"Oh, they're not bad long as you can get them turned upward right after they hit. But you let even a small one get back down in the rocks and hole up and you're going to lose your tackle and a lot of line. Ask Henry. Long as he's been grouper fishing, one got him today. Claimed it was a fifty-pounder."

"That right, Henry?" Cassidy called across the boats. "Grouper get your goat today?"

"Or the Loch Ness monster one." Henry thumbed his Panama hat back from his forehead. He was hunkered over his stove stirring another batch of fish. "I fumbled with the drag for a second and that's all it took. Got himself all wedged in and I had to break him off. But he was trophy-sized, I know that all right all right."

"Or a two-pound rock hind," Joe Kern muttered to himself. "Kept telling him about that drag."

Joe was the best fisherman Cassidy had ever known. Trim and tanned, though he was in his mid-fifties, he could have passed for young forties. Once Cassidy had been amazed to see him playing very rough basketball at the Y with twenty-year-olds. He was fourth-generation Palm Beach County and before he turned ten he had caught his family's dinner many times with a hand line out of Lake Worth. He had ancestors who had lived and died without ever having traveled to Miami except by boat. Cassidy's father and Joe had been childhood friends; Cassidy had grown up calling him Uncle Joe.

All the while dinner was making, boats came and went. Some arrived and tied on, some went back and forth to the dock, or on other errands, some pulled up close by and dropped anchor, not wanting to get hemmed in. But soon there were more than a dozen of the little boats all together and the laughter and chatter echoed far out across the water.

Cassidy made his way over three boats to where John Kern sat in the stern on a cooler, using the driver's chair as a table. A slighter, younger version of his dad, save for the sun-bleached beard, he was entertaining two young ladies Cassidy hadn't seen before, both redheads and possibly sisters, and Cassidy introduced himself while John was up under his bow canopy fetching something.

"Can I be of some use?" Cassidy asked John.

"Not in the least. I'm just chopping for salad. You okay on beer? I was explaining to Susan and Stacey here about the dinnertime division of labor among the boats."

"It's impressive to see men so apparently useful," Susan said. She was smiling at Cassidy, tapping her wineglass fetchingly against a white incisor.

"Better save your judgment until you've had dinner," Cassidy said.

"Oh, we already had some fish that charming fellow brought by. Harry, was it?"

"Henry. Yeah, you're right. My dad used to say that no one ever lost any weight on one of these trips unless they got a leg bitten off by a shark."

"So, every boat cooks something different. It's like a movable feast except we don't go anywhere," she said.

"Right," John Kern said, returning with a bottle of olive oil. "And you try to end up cooking what you caught during the day.

Or at least you do if it works out. It's very satisfying shepherd-
ing the whole process from ocean to plate. Or at least that's the
theory. Some people just aren't any damn good at fishing or diving, so they make side dishes. That's why I'm chopping lettuce
and carrots right now."

Cassidy rolled his eyes. John Kern was only slightly less of a
fisherman than his father.

"What if your boat didn't catch anything and you can't
cook?" asked Stacey.

"Your boat tells knock-knock jokes," said John Kern.

"Hey, speaking of which, I appreciate your taking Roland
today," Cassidy said.

"Hush now," said John. "I didn't need to be on the same
boat with Dad and Henry when they get going. Besides, we had
a great time. He knows more about tropicals even than Mr.
Branch. And plus it gave us a good excuse to hang out with
Susan and Stacey. Everyone on Dr. Mortinson's boat wanted to
snorkel shallow too."

"Oh, *you're* Roland's . . ." Stacey said.

Just then the boat tipped alarmingly in Roland's direction
as he stepped on the gunnel and squirmed laboriously down
beside Cassidy, huge smile on his face. John Kern looked around
in mock alarm at the comically overcrowded boat. "Man the
pumps," he called.

"Clever," said Roland. "I see you've met these gorgeous
creatures." He was smiling benevolently at them, and they in
turn seemed all atwitter.

Cassidy looked at John Kern, who smiled back. It was this
thing about Roland and women, though to Cassidy's knowledge
he'd never been on a date.

Roland wore flip-flops, Bermuda shorts, and for some reason a huge floral kimono that seemed perfect for the occasion.
There was a red blotch in the middle of his forehead where he
had missed with the sunscreen, and he carried an umbrella and
large tumbler of ice and some pinkish orange fluid.

"Whatcha got there?" Cassidy asked.

"Beefeaters and tonic, dash of bitters, half a Key lime. Don't know what you call it. Joe Kern made it for me. What *do* you call it, John?"

"Beefeaters and tonic, dash of bitters, half a Key lime," said John Kern.

"Ah," said Roland, taking a healthy slug.

"So, Roland," said Stacey, "John and Quenton were explaining about how all the boats contribute to dinner. What is your boat doing?"

"An excellent question, Miss Parsons. Mr. Cassidy, what is our boat contributing to this repast?" This without a trace of irony.

"We are providing the *Panulirus argus,*" Cassidy said. "We call them bugs or sometimes crawfish. They are, in fact, the elusive spiny lobster. Harry Winkler just set them a-boilin' a little while ago and they should be just about close to perfect. And none too soon if you want my opinion. I could eat a horseshoe crab."

The platters went back and forth and round and round. Because the stoves were small, the cooking went on for some time, and some of the cooks stood down and were relieved so they could eat. From near and far one could hear exclamations of gastronomical wonder, particularly from diners on their first trip over. There were pearly white lobster tails boiled simply and quickly in seawater, served with melted butter and Key lime halves. There was more of the fried grouper, big golden chunks, served with tartar sauce and lemon wedges. From Bill Eaton's boat Cassidy was delighted to see some wonderfully fragrant pieces of hog snapper grilled delicately on mesquite coals. Dr. Mortinson, no fisherman or diver, had made his usual huge bowl of pigeon peas and rice, and the modest John Kern turned in an excellent salad of young greens with chopped yellow squash, snow peas, and vine-ripened tomatoes, fetched fresh that morning from Miss Emily's roadside stand. Someone had gone to see the conch man that morning and there was a wonderfully tangy ceviche.

Beverages were served. Everyone had a killer you had to try. Drinks made with Mount Gay Rum, or RonRico Coconut or Cockspur, Appleton or Havana Club. There were drinks with coconut milk and gin, drinks with vodka and star fruit, drinks with anything and pineapple juice. There was Red Stripe beer, St. Pauli Girl, Heineken, and Kubuli from the Dominican Republic.

There might have been alcoholics in the group, Cassidy knew, but most of them were too young to know it yet. Cassidy didn't think he was one, but he wasn't sure. He was certainly capable of overdoing things, and not just booze. He figured it was that thing—the thing about going too far—that maybe made him a good runner and a good diver and sometimes a harebrained poet. It made his life exhilarating and sometimes ridiculous at the same time.

It was getting to be homegrown entertainment time, which usually started with some well-worn limericks. There was the old hermit named Dave who lived in a cave and had sexual proclivities best left undiscussed.

"I've got a new one," John Kern said. "Been working on it for a month."

"Better be real rhymes this time," called out Jim Branch. "None of this *unwillingness-cunnilingus* business."

John Kern grinned bravely into the laughter. "Okay, here goes: there was a young man named Cantino . . . who wooed the fair maids *with the vino* . . ." Some snickers here. "But he ran out of *bread* . . . so he made do *instead* . . ."—an appropriate pause—". . . *with a mail-order device from Encino!*"

Hilarity ensued and Cassidy realized how tired he was when he could not work up much more than a chuckle. Since there were a number of first-timers on the boats, someone was egging Roland on to tell his Robert Vesco story.

"This is true?" asked one of the redheaded young ladies.

"Oh absolutely," Roland said. "Summers in high school and college I used to work for my uncle Stafford, who was a fabulous and well-known chef, mostly northern Italian cuisine. He was working in Miami when Vesco persuaded him to come over here as his personal chef. At the time Vesco was an absolute fugitive, holed up in the top floor of a hotel in Nassau. He had been booted out of most civilized countries, but he had greased every Bahamian palm in sight and he was buds with Bebe Rebozo and Nixon, so he was snug as a bug in a rug."

Cassidy saw some backstory whispering going on.

"Anyway, since Vesco couldn't risk leaving the Bahamas, he would send his Learjet back to the States to run errands, particularly to make food runs, fresh vegetables and the like. He'd occasionally send it all the way to Omaha to get a load of prime steaks. He believed in living well while remaining out of the clutches of the *gendarmerie*."

Warming to his story, Roland took a healthy slug of his drink.

"Anyway, Uncle Stafford would sometimes go on these steak runs and one time they got back to Nassau very late at night and on the way back to Paradise Island from the airport, he told the van driver to stop at his house. The other guy, one of Vesco's bodyguards who was running the operation, says, Stafford, what are you doing? Nothing, he says, and unceremoniously hauls a Styrofoam cooler of about forty pounds of filet mignon into his house."

There is much good-natured murmuring and catcalling from the boats.

"This is a true story, swear to God?" said one of the new guys on Dr. Mortinson's boat.

"Absolutely true. I was there in the kitchen doing prep work for dinner the next afternoon when Vesco himself marches in, Israeli bodyguards on each shoulder. He marches up to my uncle, who's a ponderous huge man, by the way, a Falstaffian sort of man . . ."

"Gee, that's hard to imagine," Cassidy murmured.

"And Vesco says, Stafford, you're the best chef I've ever had and I'd hate like hell to lose you. I don't know what's come over you or how you thought you'd ever get away with this, but I've thought it over and I've decided to let it go this time. You return the steaks and promise never to do such a thing again and you can keep your job."

"My uncle looked Vesco in the eye and said: '*Mister Vesco,*' very crisply, he said, '*Mister Vesco,* if you'll return the $224 million you stole from all those people through Overseas Investments Limited, I'll return the steaks *I stole.*' "

Even the people who had heard the story many times were roaring, and the rum didn't hurt, but it was mostly Roland's performance, wrought smooth from the years of telling, that made it so funny.

When the hubbub had settled down, the new people began asking the usual questions, the first being, *Did he keep his job?*

"That's only in Hollywood," Roland said. "We were both fired at once and escorted off the island with the clothes on our backs. I was scared to death but Uncle Stafford seemed to be having the time of his life, joking with the pilots about whether we were supposed to be *dropped off* in the middle of the Gulf Stream. When we got back to Miami, it took him exactly three phone calls to get us both hired at a very nice restaurant in Coral Gables."

"Where is your uncle now?" someone asked.

"No longer with us." Roland smiled sweetly. "But that's a whole 'nother story, as they say. Mr. Vesco is currently trying to buy his own island in Antigua, and is also making eyes at Fidel Castro."

Cassidy would have liked to have stayed for the music but he knew he was done for, nap or no nap. Joe Kern was getting out his ukulele and Jim Branch his guitar when one of the interior boats next to Cassidy needed to detach and Cassidy used the opportunity to make his exit, after making sure Roland had a ride back to the dock.

"Don't worry about me," Roland said, toasting him with his tumbler. "I am an excellent swimmer."

"Roland," Cassidy said, "I'm pretty sure you're kidding, but just in case you're not, get Joe to tell you about some of the sharks we've caught in here at night."

"No doubt," said Roland, looking serious.

Joe was grinning as he tuned his ukulele. "It's one time fishing you don't want to catch anything unless you're armed."

Cassidy cranked the Mercurys and puttered just far enough from land to be out of mosquito range. As the boat swung gently around on the anchor rope and hung, he could hear the hum of the hotel's generator across the water, the faint singing and laughter from the boats, and the occasional sudden panicky splash of something big chasing something small.

The clean cotton case on the camping pillow felt cool and delicious on his sun-fevery face as he sensed a tidal wave of sleep coming on relentlessly and pleasantly, strains of distant and familiar lyrics coming to him across the smooth water as if from a child's nap dream:

Now de fishing's good near your island . . .
dat's why I come back for more . . .
but when you swim me boat 'round naked . . .
I follow you back to de shore . . .
singing island woman . . . island woman . . .
making me forget who I am . . .

11

Out by the Buoy

ROLAND WASN'T IN his room so Cassidy wandered around to the coffee shop in the lobby to find him working on a double order of French toast and fresh strawberries.

"You missed it last night at the Sit and Be Damned Lounge," Roland said, pouring him a cup of coffee from the carafe. "More than acceptable steel drum group called Bimini Traffic Jam, shamelessly drunken limbo contest, many young ladies." He crunched a piece of bacon thoughtfully. "Mostly Canadian schoolteachers on holiday package tours. Also the two from our group, who asked about you, by the bye."

"I wouldn't have been any good to anybody. I slept so hard that when I woke up I thought I was camping on the coast up in Maine. Took me a good thirty seconds to remember my name."

Roland offered—without much enthusiasm—a piece of French toast.

"No, thanks. Still full from dinner. Bimini Traffic Jam, huh? That's pretty good. Those guys always come up with good names.

Heard a group in Nassau once called Square Grouper Bonfire. So what are you thinking about doing today? More pictures?"

"John Kern said you two were going fishing?"

"We talked about going out by the buoy and casting some tube lures. Why?"

"May I join you?"

"Roland! Of course you can join us! I've never known you to show any interest in fishing at all at all, other than just hoping something would end up in the pan."

"It occurred to me that I ought not remain so completely ignorant of the process, repugnant though it may be in some aspects. I assume we will be going after one of your *bill*fishes? Your majestic blue marlin, perhaps?"

Hmmm. Cassidy eyed him carefully. Had he been reading Hemingway?

"Nothing so elaborate today. This is just messing-around kind of fishing. Out by the buoy there are always some big barracuda or jacks maybe, and they just *love* tube lures. It's as close to sure-thing fishing as you can get. It's like if your cousin is visiting from Ohio and you want to be sure to hook him up to something that feels like it's going to pull his ass overboard so he can go back and tell everybody in Akron about it, well, this is what you'd do."

"What can you do with barracuda? Are they edible?"

"Well, you can eat the smaller ones if you're hard up. They're oily and fishy, though. They smoke up okay if you have the time, sort of like sailfish or jacks or something like that. The bigger ones aren't worth the risk. They sometimes have this toxin called ciguatera, which will make you sick as hell."

"Hmmm." Roland sniffed.

"Or kill you," Cassidy added cheerfully. "But they're fun to catch!"

"I would have preferred the majestic blue marlin, but . . . Say, this form of fishing doesn't have anything to do with worms, does it?"

"Only to the extent that they are the end to which all fishermen come."

"Eh?"

"Go get your zinc oxide and meet us down at the concrete pier. I'm going to go over to government dock to top off the tanks and get some ice. John Kern will be waiting."

By the time they got out to the orange and white buoy the tide was peaking, so Cassidy turned the engines off and let the boat drift. The three of them sat for a moment, enjoying that sudden tranquil state when internal combustion is instantly replaced by the cry of gulls, lapping water, and the muted thunk of a rusty buoy.

It was still early enough to be coolish, and even Roland was enjoying sitting out from under the Bimini top, his closed eyes upturned to the warming sun. His nose was hidden under a layer of zinc oxide but for once he wasn't wearing some kind of huge headgear. Cassidy thought that he heard him purring.

Cassidy nudged John Kern, who smiled when he saw Roland's rather regal pose.

"Do you have any lures made up?" he whispered to Cassidy.

"Don't think so. We'll have to do some. There's a spool of tubing under the platform, and I've got wire and hooks in the tacklebox."

"What are you two whispering about?"

"Nothing. We didn't want to disturb you. We've got to make some tube lures before we can do anything."

"Make them? Are they not commercially available?"

John Kern and Cassidy looked at each other. In fact, neither of them knew.

"I doubt it," Cassidy said. "There's nothing to them really. I guess maybe a Yankee would pay for one, but nobody else. We'll show you how to do it."

Roland actually paid attention as they set up a little assembly line. Using a well-worn pair of needle-nose pliers, John Kern cut lengths of leader wire three feet long while Cassidy cut eighteen-inch lengths of orange surgical tubing with a fillet knife. Then they both set to work pulling the wire lengthways through the tubing and twisting big treble hooks onto the ends. On the other end of the wire, they made a loop for the connector and wrapped the excess wire around and around. Using the needle-nose pliers, John Kern put a little lock knot on both ends of each lure and they were done. In a few minutes they had made a dozen.

"There you have it, my friend, several weeks' supply of tube lures." Cassidy handed one to Roland.

"I'm sure I don't understand." Roland looked at it from different angles. "What do the fish think it is?"

John Kern and Cassidy wrinkled their brows.

"Hmmm," said John Kern. "That's a good question. Nobody knows really. All we know is that barracudas go completely wild for them. Other things too. Big jack crevalles, pompano, lots of things. But nobody has any idea what the fish think they are. Some kind of eel, maybe? All I know is that my dad taught me how to make one when I was about eight years old and that they work great."

Roland's face clouded over.

"What's wrong?" Cassidy asked.

"I'm beginning to think that I've been brought on some kind of nautical snipe hunt," he said unhappily.

"What are you talking about?" Cassidy said.

"I've never heard of a fishing trip where a catch was almost guaranteed, and even the variety of fish and the very type of unlikely lure specified in advance. I can see that I am to be made an object of your japery."

"What's he saying?" John Kern whispered.

"He thinks we're making fun of him," Cassidy said. "That it's a practical joke."

"There's one way to find out," said John Kern, handing

Roland his Penn Senator casting rod, now rigged with a tube lure. "If you can get that lure to land within ten feet of the buoy and get it back on board this boat without having a fish at least hit it, then I'll buy your first drink at the Sit and Be Damned Lounge tonight. Here, let me show you an easy way to cast . . ."

Cassidy watched entranced as Roland readily took the rod and allowed John Kern to guide his first cast.

"Roland, you've been on dozens of fishing trips with me and I've never—"

"Oh, I don't mind playing the fool in your little farce, but I want you to remember in the telling that I most assuredly was *not*— Oh my!"

The lure had landed with a splash very near the buoy and instantly disappeared in a violent flash of white-bellied scales and splashing water.

"'Cuda," said John Kern quietly. The new fisherman was doing some kind of excited little two-step jig.

"Stand still and get your rod tip up," said Cassidy, placing his hand in the small of Roland's back to guide him. "Yank back on the rod a couple of times to set the hook. That's it, really hard. Once more. Okay, you got him. John, you want to take over while I get the boat?"

Cassidy got the engines started. The fish was taking line off the reel in steady rasping jerks and Cassidy knew that John Kern would have set the drag correctly and that the fish would be paying the maximum price for all the line he got on this first run. The barracuda was heading toward open water, away from both the buoy chain and the boat, so Cassidy kept the boat in neutral.

"Ho ho ho!" Roland said, grinning hugely. Cassidy had to smile too.

"That's right," said John Kern, "he's slowing now. When he stops for a second, pull up on the rod and try to get some line back. That's it, just a little at a time. He'll take off again once he's had a little rest, but at least you've made him pay for it. That's it, get a little more. *Here he goes again!*"

The drag began its high-pitched pulsing screams as the fish sensed itself going in the direction of danger.

"Whee!" Roland said.

But John Kern glanced back at Cassidy, who nodded, put the boat in gear, and began following the fish.

Cassidy and John knew what Roland did not: there wasn't a great deal of the thirty-pound test filament left and a fish like this was perfectly capable of running every bit of line off a reel, snapping it off, and swimming happily out to sea dragging a few hundred feet of line. Putting the boat into the equation could give Roland a little extra margin, as long as the fish didn't go straight down, which was unlikely.

"That's it," said John Kern. "He'll get tired again, then you can get some back." John went to the front of the boat, put on some sunscreen, and got a baseball cap out of his bag. He came back to Roland's side and put his fingertips under the rod to feel the pressure.

"Okay, he's about done. Get some of your line back."

"This is . . . this is . . ." sputtered Roland happily, out of breath.

"I know." John smiled. "Don't talk, keep reeling. Cass, he's coming back."

Cassidy put the boat in reverse as he watched the line come more and more vertical. But the fish was staying very deep and there was a huge belly of line out by now, so Roland wasn't able to get any more line back. John Kern was watching the angle of the line intently and realized what the fish was doing.

"It's okay," John said. "He's going under the boat. Go ahead, just keep following him. Don't try to reel yet. Put the tip of the rod right down into the water if you need to. That's it, lean over the side a bit, I've got you. Cass will get him squared away. Try to keep the line off the boat hull if you can."

"*This fish!* This fish is . . ." The thrill was still there but Cassidy knew that Roland was beginning to really understand the strength and stamina of the animal on the other end of the line. There was both admiration and frustration in his voice.

Cassidy backed off and away from the line and now Roland was standing back up and playing the fish straight off the side of the boat, though now they were facing back toward the buoy and the island.

"Okay, Roland, you're doing great. But we've got a big loop of line out there in the water, and we can get a lot of that back. He's going to try to make it back to the buoy chain and we've got to stop him, so go to work on him."

Roland was pumping and reeling as fast as he could, panting and red, and Cassidy thought for the first time that this might not be the safest activity in the world for his overweight friend. But John Kern had done this many times with friends of his dad's who were not exactly endurance athletes, and Cassidy trusted his judgment. Besides, Cassidy had watched Roland's behavior and knew very well the fish wasn't the only one hooked. He wouldn't want to be the one to try to take the rod out of his hands.

Roland was facing the buoy getting line back steadily now and so he was surprised when there was a noisy thrashing right behind the boat.

"Another one!" he said.

"No," said John, tracing out a pattern over the water with his finger. "That's your fish. See, here's the way the line's looping through the water. It's all excess. We call it a belly of line. The friction of the water makes it hard to reel in, but you can do it. He's getting pretty tired now. Here he comes again!"

The fish flashed on the surface again and gave a halfhearted jump that brought his muscular dark green back out of the water. He was over a yard long and as thick as a rolled-up *Sunday Times*.

"Wow!" said Roland.

"They don't really jump much," said John Kern. "That's

about all you're probably going to get out of him. He's a pretty big boy, maybe thirty-five, maybe forty pounds."

"He's a champion! I am going to have my picture taken with him before I let him go!" He was reeling joyously now, rhythmically pulling the big rod into a bow then lowering and reeling, over and over.

"Well, uh, Roland . . ." John Kern looked back at Cassidy and shook his head. Cassidy gave him a little shrug.

"I don't need to have him mounted or anything. No trophies or any—"

"Roland . . ."

Just as he was starting another pull the line went slack so suddenly that Roland would have fallen right on his backside had John Kern not been standing there braced and ready to catch him.

"What did I . . ."

"It's okay, he didn't break off. You did good . . ." John Kern reassured him.

"Wait, hold on, I think he's still on!" Roland continued to reel, and was now feeling some resistance. Nothing like before, but he could tell something was still on his line.

"No, Roland. We should have told you. There's not anything you could have done about it. It happens a lot, particularly on the first fish."

Roland kept reeling, and looked back at Cassidy.

"He's right," Cassidy said. "I'm sorry, Roland. A shark got him, is all. Sorry."

"A shark?"

"Yeah. They hang out here. Blues, makos. They could never catch a barracuda normally, but one gets on a line and gets tired, it's no contest really. I'm sorry, Roland."

"But are you sure? It still feels like I've got . . ."

Then the tube lure showed on the surface and Roland pulled in a perfectly ferocious razor-toothed five-pound barracuda head.

12

Real World

A S USUAL IT took several days back in the world to grind away all the mellow from the islands.

He had caught himself idly studying the feral parakeets chattering away in the kumquat trees outside his office. When he came to he had no idea how much time had gone by.

It was good to be back running again, which he couldn't do when they were in the islands living on the boats, but that was the only good thing he could say for being back on dry land.

He thought of how happy Roland had been, despite a very rough crossing coming back, and that made him happy too. They had dodged squalls and pounded hard over and through twenty-foot rollers for more than four hours before they saw the gray outlines of condos marching up the coast from Boca toward Vero. The trip took twice as long coming back and was a lot more uncomfortable. Scary too, crossing the Gulf Stream like that in small boats. Yet Roland hadn't complained a single time. In fact, he seemed invigorated.

"It always goes like this!" Cassidy had called, shouting over the wind. "Easy over, rough back. Or vice versa." He pulled back on the throttles to avoid overshooting a big roller out into the void, then sped up again to keep from being overtaken by the following one.

Roland, standing beside him at the center console holding fast to a rail, using his knees as shock absorbers as the little boat rose and plunged, looked over with a smile: "It's a karma thing! Seems only fair!"

Cassidy was surprised at the change in him. On their last evening in the islands Roland had begun talking about getting a boat, something Cassidy gently counseled against.

"Why?" Roland asked, mixing drinks for the guests on their boat.

"Because as a general rule people should not be taking up boats or motorcycles or skydiving for the first time during their prime earning years," Cassidy said, getting a general affirmative murmur from the cocktail crowd. "It bespeaks bohemianism."

Roland regarded Cassidy curiously. "You usually don't talk that way until three drinks," he said.

"Much better to have friends with boats than to have boats," Joe Kern said, holding his drink up in a toast to Roland. "And you have lots of friends with boats!"

"Here's to them and those like them!" said Roland, holding up his own elegant goblet of sauvignon blanc. Where in the world he had come up with a crystal wineglass Cassidy had no idea. Everyone else was drinking from plastic tumblers.

"Damn right," said Joe Kern.

"Damn right," said Cassidy.

"In fact, if no one has any objections, I'd like to sell mine and just go with one of you bastards," said Joe Kern, holding his glass up again.

"To us bastards!" cried Jim Branch. "Damn few left!"

Back on the mainland Roland jumped into his daily routine with irritatingly good cheer. Cassidy slogged through a melancholy readjustment, lost in an ocean of daydreams, daydreams of oceans. There were occasional frenetic bursts of focus and coffee-fueled activity but he just found it more difficult than usual to take seriously the infernal residue of conflict, greed, hate, and willfulness that bubbled to the top of the fermenting tank of American jurisprudence. It was his job and sworn duty to man the pumps and skimmers that would process the acrid stuff into legally cognizable compromise, triumph, or regret that was only slightly more palatable to the contestants than armed combat. And occasionally not.

He was grateful that at least his group rarely did family law, eschewing as it were the statistically significant possibility that a case might end in gunplay.

But an island trip temporarily wrapped him in a cocoon of serenity that slowed and blurred life like a wonderful drug. Midmorning found him in a deposition on the ninth floor of an office building across the bridge in West Palm. Mentally, though, he was barefoot, on the deck of that bare-masted forty-foot trimaran about to motor under the Flagler Bridge. From the court reporter's corner office he had a view of a good stretch of the Intracoastal and at this moment he was picking up the grainy tactile sense of the deck's pebble-grain fiberglass surface on the soles of his feet. From a mile away in his air-conditioned glass box he could have sworn his ears had picked up the metallic clang of the halyard hardware on the hollow aluminum mast. Instead of the musty books and paper and copier fluid that made up *eau de office,* his nose was processing wind, salt, fish.

Later in his own office he was leaning back in his leather Execucliner, hands behind his head, open transcript in his lap— mostly as a prop—still thinking about the trimaran when he realized that Roland had been standing in the doorway, for how long he didn't know.

"Sorry?" he said, looking over, still tapping the bridge of his nose with the pencil he had been making margin notes with.

"Mission control to Major Tom. I was just inquiring . . ." said Roland. Sans jacket, his elegant suspenders perfectly matched the dominant colors of his floral necktie. He had a volume of ALR under his arm.

"Something about fishing, sorry. Ah, you've been in the library researching *the law,*" he said, gesturing at the book.

"Amazingly enough, a thing that might actually involve the Rule in Shelley's Case. Tangentially, of course, but what are the chances? Not three people in my real property class understood it properly, including the professor. But I was asking what kinds of fish you are able to go after on your boat."

"Do you mean, do we have different kinds of tackle?"

"No, I realize you have an enormous variety of equipment. But I've often noticed much larger craft out there pursuing the creatures."

"So what you're asking is, are our boats capable of going after really big fish?"

"Yes, your gallant sailfish, your noble blue marlin. Successfully, I mean. Or do you truly need the larger craft?" He pronounced it *guh-lont.*

"Oh no, not at all. Our boats are perfectly capable. You realize that I'm more of a diver than a fisherman. But Joe and John Kern go all the time. Jim Branch, Frates, Bill Eaton, all those guys are excellent. They can catch just about anything from their boats. I don't fish nearly as much as they do but mine is outfitted pretty much the same. You need outriggers, of course, a good fighting chair. And the right tackle, always. The rest is just know-how. Those guys have been doing it almost their whole lives. It's second nature to them."

"But you abjure the sport?"

"Lord, no! I grew up with it too. But given the choice, I'd rather be below the waterline, hunting instead of trapping. Harry's the same. Don't get me wrong, I love being on the water doing just about anything, and I've fished plenty, back with my dad when I was a kid and lots of times with those guys. But I just don't get quite the same thrill from it they seem to. With me it's diving. Hunting fish in deep water with no tanks. Lots of times there'll be six or seven boats out and Harry and I will be the only ones diving. Everyone else will fish."

"Diving seems like more work," Roland said.

"Often, but not always, particularly with the ones you're talking about, the big ones. They'll wear you out pretty good. Funny thing, though."

"What?"

"Lots of times a boat will come back blanked, even in the islands. Doesn't happen often with those guys, but it does happen, even to the best. They'll just turn up empty. Sunburned and tired, embarrassed as hell. But completely aced."

"Hmmm."

"But not Harry and me. We always seem to bring back something or the other."

"Why is that?"

"Just the nature of things." Cassidy laughed. "Other than their electronics, fishermen are blind. But Harry and me, if we go someplace to get fish or lobster, and there aren't any there, we just go someplace else."

"Sounds reasonable enough. But frankly this business about spearing things seems ghastly to me. The battle of wills with hook and line, that's something else!"

"So you're really interested in sportfishing? Billfish, or wahoo, cobia, things like that?"

"I was just wondering what the process was like. An overview, I mean." He placed the big green volume down on a corner of Cassidy's desk and sat down in one of the client chairs. Cassidy didn't see any bookmarks and wondered if the library trip might well have been a ruse. Rule in Shelley's Case indeed.

Cassidy looked at his watch.

"Look, it's almost lunch and I'm spinning wheels here. Let's go over to the Ocean Grille and get an outside table where we can see the water and I'll tell you about it."

Roland sprang to his feet. "Let me drop this off and I'll meet you in the courtyard."

It was a perfect fall day for outdoor dining. Still warm, with a gentle ocean breeze rocking the green-and-ecru-striped canvas umbrella over their table, bringing the familiar heady salt-fish-Coppertone fragrance that to Cassidy always seemed unnatural in the middle of the week when you were wearing a suit.

It was early but the patio was already half full, mostly men, some in business attire, some ready for golf or boating, lots of Guccis and Topsiders with no socks. The rich and the trying-to-be-rich, Cassidy thought. But looks could be deceiving. Some of the "golfers" were in fact Palm Beach attorneys who dressed like their clients on days when they didn't have to go to court, which was most of the time. On occasion you might see a Kennedy or a former governor or ambassador casually working the tables. Cassidy waved to the elegant, gangly Earl E. T. Smith, semiretired from investment banking and the current mayor of Palm Beach. He had been the last American ambassador to Cuba before the unpleasantness. A client of Joe Kern's, he smiled and waved back, on his way to dine inside. He was with people, so to Cassidy's relief he made an apologetic gesture to Cassidy and Roland and didn't come over. Roland acknowledged with a sympathetic smile and shrug. The mayor was getting on in years and on his bad days conversations with him could be comically repetitive.

"Imagine it!" Roland said. "The man was appointed to the War Production Board by Roosevelt!"

"He occasionally comes up with the damnedest things," Cassidy said. "If you didn't know better, you'd think he was just a loony old guy. Once I was having dinner at Joe's and the mayor and his wife were there. We were talking politics and I said something about the Kennedys—I can't recall what—and the old gent looked me in the eye and said, 'Well, I'm a Republican, of course. Eisenhower was my guy. Golfed together and all that. You're probably more of a Kennedy type. I don't know them well. Well, I knew *John* quite well, but not the rest.'" Cassidy tried to do that lockjaw Exeter–Beacon Hill–Harvard thing with his voice.

"So much for dropping over to Rose's place to borrow a cup of sugar," said Roland.

"Well, you know, their cottages are next to each other on North Ocean Boulevard."

"Yes, *cottages* indeed. What else did he say?"

"He said, 'They wanted my scalp over Castro. They held hearings. Oh, they came at me hammer and tong.'"

"What happened?"

"He basically skated. A good friend of his had told him to keep copies of all his cables. Said it would be good insurance. Earl said it was the best advice he ever got. After the revolution when all the jackasses in Congress started looking around for scapegoats, he pulled out a fistful of cables showing where he had been warning the weenies in the State Department about Castro for years. Said it was the career people, the fourth floor they call it, that bollixed the whole thing. He said, 'They *adored* Fidel, thought he was a romantic figure. They live in their own little world up there. But they weren't alone. At first everyone thought he was wonderful. They sent me over personally to tell Batista it was time to go.'"

"My God! He's telling you American history at dinner!"

"But then Lesly goes, 'Earl! Leave Quenton alone about politics!' And I've noticed that those old guys with young wives always do what they say," said Cassidy.

"Assuredly."

"But then he whispered to me, 'It's all in my book. I'll send you a copy.' Sure enough, *The Fourth Floor* by Earl E. T. Smith arrived at the office the next day by courier. It's pretty good too," said Cassidy.

From their perch on the patio of the Ocean Grille, the growing throng seemed something like a living socioanthropological diorama. There were a handful from families who'd had so much money for so long that the last several generations didn't know what anything cost and didn't really understand the difference between a hundred-dollar bill and a quarter. Their great-great-grandfathers had started a railroad or a coal mine or an insurance company, or their great-grandfathers had invented the flow-through tea bag or the cornflake, or their grandfathers had mastered the engineering of the aerosol spray valve or the sanitary napkin. Some of the snootiest owed their status to ancestors who had smuggled booze or sold patent medicines. Some not-so-uppity nouveaus had made millions in the burger wars, starting rabid HMOs, or selling shrunken heads by direct mail. They came to Palm Beach seeking high society, only to find they couldn't draw flies at a goat dipping.

But a common denominator of the true old-money crowd was simply that some perceptive soul along the way—an early generation before all the fear and ambition had been bred out of the gene pool—had set up the kind of corporations, trusts, leases, and foundations that would prevent any single particularly flagitious generation from pissing it all away.

Many of the smiling gray heads on the patio had been raised by servants and retainers of various kinds and during their childhoods thought of their parents as some kind of visiting international dignitaries, and now though they listed their occupations as investment banking or "finance," when they had anything to do with business at all it was only through trustees and lawyers.

The ones with some brains or spunk might have gotten into an Ivy League school and done politics or philanthropy. The others knew that even as legacies they couldn't compete with the turbocharged and outrageously ambitious scions of the professional classes and so were caught in a soul-draining no-man's-land. They went to Rollins or College of the Atlantic where they dressed like Copenhagen drug dealers, and would later champion some variety of sea mammal or an obscure species of bat. In

Palm Beach some of the women would occasionally attach themselves to fashionable charities or causes that seemed to require
elaborate balls. These were among the more admirable ones.

The Ocean Grille crowd contained some of the strangest
and most miserable and most useless people Cassidy knew of,
but there were others on the island much worse: ghouls and
psychopaths who would have been locked up anywhere else in
the world. Many would not even be up at this hour. Others were
just lost souls who would disappear on occasion into rehab, go
off chasing swamis, or suddenly discover Scientology or herbal
tea. The alky-druggie-sex fetishists and vampires were often
the much-prized clients of Cassidy and Roland's brethren in
the local criminal and family law bar, unless the really big guns
from Miami were imported.

The raree-show on the patio was entertaining as always, but
to Cassidy the important thing was that he was near the ocean
and there was a pleasant breeze. He hung his jacket on the back
of the chair and loosened his tie and enjoyed the salty air and
the gulls cawing and Roland's infectious happiness, this little
guilty slice of wind and sun stolen in the middle of a weekday.

The waitress brought iced tea, unsweetened, and a basket of
rolls, which they fell to hungrily.

"So, the boats are big enough?" Roland asked, buttering a
roll, trying to get back on subject.

"Sure. That chair in the back, there's a reason they call it
a fighting chair. You use it when you go after really big fish.
The boats themselves are called open fishermen. They're made
for doing just that. The other stuff we put on them, the front
canopies, the sleeping cushions, the diving platforms, that's all
just housekeeping stuff to make them comfortable for island-
hopping and diving. When they come from the factory all they
really have are live wells and space to fish."

They had finished all the rolls when the waitress brought
Cassidy's broiled red snapper and Roland's shrimp scampi. The
sea air had made them both ravenous.

"So you said the process was more involved," Roland said. "Do you use those tube things or do you have to make other kinds of lures?"

"No. Mostly you use live bait, which is much preferred. If you can't get live, you might use frozen ones, which also work pretty well. To get live ones we go out just beyond the mouth of the inlet and putter along by the rocks of the jetty. Did you notice those smaller rods on the boat, the ones with the open-faced reels and really thin line?"

"I think so." Roland was thoroughly into his scampi, but paying attention. "They had little feather things on the end. I think that's what John Kern used one day to catch some little mangrove snappers for dinner."

"Right, that's really light tackle for catching smaller fish like those snappers, and also for going after blue runners and such for bait. You can buy different things at the marinas, greenies or look-downs and such, but we like to get our own. You use that little feather lure tied directly to the line, no leader or anything, and just cast it out around the rocks. There are usually schools of baitfish. It doesn't take too long to pull in a few. It's kind of fun. We've had new people go out with us who thought that was the whole trip. They'd get all excited pulling in a feisty little blue runner and say things like 'I never knew deep-sea fishing was so much fun!' They thought getting the bait was the fishing!"

"That would have been me, I'm sure. One of your basic tyros," said Roland.

"Naw. You've caught your first barracuda head. You're a veteran! Anyway, once you have a few blue runners swimming in your live well, you head out to sea, out to the Gulf Stream or a little beyond. You use a really big rig and you drag the bait behind the boat. You go kind of slow, and the speed is important. You lower the outriggers—those long antenna-looking poles—out to the side of the boat so that the bait is towed clear of the wake where the fish can see it. The line is just clipped out there with a clothespin thingie, so when a fish takes the bait the line falls down. Then it's just you and the fish."

"And then does a shark leave you just the head?"

Cassidy laughed. "No, not usually. For one thing, these are much bigger fish than barracuda, and they have their own weapons. And for another it's farther out in open water, not in close-in places where predators usually hang out."

"But in *The Old Man and the Sea*—"

"Aha!"

"What?"

"I knew it!"

"Knew what?"

"That you'd been reading Hemingway!"

Roland was indignant. "Certainly. Junior-year American literature seminar. Remember Smith Kirkpatrick? He was published himself, as I recall, and a navy man. I liked him quite well and he was the one who brought in Harry Crews. Anyway, he was gaga for Hemingway and I frankly did not understand the fuss. But that was a marlin in that story, was it not?"

"Yes, a blue marlin, I think."

"And wasn't the whole idea that the sharks got the fish in the end, much as mine was lost, despite a quotidian struggle?"

"Hmmm. I hadn't thought of it that way. It's just that in real sportfishing with a rod and reel out in open water, even if the fight takes several hours it's usually over and the fish is either on the boat or gets away before any really big sharks can get into the act. Not that it doesn't happen, but just not usually. Even after they're hooked, they can still defend themselves, except right at the end when they're completely exhausted. And then things happen pretty fast. You get them up to the boat and gaff them and it's over."

"So you're saying it was built around a *false premise*, this Hemingway plot?"

"No, no. Not at all. It was a different situation altogether. The old man was fishing with a handline. That's the old-timey way commercial fishermen did it for hundreds of years, from the Maritimes down to Key West, just a guy alone in a little wooden boat, usually out of sight of land, sometimes in the rain and fog, hauling in enough of these big old fish to make a living."

Cassidy was lost in thought for a moment, eating his red snapper and picturing again the woodworking shop he'd visited in Shelburne where for nearly two hundred years they made those double-ended Nova Scotia dories, and still did. For tourist displays, now that the fishermen were long gone, and the fish too.

Roland recognized this look.

"Hearty souls, no doubt. And the old man not the least of them, I'm sure, but he still lost his quarry," he said, trying to bring Cassidy back.

"Yes, he battled the marlin for I don't know how long before he finally hauled him in. He was just huge, this fish. He wouldn't even fit in this little boat the old man had, so he had to lash him to the side. After it was dead, I mean. It was only then that the sharks came on, and even then it was a while before they showed up. At least that's the way I remember it. It's a different situation altogether."

"It's coming back to me now and I believe you're right."

"Something similar used to happen when whalers would have a big one lashed up to their side and they'd have to hurry to strip off the blubber before the sharks got it all. Some guys would be bashing at the sharks with clubs while other guys cut the whale up. It could be a real donnybrook out there, Roland."

"What do you mean 'out there'? I've got a will contest coming into the office next week involving a corpus of about nineteen million, a young widow of short duration, and half a dozen grief-stricken nieces, nephews, and cousins. Sharks have nothing on these people."

"And you represent . . . who?"

"Does it matter?" Roland said, signaling for the check. "Just one of the participants at the feeding frenzy."

It was several weeks before Cassidy began to realize that something more basic than post-island ennui was at play. He assumed he would soon shake it off after a few days and get back into the mundane slipstream of everyday life, but it persisted. Roland noticed it and took to asking him if he was all right, the query accompanied by poorly disguised scrutiny.

Winkler noticed it too, but he had weathered many of Cassidy's moods with equanimity and knew well how they came and went.

It was a do-nothing Wednesday evening when Cassidy jogged in from his run and walked around to the back of the house to hose off. He found Winkler already sitting on one of the lawn chairs in the courtyard, shirtless, towel around his neck, cooling off from his own workout. He had a net bag of Key limes in the chair next to him. Cassidy took off his shoes and ran the coolish hose water over his head for a few minutes. He was already drenched with sweat, so he couldn't get any wetter. Then he moved the limes and sat down with a squish next to his roommate.

"Doing some picking?" Cassidy asked, squeegeeing water off with his hands.

"Mmmm. Tree's loaded. Thought I'd do something useful. Loquats are in too, and the star fruit. But you got to draw the line. Get a good run in?"

"Not bad. Pretty humid, though. I ran up to the middle bridge and then across. Then back down on the other side. Almost got arrested for no shirt over there."

"They still have that?"

"Yeah. A cop actually stopped me. He was nice about it and said it was just a warning. I told him to go ahead and write me up because I wasn't going to wear a shirt and get heat prostration and that his ordinance was unconstitutional anyway."

"What'd he say?"

"He laughed. Said how did I know. I said because Roland Menduni Esquire told me. Which he did. He's pretty good on state constitutional stuff. Taught a course on it one summer at Stetson Law. Anyway, the cop said he didn't know about that, and that normally he would be more than happy to give me the ticket, but that he was going on vacation in two weeks and he'd be damned if he was going to come back from fly fishing in Montana for court. I said I didn't blame him."

"He let you go?"

"What else could he do? I told him he could give me the ticket just about anytime, because I'd still be running and I'd still be shirtless when he got back. Hey, you want to get some dinner? The Crab Pot, maybe?"

"Think I'll pass," Winkler said. "I hit the weights pretty hard and I'm kind of pooped. And not particularly hungry either."

"This is a first. How about we do something simple here? I've got some conch defrosted. We can do fritters."

"Hmmm. That actually sounds pretty good."

"What else?"

"We've got romaine, I could make a big salad. There are a zillion cherry tomatoes on the bush, and I think we've got black olives and croutons. Maybe use some of those limes with olive oil and wine vinegar for a dressing. We could do anchovies on the side. There's feta, which I know you hate."

"I don't hate it, I just call it by its real name."

"Flotation material?"

"Exactly."

"Are there any of those hard rolls left?"

"I think so. There are more in the freezer. I thought you weren't hungry."

"I'm talking myself into it."

The fritters took a few minutes, but it wasn't long before they were eating on the little screened-in porch. Freshly showered, they had both dressed in clean running shorts and T-shirts, and were barefoot on the cool tile floor.

"I hadn't thought about Mize in quite a while," Cassidy said. "Then when I was running today I saw a little helicopter coming across the Intracoastal and it all came back."

"He was a good guy."

"I've still got some of his letters. They started out pretty optimistic, but you read them, you can see him getting down. He said most of the Americans were oblivious or downright hostile to the people there. He heard guys referring to the Vietnamese as 'foreigners.' Believe that?"

"Yeah, I believe it. I still don't know why he wanted to go," Winkler said.

"He didn't want to exactly. He went in ROTC mostly because his old man and his uncles had been in the military, and plus he thought he was going to need some kind of deferment so he could stay in school. He redshirted his sophomore year with that fatigue fracture in his shin, so he had a year of eligibility he could have used to go to graduate school if he could keep from being drafted."

"They would draft you out of graduate school?"

"In a heartbeat. Don't you remember? As soon as you graduated, you'd get your preinduction physical notice and then you'd be right in the middle of 'Alice's Restaurant.' Then they put in the lottery, and it turned out he got a pretty high number so he wouldn't have had to go anyway, but by that time it didn't make any difference to him. He was all gung ho. I tried to talk to him about it, but you know Mize."

"Not really."

"He disguised it pretty well. With his sense of humor and all you might think he was a kind of cynical guy, but he had a spiritual side. He had a lot of doubts about the war early on, but he still felt a sense of obligation. They were talking to him about the Army track team and he was plenty good enough. Lots of track guys we knew did that. Some of them never even went through basic training, just changed jerseys and kept running. But Mize turned it down and went to helicopter school in Texas. Said if he didn't go, someone else would have to."

"Man, I was never that gung ho," said Winkler. "When they came to me with the team handball thing, I couldn't sign up fast enough. I had my PE degree, so they said I could coach the women's team, and if I made the cut, I could play for the men's. And since nobody outside the military knew what the hell team handball was, they told us we'd probably all go to the Olympics. They were right."

"Pretty nice gig."

"Darn right. Despite all the smoke Cornwall was blowing, I'd have never made the team in the decathlon. I was only ranked eighth or ninth, and I just wasn't ever going to vault much over sixteen feet, period. I couldn't make up the points in the other events, so that was that."

"Yeah, the competition for those three places is pretty fierce."

"You ought to know."

They ate in silence for a while.

"So what did you end up thinking?" Winkler asked.

"About what?"

"Mizner."

"I don't know, Wink. I can't think of one good thing about it. It just seems like a giant waste, is all."

"Is that the kind of thing you're always writing about in your journal book all the time?"

"No. That's something else."

13

Orange-Scented Night

CASSIDY LAY FORWARD on the tank of the Vincent Black Shadow motorcycle with his chin just above the speedometer and bore on through the warm central Florida night, the hallucinogenic scent of orange blossoms ramjetting directly into his brain, making him dizzy with high school nostalgia. Soft chilly-warm spring evenings when your brow was fevered from sun and hormones and you were heading to the beach after the prom in David Harper's Volvo 450 with a dark-skinned girl with very white teeth. You were all-state in basketball and the state mile champion and had college offers. You were something of a king bee, he thought, and all in all you felt very, very good.

It was all so remote from him now. Drive-in movies, the Big Game, fourth-period English, waterskiing at the lake behind Caldwell Smith's house, what college you were going to pick.

It hit him like a bouncer's slap: at one time there were hundreds if not thousands of grown-ups all around south Florida who were *keenly* interested in which college he was going to pick and which sport he was going to play. The most natural thing in the world at the time and now positively odd, like some abandoned religious ritual or discredited superstition.

It really wasn't that many years ago, growing up in that crew-cut era. You could still feel the momentum from the Second World War; Korea was a hiccup and Vietnam a rumor they called "Indochina." The future was all Mohawk carpeting and Amana freezers as far as the eye could see. Oh, it could all end in an atomic fireball at any instant, but you had done the drills and knew how to stick your head under your desk. There were neighbors with bomb shelters and people like Arthur Miller and Rod Serling hinted that there might be a dark edge to the American Century, but that was the minority report. Everyone else saw clear skies ahead, Cassidy among them. His yearbook held many inscribed references to things like opening ad agencies or working for "major corporations." These weren't condemnations; they were signals of unarguable success, the absolute brass ring. That, and raising a houseful of progeny.

He could hardly believe he had once looked at the world with such naïveté and he marveled that it took as little as an evening whiff of orange blossom to recall perfectly that innocence, that simple-minded happiness. And yet.

And yet he had been happy. He was sure of that. Everything he had done until then had been in preparation, a teeing up. His life was all possibility then, all good things to come. Maybe that is the false clarity that sports gives to the young, he thought. You did your running over the summer, you lifted weights, you did your layups. Then the season started and you won or you lost and the season was over and you went to the team banquet and slapped the guys on the shoulder and said, "Way to go, Joe" and "All right, Kent." And then summer came and you did your running . . .

It seemed too good, Cassidy thought, and it was.

In high school he had thought of sports as a way of life, but years later when he finally left Kernsville with his two degrees,

he had come to think of sports as a refuge—a welcome one—
from life.

There were a lot of bugs out tonight and one with a particularly hard shell would occasionally pop him pretty good on the
cheek or forehead. He thought about stopping and putting on
the little butterfly windshield, or maybe the faceplate on his
helmet, but they were buried in his saddlebags and it would be
dawn soon and the bugs would go to earth as all things do.

Big Jim Pegram was dead. Cassidy would get used to it, he
supposed, and it was a long way up to North Carolina and there
would be time to think about it. Time for decisions and revisions.
He had buried his best friend so recently he could still smell the
freshly dug earth. Now he was going to bury his grandfather. He
couldn't shake the feeling that it wasn't supposed to be like this,
that there was something important he had forgotten to do that
had caused everything to go wrong.

Is it possible, he thought, that getting older is a process of
losing pieces of yourself along the way, and that it just goes on
until there isn't anything left?

A glint of mango dawn light was showing as he hit the Sanford exit for the diner where he was to meet Andrea. Well, here
is a dusty carton from the attic, he thought.

14

Andrea

H IS HEART THUNKED just a little as he watched her get out of her car and walk to the entrance, and he was probably the only one who would have noticed the hint of anything wrong with her gait. It was the flawed-perfection thing that had rendered him helpless from the beginning. Her blond hair was in a fetching ponytail and despite the floppy green scrubs you could tell she stayed in shape. She wasn't really all that tall, but the authority of her movement gave that impression.

He definitely was not the only one who watched her make her way to his booth, as several dozen seed corn and John Deere baseball cap bills swung around like radar wings and tracked her right to where he kissed her on the mouth briefly and held her a second too long.

A biker among truckers, he had been ignored up until then and now he was merely hated; you could cut the testosterone-laced hostility with a spatula.

"You," she said.

"I'd like to drag you right under the table right now."

"Always the romantic. What are you working on?"

"Just jotting down some notes."

"Like a journal?"

"Sort of. So, how're things?"

"Good. Busy. I'm operating this morning in fact."

"How's he doing?"

"He's fine, Quenton. And he's . . . He's fine, Quenton."

"Ah."

"Come on."

"No kids yet?"

"Quenton, we're separated. We have been for almost a year."

"You're not serious."

She just looked at him.

"Why didn't you . . ." He was shaking his head at her, unbelieving.

"Sure. I'm going to call you up and say, *Hey, guess what, Quenton? I'm available again.*"

"Yes. That."

"No. And I wasn't really. And still not. I needed some alone time."

"Okay."

Her sad little smile caused some kind of physical sensation in his chest and he thought no wonder they talk about the heart this and the heart that. He was perhaps channeling a little of her pain and he realized for the first time something startling: that everyone, every single last one of us who isn't still a child, is carrying some kind of very heavy burden.

"Tell me about what you do," he said. "You still like fixing eyeballs?"

"Oh, it's wonderful. You can't imagine how grateful people can be if you can keep them from going blind."

"Oh yes I can."

"I find that I have some kind of innate talent for moving a laser beam around with my chin. We have three others in the practice and that spreads it around so there's less on call. Plus retinal surgery is not one of those really hectic specialties. You can have a life. Like right now. I don't have to be in until ten this morning. It's lovely."

"It's nice to know exactly who to call if my eyeball falls out."

"Not your eyeball. Just your retina. And you keep riding those things and you'll need some kind of medical attention sooner or later."

"I'm on my way to North Carolina. Big Jim died yesterday morning."

"I know. I talked to Roland."

"That busybody."

"Cass, I called him and made him. Your message was cryptic as usual and I was worried. And I *like* Roland."

"Everyone does. It's okay."

"But why are you riding that thing? Surely you own a car by now."

"It wouldn't start and I just got mad and hopped on the bike. Besides, it gives you time to think. Inside the helmet that's all there is to do. That, or sing."

She flashed to one of the times long ago when they had still been together.

A glorious spring Saturday morning he had run early and they'd rented a tandem bike and were riding the narrow little asphalt bike trail from Kernsville to Payne's Prairie. She was in front, getting tired after ten fast miles and on the verge of turning to suggest that maybe they ought to slow down or even stop and rest for a minute, when she noticed that they were going faster.

It was her job to steer and there were cyclists coming from the other direction so she had to pay attention. He's trying to prove something to me, the son of a bitch, she thought. He noticed that I was slacking off and now he's going to show me.

Within a few moments, though, they were seriously moving and they were also beginning to encounter more traffic both coming and going. She had to swing out and get around slower bikers—which was everyone—and to stay well over from oncoming traffic. Still their speed was increasing and she was perspiring, not from effort, but from nerves and concentration. She glanced hurriedly down at the little speedometer and her eyes went wide when she saw that the needle was almost on thirty and by now she had stopped pedaling altogether.

Goddammit, she said to herself. She was really angry now and just waiting for a clear space so she could turn and tell him what brand of asshole he was. That's when she heard it.

At first she thought he was mumbling something to her, maybe a taunt of some kind, but then she recognized the words: *"He's not a gypsy my father, she said, but lord of these lands all over and I will stay to my dyin' day with my whistle-uh-ing gy-uh-psy roh-oh-oh-ver."*

She couldn't help it, she laughed despite her fear, which quickly went away and was replaced by something else. They passed another couple on a tandem so quickly that the girl looked up at them with wild eyes and jumped.

Then it was clear ahead for a while and Andrea turned to look at him and sure enough his head was down and he was grinding happily away paying no attention whatever.

And he was singing.

And Cassidy never figured out why she started braking and signaling to him and finally bringing them to a stop where she pushed the bike over and held him quietly for some unfathomable reason as he kept saying what's wrong what's wrong and she said shut up shut up.

And now here they were looking across the table from each other at an angry truck stop in central Florida and he was again trying to figure out what he had done wrong.

15

Cedar Mountain

I T WAS GETTING late in the afternoon when he pointed the Vincent into the switchbacks up and over Caesar's Head from South to North Carolina. Scraps of whitish mist blew across the mountain road more and more thickly until it finally became just a normal fog bank. It was that same mist that had hidden the top of the mountain since before Greenville. When you were in it, it was fog, but from down below it was just another cloud in the sky. He had made this trip up over Caesar's Head a thousand times since that first boyhood summer, joyfully fleeing the insane heat of the Florida flatlands. It felt like a return to something cooler and simpler, these homecomings to a little town that lived in the clouds.

After several minutes of negotiating misty hairpin turns—flicking his sunglasses clear every few seconds with a windshield-wiper motion of his pointing finger—he broke through into the gray moist landscape that had been up there all along, redolent of sweet pine needles, chimney smoke, and the earthy decay of wet mountain forest. He got the usual little lift from the bright red, white, and green WELCOME sign as he crossed the border between the Carolinas, then rumbled along through thick forest for a while before he began passing the occasional homey little cottage tucked snugly back in the deep green laurel and junipers, curling smoke from brick chimneys anticipating a chilly evening coming on. Everything around including him and his motorcycle was dripping as if from rain, but he knew it was just the pervasive mist. Sometimes it would be like that in the morning and it would be hard to convince yourself that it would burn off later and turn out to be a perfectly gorgeous day. Or not. Those were good days to keep the kettle on the hob.

Cassidy sighed and hunched over the gas tank wetly, putting his left hand into his jacket pocket, and homed in on Cedar Mountain like the motorized prodigal that he was.

The house had always been there.

There was nothing special about it to a stranger, he supposed, just a big two-story white clapboard farmhouse built up off the ground on a brick foundation, an old house of no particular era or architectural style, handsome and solid, the cupped brick steps on the front porch a worn monument to the comings and goings of several generations. Gleeful kids, young soldiers, prideful graduates, grieving widows had worn down the hardened clay in all seasons and all weathers and were all the same people making different trips.

It was the kind of house you saw off in the distance when driving out in the country, far away from cities and interstates. The house had a big front porch with a swing hanging from chains and several metal motel chairs, a porch that got used. The front yard with its lush cool grass and single cherry tree was perfect for chasing lightning bugs and playing tag on long summer evenings while the grown-ups sat on the porch watching the occasional car go by, fanning themselves and gossiping.

There was a scary basement full of rusty old chains and

imponderable farm implements from a horse-drawn era. For some reason only half the floor was concrete; the remainder was dusty earth that had not seen direct sunlight in a hundred years. Down there you could see how strongly built the house was, with thick ax-marked joists that bespoke an age when nature did not easily give up the goods in smoothly geometric forms. Squared-off handmade nails could be seen down there, bullied with great effort into the dense wood.

All of the space down there was used for something. There were sacks of black walnuts, strings of apples hung up to dry, burlap bags of onions, potatoes, beets, and whatnot. There were dozens of rough plank shelves along the back wall holding row on row of Mason jars, what the old woman called her "perserves": pickled pears, onions, watermelon rind, beets, apricots, peaches. There were just plain pickles too, of several different varieties and levels of pungency. Also: stewed tomatoes, chopped okra, strange yellow beans, blackberry jam from the fields down by the pond, apple butter, peach butter, raspberry jam, rhubarb, pawpaw, cherry jam made from the bright sour billy cherries in the front yard. They went on and on, the dusty labels, mostly in his grandmother's scratchy hand, but many with notations from aunts, cousins, neighbors, or friends, some of whom were still alive. As a child he had been mystified by this dusty bounty. He knew very well that food came from grocery stores and he theorized that this subterranean hoarding had something to do with the Cold War. He decided that when the Russians finally bombed his family, they'd all live in this basement, surviving happily on jam and walnuts. His big fear was that he would eventually be enjoined to sup on cold okra or those strange yellow beans and he could imagine civilization coming to no worse end.

There was an old saddle and horse tack from when his uncles had gone through their western phase, and there were water skis and snow skis, golf clubs, fishing tackle, ball gloves, pitons, and various-shaped rackets from their other phases. Grandma's incongruously new and modern washer and dryer stood in a neat, well-lit corner, and beside them a freezer full of wild meat that had mostly been shot, hooked, trapped, or run over within three miles of where it now sat in icy repose.

The house also had an attic, which the other children thought was nearly as scary as the basement, but Cassidy found fascinating. He spent hours spelunking up there in the boxes of sepia photographs, unlikely clothing, spooky-eyed hunting trophies, and endless musty boxes of brittle papers, books, and magazines.

The warp and weave of the house exuded the institutional memory of the family and he always thought of it as whirring with communal activity: cooking, mending, making, cleaning: an ancestral hive. So Cassidy was surprised to see no cars in the gravel driveway, just his grandfather's familiar pickup. Then he recalled that some years back they had stopped doing things the old way and that they probably were not *sitting with the body* anymore. So he wouldn't have to deal with his grandfather laid out in a gardenia-infused haze in the same parlor he associated with visiting pastors and rainy-day Parcheesi games. The funeral home was the new way and the more affluent mountain families had been only too happy to get away from the grisly customs. It was now more or less acceptable to export a portion of your grief out to an establishment that specialized in repackaging it and selling it back to you.

Cassidy switched off the bike and sat still, stiff and tired for a moment, heaving a huge sigh in the ringing silence now interrupted only by the clicking of the hot engine cooling. As he gingerly climbed the back stairs up to the screened-in porch off the kitchen it occurred to him that everyone might be gone. She didn't drive anymore, but someone might have come by to take her down to the funeral home.

The house looked the same and he became light-headed with nostalgia at the familiar smells of wood smoke, breakfast sausage, boiled coffee, simmering green beans, old paper, heart-of-pine paneling, and something fine, musty, and pillowy from the feathers of the huge stuffed great horned owl that presided fiercely over his grandfather's darkened den. The furniture was the same; the upright piano, the paintings of hunting scenes, the doilies, all the same for as long as he could remember. Time was hamstrung at least in this one place, he thought, hobbled and brought to heel.

All the prepared food in the unfamiliar dishes were the give-away that this was a house of death. The kitchen table and all the counter space was covered with casseroles, bowls of vegetables and coleslaw, big jars of tea, plates of cookies, frothy cakes, and several varieties of pies and cobblers. He expected the food but not the emptiness.

"Hello? Grandma? Anybody home?" he called out. No answer, but he heard steps on the basement stairs and after a steady, determined upward march she emerged from the stair-well gloom and came to him, drying her hands on her apron, making little throaty coos that were the closest thing to emotion he usually ever saw from her. She was a mutterer and no one could ever tell if she was really saying anything or just making a little white noise for herself, like a nesting bird.

She was a little wiry bent-over question mark of a woman with silver wire-rimmed old-lady glasses; her once black hair was now flecked with steely gray, pulled back in some kind of eternal grandmother bob. As he reached his arms around her and lifted her slightly it occurred to him that she had looked pretty much the same the first time he looked up at her so many years ago in this very kitchen. She had exclaimed, lifting him high into the air, "The first one! The first one!" and his mother had to explain later that she meant he was the first grandchild.

He couldn't ever remember seeing her when she was not in motion. Even as she got older and spent more time watching her maddening daytime television shows, she would not sit in furniture that didn't move in some way: rocking chair, glider, porch swing. Her hands too were always tatting, knitting, writing, mending, or just washing themselves in the air. Even if she perched somewhere, in a moment she would come to her senses, heave herself up, deposit her handiwork in a heap on her seat, and scurry off to tend to laundry, make a bed, change a lightbulb, fry an egg, or bring back a bowl of beans to snap, anything to occupy those whirring hands. Sometimes she would have projects all piled around her in heaps, and Cassidy thought this was when she seemed the happiest.

"Don't you have you a car?" she asked, still in his grip.

"It didn't want to start so I rode on the bike. Don't worry, I brought a suit." She sniffed in mild disapproval as he let her go and held her back to look at her.

"Funeral's tomorrow. Your momma'n them is down at Cooley Brothers. I said I'd wait for you," she said.

"You didn't have to . . ."

"You sit you down and eat."

"Grandma . . ." He started to protest, but she just pushed him down into the chair and cleared a space in front of him. So he did what he was told. He had long since learned it was easier to sit down and eat something no matter how little appetite he had. She wouldn't leave you alone until you did. It was the same with her own grown children, as well as pastors, neighbors, Grandpa's employees or business associates, and anyone else who entered the house through her kitchen, which was almost everyone. He noticed that most people just complied as he did, and sat right down and helped themselves to, if nothing else, a few cucumber slices in wine vinegar. It didn't matter to her what you ate, as long as you took the sacrament. She'd try to force something else on you before you got up, just to make sure you weren't still hungry and were just trying to be polite. His grandmother, he learned, was steeped in the Great Depression, when lots of people were hungry but pretended not to be.

Cassidy took some tomato slices, a cold biscuit, and a sausage patty no doubt left over from that morning's predawn breakfast. She offered to warm up the biscuits but he said he'd rather have them cold so she sat down across the table from him to watch him eat. But then she hopped up and came back with a bowl, a grater, and a head of cabbage. She had made at least one huge bowl of coleslaw nearly every day of her life. Cassidy watched her as she sliced the cabbage head in quarters and began grating it, making her little nesting noises. She seemed mostly dry-eyed, though she snuffled occasionally into a ridiculously tattered tissue from her apron pocket.

"Are you okay?" he asked finally.

"Your momma'n them got in day before yestiddy. Took the airplane to Asheville."

It was something of a reproach, he knew. She was always getting in everyone's business, irritating the bejeebers out of most of them, but it never bothered Cassidy.

"I know, I talked to her. I wanted to drive so I could visit some folks while I'm up here."

She nodded and went back to grating.

"Do you want me to carry you down there now? I could drive you in Grandpa's truck." He was already slipping back into the argot.

"Naw, your momma'n them'll be back directly. They left right after dinner."

He remembered after a moment of confusion that dinner was lunch and supper was dinner in these parts. Or at least it was in the Piedmont, from which the Pegrams had brought their colloquialisms shortly after the Civil War.

"All right then. I'll just go up the hill for a bit and then come back and rest. Do you want me in Mom's room?"

"It don't make no difference."

He always stayed in his mother's old bedroom upstairs in the back, with the view of Panther Mountain, and he knew that his grandmother wouldn't have let anyone else have it if she knew he was coming. His mother seemingly had no interest in it and would stay in a larger room downstairs, or sometimes with one of her brothers or sisters nearby in their more modern homes.

But since his childhood Cassidy had wanted to be nowhere else. It was a room in which time had not merely been tamed, but actually stopped cold at the very moment in 1941 when his mother, a new high school graduate, left the house for the drive to Asheville to become a Coast Guard SPAR, to the shock of her parents and nearly everyone else in Cedar Mountain.

Dominating the tiny space was a bouncy, squeaky, old-fashioned poster bed with a dotted Swiss bedspread that would pockmark your face if you fell asleep on it. There were doilies all over the place that showed off his grandmother's tatting. There was the old ginger jar lamp on the bedside table and he knew she would have checked the bulb because she knew he would want to read. There was his mother's scant library still there in the dark oak bookcase: several hardcover 1930s mysteries by Mary Roberts Rinehart, some Nancy Drew, her high school annual, one book of Hemingway short stories, and *Tender Is the Night*.

He slid her annual off the shelf and sat on the bed with it open in his lap. It was incomprehensible to him that there was such scant mention of World War II except in a few bravado-laced inscriptions from her male classmates who seemed eager to get the show on the road. It was the strangest thing to imagine his mom as a high school girl starting her senior year a few months before Pearl Harbor.

Over the years he had asked her about some of her classmates. Whatever happened to ol' Rollo Scudnick, he would say, the book open to a page showing a young rake standing proudly, ducktailed, with one foot on the running board of his much-doted-on roadster, a confidently scrawled inscription indicating that the yearbook's owner had at least on one occasion been a passenger.

In response to these odd questions, she would give her son a curious look, think for a moment, and then say something like: "He fought in the Pacific. He still runs the service station down by Short Sugars. Or his sons run it, rather. He sits in there and reads the Asheville newspaper and what *he* runs is his mouth."

Sometimes when he asked about someone, she would get a wistful look and say something like: "Oh, he was in France. He didn't come back." A pause, then: "A lot of those boys didn't."

Cassidy put the yearbook back and dumped the meager contents of the canvas saddlebags onto the bed, unrolled and hung up the suit pants and jacket that he had had the foresight to store rolled up navy-style. He put the rest in the dresser, and then—for the umpteen thousandth time in his life—pulled on his shorts and running shoes.

A very few minutes later he was on the trail halfway up Panther Mountain, headed toward the Feedrock Trail and Thunder Lake.

When he got back from his run the house was empty. He walked down the dark first-floor hallway looking for his grandmother. The portraits on the walls always seemed to Cassidy to constitute a dour sepia jury of his ancestors.

From his oval universe of dark walnut stared the sad eyes of his great-uncle Neal, the eternal doughboy, lost in the mud of the Great War and—like a hundred thousand others—forever eighteen up there in his lumpy brown uniform, dustily observing the days and ways of the cascading generations. As a child Cassidy had been fascinated and frightened by this visage from an unfathomable past, and assumed that the almost fierce seriousness of his relative's expression connoted hard-won wisdom and insight and a willingness to judge others—harshly it would seem. Cassidy was still very young when—rambling in the attic one rainy summer day—he found a box containing among other yellowing items a stereopticon and a stack of view cards from the war; scenes of black-and-white three-dimensional carnage so grotesque they became merely interesting—look, that rotting corpse appears to be pointing a bony finger at a road sign that says PARIS-36K! Under a single bare bulb he sat in an old rocking chair and read a letter from Neal the doughboy to his sister, Beatrice, Cassidy's grandmother, dated March 2, 1917, two months before his death. It was written in pencil, filled with misspellings and trite observations about strange-talking foreigners and their curious customs. He commented enthusiastically on the good humor of his trench mates, some of whom were from exotic places like Corvallis, Oregon, or Paterson, New Jersey. The four pages contained little wisdom or judgment of others whatsoever, and connoted mostly boredom, fear, and a palpable though bravely disguised homesickness. Even as a child himself, Cassidy recognized something familiar there: the workings of the mind of another kid, not much older than himself. And something else: this was a kid caught up in some kind of feverish and confusing nightmare from which he wanted only to awaken, to return to something safer and simpler and happier. But the way he writes about it, he's not sure if that happier time wasn't a dream too, and to dispel that notion he recalls scraps of memories: a pretty girl he had spoken to in Sunday school, a bonfire before the big game, a picnic down by the pond. Cassidy had folded the letter carefully and returned it to its cardboard box, and from then on he no longer looked at the face in the dark oval frame the same way.

His newfound understanding spilled over to the other pictures on the wall as well, and he began to see not simply the humorless Bible-toting icons rendered stiffly in black-and-white, but actual pink-cheeked folk who lived their lives as he did, in color. Proud of their hardscrabble little houses and bare-dirt yards and scrawny kids, but ill at ease as they tried to sit perfectly still in their best Sunday clothes, and *definitely* worried about how much all this was going to cost.

There was Cassidy's great-great-grandfather, William Allen Pegram, who had lost his first wife, one of the Dye girls, when she bore their fourth child, and then famously married her sister and churned out another flight of feisty redheaded Pegrams, one of whom, John Allen, had been the sheriff of Rockingham County until he tried to board, uninvited, a moonshiner's speeding automobile. The roads being what they were in those days, they probably weren't doing more than forty when he sprang from his patrol car to the running board of the speeding male-factor, but it was enough to end the sheriff's law enforcement career and his life abruptly in the early-morning hours of October 31, 1929.

Cassidy thought, I used to believe that if I were in a room with all the generations of Pegrams back to old George in Colonial Williamsburg, it would be little different than being cooped up with a bunch of total strangers. Now he was sure that wasn't true. We would *smell* alike, he thought. We would surely recognize each other as kin despite the strange collars or the mutton-chops or the bustles on the ladies. And how could we help but take each other in, feed each other, bind each other's wounds? How could we not love each other?

He realized suddenly that he would have more physically in common with the men's wives than their very husbands, for he would have the blood of both flowing through his veins and their husbands would not, in theory at least.

At this gathering of long-dead and short-dead Pegrams he would be able to ask his great-great-great-grandfather Henry J. how he had met Clarissa, and why they had moved to Rockingham County. How much different from Warren County could it possibly have been in those days? Was it bad blood in the old place, cheap land in the new? Maybe just a good old American itch to get on down the road?

He would respectfully shake old George's hand, thinking perhaps this gentleman was never even an American, there being no such country then. Cassidy could imagine gesturing at the large gathering of Pegrams and congratulating the English-man on planting such a fortuitous acorn in the colonial soil.

And there would be a few whom he knew personally.

He would again get to see his cousin Connie Jo, with whom he had spent barefoot childhood summers scampering in the creeks of her father's farm, getting in daily trouble with her mother, Cassidy's great-aunt Mary, a quick-witted white-haired beauty who had a wonderful sense of humor but who brooked no nonsense from any child.

Connie had been a pilot for Delta, and had left them one bright sunny day at an air show in Ohio when she had to crash-land a P-51 with a stuck landing gear. She very nearly pulled it off, bringing the restored plane in softly and almost to a stop when it had veered at the last second into the control tower and crushed the fuselage and pilot.

He would get to look into his aunt Betsy's sweet face again. He would tell her that she was the first person he had ever lost. That her leaving had been his untimely introduction to real grief.

He had towered over her though he was barely a teenager and she was a young mother with what, her whole life in front of her?

But of course there is no one older than someone getting ready to die and so she was all but ancient lying there in that hospital bed with her head splitting and her brain understanding its own plight so much better than the doctors did. Understanding well enough to make a solemn request of everyone there: take care of my Ralph, take care of my baby girl . . .

It nearly killed your brother, he would tell her. All of them really. I never saw Big Jim cry, but I saw him turn away. Grandma bustled around, making jars of tea and putting out the food the ladies brought. People wouldn't stop bringing it though she begged them to quit. She stayed in constant motion pretty much like she always did, sometimes nibbling on a ham biscuit as she worried the linoleum from room to room.

That was his introduction to the huge bounty of a house of death, piled up there on the dining room table beneath that fierce giant stuffed owl with spread wings, and on the kitchen table and on all the kitchen counters, these casseroles and baked goods of helplessness and loss.

In his dreamscape reunion, he would tell his long-dead aunt: I didn't understand. I thought you'd come back someday. I felt grief mostly through the others. I felt it through Ralph especially. Neal and Leroy were on either side of him and of course they were very strong and they just basically carried him into Grandma's living room and up there to look at you for the last time. Lying there where they had taken the piano out to make room. The last time any of us would see you. As they were carrying him up there he was making sounds I had not known a grown man could make.

In his vision he would say: his feet were just *dragging*, Betsy.

I know, she would say.

16

The Poutin' House

THE GRASS WAS crinkly with frost as he made his way up the pasture as the sun was just showing over Panther Mountain. He didn't like running this early but it was the only time he could decently do it on this of all days. It would have been way too awkward sneaking out later after the funeral, and he was already considered enough of an oddball by these good people. Plus he figured the mild fatigue and the endorphins would help get him through it all.

He had come back to Cedar Mountain to bury his grandfather and he had to face the fact that before long he would be back to bury his grandmother, and then that would be that.

He couldn't imagine what would become of the old house when she was gone from it. He had a vague notion that everything would somehow be magically preserved as she had left it, that family members like himself could come from time to time as if to a museum.

But who would be there to bustle around, endlessly drying her hands in her apron; who would be there to clean, tat, cook, force food and advice on visitors?

No, time would no longer simply be hobbled or stopped in that place, it would go away altogether. And whoever lived there next would never understand that they inhabited a dwelling whose most vital reality was woven into the mental tapestries of others.

There was another old place on the property that had long informed him on such things. Ramshackle and lonely looking, it sat in a hollow in the upper end of the pasture up behind his grandmother's house, not far from where his favorite running trail edged into the forest. It was the old log cabin his grandfather had lived in as a child. Cassidy had always heard it referred to as "the old place," but then in recent years an occasional uncle or cousin, owing to a marital spat or a return from a faraway war or an ill-starred employment foray, would take up temporary residence. Cassidy noticed that his grandmother and then most of the others took to calling it the Poutin' House.

Most didn't stay long. There was no electricity, and the only plumbing consisted of an iron-handled pump mounted in the kitchen. The outhouse was so long disused that it didn't smell anymore, and there wasn't even a decent road to escape on. Wagons had been the transport of choice in its day and most people then had simply come and gone on foot.

For several years before the new barn was built the cabin had been used to store bales of hay, and because of the indifferent housekeeping of its few male guests over the years tufts of the stuff was scattered around, and the place smelled pleasantly chlorophyllous, the essence of clover and alfalfa from springs and summers past now driven deeply into its cracked and ancient timbers.

When not occupied the old cabin had been a forbidden and alluring play place in his childhood, but in later years he had passed it so often heading into the woods on his runs that the old pile of logs had become to him almost a part of nature, of no more note than a clay bank or a granite outcropping.

Running past it this morning, he saw that this old homestead was what happens to places where time goes away. He circled the cabin once, looking into its dusty hardscrabble windows. They take in troubled transients or they shelter cow feed and bored children.

Such places dotted the pastures and countryside of America, most not even put to such trivial or occasional uses but simply left to collapse in on themselves out of sheer irrelevance.

As he made his way into the trees, the tops of which were now gilded with morning, he wondered if his grandfather ever thought much about the old place all those years going about his chores on the farm. Did he look at those dried logs with their mud chinking and remember the days when he played in the dirt beside them? Perhaps it was some little-understood spark of sentiment that kept him from bulldozing the place, some wisp of nostalgia that fueled at least the scant moments of attention over the decades that kept the rusty roof more or less intact, the broken windows repaired or covered.

Shortly before Cassidy came to the intersection of the Feedrock Trail, his path dropped briefly into a dark ravine where the air turned earthy, mossy, somehow primordial; fecund air understood by both gardeners and undertakers. It was enough chillier down here that his breath became visible.

It was then he noticed for the first time that the leaves were already turning.

17

Henry

THE NEXT AFTERNOON it was rainy-dreary and after lunch Cassidy was plinking on the piano in his grandmother's living room—not a coherent thought in his head—when he looked out the plate-glass window and saw Henry's immaculate black '57 Chevy turn off the highway and head up the drive.

Henry came through the front door to avoid his aunt, shedding his wet jacket and grinning at Cassidy as he plopped down in Grandpa's worn recliner, jacking himself back into the maximum comfort position. He was short, solidly built, and still looked vaguely military with a buzz cut left over from the marines. A first cousin once removed, he was enough older than Cassidy to have always been known as Uncle Henry.

"Play me somethin', maestro," he said.

"What's your pleasure? Most of my repertoire is free, but 'Feelings' costs sixteen thousand dollars."

" 'Feelings' it is, then."

Cassidy assumed the stiff-backed formal posture of a concert pianist, hands poised dramatically above the keys. When they finally plunged downward, Henry was surprised to hear the first ten very loud and dramatic chords of "Exodus," rendered with great flourish and full-sustain pedal.

Grandma leaned in, drying her hands on her apron, took in the scene, and withdrew.

While he still had surprise on his side and a bare minimum of credibility, Cassidy snapped the lid down on the keys, lifted his feet off the pedals, and, using his left butt cheek as a fulcrum on the polished bench, rotated expertly the precise half circle necessary to face Henry.

"So, whatcha know good?" he asked.

"I take it the concert's over?"

"Believe me, it would only go downhill from there."

"Sounded good to me. Can't play a lick myself. Patsy, though. That girl can sit down and play anything you'd ever want to hear. Has since she was a little girl. Doesn't read a note."

"I know. I've seen her do it. How's she getting along? I hardly had a chance to say two words to her."

"She's making it okay. She saw you there but didn't want to go over, so I told her, 'Go hug his neck,' and she did."

"I appreciated it. I had forgotten how it was with all the old ladies coming up wantin' to hug on you, explain who they are. 'I'm Loretta's mama's best friend's neighbor from when they lived on Barnes Street.' And I'm wondering who the hell is Loretta and where the hell is Barnes Street. After a while I'm just standing there grinning and bobbing my head like one of those plastic dogs in the back windows of people's cars."

Henry cackled. He heaved on the recliner's lever and brought the chair upright with a thud. Slapping his denimed knee, he said, "You had any stew since you been here?" He pronounced it sti-yew.

Cassidy called out, "Grandma! Henry'n me're goin' for sti-yew!"

"Go on then," she called. He could hear her starting to mutter, no doubt about spending money on food when there was a gracious plenty sitting around for free that was probably going to have to be thrown out. She usually muttered loud enough for people even in another room to get the general idea but these two were already out the door.

As they approached the glistening car, Cassidy looked over at Henry and raised his eyebrows. Henry rolled his eyes and gave Cassidy a weary look. Then he tossed the keys over with a laugh and headed toward the passenger's side.

Cassidy pulled out onto the highway with just a tad of rear-wheel slippage on the slick road, winding up to near red line before hauling on the eight ball of the Hurst shifter.

"Drive it like you own it," Henry said.

"I sure wouldn't mind. Make you an offer if I didn't know I'd be wasting my breath."

"Your kinda money, don't be too sure."

Henry had been Cassidy's lifelong internal combustion mentor. When Cassidy was only eleven years old, Henry had sat him in his lap and let him more or less drive a front-end loader around the farm. In Cassidy's young mind that pretty much cemented the relationship. But then one summer when he was fourteen and had owned his learner's permit a scant two months, Cassidy was astounded when Henry casually tossed him the keys to his car-of-the-moment, a red and white '58 Corvette convertible. They didn't go far, and Henry kept him on deserted country roads, but as far as Cassidy was concerned this was a blood brotherhood. Recounting the experience the next year in school had brought on two fistfights and numerous shouting matches. He only wished that he'd gotten photographs.

They headed down Cedar Mountain toward Rosman, but Henry soon had Cassidy taking obscure turnoffs into hollows and ravines he'd never seen before. In a matter of minutes he was completely lost. But the rain had stopped and it seemed to be clearing.

"It was quite a to-do, wadn't it?" Henry said.

"As befitting a man of his stature."

"I never saw the church that full before," Henry said.

"Christmas and Easter, like the preacher said. Probably half the people in there, he built their houses. *Started* the church, him and Doc Coates."

"If the people were too poor for banks he carried the paper. If they didn't have the cash of a month, he'd take chickens or tomaters. Which he didn't need, usually."

"I never knew him to slow down until he had his stroke. All those years he'd have two or three construction sites going, not to mention his tobacco allotment and the rest of the farm to tend to, and on the weekends his fishing, and the turtle trotlines and the squirrels."

"You ever eat squirrel?" Henry asked.

"Not on purpose."

"I *know* you ate turtle."

"Only for cash money. I used to go watch them clean them when they came in. Scared me to death when they'd dump out those muddy burlap bags. They'd hold out a stick for the turtle to bite down on, then pull on it and stretch out his neck, then chop his head off. But what scared me the most was when they told me not to even mess with the heads, because they could still bite you."

"And they can too." Henry cackled. "Turn in right up here past the mailbox."

Cassidy turned in to the gravel drive of a small white clapboard house, the kind his grandfather had built hundreds of, perhaps this one. The house was so hard up against the side of a steep hill that it had almost no backyard at all, though you couldn't see a neighbor on either side for the thick trees. Wood smoke drifted out of the chimney. There was a small screened-in shelter in the side yard containing a pair of picnic tables.

"Will Spell's place," Henry said as they walked toward the shelter. A skinny man stuck his head out the front door and

Henry stuck a hand up in what Cassidy thought was a *V* for victory sign, then realized it was a *two* for the number of diners. A few rays of actual sunshine poked through the clouds, which gave Cassidy an instant and wholly unsupportable feeling of optimism.

They had barely seated themselves at one of the tables when the old farmer brought out a tray with two steaming paper bowls of Brunswick stew, an unopened loaf of white bread, and two big Dixie cups of sweet tea. He didn't make eye contact with either of them, said nothing. He placed the tray on the table, expertly split the loaf of bread in half and turned both opened ends up side by side on the table, produced two different kinds of hot sauce, nodded at Henry, and departed.

Henry carefully handed the brimming bowl across and grinned at Cassidy. "Hadn't I ever brought you out here for sti-yew?"

Cassidy shook his head, trying to slurp the delicious tomatoey pork soup from the big plastic spoon without burning himself.

"Naw, we went to a place down toward Caesar's Head off Highway 8. Lady whose husband made those mechanical lawn ornament things. I loved going there when I was a kid. All those little airplanes with spinning propellers, old-timey guys riding those funny-looking bicycles, everything whirring away in the wind to beat the band."

Henry nodded. "Virginia Coldiron's twin sister, Victoria. Died a few years back. Husband a few years before. But she made the best Brunswick stew I ever ate. Will's is close, though. Like it?"

"Can't stand it," Cassidy said, blowing his nose on a paper napkin. He was eating so fast the fumes and hot sauce had activated his sinuses.

"They never stop cooking it," Henry said. "That's the secret, just keep adding ingredients. Why, we might be eating a kernel of corn or a piece of okra two, three years old."

"If you're trying to discourage me it won't take. Is there any such a thing as seconds?"

Without looking back toward the house Henry threw his left arm in the air with two fingers extended, and in a very few minutes the old man was backing out of the screen door with another tray.

"He sets in there watching the teevee," said Henry, "but he keeps an eye out the window."

The sky had darkened again as they got in the car and before the souped-up engine roared to life, several fat raindrops had already splatted on the gleaming black lacquer of the hood. After two bowls of stew, Cassidy was sleepy and content to let Henry drive. The temperature had dropped while they were eating and Cassidy was chilled in his thin jacket, but it wasn't long before the heater had the interior toasty.

Henry seemed lost in thought, humming along with the radio, one muscular arm attached to the suicide knob on the heavy wheel.

Cassidy leaned back against the window, watching the darkened trees and hills pass by in the heavy downpour. Chad and Jeremy were singing "A Summer Song" softly on the radio and Cassidy suddenly had one of his rain-induced moments of faux nostalgia over things he had never experienced.

But what brought this on? Ladies named Coldiron who no longer served stew among a windy throng of spinning gewgaws? Abandoned cabins moldering away back up in these dark hills? Big sturdy men in overalls who once built houses and churches with their own hands, who teased little boys with fierce turtle heads, substantial men who nonetheless were no more?

Whatever it was, it seemed to have captured Henry as well. When the song was over he reached down and turned off the radio, leaving only the rhythmic slap-slapping of the wipers keeping time to nothing.

"Lawdy, lawdy," he said to no one in particular, "what does it all mean anyway?"

C

The Dickinson Legg series 600 cutter was big enough for two grown men to work inside, which was good because it took two millwrights to get the blade sets off. There were four of the huge machines side by side in the American Tobacco Company facility in Rosman where Henry worked, as had his father before him.

Each of these units could process a ton and a half of leaf tobacco in less than eight minutes, the big blade sets beginning to spin very slowly at first, turning the leaves into salad-sized strips, but gaining speed so rapidly that in the old days before they had density sensors, the operators would occasionally run the machine too long and ruin a batch. It was known as "powdering a load," and though you'd catch a ration from your coworkers, management didn't get all that upset because they had a standing deal with the Skoal plant just down the road in Silva.

But now that the sensors had been perfected the machines shut off on their own after reducing the broad cured leaves into so much pungent confetti, ready to haul off to the blenders where the different types of tobacco would be mixed together, and a highly paid lab-coated chemist would carefully pour in a supersecret recipe of rum, bourbon, honey, licorice, sage, pepper, cumin, cinnamon, nicotine, ammonia, and whatever else the vampire-scientists in Winston-Salem had come up with to help turn Bud and Sis and Junior and Mary Jane from sixth graders into lifetime addicts.

One thing about the sensors, they cost several people their jobs back in the early sixties. The machines no longer needed full-time operators to turn out a perfectly chopped batch, so they were all moved to other positions or retired out and not replaced. The loaders stacked their eighty-pound bundles inside, cut and pulled as many of the binding strings as they could easily remove, and closed the safety gates. They always worked in pairs, and the rule was that before they were allowed to set the timer and hit the red start button they both had to be outside the threshing housing and in direct eyeball contact with each other. For obvious reasons.

Henry didn't smoke. He didn't need to, actually, because he and the rest of the 243 employees at the plant got a contact high the second they walked through the doors of the big plant. In fact, there was so much of the stuff in the air that they would start to get a buzz in their cars every day as they got closer to the plant. Of the ones who didn't actually smoke cigarettes, not a single one of them could figure out why they always started to feel lousy whenever they went on vacation or drove off somewhere to visit relatives. They had no idea that they were going through withdrawal.

When he returned from his stint in Korea, Henry's father had landed him a job as a loader. Then one day when the millwright in his section was out sick, Henry got some tools out of his car and before his supervisor could pitch a fit and stop him, he had repaired a broken hydraulic line on one of the huge forklifts. The next day when he came to work they told him he was now an apprentice millwright. A little over a year later, they made him a master millwright and Henry knew he had found his purpose in life. By that time he could take any of the Dickinson Leggs—and most of the other machines in the plant—apart and put them back together one-handed and blindfolded. But as is true of any industry that can count on a truly motivated customer base, his company lavished funds on backup machinery and routine maintenance of all kinds. It cost the company in the six figures per hour when any of the lines went down so it was just good business to see that the machines were babied. They rarely broke down, and when they did they were quickly repaired and back running. A large parts inventory and a fair-sized machine shop allowed Henry and his more creative colleagues to repair or even invent what they needed by milling, stamping, bending, or drilling some piece of stock metal into a reasonable facsimile of a tricky proprietary item. Failing that, a courier could be dispatched from just about anywhere to fly some obscure and inimitable gasket or gear to the hills of North Carolina, all to squelch any potential hiccup in the three-shift-a-day process that fed the red-eyed beast that was the American Nicotine Junkie. Countless millions of them expected nothing less than a smooth yet full-bodied smoke, and by God the American nicotine industry aimed to give it to them. And then some.

So it was that the Monday after Henry and Cassidy went for stew, Henry and his apprentice were inside the number four cutter, both wearing thick cowhide gloves with elbow-length gauntlets to keep from slicing and dicing themselves as they removed the stainless-steel blades. They were self-sharpening, but when the metal got worn enough they had to be replaced. This was regularly scheduled maintenance and they worked quickly, unbolting the sleeves on either end and lifting the heavy blade set by the axles on each end. Henry's apprentice was a high school dropout named J. T. Samples, who always introduced himself as "J. T. Samples and the J.T. don't stand for nuthin' except the letters so no need to ast." He was an affable, dense young man who both amused and exasperated Henry. When asked by his section supervisor how the young man was doing, Henry would say, "Well, he's doing. He's a nice fella and I like him. But sometimes he don't seem to have the good sense God give a billy goat."

The millwrights had their own safety procedures, and no one else was allowed around the cutters during maintenance. The machines came from the factory in Richmond with a built-in fail-safe mechanism to prevent catastrophes. The safety switch was designed to keep anyone from accidentally turning the machine on unless both the inner and outer hatches to the hopper were closed and locked, which could only be done from the outside.

Over the years the millwrights had overridden the fail-safe

mechanisms on all but one of the machines because of some repair or another that required activation of the mechanism so that someone could observe or make an adjustment from outside an open hatch. Naturally, no one would have ever dreamed of trying anything like that with the blades installed, and usually the first thing they did when working on a machine was to remove the blade sets and stand them on end outside the hopper. But there were some jobs that simply couldn't be completed without keeping the gates open, so the millwrights developed their own procedures when working on the three machines that no longer had fail-safe mechanisms. First, they placed one of their huge toolboxes on the floor in front of the operator's area so that any passing idiot could see someone was working on the machine. Second, they hung a pair of pliers over the safety switch in such a way that you couldn't flip it without removing them. Third, they took two strips of silver duct tape and taped a big *X* across the red cover cap over the start button. After coming up with the scheme, the wrights used to joke about how some addlepated loader might manage to trip over the toolbox, flip the pliers off the safety switch with one hand and the tape off the start cap with the other, before tripping the heavy-gauge spring-loaded start switch with his stone-hard forehead on the way down.

"I feel right secure about it," said Henry one day. "I believe all of the loaders with that kind of talent work down in *South Carolina.*"

For consistency, they used the same procedure on all four shredding machines, including the newest, the number four machine on the end. That way, you didn't have to stop and try to remember what machine you were working on, you just left the damn toolbox in the damn doorway, you hung the pliers on the safety, and you duct-taped the damn cap on the damn switch. Period. If you were on the number four machine, you did it anyway, just to keep in practice. They figured they were just doubly safe when working on number four.

A month earlier, J.T. had been gone for four days down to Anderson, South Carolina, for his wife's mother's funeral. While he was gone, the number four machine was removed from the line and dismantled so it could be trucked to Reidsville, where they were starting a new line. It was replaced by an older machine they had rebuilt in the machine shop. At that point, all four cutters on the line were older machines with the fail-safe devices overridden. J.T. was told about the exchange when he returned, but he was still in a daze from the travel and all the unfamiliar people he had tried to make small talk with, and truth be known he wasn't that good a listener anyway.

That was one of the reasons it happened.

It was right at lunchtime Monday when they finished up the monthly lubrication and blade set exchange on number four.

"Short Sugars better start pullin' some pork out the smoker," said J.T. after they had tightened the sleeves on the second blade set. All the shopwrights went to the barbecue place on Mondays, the theory being that it would give them something to look forward to on the most depressing day of the week.

"I could eat if I had to," Henry admitted. "We'll do the run-up when we get back. They said they don't need it till midafternoon anyway." It was hot in the shredding chamber, and J.T. was wiping sweat off his forehead and neck with a pink rag as they emerged from the machine. Henry closed the inner and outer hatches to the chamber.

"You might as well go warsh. I got to take my toolbox back and then go get the keys to my truck," Henry said.

"I can drive," J.T. said.

"I know it but I can't leave this box and besides I have to go by Aunt Bea's and take her some snap beans that Patsy put up and they in my truck."

Before leaving, Henry stripped the duct tape off the switch, then hoisted the heavy toolbox and started toward the machine shop. He got about halfway there when he got a notion that he had left his long-handled three-quarter-inch ratchet handle in number four. J.T. didn't have his and had asked to borrow Henry's. After giving him a look, Henry handed it across so that J.T. could tighten the sleeves that held the axle in place on his side of the blade set. Henry was almost positive J.T. hadn't given it back, which Henry figured, frowning now, was about par for the course. That boy, he thought.

He could have taken his toolbox back to the shop and gone through it, but Henry figured it would just be faster to leave the box right there and go back and check. He was pretty sure he wouldn't forget it, but on the other hand, nothing would ruin their day faster than a half-pound chunk of foreign metal whirling around inside their multimillion-dollar cutting machine.

J.T. was in the locker room washing up next to their section supervisor, Buck Fannin, who was combing his hair and admiring how nicely his red 'Bama tie went with his short-sleeved fifty-fifty blend pinstripe.

"Four ready yet, J.T.? We could get a load done before second lunch shift."

"Done but not tried," said J.T. "Henry thought we'd run it up when we got back from Short Sugars."

"Hmmm. Hit it a lick before you leave, would you? I've got to walk over to admin. If she's not ready for some reason, just leave the tape on the switch and we'll wait on y'all to get back from lunch."

Dammit, thought J.T., hurrying back to the line. Henry was probably sitting in his truck waiting on him and Henry wasn't known for his patience.

As he stepped up to the operator's panel, a thought flashed in his mind that he ought to do the normal procedure and check the gates before throwing the switch. It would have taken all of two seconds to walk seven steps around the side of the machine, but then he thought, Naw, it's number four. Wouldn't crank anyway if the hatches ain't shut.

Plus, he thought, there's no pliers, no tape, and no toolbox. She's good to go.

It was only after he flipped the switch that he knew something was terribly, terribly wrong.

18

The Noonday Demon

THE HORSE'S HOOVES kept pace as they ran along State Road 12 in Kernsville, Cassidy and some of his old teammates. The dappled gray was pastured across the highway, and some mornings he trotted over to the fence line and paralleled the runners for a mile or so. This morning no one seemed to notice.

There were guys in the group he hadn't seen for years and running with them again made him happy, though there was something troubling floating around in the back of his mind.

Old Nubbins was up ahead, as usual, but behaving himself for once, and there was dour old Hosford, and the half-miler Benny Vaughn, and tough little A. W. Smith from Tenille, Georgia, and Mark Burr from Indiana, all running in a group while Benny did one of his commentator voice-overs, pretending they were in the final straightaway of some fantasy Olympic finals.

Then he noticed that to his surprise Mizner was right there at his elbow, cruising along with his precise, efficient stride, his fine-featured brown face glowing in the early-morning sun.

"Mize!" Cassidy said. "I thought you were dead!"

"Well, technically I am," Mizner said. "But you know I'd never miss a morning run."

"Oh right," Cassidy said. It made perfect sense. But he noticed that the sound of the galloping horse was getting louder even as he awoke and tried to clear the disturbing cobwebs from his brain. He had moved his cot to the front room of the old cabin, and all he had to do to look out the front window was raise his head up on an elbow. His uncle Leroy was riding up on his big gelding, Luther.

He pulled on a sweatshirt and limped out to the front porch.

"Morning," Cassidy said. "With that hat and those snakeskin boots, you sort of look like a large economy-sized Gene Autry."

"Can't sing a lick, though. Probably wouldn't let me in the cowboy union. And they're ostrich, by the way."

"If you'll set a minute I'll put some coffee on."

"Sounds good to me. Didn't have any before we set out at first light."

"Where've you been to?"

"Up Feedrock and down and around Thunder Lake and back."

"How's the lake?"

"Still there."

"Isn't it? I ran down there yesterday and I've never seen it so high."

"All the rain last month."

He followed Cassidy into the cabin and sat down at the battered table while Cassidy pumped some water into the blackened pot and lit the little propane camp stove. After he put the pot on to perk, he excused himself.

"How's everyone down there doing?" he called from the bedroom.

"About like you'd expect. Patsy's a mess. Most of 'em are about half numb."

"Yeah, well, that would be me, I guess," Cassidy said, coming back from the bedroom dressed.

"Me too," said Leroy. "They're going to do the funeral on Friday, but nobody seems to quite believe it."

"Can you make any sense of it?"

"Not hardly," he said, studying the burbling coffeepot. "Few years back this neighbor of Gloria's mama over in Roxboro came home from her own mama's funeral. She was in her forties, this lady. It come up a blow and she went out to the yard to get some lawn chairs in when a big old lightning bolt hit a tree. Knocked off a limb and it fell and killed her dead right there where she stood. Not hardly middle-aged and just back from burying her mama. People still talk about that over there."

"I guess that's why the preachers are always talking about God and His mysterious ways, like there's some really complicated master plan that we all just don't get."

"That *is* the master plan."

"What's that?"

"We're *all* gonna get it."

"What was Henry, thirty-eight?"

"Thirty-seven."

Cassidy shook his head, pouring the coffee.

His uncle was a big man, as tall as Big Jim had been, but leaner. He was deeply tanned from years of hard outdoor work and play. Leaning back slightly in his chair, denimed legs sprawled in front of him for balance, he took up fully half the kitchen. Well into his sixties, but for his steel-rimmed bifocals, he really did look to Cassidy like a movie cowboy.

"How are you making it up here?" he asked, wrapping rough hands around the heavy mug, blowing steam off the top.

"Not bad. Like living in a different century, though."

Lee nodded, still blowing on his coffee. "We thought about running electricity out here a while back, but then the tenant moved out. Man worked for your grandpa we thought might stay a while. Had a wife and a little boy."

"What happened?"

His uncle sipped his coffee and smiled at him.

"Can't say. One morning they were gone without so much as a kiss my foot."

"Well, don't worry, I'll at least leave a note to that effect."

His uncle rocked back in the chair, chuckling. "So it hasn't been too quiet for you up here, city boy like you?"

"It's okay. It's like camping indoors. I don't even mind the outhouse."

"Gives you some appreciation for the way folks used to have to do."

"There were a few critters, but I set some traps out and got most of them. Can't blame them, though. They had a good thing going for years and then I show up . . ."

Leroy set his cup on the table and settled the chair on all fours.

"Well, I told Bea I'd ride by. You know how she is."

"Indeed I do, Uncle Lee. I was meaning all day yesterday to get down the hill to visit, but then I just didn't. "

His uncle laughed.

"You're welcome as long as you like of course. Or there's our house, or Mama's, or any of them. All the comforts of home and no one would bother you."

"I appreciate it. I'm fine, really. Right now this is just my speed. They're going to give me some time off from down there and this quiet here is about the only thing that seems to help. I know folks probably think I'm about half nuts . . ."

"Half?"

Cassidy laughed.

"Don't matter what they think. They call it nerves around here. When Betsy died I got so I didn't know if I was going to make it or not. I got so I just couldn't think straight, and I didn't care about a thing. There wasn't one thing in this world that held any interest for me. Not one thing."

"What did you do?"

"Well, I came out here for a while. It was before Gloria and

I got married. They said, 'It's his nerves. He'll be all right.' I always wondered what nerves had to do with it."

"How long did you stay?"

"Almost a month. I worked around the place, one of the reasons it's in as good a shape as it is. Put glass back in those front windows, got the pump working again. We still kept hay in here then and I used some of the bales for furniture. I still tell people they don't know what a good night's sleep is until they sleep on hay bales."

"It still smells pretty good in here. And the cot isn't bad, but I may try that hay bale thing."

"Henry brought the cot and some other things in. He lived here for a while when he got back from Korea and he and Patsy had a rough patch. That mighta been when they started calling it the Poutin' House."

"It's a good name," Cassidy said. "Maybe that's what I'm doing, pouting."

"Naw," said Leroy, standing and putting his cup in the sink. "It's your *nerves*."

19

Mexican Cuisine

C ASSIDY WAS ALMOST on time as he banked the Vincent
 Black Shadow into the La Fiesta parking lot on the out-
skirts of Raleigh. Assistant Professor Bruce Denton, ever the
scientist, had given very precise directions.

Within a very few minutes they were holed up in a comfortable booth and equipped with a pitcher of margaritas and a
hot oily basket of chips, Cassidy munching happily, still buzzed
from the ride down the interstate.

"You're looking pretty darned fit for a guy can't run," Cassidy said, redundantly salting a handful of chips.

Denton looked chagrined.

"I bet I haven't gone more than three miles in five years,"
he said. "It's this thing they call pseudogout. It's this buildup
of calcium pyrophosphate in the joints. Took forever to figure it
out. Finally an orthopod whiz at Duke nailed it. It sounds kind
of silly, but when I'd try to run the pain would wake me up at
night."

"Jesus."

"Yeah. They told me I don't behave, pretty soon I'll have titanium hips," Denton said.

"Seriously?"

"Damn right seriously. I do the stair machine and this rowing thing that's pretty good. And I eat an amount of food that would barely keep a starling aloft."

"That can't be easy for someone like you. You were a garbage disposal."

"You don't know."

"Remember the all-you-can-eat fried-chicken things at Morrison's on Tuesdays and Thursdays? We'd have three or four skinny guys down there . . ."

"Pile the bones up in a heap in the middle of the table like a bunch of Vikings?"

"People walking by staring. The waiters thought it was hilarious and would keep hauling out these platters . . ."

"Yeah, the managers were kind of nervous though. Sure I remember it. I have dreams about it," Denton said.

"Night after Callaway Gardens that one fall you and Jerry Slavin went one-on-one at one of those Red Lobster crab-claw deals, shells and melted butter all over the place. And after all the carnage Slavin throws down his napkin, says, 'That's it. One more, my eyes are gonna grow out on stalks.' "

"He was a pretty big boy for a runner," Denton said. "He could put it away."

"And then on the way out you casually buy a Three Musketeers bar at the counter."

"Rub it in a little." Denton grinned.

"Jerry still talks about it. Saw him not too long ago at the federal courthouse in Miami. He's a parole officer in Tampa, had a case. Looked good though, still running a lot."

"I know. We do Christmas cards. I've also run across him at a couple of road races when I've taken some kids. Jacksonville River Run last year he was there. He's hanging tough. Finished in the age-group money."

"I bet he *still* goes to all-you-can-eat places. Probably does some serious damage," Cassidy said.

"Probably. But have you noticed how they've changed the wording? It's a subtle thing, but nowadays the signs say ALL YOU CARE TO EAT."

"Yeah, like they're trying to take the challenge out of the thing. 'Hey, Bozo, it's not a competition. It's dinner!' "

"Yeah, but to a five-foot-ten one-hundred-thirty-five-pound kid with three percent body fat who's just put in a twenty-two-mile day, it's pretty much the same thing."

"Was for me. Used to finish *all* the leftovers on the table. Not anymore," Cassidy said. "Nowadays I eat an orange I look like a snake swallowed a golf ball."

Denton laughed. "All that can change pretty fast. It can catch up with guys who don't figure it out quick enough. Stop running and turn into little butterballs. Remember Chris Holman?"

"Pale literary type?"

"No, that was Chris *Hosford*. Holman was the nine-flat two-miler from Indiana."

"Oh yeah! Cornwall called him Hoosier. Nice kid. Went to this dinky little high school with no program. He got his workouts by mail from Fred Wilt, also a Hoosier," said Cassidy.

"Right, the FBI agent who went to the Olympics in the forties. Steeple or something. He became a student of training techniques before there were any physiologists. Did all those books where he wrote to guys and got their workouts and published them. Everyone sent in their most ungodly sessions and said they were just typical days. Tried to psych everybody out. Anyway, a few years back Holman did graduate work up here, civil engineering or something. I guess he got hurt and stopped running. Had really bad bunions and had to get them cut off or something. Never really came back from it. Anyway, I saw him on campus one day and walked right by him."

"Put on a few, did he?"

"He was about five-six if you remember. And Quenton, he was about a ham sandwich short of three hundred pounds."

Cassidy whistled, unironically reaching for chips from a freshly delivered basket, salting them again while gazing thoughtfully into the middle distance.

"All this salt tells me you're getting in some miles," Denton said.

"Mmmm?"

Denton knew he was probably in a reverie of old teammates, friends once as familiar as family members, now rarely thought of. Cassidy came back to earth when Denton pointedly cleared his throat.

"Sorry." Cassidy smiled. "Brain just took a little sabbatical."

"No kidding."

Cassidy looked at his old friend and decided that he did look pretty good. The still-boyish face was etched a bit by time, but was tan and taut. There were flecks of gray at the temples, but the eyes still shone with amusement and irony.

"So what's it like being a professor?"

"Quenton, I still keep *Mad* magazines under my bed, if that tells you anything. Most of the guys in the department are like that. Once your geek self-image is formed, all the degrees and Olympic medals in the world won't change it."

Cassidy knew that there were probably people in Denton's department who had worked with him for years before they found out he had been an athlete, much less an Olympic gold medalist.

"But all in all the academy is not a bad place, if you don't let the politics get you down."

"Politics?"

"You have no idea. You get a bunch of nerds together with too much time on their hands and you're going to get politics coming out of your eye sockets."

"You doing much teaching?" Cassidy asked.

"Hardly any. This semester none. Half my time is research,

genetically induced pest resistance, which is the latest rage. The other half is extension work, out in the field with the growers and other ag specialists, so I'm usually on the road several days a week. Cotton is king around here, and the boll weevil is my sworn enemy."

"That explains the tan, I guess. And you have a pretty good group in the afternoons?"

Bruce brightened, refilling their salt-rimmed glasses.

"You'll meet them tomorrow. Yes, when I was still running, they'd just do my stuff, kind of like the old days in Kernsville. Now I'm more of a typical clipboard kind of guy. I head to the stair machine when they're out on the roads. Sometimes I mountain-bike with them just for grins."

"Pretty good group, talentwise?"

"Hmmm. Not bad. Some grad students trying to stretch it out, maybe make the trials. One kid, Endris, getting his Ph.D. in Kernsville, is taking a semester off to train with us. He's a miler type. Some marathoners. A few older age-groupers and outright joggers who just like the organization of the thing. Oh, and a handful of kids from the school team that Henderson turned over to me. You've heard of the Shea sisters?"

"Sure. They still have eligibility?"

"Julie's a senior, Mary's a year back. They could go one–two in cross-country this year. In track we'll probably split them up. Lots of talent, great kids."

The waitress had been back several times so they really tried to concentrate on the menus.

"What's good here?" Cassidy asked.

"Well, it's a Mexican restaurant in North Carolina, so it doesn't really matter what you order, you're going to get basically the same meal. The different combination platters just designate the way the items are arranged on the plate. But what you can count on is your guacamole, your Spanish rice, your refried beans, and some kind of grilled meat rolled up in some kind of starchy shell."

"Bruce, you picked the restaurant," Cassidy said.

"You misunderstand me, señor. I *like* guacamole, Spanish rice, et cetera. It's the number six combination dinner for me," he said, snapping the menu shut with a flourish. "On special occasions I will order number seven. That gets you your refried beans at three o'clock on the plate."

"But with number six?"

"High noon."

They hadn't really seen each other in person in several years and Cassidy noticed how easily they had fallen into the worn groove of their friendship.

"I haven't even asked about the family unit," Cassidy said, setting his menu aside.

"They're great. Jean does computers in the math department, staff type. Matt's getting to be a bruiser, God help us, maybe a football player. Terry's leaning toward ballerina. Some of the kids from the team are around the house a lot. It can get to be quite a zoo around there. You'll see."

"Looking forward to it."

"So you've been up here for a while? I was sorry to hear about your grandfather, by the way. There was an article in the paper even over here."

"Yeah, thanks. We've had more troubles too. I'll tell you about it. I've been staying in this old house they have up the hill on the farm. It's good and quiet up there. Good place to run. Good place to think. I've been up there for a couple of weeks now. But I guess the fun's about over. The real world is calling."

"Mmm."

"You remember how at Mize's funeral we were saying that it was hard to be sad when you just plain didn't believe it?"

Denton smiled.

"Hard as it was, I don't think it really hit me about Mize until just a little while ago, that I really wouldn't ever see him again, not in this life. We wouldn't ever go out for a ten-miler and then hit the Red Lion to drink a few beers and play bumper pool," Cassidy said.

"I know."

Cassidy idly traced figure eights in the frost of his glass.

"For the last few years my grandfather cut less and less of a swath. One summer when I was in high school I was sitting with him on the porch one afternoon and one of his old cronies dropped by. Old farmer in bib overalls—'overhauls' they call them—doesn't even shake hands, just pulls up a chair like he's done a thousand times, gets out a red bandanna to wipe his forehead, and he's going, 'Lawdy, Mr. Jim, it's a hot one,' and all that. Then he says, 'Mr. Jim, how you been gettin' along?' "

"Mmm, yeah." In his extension work, Denton spent a lot of time with farmers.

"My grandfather looked at him and—I'll never forget this— he looks at the guy and he says: *'Gettin' old!'* "

"Hah."

"But I mostly remember the way he said it. He wasn't trying to be ironic. He had this tone of voice that I didn't get for a long time."

"Yeah? What was it?"

"*Surprise.* My grandfather was surprised."

Denton nodded, waiting while the waitress distributed their plates.

"Runners are much more in tune with the winding-down process," Denton said.

"You think?" Cassidy was digging in.

"Oh, yeah. Your average citizen these days isn't that connected to the physical realm. Some still are. Builders, farmers, folks like your grandfather. In an older time, with, say, manual agriculture or hunting-gathering, you always knew how much less you could carry than a year ago. Or how less far you could ride or walk. Believe me, when dinner depends on running game to ground, you notice pretty quick when it starts to get harder. You probably haven't begun to deal with it that much yet. It happens with all athletes, but with us, with the endurance sports, everything is just too damned quantifiable."

"You've done some thinking about this."

"You will too. Modern civilian though, things happen too slowly to notice. Jeeminy, when did the basement steps get me wheezing? Am I old or just out of shape? And if you were never *in* shape, is there any difference?"

"Whereas we can just watch ourselves slowing down like there's a gauge on the dashboard," Cassidy said.

"Yes, the same black-and-white numbers that we used to live and die by as runners, all those landmarks along the way, like the first time you go under 4:10, your first sub-30 10K, all that. But if you keep at it long enough, you get to play it all back in reverse. I'll never forget the first time it took me more than thirty-two minutes to finish a 10K," Denton said, amazement in his eyes.

"Hey, you used to could *win* with that!"

"I did! But thirty-two minutes!"

"People don't realize what it's like to be in a sport where you can compare yourself so easily with guys in Europe, guys in Africa," said Cassidy.

"Or even with guys from a different generation."

"Or with your own younger self."

"I have to laugh," Denton said, "when I hear some old jock talking about how the old Celtics from such and such a year would run circles around these spoiled kids today."

"I heard this guy in a bar in West Palm go on and on about the Four Horsemen, how good they would be even today."

"Dream on. Imagine if one of those athletes could magically be brought to the future—still in his prime—and could see up close what a forty-inch vertical leap looks like?"

"Or a 4.3 running back going away from you without even breaking a sweat."

"Pretty much end of discussion," Denton said.

"You played some basketball in high school," Cassidy said. "Here's a guy taking a jump shot on you, and the bottom of his sneakers are somewhere around your navel. You want to block his shot, but you're staring at his kneecaps. And he's six six or six eight to boot. Jeez!" Cassidy was getting worked up but figured it might be the margaritas.

"Well," said Denton, leaning back in the booth and licking salt from the rim of his glass, "you've got me pretty much ready to turn myself in to the abattoir. At least you can still run on both legs."

"And I don't have the hips of an eighty-year-old rodeo clown."

Denton smiled painfully.

"Sorry," Cassidy said.

"No, it's true. It's kind of a karma thing. Payback for our arrogance when we could run a hundred miles and sort of pitied people who couldn't."

"Yeah, I guess."

"You ready?" said Denton.

"Sure, but first tell me something."

"Okay."

"Do you ever miss it much?"

Denton paused as he was sliding out of the booth and looked at Cassidy.

"Quenton, you'll come to understand this eventually. I had my time, I really did. It was wonderful, no doubt about it. Stood up there blubbering like a schoolboy with my hand on my chest . . ."

"Bruce . . ."

". . . and that was then. Now I have a wonderful life. Family, career, good health . . ."

"Bruce . . ."

Denton laughed.

"More than I can tell you," he said, picking up the check and handing it to Cassidy.

20
Creepy Crawlies

D ENTON WAS DISPATCHING his minions for the afternoon. Cassidy—pretending to stretch—was lolling around like a sprinter on an expanse of indoor-outdoor carpeting in the NC State field house.

"Group one, marathoners," Denton said. "Yesterday you guys went long, so five very easy for you. And I mean *easy*. If you want to be ready for intervals Wednesday you need to start getting your glycogen back. Take off."

Five of the age-groupers departed, three women and two men, apparently in a good mood.

"Group two, milers, et cetera, standard Monday," Denton said. "Three-mile warm-up, mile of striders, three times six hundred with three hundred jog, mile jog, three times three hundred, mile jog, repeat three times, mile of striders, mile warm-down."

"How fast on the intervals?" one of them asked.

"Brisk, but don't strain. Keep them consistent. No racing. Finish with some snap in your legs."

A large group, mostly undergraduate men, prepared to leave, each one carrying a spiked racing shoe in each hand.

Denton went through the remaining assignments, making adjustments as he went: he reassigned several runners to different groups for the day, sent one young lady with a sore metatarsal and possible stress fracture to the pool for water running. Two of the age-groupers had major competitions coming up and were given truncated programs within their groups. Finally, he turned to Julie and Mary Shea, a group unto themselves, their only training companion the Kernsville transplant, Endris.

"Okay stud and studettes," Denton said to them. "Thirteen miles no faster than seven-minute pace. Mile of striders. Mile jog. That's it. Interval miles coming up on Wednesday. And Dick, no collecting." Big laugh for that as they headed to the doors.

"Huh?" said Cassidy, as Denton grabbed his mountain bike and they followed the others.

"Endris," Denton said, getting a foot situated in the pedal clip. "One I told you about getting his entomology doctorate at Southeastern? He's a fan of mixed metaphors, like you. I told him some of yours one day. 'More fun than a barrel of rotten monkeys, barking up the wrong sleeve,' the ones I could remember. Know what he said?"

"Can't imagine."

"He said, 'It's no skin off my teeth.' "

"Not bad. But what's this business about collecting?"

"Oh, on runs Dick occasionally picks up specimens. He puts them in a piece of scrap paper or a flattened Dixie cup and tucks them in his waistband."

"Like you used to do with little plants and seeds and stuff," Cassidy said.

"Still do on occasion. But Dick's an entomologist and by definition mad as a hatter," Denton said. "One Friday before spring break last year he comes across this huge female wolf spider with an egg sac on her back. Dick finds a Dixie cup and scoops her up. Wants to count the babies, he says, maybe keep her as a pet. Back in the locker room he gets gabbing, forgets all about it. He takes off and goes back to Kernsville for the week. Next thing you know, everyone's back from break and someone opens a locker and suddenly it's a creature feature in there."

They were crossing the busy campus now and the sunny afternoon was clouding up quickly. Denton started laughing at his own story, making the bike wobble.

"Remember that scene in the original *Blob,* where at one point this big crowd comes screaming out of the movie theater? I was walking into the locker room that day and it was just like that. Endris's locker was just alive with very active little *Lycosa carolinensis.* Merriment ensued."

"Ah, the high jinks."

"Rollo—the varsity coach—wasn't all that amused."

"Aww . . ."

"We're accustomed to a certain amount of weirdness—this *is* a track team after all—but after a few days most of the hilarity had worn off and we were left with a simple infestation."

It had begun to rain, but neither said anything. In their college days they had run so often in downpours that it scarcely rated comment. The heat and humidity of north Florida often made the afternoon thunderstorms the best time to run in the summer. It worked tolerably well except for the perpetually slimy training shoes.

This rain was chilly, but they generated enough heat to be comfortable, even in T-shirts. On his bike Denton easily kept up with Cassidy, who was putting some effort into it, enjoying the soft trail that snaked around the perimeter of the campus. They would only be doing seven miles and for Cassidy it would be a tempo run.

The rain slacked off to a steady drizzle and they were soon out far enough to have left the campus traffic behind. They continued in a comfortable silence for stretches at a time, each lost in thought.

"You know, Bruce," Cassidy said finally, "you've given me some pretty good advice at some critical times."

"Can you hold that thought and repeat it later to my wife?"

"I mean it."

"Okay."

"It was scary how right you were about that time afterward, after the Olympics. It's a good thing I was at least a little bit prepared for it. Going back to Kernsville, the cabin, the routine, it probably saved me."

Denton said nothing.

"But it was still hard."

"I know."

"It was slow going, coming out of it, getting back to an even keel. I heard about some of the other guys who were a mess for a long time. Maybe still are."

"Yeah, I knew some from my time too. The ones who didn't have a very broad base. You could pick them out, the ones who were going to have a hard time, win or lose," Denton said. Then he added: "Losing's tougher, of course."

"I can vouch for that."

"A silver medal is not losing."

"It is in this country."

"You know better than that. Besides, not even every gold medalist ends up on a Wheaties box."

"I suppose," Cassidy admitted.

"Look at Bob Schul."

"I know."

"Only American ever to win a five-thousand-meter gold medal and couldn't draw flies at a pig boil," Denton said.

"True."

"But you came through fine, Quenton. You were as focused as anyone, but you were never one-dimensional. You had a good athletic career, you went to the Olympics and did great. And you came back to the real world reasonably intact. You came through just fine."

"Well, that's just it, Bruce."

"What's that?"

"I don't know how fine I am anymore."

21

Fire Tower

DENTON AND CASSIDY sat high above the city on an abandoned fire tower, swinging their legs like ten-year-
olds.

"The forest service is all satellites and stuff now," Denton
was saying. "They don't need the towers anymore and now kids
come up here to drink beer and God knows what."

"And runners."

"Runners will always find the cool places," Denton said.

"Like Tobacco Road."

"And the Devil's Millhopper. And I think we were the ones
who discovered that there were alligators in Lake Alice."

"I think that was de Soto."

"Hey, no kidding, here's something. Did you know that little
park we used to warm up in when we were in Tallahassee for
cross-country, what was it called . . ."

"Lafayette?" said Cassidy.

"No, the other one, close to the capitol."

"Can't remember. Oh yeah, Myers. Myers Park."

"That's it. Year or so ago they were digging a foundation for an office building next to the park, started turning up all these buttons and stuff. Thought they were Civil War era. Turns out they were very old Spanish artifacts, and what they had discovered was the site of the first Christmas in the New World, 1538 or something."

"Jeez, those were some hardy souls," said Cassidy.

"Lot of what they found was rusty chain-mail pieces and bullets."

"That kind of advanced technology probably impressed the natives but I bet it didn't help much with the mosquitoes."

"Or the water mocassins," said Denton. "But 1538. A quarter of a millennium before there was a United States. And this is a place where we've been out for a casual jog."

"Yeah, and our casual three-mile warm-up loop that went down by Lake Alice, where Yankee students casually wandered down and got their dogs casually eaten," Cassidy said.

"They didn't believe the signs. They thought it was a gag. The Northern kids read them, rolled their eyes."

Denton lay back on the platform, hands behind his head, eyes closed against the pleasant sunshine.

"So, are you sure that it's running that's calling you back, or is it just some earlier time in your life you want to relive?" Denton said.

Cassidy studied a red-tailed hawk skimming the pine trees far below.

"I don't know," he said. "Do I have to choose?"

"Hmmm."

"I've been doing some writing for a while now, just notes to myself, like a journal thing. It has made me think a lot about those days, what they really meant to me. One of the things I figured out—and I'm pretty sure about this—is that I never took any of it for granted."

"Yeah?"

"Remember telling me after the race with Walton to never

forget that moment? You said, 'It never gets any better than this, so you'd better remember it.'"

"Yes, I remember."

"Well, I didn't say anything, but I was thinking the same thing."

"Really?"

"When I started writing about some of these things, I realized that I was doing that kind of thing all the time. I'd be, you know, running along behind the guys on the morning run on the Bacon Strip and we'd come up over a hill just as the sun was coming up and I'd see the guys up there silhouetted against the rising sun and I'd say to myself, You need to remember this, always."

"Interesting."

"So I don't think this is about regrets or squandered opportunities, or anything like that."

"Good. That's very good."

Cassidy was carefully studying the treetops below but he had lost sight of the hawk.

"I'm not saying I haven't missed it. You know, the shenanigans, the weirdness. Real life becomes . . . mundane."

"I know." Denton laughed. "Anyplace else they'd haul us off to the laughing academy."

Cassidy chuckled. "You talk to any runner and it's always the same."

"My idiot cross-country team ran right through the middle of the library one afternoon. In one door and out the other. They wanted to do something to us but they couldn't figure out—technically speaking—what rules we had broken. We were all Miami of Ohio students, entitled to use the library, so they ended up just telling us to please be good."

"Yes, you told me."

"I guess I have." Denton sat up, rubbing his eyes. "Hey, what was that one you used to tell about the train?"

"Oh yeah. Absolutely true story. We were sworn to secrecy for years but I think the statute of limitations has run out. We were over in Blacksburg after nationals one fall. Mize and I were staying with Mark Stickley. Raynor and some of the Vanderbilt guys were there too. Raynor's girlfriend was going to architecture school at Tech," Cassidy said.

"Sounds like the right cast of characters," Denton said.

"Oh yeah. So, it's us and Stickley and some of the other Tech guys, and they're showing us this really neat twelve-mile loop that goes way the hell out of town. We're coming down Peppers Ferry Road and we hear this train whistle off in the distance and Stickley looks down at his watch and says, 'Uh-oh, we need to pick it up or we'll get stuck.'"

"Of course."

"So we're all going, Sure Stickman, and he says, No really."

"Like it's a gag, like the alligators."

"He says, No, this damn train is really long and it's a big deal with them to get trapped on one side by it. And to tell the truth, even though it was a sunny day, it was pretty chilly and it wouldn't have been fun hanging around in damp T-shirts waiting all afternoon for the Orange Blossom Special to go clanking by," Cassidy said.

"So now you're sprinting toward the crossing."

"Yeah, well, cruising anyway. We were just following the Tech guys. So we come around this bend and there's the crossing a half mile down the road, and here comes the train lugging up the hill toward it. Now, I can see why the Tech guys didn't give it much thought. The train is a jillion miles long, and it's going *slow* up this grade, like casual bicycle speed. It's not like it's a death-defying thing to try to beat it across."

"Oh boy."

"So these are all decent runners and we make it okay. But still we all think it's pretty cool beating the train and all that, and even the Tech guys are enjoying that we're kind of hyped up, and that's when Raynor says, 'Hey, come on,' and he takes off after the train."

"Like you can't see this coming," Denton said.

"Uh-huh. So we're all running, laughing like maniacs, racing the train. It's this great sense of power and control, because we can easily speed up and start going faster than the train, then slow back down and let a few cars go by, whatever. It's like, we *own* this train."

Cassidy was laughing, shaking his head at the memory.

"So what happened?"

"Well, this open boxcar goes by and Raynor just flips himself up into it like he'd spent his life hopping freights. It was easy. Pretty soon the whole group is in there, and we're all laughing, slapping hands, singing 'Trailers for sale or rent,' and stuff, and even Stickley is having a good time."

"He was a pretty serious runner, wasn't he?" Denton said.

"Definitely. So it was a pretty big rush, I have to admit. And, you know, nationals were over, holidays coming up and all that. Everybody was in a good mood. And plus, we had all read Kerouac. And how many guys of our generation ever actually hopped a freight?"

"Let me get back to you on that."

"But we've all read about it though, daydreamed. It's part of our cultural heritage."

"Okay, okay. So you're having fun."

"Having a great time. Getting farther away from campus all the time, but we're all in shape, and this damn train is going about the speed of a mama pushing a baby stroller. By now we've all cooled down and some of us are getting just a tiny bit chilled, not to mention hungry. Remember, this was a twelve-miler and we were almost through when we jumped on the thing. So someone says, 'Well, we'd better be thinking about getting back.'"

"Some party pooper . . ."

"Okay, it was me. But even Raynor says, 'Yeah, let's start looking for a good place to jump down.' Well, about that time we go into this tunnel."

"Uh-oh."

"We'd been going uphill all this time and we're obviously now going through a pass in the hills, but it's not open, it's through this tunnel. So now it's completely black-cat-in-a-coal-mine dark, but still kind of cool. So guys are now hooting and calling out into the tunnel for echoes and still having a good time. At the same time, you can tell some of them are getting a tad nervous."

"Ah, I think I know where this is going . . ."

"I mean, it's still upbeat until some of us start noticing that the rhythm is changing."

"Right."

"The clickety-clack is getting faster. And faster. We've obviously crested the thing and now we're heading downhill, still inside the tunnel, still dark as pitch."

"Geniuses."

"Well, by the time we came out of the tunnel, honest to God, instead of doing five miles an hour, we're doing twenty. And getting faster," Cassidy said. "So now jumping off isn't going to be a lark anymore. Everyone is beginning to work on the equation, jumping versus not jumping. And we're beginning to figure out—topographically speaking—just what we're looking at here. What we're looking at is a long downhill run into Roanoke fifty miles away."

Denton laughed. "I can see it!"

"And here's this bunch of sweaty, skinny guys in shorts and T-shirts without a dime or a piece of ID among us. And oh yeah, one of the Tech guys is like the son of a dean or something and his life is flashing in front of his eyes."

"And what are you doing all this time?"

"I'm trying to make eye contact with Raynor, see if he's getting it. Well, he's way ahead of me. This is his party, so he's outwardly upbeat, and he goes, 'Okay, boys, time for dinner,' and he's out the door and gone like a paratrooper in a movie. I look out the door and he's tumbling and rolling through the brush like a . . . like a . . ."

"Like an ex–Vanderbilt assistant coach thrown from a train?"

"Pretty much."

"How fast do you figure you were going by then?"

"At least twenty-five, thirty. Maybe faster."

"Man oh man."

"You could just see everybody pondering. They're thinking, Jeez, I know I need to jump, but we're going so fast that it's really going to hurt when I jump, so I don't want to jump, but then it's getting faster all the time, so the longer I wait, the worse it's going to be, but still I don't really *want* to jump . . ."

"So how did it end up?"

"With bodies scattered across the countryside. Raynor swore he found Stickley planted facedown in a creek."

Denton was flat on his back, laughing.

"I mean, you should have seen us when we finally straggled back in. We looked like we'd been in a war. Clothes ripped, cuts, scrapes, bruises. One kid held his arm to his side all the way in. There wasn't a single one of us unbloodied."

"But a good time was had by all."

"Well, turned out the kid had a broken arm."

"Small price for such a good time."

"I suppose. The amazing thing is that the oath pretty much held up. Raynor made everyone swear, and I think they were all scared anyway, you know, about what laws had been broken or whatever. Raynor told them he could get fired. And he was friends with Todd, told them he might get fired too."

"Amazing."

"Fortunately, like I say, it was over break so everyone had a chance to heal up pretty much before anyone really noticed anything. Well, except for the broken-arm kid. He had to come up with some story, I guess."

"You know," Denton said, "Vinnie Lananna at Dartmouth used to tell stories like this about some of his guys' stunts over the years, and I asked him, 'Vin, how can all those magnas and summas and fifteen-hundred-plus SAT guys end up doing the same stupid stuff as everybody else?' Know what he said?"

"Can't imagine."

"He said: 'Their brains are too heavy for their skulls.' "

22

Physiology 101

C ASSIDY HAD BEEN back at the Poutin' House for several days when he looped down to his grandmother's house at the end of his afternoon run and there was a fat envelope on the hall table, along with two jars of homemade pickles from his uncle Leroy and a sack of apples dropped off by his aunt Mary, Neal's jovial wife. His grandmother was nowhere to be seen.

There were several telephone messages, one from Roland saying please call when he got a chance, not an emergency. That was a little puzzling; he had talked to Joe Kern the day before, Cassidy growing effusive in his gratitude.

"I don't understand this," Joe said.

"Joe . . ."

"Why are you even asking? It's completely up to you. There is absolutely nothing earth-shaking going on here, and even if there were, Jennifer is coming along splendidly. Roland is fine, of course. And Karl is . . . Karl. Do what you need to do and let's hear nothing more about it."

"Joe, you have no idea how—"

"Just be sure to give your best to your grandmama. She's an extraordinary woman."

"She is?"

"We've been exchanging secrets."

He had been up the hill, reading *Of Time and the River,* waiting for Denton's response, which this envelope surely now contained. And he had been running twice a day for the first time in years. He had been trying not to think about it, just going about the routine mechanically, seeing how his body would or would not adjust to it.

The sun was still high enough over the mountain by the time he got back up the hill, and it was still warm, though fall was coming on for real. There were places where bright fallen leaves now obscured the trail. He got a towel and plopped down in the old rocking chair on the front porch.

There was a photocopied report paper-clipped at the end, and the letter itself was several pages long:

Dear Quenton:

I've given this a lot of thought and have spoken with some people whose opinions I trust, particularly Vinnie, who you remember I told you dealt with something similar with one of his guys a few years back.

I also called Joe Henderson, who has a kind of encyclopedic overview of the sport that I doubt you could find with anyone else on the planet.

In a nutshell, he says there have only been three guys in history who have ever run under 4 in the mile and under 2:10 in the marathon. They are Rod Dixon, Ken Martin, and Geoff Smith.

Shorter probably had the capacity. He was 2:10-something in the marathon and in college he ran the mile a few seconds over 4, and that was when he was doubling in most of his meets. He told me once he was certain that he could have done it.

So, with certain caveats, it would seem that this might be possible. There are plenty of examples that go the other way, of course, lots of guys who tried to move up to just the five or the ten and simply got hosed. They can't take the workload, or something. I honestly think a lot of them just missed the speed. Supposedly Snell said that he thought that he could have extended his career by moving up to the five, but I don't know. Ever see the size of his thighs? Going from the half to the mile is one thing, but the five and ten are a different territory.

But Quenton, when you talk about the marathon, you're talking about something qualitatively in a different realm. I know we've always made fun of the runner mystics and their blather, and sure enough track guys cleaned their clocks when they finally moved up. But from everything I've been told (and experienced myself that one time), it is truly a different ball of wax.

One thing that almost everyone suggested is that you should get yourself tested. All the science has really changed since the time we were competing. The research is rife with red herrings, but a lot of the basic physiology seems to be pretty sound, particularly in the area of oxygen carrying capacity and utilization, muscle fiber typing, biokinetic efficiency, and so on. They've gotten pretty good at measuring things, even though at times they're not quite sure what they're measuring or even what it means.

But they know a whole lot more than they used to, which may or may not be saying much.

I've gotten to be pretty good friends with one of the physiologists, Dave Costill at Ball State. We've been talking on the phone and corresponding for a while now. I've sent some kids up to him for testing and such and I guess he considers me sympatico and so he'll occasionally bounce ideas off me.

Anyway, I'd like to send you up there and have him run you through his rat maze and see what he says. Then you'll at least be going into the thing armed with some fairly objective data.

I've talked to him and he's game. Just let me know.

I also talked to that guy I mentioned in the psych department, used to be a runner? He said that he doesn't have anything concrete to back it up, but that he has long suspected that people who gravitate toward running or other endurance activities probably self-select for manic depression. Says he thinks it's like an occupational hazard, and that what we're essentially doing with heavy training is self-medicating with endorphins and such.

I don't know, it could be so much psychobabble, but it fits in with what I've seen over the years.

And Quenton, it fits in with several people I've known who are no longer with us. My friend says you should take it very seriously and he says that you should consider talking to someone.

Nuff said. Let me know what you want to do about Costill.

Bruce

23

The Old Woman

SHE KEPT BRINGING food to the table and he knew that she would continue because she had obviously been cooking much of the day. There was country-fried steak with mashed potatoes and gravy, green beans, stewed okra, creamed corn, pickled beets, a big bowl of her tart coleslaw, and the usual assortment of small saucers containing several days' worth of leftover bits and pieces—ham, biscuits, deviled eggs, potato salad, and whatnot—that she would keep bringing out over and over until they were finally gone or else petrified into paperweights and doorstops.

"Grandma, I'm fixin' to founder." In point of fact he was still shoveling it in and he'd never been so grateful for the bounty of her table. Cooking for himself on the old woodstove had slowly worn him down to the culinary simplicity of a Trappist. A pot of pinto beans had kept him going for days now. His mileage was up and he was perpetually hungry, sometimes soon after eating.

"You skin and bones, livin' like colored upair onee mountin. Younguns and y'doin's . . . Know good and well theys rooms upstairs . . ."

She drifted into the subaudible mumble that was her medium for describing and critiquing—mostly to herself— an irrational and probably insane world. Cassidy continued eating happily as she scuttled birdlike back and forth in the warm kitchen. A clock in the shape of a rooster told Cassidy he needed to finish so she wouldn't miss the beginning of her program. Occasionally he would catch a word or two and from that deduce in a very general way which topic she was on. When he heard *hay bales* and *'lecktricity* he knew she was still on his tenure at the Poutin' House, but her discontent was muted. She liked having him stay these weeks, his longest visit since he'd been a child. There had been a summer in high school when he had worked construction for one of his uncles, but since then he had been like all the rest, a day or two at a time and then gone, back to lives lived elsewhere she could scarcely imagine. And she didn't really count that last working summer either. He had mostly stayed with cousins in town, working all day and gallivanting all night, coming by for the fried chicken on Sunday. When he left at the end of that summer she knew he too had joined the throng of infants, toddlers, kids, adolescents, and teens who had noisily grown up full- or part-time in the orbit of her hems, lolling around a Monopoly board on her clean floor, falling asleep in her lap on the porch swing as she fanned their red faces, racing breathless up her back steps with a string of hapless fish or a leaking basket of blackberries. From her point of view each would walk without a care out her back door one last time and when they returned it was as an adult, sitting politely straight up in a chair, sipping iced tea from a glass wrapped in a napkin.

When he heard the phrase *wild as red injins* in her low ruminations Cassidy knew that this serial abandonment was her topic and that if she stayed at it she could work herself into a real tizzy.

"Yes'um, you pretty much run 'em all off, hadn't you?" Cassidy asked.

"Eh?" She was startled. His breaking into her reveries did that, unaware as she was that she was talking out loud. Of all of them, Cassidy was the only one who talked to her like that.

"Now they only show up on weekends and Mother's Day and your birthday and Arbor Day and about two or three afternoons a week," he continued. "Carrying their own younguns and friends from work and sometimes their neighbors, all of them piling in here calling you Aunt Bea and Miz Bea and you running around making coleslaw and gallon jars of tea. For an abandoned woman you go through a lot of cabbages and tea bags."

"Well . . ." She was loath to concede anything, but the house did fairly buzz with visitors at times.

Still, he knew it wasn't the same for her. Once when a garrulous group departed one Sunday afternoon he had observed how stone-silent the place went in an instant, dust motes twisting languidly in weak sunbeams, bony ticks from the hallway clock sounding through the stilled rooms of doilied furniture and oval picture frames: this house had *raised* its children. All of them.

"Hey," Cassidy said cheerfully, "guess what happened to me today. I was running up around old man Stone's property, and I was about to do a loop around Thunder Lake when I saw a whole herd of deer, must have been eighteen, twenty of them, all watering at the edge of the lake. I don't know if you remember how it is, but the gravel road around the lake is mostly on an embankment ten or fifteen feet above the water. So the deer are all down below me as I get down to the road and start my way around . . ."

She was clearing things from the table and getting a pecan pie from the oven, but he knew she would always listen closely to any kind of story. She might not know whether to believe it or not, and she might find the moral to be unpersuasive or wrong-headed, but as a young girl she had grown up in a house without even a radio, and people telling "stow-rees" was about the only entertainment a lot of folks had. The stories needn't have much of a point and they didn't *have* to be funny and they most definitely didn't have to be true. In fact, locally the very word *story* might be accurately defined as "an interesting lie."

"So they had seen me on the trail heading down toward them," Cassidy continued, "and since I'm running right at them, naturally they spook and start running along the edge of the lake a little ways. Thing is, they're running counterclockwise, which is the same way I'm going. Once I'm actually on the gravel road, I'm sort of directly above them and there are some trees and bushes growing along in there, and they can't really see me unless there comes a clear patch between us."

She put a way-too-big slice of pie in front of him along with his usual cup of instant Sanka, and for once she sat down across from him, a tiny sliver of pie on a cup saucer in front of her.

"So they run for a ways, and stop and look around, and when they don't see me, they start milling around, drinking and grazing and whatnot. Pretty soon, here I come along and sure enough, they look up and see me and they take off again, going the same direction, not panicky at all, just, you know, trying to get away from this fool chasing them. This keeps going on and keeps going on and those idiot deer never do figure out that I'm just running around the lake. Before you know it, we're back to my trail, so I turn onto it and head on up out of there. When I look back, those deer are right back to where they were when I first saw them. They had run two miles clear around the lake with me."

She sat, nibbling at her pie and thinking it over.

"Deers is supposed to be smart but I don't know," she said. He sensed that she wasn't too excited about this story. She preferred stories about people, and particularly ones in which certain kinds of people got their comeuppance. Although she found it interesting the way Cassidy told it, she knew intuitively that it was one of those that she wouldn't get much mileage out of herself, given her penchant for ruthless summarizing. As she rocked on the porch with one of her friends, it would likely come out as: "That youngun of Adelaide's said some deers run clear around Thunder Lake with him."

Cassidy realized he would come across (once again, he suspected) as some kind of wondrous fool from far away. Without the subtle details, the story lost not only all meaning but also all credibility. There was no point. In her high-contrast worldview, almost every individual and nearly all human activity could be reduced to a few judgmental—and often harsh—words. A person who didn't meet her standards of morality or thrift or hard work was "sorry" or "no 'count." A child who did his or her chores and didn't waste money was "smart."

Cassidy had known for a long time that though he was of her own flesh and blood, to her he was as exotic as a lemur. Even when he was a small child she could make no sense of him. Like the other children, he would wander through the woods or go fishing at the pond, but then, in his teenage years, he would also spend whole afternoons in his grandfather's recliner, reading. When he was not around, she would pick up one of the books, note a title like *Look Homeward, Angel* or *Sometimes a Great Notion*, open to a random page and read a few sentences of what might have been protocuneiform.

But there was no denying he had the Pegram energy, and as a child he played every sport and game the house and the mountain had to offer, either alone or with herds of cousins and friends. He was always recruitable for whatever passing obsession occupied his uncles at the moment: horseback riding, reupholstering, buck dancing, deep-sea fishing, rock climbing, stained-glass making, jungle-rules volleyball, whatever. For several years in a row it was water-skiing, and at age twelve he went from two skis to slaloming to barefooting, losing several bathing suits and drinking half the lake in the process. His grandparents—to him, it seemed—turned in not long after dusk, so he would flee the darkened house in search of cousins: Linda,

Catherine, and Henry were just down the road; James Gordon and Debra were nearby; the euphonic Dobie Kay and Tena Gay were just down in the valley. His grandmother eventually contented herself with the idea that maybe he would outgrow his strangeness or that it was something only she could see in their quiet moments together.

But when all the running business started with him and he would disappear into the hills for hours at a time, she really had no reference points and could not fathom what was going on. When it was explained to her that in school this was his "sport" and furthermore that it would be paying for college, she suspected that it was herself who was being made sport of.

In the winter of his sophomore year at Southeastern he made the finals in the NCAA indoor championships, and they all gathered around in her living room to watch the race on television. Not winning, but definitely *there*, in living color, inside the box. Somehow that clicked for her. If it was on the TV, it had to be significant in some way. And she strongly suspected that everyone who got on television was paid, and probably a lot. That made sense as well.

In the end she just came to accept the idea that people did things she would never understand or relate to, in much the same way her grandchildren couldn't fathom her tatting or knitting, neither the activity nor the finished item. It was something from another time, another world, and you just had to accept that it had significance and value to others, though you didn't understand it yourself. That was the breakthrough for her, the tatting analogy, and once she had that down she began to think of herself as a reasonably sophisticated and open-minded citizen of the world.

"Well, I got to get on back and get packed," Cassidy said, rising. He saw that it was almost time for her beloved *Rockford Files*. "Come on uppee road with me," he said, observing the ritual.

"I reckon I better not," she said, rising and drying her already dry hands in her apron.

"I'll be leaving early so I won't see you till I get back. Don't forget, I'm taking Grandpa's truck so don't freak out when you see it gone." He was giving her a good-bye hug.

"Naw. Take it on. I don't drive it noways. If I need to go somewheres I'll crank up that motorsickle of yours and ride on it." She was snuffling at her tissue and not looking at him.

"You do, you get Leroy up here with a camera. I'd like to see that," he said.

She didn't look amused.

"Look," he said, "I just have to take care of some things in Florida, and I need to drive my car back up here. I'll be back in a few weeks."

"Go on then," she said, turning back to her kitchen.

The next morning he went through a brain-wrenching cultural warp: from a night of slumber in a hundred-fifty-year-old, lantern-lit log cabin in North Carolina to a vacuum-sealed high-altitude nap in a modern jetliner over Georgia. As the plane "began its descent," he awoke to observe that the clear mountain air below had morphed into a muggy, yellow-brown blanket over the New South.

Ten in the morning and it's an inferno down there already, he thought. Sherman after all only burned the place once.

He was on his way to tie up a thousand loose ends from an interrupted life, but like all Southerners going *anywhere*—San Francisco, Buenos Aires, Hell's Half Acre—he was going to have to change planes in Atlanta.

24

Leaving Palm Beach
Is Never Easy

O F COURSE ROLAND pulled up to the curb in his three-wheeled Morgan.

"Roland! You drove the Morgan!"

"It came out nicely, didn't it?"

"It's beautiful, but where am I going to put my bag?"

"Oh, it's got a boot."

"It's got a boot. When did you turn British?"

For luggage Cassidy had one half of his motorcycle saddlebags, basic enough, but still too big to fit. By taking some items out and packing them around the sides they were able to cram it into a space not much bigger than a glove box. It closed with *buckles*.

Inside the passenger's compartment Cassidy was grateful his training had burned his body fat well down into single digits because Roland virtually flowed into all the available space of the little convertible. But he buzzed out into the early-evening West Palm traffic with inordinate pride, attracting either bemused or admiring stares. He was still in tie and suspenders but had his suit jacket off, folded neatly in his lap. The car had no air-conditioning, but the air flowed around them copiously and so he was perspiring only moderately. Through the traffic fumes Cassidy picked up the familiar scents of frangipani and hibiscus with a spritz of ocean. The abrupt transition from the North Carolina mountains was unnerving and made him feel as if he had been gone a long time.

"Could you ever imagine that thirty-six horsepower could be arrayed to such advantage?" Roland chortled happily, maneuvering the tiny gearshift lever with considerable dexterity.

"No, I could not. Nor will I ever understand some people's fascination with marginal vehicles of yesteryear. But then again, as a 914 owner, I'm familiar with the concept of the small 'boot.' Speaking of which . . ."

"Yes, I told you on the phone Harry retrieved it and it's fine. It was some valve or gasket or synapse that was interfering with the fuel system, as I understand it, and Harry said it drove fine now and that in fact he had had it up over a hundred miles per hour in third gear."

"Oh he did, did he?"

"Yes, and he said that that's exactly how you would react when I told you."

"And how is the redheaded wonder boy?" Cassidy held his arm over the side, dribbling his fingertips in the soft tropical air.

"Fit as a fiddle and quite ecstatic about coaching women's team handball again. He'll tell you all about it. He's meeting us for dinner." Roland turned east, toward downtown and the Intracoastal waterway.

"The Olympics again! Goes twice as a player, and now he's going back as a coach. Talk about milking a gravy train," Cassidy said.

"Gadzooks. That was bad even for you. But yes, he's all excited. Complete mystery to me, of course. I thought that handball was a sport played against tenement walls."

"They are two different things."

"So Harry says." Roland was yawning.

"Team handball they play indoors on what looks like a basketball court, except that it has these soccer-type goals. Harry claims it's the second most popular team sport in the world, after soccer of course."

They were stopped now, watching the Flagler drawbridge rise for two huge yachts and a string of sailboats. Cassidy had forgotten how soothing these little random intersections with the maritime world were. Roland said something that was completely blotted out by a skull-rattling foghorn from one of the yachts, thanking the bridge tender as he went under.

"Eh?"

"I said, do you think it's true, this number two spectator sport thing?"

"Not spectator sport, team sport. I don't think you could lure prisoners out of solitary confinement to watch it. The ball is the size of a grapefruit, so you often can't see it. To me the whole thing looks like a bunch of guys in shorts running for the bus."

They watched the last of the sailboats motor under the bridge, an older bearded gentleman in a floppy hat looking contented at the tiller of the last, one cork-encased glass of something or other in the gimbal beside him.

"Be sure to mention that, when we see him, how one of his life's great passions is so completely ludicrous," Roland sniffed, as the bridge's jaws bit clangingly together and the little vehicle whirred into motion. Once they were on the Palm Beach side the eccentric little car would hardly raise an eyebrow.

"Oh, we've discussed it at length. In fact, we often talk about how other people's sports look silly to everyone else. Curling, for instance, or water polo. Harry loves that old Bob Newhart routine where Abner Doubleday is trying to explain baseball to somebody over the phone. The game sounds completely ludicrous, of course. But he's describing it perfectly accurately. Every game sounds like that when you deconstruct it. Harry and

I finally concluded that everybody's sport is pretty silly except your own."

"They say that there are basically only two different sports: ball and chase," said Roland.

"Right. And the ball sports are the most ridiculous."

"Why would that be?"

"We figured that out too. In order for any ball sport to work, all the participants—and spectators too for that matter—have to jointly agree for the duration of the contest that some silly inflated goat bladder is the most important object in the universe."

"Ah, a willing suspension of disbelief."

"Precisely. A game is a physical form of fiction. The instant the game is over, this magical object is suddenly just a goat bladder again. Chase, on the other hand, is a much more elemental concept."

"In what way?" Roland was pulling up to the green-striped awning in front of Petite Marmite.

"Everyone understands the idea of escaping from something that wants to eat you. There's Harry!"

As he accelerated up the ramp off Military Trail and north onto the turnpike this time it really did feel like he was leaving Palm Beach. It was hot even as the big orange disk sank below the palmetto scrub horizon, but there was just a bit of dryness in the air that hinted of a muted autumn to come, even to these latitudes.

The little bright yellow car was packed, loaded down with all the clothes and paraphernalia he would need for the duration, but it didn't complain as he wound it through five forward gears. He then settled back for the long droning emptiness of the cowbirds and soggy pastures between Stuart and the southern edges of Orlando. He fiddled up and down the radio dial for a few minutes through the country-western wasteland but he wasn't much in the mood for nasally 'plaints about abandoned women, hard-drinkin' men, and their bewildered offspring. He finally flicked the radio off and hunkered down to the meditative hum of the highway. He had kept the targa top on and the little car wasn't air-conditioned, so he had to make do with the fresh-air vents and the occasional blast of evening air he allowed himself.

How many times in his life had he made his way up the gullet of this peninsula? As a youngster with his parents there had been vacation trips back and forth to North and South Carolina and points north. Every trip it seemed just getting out of the state took a small forever. Before the turnpike and the interstates there was an endless string of Podunk towns up 441, following the long, complicated ant trail north. To a sleeping child in the backseat it was a dreamscape of late-night stoplights clicking and buzzing overhead, neon shadows ghosting across the headliner of the turquo-green Ford station wagon, the comforting murmur of his parents' voices drifting from the front seat. Occasionally he would hear his own name mentioned, and though he could never make out what was being said, he felt reassured somehow in a universe where his own tiny existence might merit a comment from grown-ups. Later he rode big yellow team buses grinding up and down the interstate, bound for away games and regional meets and—on a very few miraculous occasions—to Kernsville for state championships.

Then during his college and law school years he plied the familiar route back and forth on holiday breaks, heading south to a hometown growing increasingly unfamiliar to him and back north to the university town that felt more and more like the place he really lived. He could still remember that vague amorphous excitement and anticipation as he headed north every September for the start of a new school year. The month of promises. At the time it seemed that he would be making that journey every fall forever.

After Mr. Disney had installed his plastic hippos and faux

waterfalls in central Florida, Cassidy had been able to watch in something like real time as Orlando oozed out into the million empty acres of surrounding citrus groves and palmetto wastes.

Now as he approached it again in the night he was struck by how incredibly much more of it there was, how much of the night sky was claimed by a jillion tourist-driven lightbulbs even from a hundred miles away. It seemed to defy rationality, this economic mandate that said *images* of jolly mice and bumbling ducks would command a far greater market value than real trees growing actual grapefruit or greening pastures that fed actual cows. But there it was.

Needing fuel and a stretch, he took the I-4 exit, paying off the turnpike card and heading east into downtown Orlando. His family had lived here briefly after his father mustered out of the navy and every few years he liked to drive by the little concrete block house they had occupied off Bumby Avenue, marveling at the huge oak that had grown from the buggy whip his father planted long ago in the sandy backyard. In his memory the neighborhood was like a badly overexposed photograph, bare and sun-bleached, the grass of the lawns still showing the sod grid.

The invasion of Normandy had been planned in HO scale on a huge mock-up in the gymnasium at the air force base three miles west of where he lived, the same gym where Cassidy would ride his bike to shoot baskets, lift weights, and play badminton with the other military brats. He occasionally wondered, as he took a jump shot from the top of the key, where Omaha Beach had been done up in papier-mâché, *how* they could have missed the hedgerows. And since he had made friends with some of the old-timers, with the brashness of youth he once put it to Harrison Chase, the retired OSI cartography spook who had helped design much of the mock-up and who was then a professor of geography at Rollins. Still chagrined after all those years, he sat after his badminton match in the bleachers at the side of the court and shook his nearly bald head: "They didn't really look like all that much in the aerial photographs," he said sadly. Then he looked directly at the ball-on-hip, perspiring kid Cassidy with twinkling blue eyes and said: "But thanks for reminding me."

Most of the families in Cassidy's old Orlando neighborhood had been military or ex-military. For several early years then they could look across Highway 50 to see moo-cows grazing at the T. G. Lee Dairy.

It was getting late and his old neighborhood was shutting down as he drove past the house. He noted with satisfaction that the big old oak had now joined a veritable forest of mature shade trees of every description and that this once geometrically stark and sunbaked block now looked lived-in and organically mature, the cookie-cutter houses now distinguished by an assortment of cabanas, carports, Florida rooms, backyard pools, barbecues, and outbuildings.

On a lark he headed up Bumby Avenue toward Glenridge, his old junior high school in Winter Park. When he got there he pulled over to the side of the road, turned the engine off, and sat behind the wheel in something like shock.

He was staring through a chain-link fence at an empty field. He got out and walked along the fence until he came to a chained gate in front of the single remaining building, the auditorium. Looking back across the street toward his car, he saw what had happened. The school had moved.

There was a new complex of green soccer fields and bright baseball diamonds, a pristine running track, picnic areas, apartments, condos, and houses, all looking as if they had been airlifted in the previous day and bolted down in place, complete with walkways, water fountains, restrooms, and acres of cool Bermuda grass. Right in the middle was, supposedly, his old school, built anew.

But none of it had anything to do with him anymore. It might as well have been a photograph in a brochure, from a school in another state. Still stunned, he turned back to the gate in front of the old auditorium and managed to loosen the chain enough to slither through. He walked around back to a grassy area where the clay track had once been. He remembered a day long ago when the coaches in his gym class had stared at their stopwatches as he stood bent over on the infield, holding on to his knees and gasping for breath. He had just finished the 440 time trial required of all eighth graders who did not have a doctor's note, part of President Kennedy's new fitness program to hold the Russkies at bay.

The older of the two coaches, a tall man with red crew-cut hair and bad knees, ambled stiffly over to Cassidy and leaned down. Cassidy was wondering what he had done wrong. He knew for sure that he was in serious trouble when the coach, whose name was Vickers, asked Cassidy his name. After he told him, the coach said: "After you've changed, come up to my office."

Cassidy now found the place on the grassy field where he figured the starting post would have been and sure enough, there was the rotted stump of a four-by-four still embedded there. He stood there enjoying a rare cool breeze, wondering what his life would have been like had he not set foot on that faded red track on that long-ago morning. Perhaps he would have sooner or later been shunted onto some similar path, but maybe not. He had been a dreamy kid, an underachiever bored by memorizing the exports of South American countries. Fate does seem to swing on tiny hinges. Sometimes it swings back, sometimes not.

He had stood in many stadiums since that fall morning, holding on to his knees and gasping for breath, sometimes with thousands of roaring throats in the background. It was an amazing thing to feel that sound vibrating your brainpan and to know that it was all for something you had just done. He had wanted desperately to hear that sound in his youth and he had eventually heard more than his share of it. He had heard it enough to know that it could twist you inside and make you an adulation junkie. He had heard it enough to know that you should not try to build a life upon it.

It was genuine enough, and it was wonderful when it happened, but he had had sense enough to know that it was also temporary, and would soon be forgotten like yesterday's newspaper. He was prepared for all that. But it never occurred to him that *the places themselves* would disappear, that the stadiums of his past would become empty grass fields or shopping center parking lots. Was that why he felt that world calling to him again? Was he trying to find his way back to that rare dimension he had discovered right here so long ago? Was this precisely where the universe had clicked into alignment for him, where everything had made sense for the first time?

Well, for a while now very little in his life had made much sense. In some vague way he understood that, like an esoteric but key trace mineral or obscure but basic immunological function, his life depended on what he was doing now, on breaking away from his comfortable path of least resistance.

He got back in the little yellow car and drove away from his first running track, or from its memory. If I drive all night, he thought, I can be in North Carolina for breakfast.

25

Sort of Home Again

AMAZINGLY, HIS GRANDMOTHER didn't try to make him eat anything.

"Lee and them's up at the Poutin' House and I expect you'll want to go see what they're up to," she said, grinning for once, happy to see him back.

"What's going on?" He put his bags down by the table, and sat down, stretching his legs out. It was getting toward late morning and she wasn't cooking.

"I don't have no eye-dee. Just go on upair when you're ready and see. Do you want a cold drink or some tea?"

"Yes, ma'am, but I'll get it. You sit."

The car was no good for the wagon road up into the pasture, so he rode the Vincent and was surprised to see both his uncles' pickup trucks, along with another one he didn't recognize. That's when he noticed the power line. The noise of the motorcycle brought them out.

"Well, well," said Lee, holstering his framing hammer. The other two had nailing aprons on.

"This here's Bobby Turner," said his uncle Neal, indicating with a hammer. "Married to Shirley? Juanita's boy?" The man was in his forties.

After shaking hands and exchanging pleasantries and the basic genealogical data, Cassidy looked back and forth between his obviously pleased uncles.

"Would somebody mind telling me just what in the *hell* pardon my French is going on here?" Cassidy couldn't help smiling back, so contagious was their barely suppressed satisfaction.

"Come on and see for y'self," Lee said, stamping mud off his cowboy boots on the dry boards of the porch.

Cassidy couldn't believe what they'd done. A storage room in the back was now a more or less modern bathroom, with an old claw-footed tub and a brand-new toilet. A sink was attached to a freshly Sheetrocked wall. Cassidy was amazed when he turned on the cold-water tap and water actually flowed.

"But how . . ." He was flabbergasted.

"Got the well on a pump now," Lee said. "You don't have hot yet, but you will after we get the heater in. You'll have it in the kitchen too, but we don't have the fixtures in yet. But at least you've got a real sink, 'stead of that old tub. You're on septic, of course, but you won't have to be raising goose bumps on your heinie makin' midnight trips to the throne room."

"This is just amazing. But what possessed you all . . ."

"Oh, we've been talking about doing it for years, get some real use out of the place. Nobody has ever wanted to tear it down exactly, but nobody had much interest in doing anything with it either, so it was just nice to have an excuse to get cracking on it," said Lee.

"And you won't have to use that old pump handle, unless you want to leave it for atmosphere," said Neal.

"Oh, most definitely. This is . . . I mean, it's just . . ."

"But you haven't noticed the best part," Neal said, flicking a light switch off and on.

"Oh, of course I did. It was the first thing I noticed. I mean, I don't think I've ever even seen what the interior of this room really looks like before, it's always so dark in here, even at high noon in the middle of the summer," Cassidy said.

"You're good with the woodstove for heat," Bobby said, "and we've got a real bed and some other furnitoor for in here, so you won't have to bed down on those hay bales anymore. We'll get all that in tomorrow or next day, after we finish the kitchen."

"Well, you can forget that bed. I like my hay bales. But you fellas are looking a little peaked. How would it be if I was to stand us all to some dinner at Short Sugar's, assuming we can sneak past Grandma's without alerting her."

"I heard that," said Bobby, working on the knot on his nail apron.

"Lord, there's a way out of here she don't know a thing in this world about," said Neal. "And it's a good time to use it. She's got some leftover okra she's been trying to sell for nigh onto a month now."

The next day, Saturday morning, Denton showed up early, pedaling his mountain bike up from the main house.

"Hey, nice improvements. When did you have time to do all this?" Denton was walking around the little house, exuding admiration.

"I didn't. Lee and Neal did it while I was gone. They seem to think I'm going to be here longer than I think I'm going to be here."

"If they have much snow up here this winter you won't want to be on those trails. We might as well plan for the contingency and have you come down to Raleigh. It'll do you good to run with my guys for a while anyway, get some miles in with some company and keep from going stir-crazy," Denton said, digging around in his backpack.

"Actually, I was thinking about Kernsville," Cassidy said.

"Hmmm. Not a bad idea. The A-frame's still available, and in much better shape than you ever saw it in. And Endris is headed back down to finish his dissertation. You could hook up with him for intervals and such," Denton said, still poking in the backpack.

He finally dug out two identical plastic-bound booklets, each about thirty pages, of the kind Cassidy associated with overly enthusiastic business plans.

"Here's the stuff Costill came up with," Denton said, tossing one over to Cassidy. "You can study it at your leisure, but I can give you the high points pretty quick."

"Okay, high points then," said Cassidy, opening the report to the title page, which read "Biophysiological Profile of Quenton Cassidy." On the same page was the logo and contact information for the Human Performance Laboratory at Ball State University, where Costill was a professor of exercise physiology.

"Okay, basically it says that you might have lost a point or two of your VO2 Max, though that is far from certain because you never had it tested at your peak. It says that you've lost exactly two beats from your max heart rate, which now stands at 205, and *that* they do know about. The muscle biopsy shows the breakdown of your muscle fiber types in that graph on page twelve. Surprise, surprise, it shows a high percentage of the highly prized red fast-twitch fellows that we would expect in a world-class miler."

"Seems reasonable," said Cassidy, looking at the graph and the accompanying photograph of a selection of his own painfully extracted calf muscle cells.

"What's not so reasonable is your plan. When I told him in a very general way that you were thinking of returning to active training, he assumed you'd be moving up to the 5000. You'll see there at the end where he concludes you'd make an excellent three-miler."

"I think I see where this is going," Cassidy said.

"Can't blame a guy for trying," said Denton, tossing the report onto the table and rocking back in his chair. "Got any coffee?"

"Well, Bruce, I appreciate it, but we've already been through this." Cassidy got up to put the pot on to reheat.

"You have got a point. For sure nobody gives much of a damn about the five. I can attest to that. Hell, old Schul would tell you too."

"Billy Mills got all the attention that year."

"Yeah, and well deserved. But where does it say there's only room for one hero?" Denton said.

"You're not thinking like a sportswriter. Billy Mills was a feature story on legs. Native American, grew up on a reservation, complete long shot, comes from behind. They didn't even have their casinos back then. Jeez, Schul was just a schoolteacher from Ohio."

"Hey, don't knock America's breadbasket."

"Ohio?"

"I was referring to the Midwest in general."

"Well, anyway, does Costill think I'm totally nuts?" Cassidy was pouring the coffee.

"Actually not completely. You can read it, but basically he says that your profile is very similar to both Rod Dixon's and Ken Martin's. Both of them have been through his lab. He thinks that's pretty interesting."

"And that would be because . . ."

"I told you before. Both those guys—and Geoff Smith too, but Costill didn't test him—are among a very select and very tiny club, runners who have run under four minutes for the mile and under 2:10 for the marathon."

"So save me the suspense. What's Costill's bottom line on my making the Olympic team in the marathon?"

"He says he thinks if you do it right you are probably *capable* of running a good marathon . . ."

"But?"

"But it will hurt like hell."

The next morning, after a leisurely ten-miler, they sat back down at the kitchen table to begin mapping out a strategy. Denton produced a sheath of calendar pages laid out one month per page, his preferred way to plan long-term training programs, as well as to keep training logs.

"Okay, I've blocked out a few months in a very general way." He handed the calendar sheets to Cassidy, each square filled with meticulous notations. Cassidy whistled. Seeing it all laid out like that would have been intimidating had he not seen so many like them before.

"Looks like a lot of overdistance."

"You're not kidding. I'm still hoping you'll take a look at this workload and reconsider."

"You're still on that kick?"

"Well, think about it this way. I don't really *know* anything about this event. My specialty is middle distances. Most of what you see there comes from picking the brains of anybody I could think of. I've run up a helluva phone bill talking to Shorter, Bacheler, Billy, Benji, Kenny Moore, Dave Costill, Dave Martin, Jack Daniels—the physiologist, not the distiller—and a whole bunch of other people. Oh, Joe Vigil, I called him out in Alamosa. Woke him up."

"Bruce, you've run 10Ks, half-marathons, you understand the basic principles. Hell, you've run *marathons!*"

"I ran *a* marathon. I ran a 2:14 and I considered myself very lucky to have gotten out of there alive. As it was, it may have been what crippled me for good. And Quenton, I've coached some fairly decent age-grouper marathoners in the past few years, but this is a whole different deal. World-class level, I think I have a pretty good handle on everything from the 800 through 10,000 meters, through ten miles, even. But I don't think there really are any experts on this distance yet. I'll help as best I can, but I want you to realize that I'm pretty much flying blind here."

"Well, I don't know anyone else that I'd—"

"And there's something else, something every single one of those guys said to me when I told them what was going on."

"Yeah, what was that?"

"They all said: don't let him do it."

26

Leafy Trails

EVEN THE COLOR-BLIND could tell fall had come to Cedar Mountain. The cars carefully winding their way up and down the switchbacks were all big land yachts with the women in the back and the gents in the front, and they all had Florida or Georgia plates. Cassidy's trails were now awash with fallen leaves, which seemed charming at first, then annoying, then downright perilous. One afternoon as he started to make the left turn at the Harmony Farms trail down toward Thunder Lake he was brutally reminded to pay closer attention.

Because it was a tempo day and he was feeling his oats again, he was moving along at 5:45 pace, feeling nothing but the primal animal joy of the wind rushing by his ears when his left toe caught the nub of a mountain laurel root hidden by leaves in the middle of the trail. It was one he knew well and had cursed before and had meant to bring implements up to remove. But he hadn't. His chest hit the trail with a harsh explosion of breath and he felt himself skidding along like a cartoon mouse, plowing a Quenton-sized furrow in the fragrant earth.

Even though he had hit hard he was pretty sure he wasn't injured, so a bizarre thought popped into his head even as he was still skidding. He had often wondered what it must have felt like when Lasse Viren popped up from a hard fall in the 10,000 finals in Munich. He caught back up to the pack and went on to win the race, a demonstration of dominance scarcely fathomable at that level of competition. So here was the perfect opportunity for an impromptu experiment, he thought, as he forced himself quickly back to his feet and, without even taking time to brush off the considerable debris, willed his body back into motion immediately.

What he found was shocking. He was so stiff that no matter how hard he tried, he could not make himself go any faster than a bamboo-legged jog, and even that was painful and surreal. Though he was sure he hadn't done any permanent damage, his body was still traumatized by the tumble. It simply wouldn't function. He felt a hundred years old.

After a quarter of a mile or so he gave up, slowed to a walk, and finally stopped to brush the dirt and debris off as best he could. He started back jogging very slowly, building up to the point where he was finally running again, and after several miles he was back to his original pace. This time with considerably more regard for the fabled Finn.

That was the high point of October, which turned out to be an Indian-summer month of warm days and coolish nights that saw him lighting the woodstove only a few times.

Denton's plan called for a cautious early buildup of mileage, most of it at a very slow pace, with a few well-placed tempo runs thrown in for mostly psychological reasons. Sanity runs, he called them. Otherwise, it was seven-minute miles with some striders at the end. He also did a thirty-minute upper-body routine in the afternoons with some very light stretching. The morning run was only four miles, but he no longer considered it optional. In the afternoons he usually went anywhere from six to fourteen miles, with the first several miles at a very slow pace in lieu of a warm-up.

It was a lot different from the kind of running he had been doing for years now, a sort of carefree out-the-door four- or five-miler at close to all-out effort, with liberal days off now and again when work at the office caught up with him or when he had overdone the previous day's run.

"That's just running," Denton told him. "It's not the same as training. Training takes discipline and consistency and it's not nearly as much fun. Also, it won't be easy. It never was before and it won't be now, no matter what you think you remember. I won't be here to slow you down, so I want you to figure out what various paces translate to on your different courses. When the schedule calls for a seven-minute pace, I want a seven-minute pace. You show back up here four minutes early, well, you record it accurately in your log, but just know I'm not going to be happy. When you send your weekly reports I'm going to bring it up. I'm going to keep on bringing it up until you're sick of hearing about it. When you get sick enough of hearing about it you'll straighten out just to get me off your back."

Cassidy had indeed forgotten the strange reverse logic of Denton's training system, which called for running hundreds of miles, but many of them at maddeningly slow paces. The advantage they'd had in the old days in Kernsville had been that Denton had been there every step of the way. And since he was by far the most accomplished runner in the group, it would have been not only presumptuous but risky for one of the pipsqueaks to spit out the bit and head for the hills. It happened on occasion, and when it did the pipsqueak usually found himself in an all-out race that he could never win.

As one of the milers in the group, Cassidy had been among those who most ached to break out of what felt like a boring and ineffectual jog. Now that his race distance was to be more than twenty-six miles, Denton's program called for an even bigger buildup of aerobic miles.

The real saving grace of the system at Kernsville was that they were all in it together, the varsity runners who had joined them as well as the graduate students who had journeyed south to train with an Olympic gold medalist. But not a single one of them could believe how slow Denton wanted them to run on that first morning. They thought it was a joke, that they were on some runner's equivalent of a snipe hunt.

Still, they stuck with the program and they learned to distract themselves with chatter to help pass the time. It became a very social little group of raconteurs and jokesters who looked forward to the afternoon workouts.

But the thing that really made it work was simple success. Everyone who stuck did well. The system was no joke, and the performances were no fluke. The miles piled up, but then so did other kinds of running, all nicely integrated into the program and interspersed through the training weeks. Everyone stayed boringly healthy and uninjured and before long they were running better than they ever had before. Cassidy didn't need to be convinced all over again. He had been through all that and he knew how tough a grind it could become.

He just needed to find a way to keep from going crazy while he was undertaking this strange and brutal process one more time, to try to make his last Olympic team.

27

Correspondence

Dear Andrea,

*The place has been pretty damn quiet and frankly a little lonely
since I got back up here. The accommodations are no longer as
primitive as I described, and in fact I now can boast of indoor
plumbing! On the other hand I don't think I've ever heard of a
runner complaining about free lodgings, and I give you by way
of example Don Kardong's old teammate who lived in the bushes
outside his dorm one summer at Stanford.*

*Anyway, I know I wasn't very articulate and that was a good
idea you had about trying to get it down on paper, so that's what
I'm doing right now. Probably as much for my benefit as for yours.*

*It's turning out to be more difficult than I would have
expected, as evidenced by the wads of false starts littering my
"breakfast nook" here. Maybe if and when I finish it, I can get
it published in one of the running magazines or maybe a book or
something. I could call it "Existential Meanderings of a Long-
Distance Has-Been." Anyway.*

First, I was as serious as I could be all those years ago when

I quit. I know we talked about it at the time, but I don't think I ever told you about those last few meets in Europe before I came home. They were decent performances—I was still really fit of course—but they were the strangest experiences I've ever had in athletics. It was like I was running those races in someone else's dreams. I didn't have it anymore, mentally, and nothing I could do could get it back: the tank was empty.

I know now that it wasn't just the so-called stresses of training or competition or travel or any of that. I really hadn't been at it long enough for that. Nor was I undone by not winning, which I've read some people speculating about. As you well know, and as un-American as it may seem, I have always been extraordinarily proud of my finish in that race, as well as just about every other race I've run since I was thirteen years old. I discovered early on that the truly great advantage of going <u>all-out every time</u> is that later you don't have to waste a single instant second-guessing yourself.

For anyone who didn't live through it, it's difficult to remember what it was like with the war and the draft and the protests and all that. (I remember being downright envious of the clarity with which our parents' generation viewed their nonoptional war.) It seemed like things were coming apart at the seams and of course all the idiotic stuff with Dick Doobey and the athletic department's grooming and dress code was just one local manifestation of it, all part of the general lunacy of the time.

Since my early teens when I discovered I had this weird ability, being an athlete has always been at the core of my identity, my self-image. I had always been proud of that, being able to wear a letter sweater and an Honor Society pin at the same time. Corny as it sounds, I always believed the old Greeks had it right and I readily admit that I ate it up with a big spoon. I loved having girls glance at you in the hallway and guys slapping hands and even the teachers being deferential, particularly when they found out you weren't just a dumb jock.

We were the leading edge of the baby boom generation and grew up with hardly any memory of war and with a future of one-earner prosperity as far as the eye could see—as long as we didn't get nuked. All the way through high school and those first years in college I look back now on as this golden time when everything was going pretty much by the script, like everyone said it was supposed to.

I know what you would say if you were here. A lot of this is the blissful myopia of youth, and the athletics part just makes it more poignant. Granted and granted. It's a Fool's Paradise, all right, but my point is that it's a paradise nonetheless. And what's a better alternative than even an idiot's euphoria when you're young and happy and you're fairly certain that one day in the near future you're going to run a four-minute mile?

Well, the alternative is precisely what we got. In my memory it seemed like it happened just about overnight. All of a sudden the whole world was upside down, buildings burning, kids shot on their way to class, and the whole culture bifurcating along a single fault line. As privileged recipients of the largesse and the esteem of the System, athletes were expected to be either morons or Establishment lackeys or both. I can still remember a political science class discussion of the war and how surprised some students were—this was early on—when I railed against it.

"But you're a scholarship athlete, aren't you?" they said. I said, "So what?" And they just looked dumbfounded. It wasn't long after that you started seeing football players in the middle of antiwar rallies at places like the University of Kansas.

Anyway, when I got back from the Olympics all of that stuff was all jumbled up together in my head and one thing I knew for certain was that I just had to get away from all of it in some way. I needed to "drop out" as ol' Tim Leary used to say, and while law school might seem like a weird form of escapism, at least half of my first-year class back then had a distinctly countercultural aura to it (the other half was the usual selection of crew-cut knuckleheads), so I guess I wasn't the only one.

Then of course came that awful day when we heard about
Jerry. And there were others too, guys you probably remember.
That pole vaulter from Bradenton, remember him? ROTC guy
with a tattoo of a parachute on his calf? He was in the Special
Forces and was killed near the Cambodian border. And Ed
Demski, half-miler, also killed flying. Fifty-some thousand of
them but of course the ones that get to you are the ones who were
on your team or had the locker next to yours. You can't process
thousands but you can sure as hell understand one guy that you
knew dying.

And then all of a sudden here we are butt-stroking the last
clinging U.S. sympathizer off the skids of the last departing
chopper from the roof of the American embassy, and it's good-bye
to all that. By that time everyone who had been protesting that
idiotic war was essentially comatose, myself included. Half the
country was in denial and the other half was just numb. Then of
course we had that incredible raree-show put on by Nixon and his
various well-wishers, and the thing that surprised me the most
was how _shocked_ the silent majority was that the wheels had come
off.

I don't know why I feel like I need to do this little minihistory
for you, except that in my mind it's all of a piece and it's pretty
hard to talk about how I got here without it.

Okay, now, fast-forward a few years and for all practical
purposes life is pretty good. I have a career with the appropriate
material compensation and a so-called bright future. There's no
"special someone" (you're still married) but there's plenty of time
for that and the good times are rolling. Winkler and I used to
come in from a Saturday fishing trip when we'd tied into a school
of dolphin (I think they're calling them mahimahi now) and
we would get on the phone and have twenty-five people over for
dinner, spur of the moment. And think nothing of it.

We all got together at Joe Kern's place in Jupiter after fishing
or diving on the weekends, and there were the weekly Sunday-
afternoon volleyball games in Bill Eaton's backyard in North

Palm, and the Wednesday young lawyers' flag football games at Palm Beach High, and all the island trips in the summer, and cocktails after work at the Greenhouse, and lunch on the patio at the Ocean Grille, and drinks and dinner at Taboo, and on and on.

There were lots and lots of girls and everyone seemed to be tanned and played tennis or water-skied or some damned thing. We weren't complete debauchers, but we didn't mind having fun. And why not? All through college all the runners I knew pretty much toed the line. We weren't monks surely, but we were darned serious about training. You remember it. You used to kid about what a bunch of wet blankets we were. Or half kidded, I should say.

I loosened up a little in law school, but I guess living out in the little place in Newberry I kept the same mind-set, kept running, kept hitting the books. I was still semitraumatized, still trying to digest everything that had happened, and that thing Bruce told me was the best advice anyone ever gave me, to keep to the old routines, to live like a clock.

Then finally I was done and back home in south Florida and all that ridiculous energy I had been channeling for years shot out in every direction. Hell, Winkler and I used to joke that it hadn't been a good weekend unless you woke up Monday morning in a foreign country at the end of the bus line dressed in a dashiki, with no passport.

Life was like the title of that surfing movie, Endless Summer, except we had day jobs. But life is like that down there: You have to pay attention to notice the seasons changing. And it really did seem like it would never end.

Then a few years ago I got this nagging feeling, not that something was wrong but that something was missing. I got it when Harry would go to team handball events in the summers, or even when he would go on an away trip with his high school teams. It was an emotion so rare to me that I couldn't identify it at first, but then I finally came to grips with it, and it was as obvious as an avocado pit: it was envy.

I was shocked. I was envious of my friend and roommate

*because he was still an athlete and I wasn't. Oh, I was <u>athletic</u>.
I was as sporty as all get-out. Most days I ran five or six miles
and I played lots of games, hard. But that component, whatever it
was, was still missing.*

*Then I did that little training buildup for that silly mile-
relay stunt I told you about. It was just a taste, a little window
into my old days and ways; the discipline, the deep day-after
satisfying ache of serious effort. And especially the intervals. I
would go out and run quarters barefoot alone on a grass field
and somewhere along in there I would be really moving on the
backstretch and I'd be thinking, Now if this was the last lap and
there was a guy ten yards in front of me right now . . .*

*And just by thinking like that, telling myself, <u>I can win!</u> the
hair would actually stand up on the back of my neck and I would
feel that old excitement again, the literal thrill of the literal
chase.*

*So this relay thing, which started out as a kind of prolonged
joke, became kind of serious to me and the more I got back into
training the more it brought back things from my past that I
hadn't thought about in years.*

*I started remembering the camaraderie, of course, the
tomfoolery and all the stuff that goes along with being on a team
of kindred souls, everyone on the same vision quest. That was a
rare and special thing, to be sure, those years with the guys in
Doobey Hall.*

*But after I graduated I still had lots of friends and still
played on lots of teams, so although it wasn't the same thing, it
also wasn't something I thought much about or ever really missed
much.*

*But there was one thing I did miss, and when I realized what
it was and thought about it, it became something of an obsession.
It's something I've never talked to you about, nor anyone else
for that matter. It's strictly a runner thing, I think, so I never
mentioned it to Winkler, or to any of the other guys I hung out
with down there, none of whom had been distance runners.*

What it was was this: when you're a competitive runner in training you are constantly in a process of ascending.

That's it.

It's a simple idea, but the more I thought about it, the more profound it became to me.

It's not something most human beings would give a moment of consideration to, that it is actually possible to be living for years in a state of constant betterment. To consider that you are better today than you were yesterday or a year ago, and that you will be better still tomorrow or next week or at tournament time your senior year. That if you're doing it right you are an organism constantly evolving toward some agreed-upon approximation of excellence. Wouldn't that be at least one definition of a spiritual state?

When I was a runner it was something we lived every second of our lives. It was such a part of us that if we had ever given it any thought, it would have been a mental lapse, a sign of weakness. Of course I am getting better every day, I would have said, what the hell am I training for otherwise? As if there were only one alternative, as if the arrow of improvement necessarily parallels the arrow of time, and in only one direction.

You might say—again—that we're just talking about an artifact of youth. That when you're young it is only natural to grow larger and stronger, to learn things, to master more and more of the skills and techniques of life, to get better, to improve.

If that's true then how do we end up with so many monsters, trolls, dickheads, and psychopaths? So many Pol Pots, Joe McCarthys, Ted Bundys, and Lee Harvey Oswalds? Or Nixons for that matter? They were all young once and relatively harmless, and in a better universe they would have stayed that way.

Or consider the religious aesthete whose piety and serenity and good works increase and multiply as the years go by, into middle age, into old age, onto the deathbed. She's working on it too, and what keeps her going is the absolute conviction that every day she's getting better, saving more souls, that she's getting closer to God.

My point is that this way of living that we once took for granted isn't necessarily a "natural" process at all. It's not like water flowing down to the sea, not like aging. It takes effort, determination, conviction. But mostly it takes will. It takes a conscious decision to follow one difficult uphill path, and then the will to stay with it and not waver, to not give up.

Our fellow students at Southeastern back then—there were about twenty-five thousand of them at the time, undergraduate and graduate—were getting better some days and worse some days, and they were doing so at different things and at different times. There were athletes in other sports who had better sophomore years than they had junior years. There were athletes— some runners—who were better in high school than they would ever be in college. There were some who were good or at least average students when they arrived and then discovered beer or the opposite sex or both and were never good at anything else in their lives. Generally speaking, most of them probably knew more when they left than when they arrived, but then again what they ended up knowing might have been wrong. Someone studying medicine in the 1800s was more dangerous to patients when he graduated than when he started. A scholar in physics or astronomy or biology in 1900 knew quite a bit, and a lot of it was wrong.

I'm not saying that we ourselves did not have setbacks, doldrums, bad luck, and reversals of all kinds. We got sick and we got hurt, certainly, often <u>because</u> of our quest. We got waylaid and distracted by fads, false idols, wars, and rumors of wars. I'm not saying we weren't human in every way you can be human. I'm just saying that all things being equal, by and large each and every day we were getting better at that one singularly difficult task and goal we had set for ourselves.

And I'm also saying that win, lose, or draw, just being involved in such an undertaking was itself ennobling. It was an uplifting enterprise that we all intuitively understood to be such, and I now know that almost incidentally the spiritual force of our effort created a slipstream that drew all else in our lives along with it and made us better in other ways as well. Better, happier, more complete human beings than we would have been otherwise.

And Andrea, I missed all that.

The arrow of my life was going one direction one day, another direction another day. I had people who thought I was wonderful when I won their appeal, or secured custody of their child, and I had legatees who hated me because they didn't end up quite as rich as they thought they would. Some of it is satisfying, some interesting, but precious little is in the least bit ennobling.

This is not ennui, not nostalgia. I am not numb or jaded. I've had revelations in deep waters and gone all light and airy inside listening to good music made by friends. I appreciate things, I really do. I can be made happy on a cloudy day by as little a thing as a stray sunbeam on a branch of elkhorn coral. All of that. I've been blessed and blessed and blessed and only a scoundrel and ingrate would complain about any of it and I'm certainly not doing that.

But still, I miss the spiritual certainty in the direction of that arrow.

And when recently I looked around and saw people in my life dying of natural and unnatural causes it occurred to me that I myself would not live forever and that I had long ago given up the certainty of that arrow before I had to. It also occurred to me that I had a little bit of time left to reclaim it. To be a runner again, to know precisely what it is I'm trying to accomplish every day. It won't be the same, I know. It can't be. But it can be something.

That is what this is all about.

That said, I miss you. I've always missed you.

Quenton

28

Feedrock Trail

CASSIDY WAS WORKING hard up the trail from Thunder Lake, slinging sweat with every stride despite the coolish bite in the air on the sundown side of the mountain. The schedule called for ten miles, with the first three easy, then five at a ninety percent tempo effort, and the final two miles as a cooldown.

Early on he had felt "pretty much like dog-doo" (as he would write in his log) and was dreading the fast part, but then it had gone surprisingly well once he got into the rhythm. Workouts often unspooled like that. Years ago he had come up with what he called the Two-Mile Rule, which said simply that you shouldn't try to figure out how you're feeling until at least two miles into the workout. The phenomenon seemed to apply in the other direction too: some days he felt great out the door and then just fell apart a few minutes later.

Today he had been *really* fooled. An involuntary afternoon nap went on too long and too hard, with lots of crazy dreaming and the porpoising slumber of continual near wakenings. He finally woke for good late and grumpy to find the autumn sun alarmingly close to the tops of the Blue Ridge Mountains to the west.

Dammit, he thought, all I'm doing up here is running and if I don't get that done I'm not doing *anything*.

He bolted out of his hay-bale bed, pulled damp shoes onto his sockless feet, bolted out the door, and was still wiping sleep from his eyes as he hit seven-minute pace on the uphill through the pasture before plunging into the already darkening woods, there slowing down finally, remembering that he was supposed to be warming up.

But there was no night running out here, and if you didn't do it before sundown you didn't do it. His nap dreams had been vaguely disturbing but he couldn't for the life of him remember more than scraps. Something to do with dogs, feral dogs, and an old girlfriend he couldn't quite place, a chilly apartment. Something about a pilot light going out. Oh well.

As soon as he hit the long downhill slope toward Thunder Lake, he picked up the pace and knew immediately that it would be a good tempo run. Another mile farther on he was fairly flying down the gentle incline at better-than-five-minute pace, and he could tell it was going to be one of those wonderful days when he would not be able to make himself tired.

It occurred to him that days like this didn't happen as much as they used to, and for that reason he should surely cherish them. He flew around Thunder Lake in the waning light, feeling only the joy of nearly effortless speed, surprised to feel his foot strikes digging in so smartly that he was throwing chunks of gravel out behind him.

He left the lake road and started back up the hill, amazed to find that his pace was hardly affected by the grade. The lower parts of the woods were getting darker now, but at this pace he would break into the light soon enough.

The trail got slightly steeper and the forest lighter as he got closer to the top of the hill, and when he came to the intersection with the Feedrock Trail, he slowed to a trot, the tempo portion over. Then, oddly, he walked. It was getting late and he didn't have a lot of light left, but the fast run had left him exhilarated and for some reason he felt the urge to find the old place.

He turned into the trees and started poking around. Within minutes he found the pile of stones now unrecognizable as a chimney. From there he triangulated the makeshift corral, and tested with his fingers the reality of the strands of rusted barbed wire now growing remarkably through the middle of mature trees. Those hard and tough remnants were all that was left of a difficult life lived way out here.

It was a rugged spot even today, typical of places you can only get to on foot. The homestead cabin had been built long before the turn of the century, back even before the Confederate lead mine operated in here somewhere. A hundred years before, this same trail had borne mule carts of supplies to keep wretched Confederate miners alive and the same carts carried out deadly marbles to make wretched Yankees dead.

The whole hillside was roiling with shades, according to "sensitive" people in town. They spoke in low tones of Indian massacres, bushwhackings, lynchings. Then later, the relative serenity of a homestead family. But it must have been a hard and lonely life. Everyone said there was a little girl who took sick and died out here one bleak winter and was buried on the mountain. Even serenity has its casualties, he thought.

In summers past Cassidy had searched in vain for anything that might have been a grave marker. In this light he was not likely to stumble on one now. It was time to go. Wiping the reddish stain of the barbed wire on the back of his shorts, he started running again, high-stepping until he was out of the brush and back on the Feedrock, then slowing to cooldown pace again on the gentle downhill stretch back toward the pasture.

Years ago when he'd heard the story of the little girl, Cassidy would think about her when he came by this spot, particularly on rainy afternoons when both the hill and the runner were chilled and the air was damp and timeless. At such times redemption was hard to imagine, much less aspire to.

He had seen in little local museums and craft shops some of the homemade toys of that era, sad little corncob dolls dressed in flour sacking and scraps of gingham. Trying to imagine her life out here, bleached of color on such dreary days, brought a lonely feeling in him that sometimes jelled into something like despair. He thought at first that he was channeling her own grief then, but after a while he knew better.

On a bright fall day like this, though, he could imagine her delighting in the ludicrously colored leaves splashing against a ludicrously blue sky. He could sense her rapture as she breathed in peppery cool air, hugging her doll and edging closer to family and hearth as dark shadows slipped down the hillside. There would have been panthers out here then for sure, and bears. And ghosts, always. The fire inside would have been soothing then, the reassurance of her mother's touch, the warmth of her featherbed.

On the home leg now, Cassidy cruised easily along the rocky trail just below the ridge, admiring how the undersides of the taller trees reflected liquid gold down onto the pine-needle forest floor, glowing reddish itself now. He was flushed with a warmish contentment; during the tempo run he had found himself on some of the shorter, steeper sections doing a bit of, no other word for it, *scampering,* throwing himself up the grade with bounding strides.

When he came to a big spruce by a scree scattered across the trail, he succumbed to another lark, coasted to a stop, turned, and jogged back. Why not, he thought. It has turned out to be a wonderful day after all. A day of taking stock.

There was a very steep face of bare rock leading up to a lightly timbered lookout ridge, and he took to the granite face with powerful, lunging strides, feeling his quadriceps burning instantly and his calves stretching as he powered up what seemed like a near-vertical wall. Three quarters of the way up he gave up the heroics and hiked the remaining few feet to the crest, breathing hard again. A narrow path led into the thin edge of trees and out the other side into the thin blue air.

He cleared the shadows and stepped out into the sunlight of the ledge, puffing hard from the sudden effort and stood, hands on hips, taking in the entire Cedar Mountain valley, flecked in the high places with splashes of yellow but mostly suffused now in a smoky blue-gray haze. An orange plush toy of sun liquefied at the dark edge of the Blue Ridge Parkway and the miniaturized tableau below was faded but recognizable: there was the tiny volunteer fire station three miles away, Sarah Sneedon's little craft store and some other places along the dark thread of highway, and beyond that his grandmother's house leaking wood smoke, and beyond that her neighbor Virginia Coldiron's snug little place up in a dark hollow toward Connestee Falls.

He thought, not for the first time, Doing this thing you occasionally get to a rare overlook. He realized that as long as he could remember as a runner he had judged every landscape he encountered as to whether or not he would like to run in it. That was what nature had been to him: somewhere you run. When he passed a lovely grass meadow beside a highway, he would imagine how it would feel to fly barefoot down its gentle slope at four-minute-mile pace, to trod its deliciously smooth turf as the world-record-holder, the fastest human ever. Running was simply how he related to nature, to the aesthetics of the natural world, and thus the most beautiful landscapes to him were those with room to amble: easy passageways or smooth footpaths disappearing into the distance. Lovely flora and fauna, moving waters, azure skies, all were desirable, of course, but good footing was truly essential.

It was difficult for him to imagine that his capacity to move quickly through landscapes meant that within half an hour he would be inside that distant miniature house sitting at an old applewood kitchen table, eating his grandmother's chicken livers and mashed potatoes and gravy. It seemed contrary to the laws of physics and the plain evidence of his senses.

And yet as he stood there still glistening, breathing deeply—though no longer panting—he knew for a fact that failing a broken leg or some act of God it was true, and it would not even require an unusual effort. It would require only the well-worn routine: jog, shower, dress, and then the quick chilly motorcycle ride down the hollow.

That mental image of chicken livers made him suddenly woozy with hunger and he turned from the glowing ledge. Backpedaling his gravity-driven way slowly and carefully down the rock face, he repeatedly jammed already sore toes into the ends of his Tiger Cortez training shoes before hitting the shadowy trail below and starting back into it slowly, allowing his eyes to adjust again to the gloom.

Picking his way carefully along the trail, he remembered something he had read about the great alpine climbers. As children they grew up surrounded by a vast landscape of snowy unattainable peaks. As they grew older, stronger, and more skillful, when they looked up, they saw more and more places they had been to and to which they could return at will. That zone of accessibility would grow and grow over the years until the very best of the guides could stand in their village squares and turn full circle, searching the horizon in vain for some tiny forbidden aerie they had not conquered, some remote crag beyond their powers.

It would have to be a wonderful and prideful thing, to feel so thoroughly at home in such a daunting and beautiful landscape. But as they grew older, the climbers who survived would find that some peaks were difficult again, some climbs strangely taxing, some routes quite impossible. They would realize to their surprise that the process was reversible; that it was, in fact, reversing.

You could see them, the aged former heroes sitting sadly in

the village square, turning full circle to gaze at a frozen world once again inaccessible to them.

Lit orange now by the last of the sun, Quenton Cassidy cruised down the darkening hillside with languid strides, thinking, I may be older and I may nap too long, but I can still scald dogs down to Thunder Lake and back.

Breaking out into the thin sunlight of the open pasture above his cabin, he thought: I can still have a day like this.

29

Migrating

A SOCIAL OCCASION WITH no alcohol of any kind; that felt pretty strange. People making small talk cold sober on a weekday evening might be almost painful to watch in some circumstances, but anyone bringing so much as a rum baba into his grandmother's house almost certainly would have been dealing with the high sheriff pronto, so folks were used to it. The kids ran around in the yard like banshees and the grown-ups inside made do.

They were throwing him a going-away party though his grandmother couldn't get it through her head that it didn't have anything to do with anyone's birthday, and seeing as how he had known about it for more than two weeks it was hardly a surprise either.

Well, anyway, she said, many happy returns.

Cassidy, smiling sweetly, said, Thank you, ma'am, and wondered, Where did she get that from?

"You sure you're all right?" said his cousin Dobie Kay, putting the back of her hand to his forehead in a motherly fashion. "You feel warmish. Sure you're not coming down with something?"

They found places in the living room on the piano bench, backs to the instrument, drinking instant decaf and balancing paper plates of birthday-looking cake on their knees.

"I'm fine. This peakedness kind of goes with the territory. I forgot how much training is sort of like being ill."

Dobie, blond head cocked like a parrot, tried to discern if he was kidding.

He wasn't. He had misplaced the memories of the physical uproar caused by the kind of schedule he'd been keeping. As active as he had been in the intervening years he now understood clearly how removed it was from the life of a serious runner. He would describe it as an ongoing delicate brutal dance, the pushing of your body right up to the edge, close to injury, to collapse, day after day. As he had approached and then surpassed a hundred miles a week, it had all come back to him: the night sweats, the muscles twitching in bed like different wild animals somehow alive on him, the searing panicky thirsts out of nowhere, the random cravings for pickled beets, chicken-fried steak, artichoke hearts, herrings in sour cream, carrot juice. Just the general feverish nervous physical anxiety that seemed to animate a blob of protoplasm vibrating itself into a higher state of physical grace. It did indeed seem to have something in common with illness, or pregnancy.

"Well, Grandmaw has loved having someone to cook for again. I reckon now we'll all just have to keep coming around ourselves for a while to ease her back down. Else she's liable to run herself out of her own kitchen with leftovers. I've never seen her measure anything. I don't think she understands the idea of portions."

"No, and I did my best to destroy any notions she had of how much one adult is supposed to eat. She probably thought she was back cooking for Grandpa's crew plus the boys too."

"Now, what are you two cuttin' up about?" Dobie asked her father and uncle, who had wandered up in an obvious good mood, cake in hand.

"Neal was just saying how we tried for so many years to talk that Poutin' House into some kind of livable condition, but it took kin trying to live there to actually shame us into doing something about it," Lee said. "And then Quenton goes and shames his own self into Sheetrocking the bathroom. We keep embarrassing ourselves and we'll get a modern house out of it yet."

"You don't know shame until you see me handle a mud knife. Fortunately a good latex-based paint can hide a multitude of sins," Cassidy said.

"Well, any potential renters or guests or squatters out there, believe me, won't be noticing any flaws of a cosmetic nature," said Neal. "And if they do we can always remind them that the little building in back with the hole in the floor is still available and open for bidness."

Someone else had wandered up and now had an outhouse story to tell, and before it was over a small crowd gathered and every other person had some kind of anecdote about outdoor plumbing.

Cassidy leaned back against the piano, abstracted himself somewhat, and—silly grin fixed on his, let's face it, *glowing* countenance—sat and watched this crowd of animated, freckle-faced, redheaded, what?, *Pegrams* work themselves into paroxysms of laughter over stories worn smooth from the telling, stories about relatives present and long gone, stories concerning the lingerie section in the Sears wishbook (a precursor of store-bought toilet paper, someone explained, just to be sure), about various critters that like to hang around loosely constructed outbuildings, stories, in short, about the inevitable assaults on human dignity common in the days before polyvinyl chloride and the ball float.

I have not the slightest desire to leave this place, he thought, but the days are growing shorter and this very morning my shoes crunched several times through thin sheets of colorful fall leaves suspended in clear ice. My log now shows five morning

runs marked by snow and ice that were more than just orna-
mental. It is time.

His grandmother slipped in and sat on the piano bench
beside him, in her faux surreptitious manner fishing his hand
up from between them and slipping something into it, ceremo-
niously closing his fist and returning it to him before slipping off
the bench and wending her stooped way back through the crowd
to the kitchen. He was fairly sure she was wiping her eye with
the hem of her apron as she left. He looked in his hand and was
not surprised to find the tightly folded square of a ten-dollar bill.
He unfolded it and showed it to Dobie, who smiled and nodded.
Inflation had not taken hold here: he was pretty sure it was what
she used to give departing children back in the fifties. He had
a sudden passing intimation of mortality, of changeless things
changing. One day your parents are laughing twentysomethings
aiming a garden hose at this skinny turbocharged brown buzz-
cut ninny hopping around a plastic wading pool. Then all that
exists only in jerky black-and-white eight-millimeter reels and
faded prints and maybe it never happened at all.

After the last scatological anecdote was trotted out, Cassidy
set his empty paper plate between his feet and embarrassed
the bejeebers out of everyone trying to tell them how much he
appreciated everything, how great it was to spend time back
home again, how peaceful and good it all was. And blah blah
blah.

Then, after a short and heavy silence:

"Well," said Lee, slightly red-faced, rocking gently in his
cowboy boots, right hand jammed flat in his back pocket. Trying
to think of something appropriate but not too sentimental or
formal, he finally came up with: "Y'all come back!"

30
Raleigh Redux

B RIGHT CHILL MORNING, more like winter than fall, and the sun-yellow Porsche fairly zipped around the switchbacks coming down from Caesar's Head into Greenville, there to pick up the interstate and head east toward the Piedmont, making into a morning's drive the reverse of the migration path that had taken several generations of Pegrams to accomplish.

Saying good-bye that morning to the old woman had not been easy. She was more wound up than usual, and he asked her several times what was wrong and she ignored him in her fidgety distress. Her skin smelled like old books when he hugged her birdlike frame, and she, having heard the car idling outside, made only a token effort to get him to sit and eat something.

Each of the last several times he had taken his leave she had seemed downcast and he had only this time seen that it was because she was thinking every time now would be the last. He didn't want to be the cause of her discontent, so he kissed the parchment of her cheek and delivered a big phony smile and then he was bounding down the wooden steps waving back to her as she watched from her kitchen window one more time, the absconding firstborn of the firstborn.

The person lowering off this mountain is a horse of a whole different color, he thought. A different entity from the one who drove up it months ago. He was now within two pounds of his old racing weight. Eleven extra pounds had scarcely been noticeable on a frame two inches taller than six feet, but he knew the difference and so did anyone who knew anything about single-digit body fat. Size medium shorts ballooned on him once again.

He looked, even to himself, younger and hungrier, and it occurred to him that one thing coming out of all this was a kind of second childhood. It might end up costing him in the long run, but for the life of him he couldn't figure out why it was not a good deal, possibly the best deal in the world. You could argue that it wasn't real, that it was self-indulgent, that it was irresponsible, all of that, but in the final analysis who, given the chance, wouldn't take it?

Just before the entrance ramp he spotted a familiar-looking sign and pulled into the parking lot of a franchised barbecue restaurant. It wasn't quite eleven in the morning but certainly high time for an early feeding. It was in this very restaurant he had once heard a heavyset waitress in pedal pushers telling a bored cashier: "If I could just get myself a consolidation loan, I'd be on easy street."

Quenton Cassidy liked the idea of occasionally setting your sights low. A person ought to be able to achieve some modicum of satisfaction in this world without necessarily straining a gut. Right now he would settle for a decent pulled-pork sandwich and some fried okra.

Put some South in your mouth, he said to himself, closing the door of the little yellow car and backing against it to bump it closed with his butt.

A very hard butt too.

⊄

Denton sat at the kitchen table with the logs and schedules, making notes on a legal pad as Cassidy lolled a few feet away on the carpeted floor on the other side of the tiled bar, allegedly doing a hurdler's stretch.

"So these elapsed times are pretty accurate, and the distance themselves you're pretty sure of?" Denton said.

"Yeah. You measured most of them yourself on the bike, remember? And I behaved. I even stopped the watch during pee breaks."

"Hmmm. Looks pretty darned consistent here."

"I *told* you."

"I know."

"And you've been seeing the weekly logs I've sent."

"I know, but it's something else to see it all mapped out on the monthly calendar sheets like this, the weekly mileage tallies: 111, 124, 104, 128."

"That 104 I had a cold," Cassidy said quietly.

"Quenton, this is a respectable amount of base on pretty challenging terrain without apparently a lot of wear and tear. How is the Achilles, by the way?"

Cassidy reached down and pinched the left one and winced. Sore as a boil.

"It doesn't hurt running anymore, but it's still there all right," he said. "I've been using heel pads and I've been doing self-massage, but it was hard to get enough ice on it in my little place up there. I only have a little dorm-type refrigerator."

"Well, you wouldn't have that problem now. They really caught it last weekend, and they're supposed to catch it all winter, according to the fur on the caterpillars or the masks on the raccoons, or the moss on the forest rangers, some damn thing." Denton left the paperwork spread out on the table and plopped down in a recliner next to Cassidy's supine body.

"So what's this race next weekend all about?" Cassidy was on his stomach, face on folded arms, no longer pretending to stretch.

"It's a half-marathon, a good one. I wanted to try you on something kind of long and not too intense just to see where you are, blow the pipes out, pique your interest, and so on."

"Is it close by?"

"Dayton, Ohio. The River Corridor Classic."

"You're kidding."

"Why would I kid about a thing like that?"

"Why would they have a half-marathon in Dayton, Ohio? I've never heard of it."

"Why would they have one anywhere? Cass, a lot has changed since you were running before. I don't know if you're aware of it, but Frank really started something winning that gold medal. It's not just a trend, it's a bona fide fad. Now Mom and Pop and Bud and Sis all want to run—not just a distance race but—a *marathon,* and they want to do it next *Tuesday,* and they want to buy some flashy togs to do it in."

"Marathons?"

"Do you have any idea how many races there are around now?"

"Bruce, I barely glance at *Track and Field News* when it comes out anymore. When I do it's to check the rankings to see how far down the list I'd be if I were still running."

Denton shook his head.

"Had you not heard that last year Peachtree had twelve *thousand* runners?"

"I've heard people talking at cocktail parties and such, but I figured it was like publicity hype or something, you know, like when they used to argue about the head count at antiwar rallies."

"Well, think again, my friend. Running has become a big deal. Every chamber of commerce or corporate entity or disease foundation everywhere wants to sponsor some kind of race or other, get in on the good karma. Remember how we used to drive for hours to get to some Podunk turkey trot somewhere, we were so hard up for races? Well, there's *hundreds* of races now.

Some guys from the old days who are still in shape are so deliri-
ous they run two or three a weekend."

"You're kidding."

"I *know* guys. Think they've died and gone to heaven. They
are amassing rooms full of hardware. Occasionally merchan-
dise. Very occasionally cash money. They'll be hamburger meat
shortly, of course."

"So how about this thing in Dayton?" Cassidy said.

"It's one of the good ones, well sponsored, several years old
now. They bring in a lot of top guys. They're expecting five thousand, which is big for a half."

"Jeez, I remember thinking a cross-country race with a couple hundred was a huge race. What's it like racing five thousand
people?"

"Quenton, that's one of the strange things about it. You can
look behind you at the starting line and see five thousand people lined up, but when the gun goes off, guess what?"

"What?"

"You're still racing against the same five or six guys you
always raced against."

Cassidy sat up, wrapped his arms around his knees, and
rocked back and forth, using the floor and the edge of the area
rug to massage the insertion points of his hamstrings.

"So why do we have to go all the way to Ohio? I mean if there
are races everywhere now . . ."

"Oh, there are plenty to choose from, although damn few
will have this kind of field. But it's not for the competition. You
aren't going to be winning anything. This is pretty much of a
time trial for you. I just wanted you to see what's happened with
road racing while you've been asleep. This is a classy race with a
good field. *And* they've got a great speaker at the clinic the night
before the race."

"Oh yeah?" Cassidy asked. "Who's that?"

"You."

31

Race by a River

IT WAS AN easy week leading up to the race, but Cassidy was surprised to see that even with travel and the race on the weekend he would still end up with well over a hundred miles. That's the way it seems to go when you get to a plateau, he thought, it's a lot easier to stay than it was to get there.

Cassidy was welcomed back into the training pack with friendly ribbing and he was glad to have company again. Denton rode along on his bike on overdistance days, and Cassidy was friendly with most of them from his previous visits, particularly the forgetful entomologist, Dick Endris. When Cassidy mentioned reading *The Andromeda Strain,* he lit up. His specialty was insect disease vectors, and he had done postdoc work at the quarantine station on Plum Island. He had no end of hair-raising tales.

Denton and Cassidy flew from Raleigh-Durham to Dayton on Friday morning and checked into the Stouffer's downtown. Cassidy went right to work on his talk. He was still irritated at Denton's financing of the trip using Cassidy as clinic fodder, so he had no qualms about chasing the suddenly talkative Denton out of the room so he could get ready.

He was accustomed to talking to juries and to small groups, but after months of isolation he knew he was socially rusty and maybe a little crowd-shy. At the moment he really couldn't imagine that he would be in the spotlight in front of thousands of runners in a few hours, so he tried to put it out of his mind and just work on his presentation as if it were an academic exercise.

What to say about running that would be meaningful, useful, poignant, possibly funny? he thought. Dunno. I've had this problem before. It's an elementary activity, running. Everyone can do it at some level, at least in theory. It's so elemental an activity that nonrunners use its simplicity to poke fun: why do you need a *coach* to tell you how to run? What does he do, just keep reminding you to put one foot in front of the other? Ha ha ha.

Well, this was admittedly preaching to the choir but the question was, What do you say to the choir anyway?

He decided, finally, Screw it, I'm just going to go for yucks and the hell with it. I'm not going to stand up there and drone on about training until everyone is cross-eyed.

With the Stouffer's promotional pen from the desk drawer he wrote at the top of his legal pad: "Ten Things a Runner Has Never Said."

Cogitating, he put the point of the pen in his mouth, forgetting that it wasn't a pencil. Then he wrote:

"Number one. A runner has never said, 'Well, this course is about nine and a half miles long so what do you say we round it off and call it nine even?' "

They went through the first mile in 4:25.

Cassidy saw Denton standing by the timekeeper just shaking his head. He didn't say a word.

Well, dammit, Bruce, what did you expect? Here are guys like Jerome Drayton, Rick Rojas, Jon Sinclair, Benji Durden, even old Frank himself, who had flown in late the night before. There were at least fifteen people in that lead group and Cassidy knew every one of them. There were a bunch more he knew behind them right now and they were back there only because they were too smart to get pulled along in the slipstream as Cassidy had.

He backed way off and realized quickly that it was smart to do so. As he ran on his own through the next several mile markers, his pace began to average out closer to five flat, which is where he knew it should have been from the beginning. He saw Denton again at three and four and while he still looked miffed, he was nodding.

It was a gorgeously bright day along the river corridor, chilly only in the occasional patches of shade, which made it perfect running weather to Cassidy's way of thinking. He was accustomed from cross-country races to seeing a bunch of people in front of him, but what he was not accustomed to was being so isolated in the middle of a race. On the track everyone was right there in sight no matter how far ahead or behind they were. In cross-country you would occasionally get dropped by a group and run along by yourself for a while but usually others would come up quickly and you would have to decide whether to tag along or keep sliding.

In this race the Olympians and record holders had separated themselves from the herd in the first mile, and when Cassidy wisely and drastically dropped off the pace shortly afterward, he found himself running what he considered to be a pretty darn respectable pace in complete privacy. Then, after the fourth mile marker, he began to pick up solo runners falling back. He would spot them way ahead on the long narrow footpath, little bobbing ants that grew over the minutes and yards. They had misjudged their shape, or were picking up a bug, or had activated an old injury; some disastrous miscalculation had led them to believe they were capable of sustaining the intensity of that first mile.

One appeared now on his forward horizon, a dark-complexioned runner in a green-and-white singlet whom Cassidy didn't recognize. He appeared to be running easily, but Cassidy gained steadily.

Now within thirty yards, Cassidy realized with a start that it was Frank Shorter. He spent the next several minutes trying to think of something soothing to say, something light but appropriate for that awkward moment when the great marathoner would be overtaken by a mere miler. He came up with nothing.

Instead, as he pulled up to the smaller runner, he said, "Frank, I'm sorry. It's me."

Shorter laughed. "I did a kind of easy 2:19 a few weeks ago and thought I was getting back. Guess not."

"Well, if it makes you feel any better I'm probably running way over my head."

"I heard you were pretty funny last night. Sorry I missed it."

"Nothing like insider jokes. You know, like that one Steve Martin does about the plumber's convention where a guy does a joke about a three-quarter-inch spanner wrench."

Shorter laughed again.

"So how's Bruce doing? I saw him last night but just to say hi."

"He's good. Killing him not to run of course. But in turn he's killing some gym equipment and a mountain bike. It's a tough thing . . ."

"Yeah, injuries . . . I don't know. He's helping you now? I hear something about . . . the marathon?"

Cassidy took the next several miles and explained it as best he could.

"Hey," he said suddenly, "I can't believe this!"

"What?" said Shorter.

"We're *talking*. In the middle of a *race*. Hitting near-five-minute pace and chatting."

"Nothing like the mile, is it?"

"Not in the least."

"Well, welcome to the wide wide world of road racing," said Shorter.

"Thanks."

Cassidy sat by the plane window in a semistupor, Denton next to him doing paperwork on the tray table. They had another hour on the Dayton-Charlotte leg.

Cassidy suddenly straightened in his seat.

"I've *got* it!" he said.

"What? What?" said Denton, looking up over his reading glasses.

"A few months ago I was watching this movie director guy being interviewed on Dick Cavett, and he was saying how, you know, in the movies if they want to portray someone carrying a bag of groceries, like a lady walking down the street, or a guy in France pedaling a bicycle carrying groceries, they always show the same thing. The bag always has, like, a loaf of French bread and a stalk of celery sticking out the top. And if they ever drop the bag, you'll see oranges rolling. But the director guy says, how can they exist on just bread and celery?"

"What did Cavett say?"

"He just laughed."

"But you've just figured out this nutritional quandary?"

"No, that's not the point. The fact is, as any observant moviegoer knows, they *eat* all kinds of things. At dinner they're having meat loaf, fried chicken, spaghetti, whatever. Anything. You don't know how the food *gets* there, because all you've ever seen *in transit* is the damn French bread and damn celery. But they somehow end up with quite a varied diet, actually." Cassidy's tone was that of a tutor for a fourth grader.

Denton rolled his eyes, then again fixed them over his half-glasses on Cassidy.

"So what is it you figured out?"

"*Why* you only ever see the bread and celery in the bag."

"Which is . . . ?"

"Because they're things that *would* stick out the top of a grocery bag! They're long and skinny and easily recognizable items from a distance. The audience immediately knows that here is a person carrying groceries."

Denton continued to study Cassidy in much the same way he would eye a plant specimen in his laboratory.

"But here's what I don't get," Cassidy continued. "When they want to portray garbage, like the cops are going through a Dumpster looking for clues, and they want to portray slimy, smelly, garbagy things, what do they show you?"

"I don't think I want to be involved in this."

"Breakfast items! It's always stuff from breakfast. Coffee grounds, grapefruit halves, eggshells. Breakfast items! Why do you suppose that is?"

Denton blinked hard and was loath to admit that he was actually curious.

"Okay, I give up. Why?"

Cassidy looked surprised.

"I don't *know*," he said, "I just *told* you. I'm still working on it. You can't expect me to figure out everything at once. Jeez." He hunched contentedly up against the window with his hands clasped together between his knees and was asleep in a very few minutes.

Denton leaned his head back and closed his eyes, smiling. Something tugged at him from the back of his mind and he tried unsuccessfully to drag it out of his subconscious. He had all but given up and was slipping into a light slumber himself when it struck him. He opened his eyes and studied his companion, now in a deep slumber.

It was the old Cassidy he had seen for a few moments there. The Cassidy who mystified and bewitched his track teammates at Doobey Hall, the promoter, counselor, instigator, the moving spirit. The silly goose who was always coming up with such outlandish . . . *projects*. He who organized the contest one weekend to see how many Volkswagens the jumpers could clear; he who set up the faux Honor Court trial of Jack Nubbins; he who would interrupt a training table dinner to present tinfoil bowling trophies to befuddled freshmen.

Denton realized that he hadn't seen that old Cassidy in a while, and that the years must erode the spirit as surely as wind or rushing water worry away the earth. But he was moved in a way both sad and sweet to see that familiar life force still bubbling away there after all, still humming beneath the layers of acquired grown-up cares and worldly woes.

And it occurred to him that it was in fact that same boundless, life-affirming, free-flowing energy that had propelled Cassidy early on to innumerable schoolboy glories and then, much later, on a fine early-autumn afternoon, to a tiny sliver of modest but undeniable immortality. Cassidy was a silver medalist and no matter what he said about it, it commanded respect, even from a gold medalist.

"What did you guys finish in again?" They were making their descent and Denton was trying to finish up his notes and put his papers away.

Cassidy, yawning, turned sideways in his seat to stretch fore and aft along the fuselage.

"One oh seven something. Fifteen, I think," he said. "One oh seven fifteen. A PR for guess who."

"Yes, it's always a PR when you haven't run the distance before. Do you know Frank's PR?"

"When I asked him he just laughed. What is it?"

"He has run about 1:03 flat."

Cassidy whistled.

"Yeah, but get this . . ."

"Yeah?"

"He ran that in the first half of a full marathon. Till yesterday he'd never run a flat-out half-marathon either."

"Oh."

"So don't go getting a big head there."

"Bruce, we finished in the *teens*. Double figures. There were *thirteen* guys ahead of us."

"Right."

"So don't be talking big head."

"Okay."

"What else is on your mind? You're acting distracted."

"Hmm? Oh, nothing. I was just finishing up your training schedule for the next three months. We have not much more than a year to get ready for the trials."

"And? You didn't say much about my race."

"I . . . It was good. Very good."

"Come on, out with it. What were you looking for? What would you have been happy with?"

"Honestly?"

"No, lie to me."

"Cass, seriously, I was projecting maybe 1:10 to 1:12. I would have been happy with anything close to that. So, at this point in the program, 1:07 is good. Scary good."

"Nothing scary about good. It's the other that's scary."

32

Déjà Newberry All Over Again

THE A-FRAME WAS set against winter-dull hardwoods and conspicuous evergreens and it looked more welcoming than ever. The red-clay driveway was in such good shape, Cassidy didn't even have to circumnavigate potholes that would bottom out his little car. After all these years, he thought, another homecoming.

A pile of UPS packages awaited him damply on the screened porch, mostly training shoes and other equipment Denton had finagled out of politely dubious manufacturer's reps. Cassidy unlocked the door and stood for a moment, hands on hips, emitting a long low whistle at the changes. The Denton family had been vacationing here for a number of years now and the hippie brother-in-law carpenter from Vermont had snowbirded down these last few winters, contributing cabinetry and trim that could only have been produced by a patience and craft all but unknown outside the woodworking ambit of your Northeast Kingdom stoner.

Long gone were the stacks of Sheetrock and plywood, the

two-bys, cartons of nails, reels of Romex, and the conduit, my God, Cassidy thought, the conduit. Much of the yard-sale furniture had been replaced, including Cassidy's old lumpy cot. The back bedroom was now dominated by a nice firm queen with an antique oak headboard. At least the scarred old pine dresser remained. The best change was a nifty little deck added off the bedroom. Opening the sliding glass door seemed to double the size of the room and bring the forest into the house. Cassidy stood outside on a layer of crunchy leaves in the pungent air, arms stretched out, breathing deeply as a hound dog.

Then he went back inside to continue exploring, having a hard time remembering how it had been before, thinking how far removed he was from that chapter in his life. But the old perpetually half-finished retreat, that strange little isolated place where he had remade himself, existed only in his memory now.

The only traces he could find of his previous life here were a few of the paperbacks now ensconced on nicely dadoed pine shelves between the kitchen and living area, mixed in with a bunch of beachy page-turners: Elmore Leonard, Michael Crichton, Kurt Vonnegut. There was some pop-thought fare of a different era: Toffler, Ehrlich, the execrable Castenada. There was *Pilgrim at Tinker's Creek,* some Didion, Doris Lessing, Margaret Atwood, and, pursuant to federal statute, Erica Jong's *Fear of Flying*.

He continued wandering. Four new skylights lightened the place considerably, two high up on each wall that you could crank open with a pole. The formerly bare or stud-only interior walls were all long since Sheetrocked, papered, or painted, and most were populated with prints and paintings. One wall along the hallway to the bedroom was covered with family photos, some in montage frames, some individual snapshots, Denton family vacation fun. As he sidled down the hall the kids mysteriously lost then regained teeth, traded baby fat for height, abandoned goofy openmouthed toddler grins for sunburned preadolescent smiles, then grudging early-teen grimaces. In the natural order of things they vanished altogether in spots and then showed up again as young adults.

Bruce and Jeannie morphed in the pictures too, though not as drastically, and much of it had to do with the follicular trends of various eras. Sideburns were apparently key at one time, making all males look like refugees from a barbershop quartet. Then they were gone. Bangs and curls came and went; ditto mustaches and wispy goatees. Cassidy sidestepped along: here's a picture of me when I was younger, is what people say. Hell, *every* picture of you is a picture of you when you were younger.

Cassidy eventually broke off his reverie to drag his bags to the back, tossing them on the bed, procrastinating on unpacking the rest of the car. He had only been on the road five hours from his aunt Dot's place in Atlanta, but he had come to believe in a universal law of endurance athletics: the better shape you're in, the more crippled you become from long vehicle rides. Cars and planes were bad; team buses were the worst. He could remember guys in high school who climbed up into the overhead luggage racks to sleep. In fact, on the way back from a meet in Daytona one late night he *was* one of those guys, and it wasn't bad.

He ambled around some more, now stopping to bend and stretch, looking forward to the easy eight-miler that would reset his clock and tune up his meridians.

Then something caught his eye as he was vainly trying to touch his toes in front of the bookshelf. He squatted down to peruse the lower bookshelves and saw that it was a vaguely familiar-looking calendar tucked in with some old *National Geographics*. It was over a decade old, and as he began leafing through the months, he now recognized his own handwritten numerals and notations. It was a long-lost training log from his Olympic buildup, one he had used for a few months before transferring the information to a more permanent record.

Intrigued, he fetched a glass of ice water from the kitchen and settled back in the overstuffed chair in the living room. He studied some of the individual workouts, trying to remember

any specific day, trying to bring back something of what he had
been thinking, feeling, seeing at the time. Mostly it was futile.
These myriad numbers, repetitions, miles, recovery intervals,
all now blurred into an undifferentiated stew of toil and sweat
and raspy breathing. But the stark numbers all by themselves
told stories that even now he could interpret easily.

One workout was a Tuesday in early April that read: "AM: 7
miles slow @ 52 mins; PM: 74 degrees; 3 m. Warm-up, felt slug-
gish; 1 m. Striders; 10 x 220 w/ 110 jog: 28.5, 27.8, 27.0, 26.5,
25.7, 25.0, 25.2, 25.9, 24.8, 25.5."

There was a mile jog and then another set of 220s in similar
times, another mile, and a final half set of five, all fast, with the
last one recorded as: *"23.2!"*

Most of the workout notations on the calendar were similar,
consisting almost solely of numerals and abbreviations, with
very occasional one- or two-word comments. The true meaning of the notes from that single forgotten training day couldn't
have been clearer to him if he had written an essay. The total
mileage for the week was 127, and the intensity and volume of
work for that day were not unusual, perhaps even a bit light.
But the morning run was very slow, less than seven-minute
pace, and the warm-up must have felt awful for him to go out of
his way to comment on it. Then there was the telltale underlin-
ing and exclamation mark of the last 220, indicating surprise
and probably no small delight at such a quick time at the end of
a set of fast 220s on a day when he had obviously been feeling
his mortality.

There was probably relief in that emphasis as well, he knew;
relief that no illness was on the horizon, no long-term breakdown imminent. Relief that everything was generally okay after
all. For a few scant seconds there he had merely penetrated the
ever-present layers of grief and gloom in the bash-and-recover
cycles of his life, had reached down through all the worm-eating
mollygrubs to where the good stuff was, and had flicked on—
just briefly—the afterburners.

And they had ignited once more and sent him flying off on a spring breeze.

He stood, stretched, finished his glass of water, and walked to the counter that now separated the kitchen from the living area. As he pulled up a stool it occurred to him that a thousand peanut butter sandwiches had been served here in the interim. Sitting on the edge of the stool, he was now able to stretch his lower-back muscles as he leaned over the calendar, flipping the page to the following month where a similar 220 workout was aborted halfway through. The exclamation marks caught his attention, along with a relatively long-winded comment: "Left Achilles really bad. Had to stop. Worst training day of my life!"

The following day there was only a three-mile jog in the morning and seven easy miles in the afternoon, followed the next day by light overdistance totaling fourteen miles. The next day, two scant days after the "worst training day" of his life, it was apparently back to business as usual: a rigorous interval session of 330s and 660s on a grassy field, a total of nineteen miles for the day, and no further mention of the Achilles problem. Nor did he say anything about it for the rest of the month or during the next month either.

He remembered not a whit of this, not the workouts or the injury, and looking back on it now he found it remarkable that an incipient injury serious enough to blow off a training day could be so casually and haughtily shrugged off by the simple expedient of taking two easy days in a row.

That's one big difference between then and now, he wrote Denton that evening. "Two, actually. One is that an injury like that now would cost me a week or two at least, and two is that I can't see myself out there ever again ripping off 220s like that. God, it all came back to me there for a second: how great it was to feel that speed, an eighth of a mile at darned near eighteen miles an hour, then just a leetle rest jog across the middle of the infield and bang, off again! Twenty-five of them, three miles of that kind of speed, just like that! I remembered all of a sudden the way you could actually feel the wind just *whistling* by your ears! Man, that was just flat-out fun!"

For now he had the rest of the car to unpack and a post-travel run to get in. He closed the training calendar and put it back on the shelf next to the *Geographic*s, realizing that one of the sensations brought on by this little jaunt down memory lane was a feeling of intimidation. He had been intimidated by his younger self.

On the other hand, he thought, as he began pulling things out of the little car, I'm running about the same mileage or more now, I don't court injuries or illness by pushing things right up to the red line every day, and I handle longer runs better than I ever did. Hell, I used to dread racing anything longer than a mile back then, and now I have a semirespectable half-marathon under my belt.

As he stacked a dozen pairs of training shoes in the closet and put the last of the nylon shorts and cotton T-shirts in the pine dresser, at the edge of his consciousness he began to feel a nameless and formless sense of well-being, a pleasing sense of serenity, source unknown.

The return to the warmth and light of the South in winter had something to do with it, surely. And the nostalgia of another homecoming to this rough-hewn place of dreams; that too. Maybe the sharp, brisk air of the familiar piney flatwoods, a fragrance he associated with long winter runs, good shape, quiet evenings reading on the screened-in porch.

But it was something else too. Something that combined anticipation of the coming spring, an amorphous sense of portent, and the fitness that was endemic to his pursuit, a fitness so acute it heightened his senses like a drug. At times he could almost feel individual molecules of clean chilled north Florida air stinging his nostrils.

It was youth, he finally realized. All of that roiled up together and distilled was the essence of youth, at least to him. He had felt it then and he could feel it right now, and he intuitively sensed that as long as you could feel that, no matter what your chronological age, you would still be young.

As he pulled on a battered pair of Nike Waffle Trainers, a glance out at the sun-filled tree crowns in back of the cabin reminded him that now this latitude gave him a luxuriously longer training day; in a pinch he could even drive into Kernsville and do a night run on the civilized sidewalks of a modern university town.

As he stood in the front doorway and glanced around the now well-ordered and comfortable little hideaway, he put his finger on something else. The screen door double-slammed behind him as he high-stepped through the layer of crackling leaves between the porch and driveway, hit full stride after a few yards on the clay, and then began to work out the worst of the travel kinks on the way to the highway.

As he made the rapid but untidy physiological transition between "at rest" and "all-ahead three-quarters" and his breathing transitioned through the momentarily ragged phase before reaching a comfortable hot-blooded homeostasis, he found himself almost smiling. He wouldn't try to cook dinner tonight, he decided, nothing in the house and no time to shop. He would tool down to the old Dew Drop Inn, have a celebratory beer, maybe two. Then cheeseburger in paradise to test the furnace-is-hot-enough theorem. Then maybe another beer, what the hell.

He now had a string of hundred-mile weeks under his belt and he had raced credibly against people whose names always floated high in the agate column of open race results. More important, he was healthy and uninjured. So far, at least.

Some pundits had grumbled in print that Quenton Cassidy had some nerve trashing their comfortable memories. He'd had a respectable career, it was long since concluded and placed behind glass. It was somehow unseemly of him to come along and upset their understanding of the Way of Things. Retired heroes ought not make the rest of us uncomfortable with their unquenched fires, their reignited ambitions. It embarrassed them.

Well then, Cassidy thought, Why, just tough titty said the kitty, is all.

Hitting the trailhead and powering onto a path already imprinted by ten million of his own footsteps, he actually laughed out loud. He was no longer the speed merchant of yore, it was true. He was no longer one of those high-octane four-lappers who could blast out of the last turn and hightail it to the finish line like a springbok. That was the province of the very young and the very fortunate few, those who had won the genetic lottery and who knew what to do with it.

But what gave him great contentment now and probably would from now on was the simple knowledge that he had once been a runner.

And now as he positively bounded up Blackberry Hill in the waning north Florida warmth and sunshine, an ancient and uncomplicated joy welled up in him and told him that for the time being at least, he still was.

33

Endris and O'Bannon

THE WEARY BRICK duplex was redolent of late-night graduate-level chautauquas fueled by Gallo Hearty Burgundy and discount-house stereo systems.

The dirt yards of the old neighborhood were full of worn autos weathering peacefully under ancient live oaks. Cassidy had always liked this quiet graduate-student ghetto, with its old wooden houses, its oak trees, its duck pond. He also liked the fact that hardly anything in this part of Kernsville had changed since his own student days.

Mad for diversion and human contact, he was happy when he could do long runs with Endris and O'Bannon, who called themselves "entomology weenies." Cassidy had always liked scientist types, and had become friends with Endris, now back in Kernsville to finish his dissertation. He was presently getting in shape to do military pentathalons in the reserves. O'Bannon was younger, a good-natured surfer type, somewhat starstruck by his roommate. He had been unathletic growing up in Orlando

before discovering running, and now trained with the zeal of the
recently converted.

Cassidy pulled in next to Endris's land yacht, a battered
rust-and-gold-colored Chrysler, got out dressed to run, and
stood for a moment beside the Porsche in a deep bent-over
stretch.

Inside, Endris was naked but for an oven mitt, peering into
a big pot of something on the stove. He had been doing the
pentathalons for two years now and his upper body had developed into a most unrunnerlike amalgam of pectorals and del-
toids. It had taken Cassidy a while to figure out that Endris
wasn't particularly vain about his physique, but rather was simply indifferent to the concept of clothing. From the neck up he
was clean-cut Nordic-Germanic, a pocket protector away from
a structural engineer. But behind the steel wire-rims his clear
blue eyes danced with good humor: He was always ready to
laugh.

"Something smells good," Cassidy said, flopping down on
the couch and reaching for a recently arrived *Track & Field News*,
some shotputter on the cover.

"Simmering since this ayem," said Endris. "They're okay
now, but they'll be really good by the time we get back. And
they'll keep getting better prob'ly three, four more days.
O'Bannon went by the day-old-bread store and got about ten
loaves of Italian."

"Carb city, I'm in. I'll get the beer. Saw a sign at the Barn on
the way in. Special on one of the cheapies."

"Okay if it's Dunk's, but I can't handle Orbit. Or what's that
other one?"

"Genesee?"

"No, worse. Began with an *S*."

"Schaefer's? Ski?"

"That's the one," said Endris, gesturing with his big wooden
spoon. Bending from the waist to keep his goodies out of the
splash zone, he stirred once more before replacing the lid and

hanging up the oven mitt. Speaking over his shoulder, he headed into the back of the apartment for his running gear.

"When I first got down here the Barn had a special on that stuff and not knowing any better I bought a case," he said. "It was something like fifty-nine cents a six-pack if you bought a whole case. I had just finished a sixteen-miler in late August and I had lost about twelve pounds of water weight. I would have drunk from a radiator. So I bought this stuff and I pulled one out and sucked down about half of it before it hit me. I wish I had a picture because I'm pretty sure I went completely cross-eyed. I've never experienced a taste like that in my life."

"I think I've heard this. What was it you called it?"

"Fermented bobcat urine."

"Yes! And I've always wondered how anyone would know such a thing."

"That's a completely 'nother story," said Endris, grinning, dressed now and stooping to double-knot his Brooks Villanova's.

"I won't ask."

"Ready? John's already started. He's circling the duck pond until we get there."

"Well, I don't have a Ski beer story, or Orbit either," Cassidy said, following Endris out the door. "I just know I don't like them and God knows I tried. Oh, I take it back. I *do* have an Orbit story. That one summer we had the cross-country guys out at Nubbins's hunting camp? Remember, out near Alexander Springs in the Ocala Forest? It would have been the summer before my junior year."

"I heard about it," Endris said. They were jogging slowly, stiffly.

"Somebody brought in some Orbit and the *freshmen* wouldn't drink it."

"There you go."

"Even after an hour in the freezer, they wouldn't go near it."

"Proof positive. And Quenton?"

"Hmmm?"

"You're talking to someone who *likes* Mickey's Big Mouths."

"You're kidding."

"Nope. All this time in undergrad and grad school living on a nickel a day, you get to be a connoisseur of ghetto brews. I was an expert on aftertastes. Ah, I'd say, just a hint of Janitor in a Drum. Or, hmmm, if I'm not mistaken I'm getting a subtle note of pencil shavings."

"You're bringing back memories," said Cassidy, loosening up some now. He had done ten that morning at a very easy pace.

"I was humbled by Ski though. Took forever to get rid of the rest of that case. We kept trying to slip it to people at parties who were already drunk. You wouldn't think that taste could penetrate an alcoholic haze but you'd be wrong. Guys would take a sip and give you a look like a dog you stepped on his tail."

"What'd you finally do with it?"

"I think over time people just spilled enough of it or poured it out intentionally until it was about gone. We had a ceremony with the last bottle where we made a giant slingshot with a bike tire in the backyard and tried to launch the thing back into the parking lot of the Beer Barn. So what's the special now?"

"Dunk's ninety-nine a six."

"Excellent! A little freezer time and it goes down fine. Hey, we should send that to the company to use as a slogan. Maybe they'd give us free beer!" Endris had removed his T-shirt, exposing startling abdominals, and tucked it in the back of his shorts.

"There's O'Bannon. How about one Duck Pond loop then maybe the twelve-miler out Tobacco Road?" said Cassidy.

"Sounds good. I got zero this morning. I could use a few to get back in sync."

It was a warm afternoon and soon Cassidy had followed Endris in doffing his T-shirt. O'Bannon had started without one. Other than the fact that half the deciduous leaves had fallen, it could have been almost any time of year. Cassidy was accustomed to the kind of winter that was just a lingering autumn that went on until it was time for spring. In south Florida you didn't even get that.

The Duck Pond was bustling with jogging students, young moms pushing strollers, toddlers trying to force-feed sweaty bread balls to nervous waterfowl. The runners ambled along easily, Endris and O'Bannon chatting about entomology department gossip, Cassidy painfully aware that his training life was so devoid of interest that he had little to contribute. But the other two were talkers, and Cassidy was grateful.

Soon Endris was on the current running scene in Kernsville.

"You knew Cornwall retired, right? And the undergrad team is pretty much under the thumb of the new coach, what'shisface. You can see them en masse on some of the old routes," Endris said.

"There's still a pretty solid core of serious runners in town though," said O'Bannon. "Even after you guys left, they just kept coming down here."

"Really?" said Cassidy. "After all this time?"

"Oh, sure. Everybody thinks they might find, you know, the *secret*. Funny, as long as Bruce was here, it was actually true, I guess. He was having an effect even on the guys who didn't actually train with us all the time, just by osmosis. Now, I don't know. Everybody's doing something different. Some guys mileage. Some guys intervals. Some guys weirding out on yoga or running in combat boots."

"Well, if you're going to dick around, this is as good a place as any. What do they do to get by?"

"Lot of them are in grad school, some working part-time at slow-mo jobs, like at the new running store Cornwall started. Of course, the studs are picking up some checks here and there. Liquori and Barry Brown. Steve Foster is doing okay for himself on the roads. Sammy Bair is down from Pittsburgh. And there's a group of half-milers, Byron Dyce and Juris Luzins, Eamonn O'Keefe and those guys. They do okay indoors and over in Europe."

"It sounds more active than my time, Dick," said Cassidy.

"Sort of. But I can tell you the difference. I saw it right

away when I got back from active duty. Since Bruce left there's no nucleus anymore. Everything's scattered. Guys on different work schedules. The campus is bigger, classes miles apart sometimes. There are probably ten or twelve different groups, two or three guys each, women too, all going out at different times, different parts of town. And there's a whole lot of guys just training solo."

"That's me," said Cassidy. "The Lone Ranger. It's a lot of time to spend in your own head."

"You said it," said O'Bannon, puffing a little. "I couldn't put in the miles if I didn't have somebody to talk to. Even if it's just Dick."

"No beans for you," said Endris.

"It's true though," said Cassidy. "Not so much with intervals, but a good group sure helps the overdistance go by. Remember how Barry used to have Johnny Carson's monologue memorized from the night before? You could go ten miles laughing your ass off the whole way."

"And the stories!" Endris said. "What was that one about the bowlegged guy?"

"Oh, that one," Cassidy said. "Lee Cohee! Marathoner, my class in law school. Most bowlegged guy you've ever seen, including cowboys."

"So how did it go, I forget."

"Oh, one chilly morning run Cohee shows up wearing these really bright banana-yellow tights."

"Oh yeah, I remember," said Endris, starting to laugh.

"And Liquori says, all serious, 'Lee, I don't think it's safe wearing those tights.' Cohee is all worried. Thinks maybe there's some kind of circulation issue he doesn't know about. He says, 'Really? What's the deal?'"

"Yeah, yeah," said Endris, still bent over, struggling now to keep up the pace while laughing.

"And Liquori says, 'Well, somebody might drive under your legs and try to order a Big Mac!'"

That pretty much settled their hash for a while, and it took some time to get back into some kind of serious pace. They ran in silence through most of the middle miles and as they were finishing up, Cassidy was impressed to see O'Bannon still hanging with them. As he began to struggle a bit the last two miles, the other two relented gracefully, allowing O'Bannon to finish the twelve-mile course with them for the first time.

"Good one." Cassidy slapped O'Bannon on the rear.

"Yeah, John," Endris added, looking pleased.

"Thanks," O'Bannon said, breathing hard, looking a little distressed, but his grin was irrepressible.

When he returned to the duplex it was getting close to dark, and they could smell the simmering bean pot from several houses away. Cassidy went right to his car for his wallet and kept on jogging to the beer place up on University Avenue.

By the time he got back with a six-pack under each arm, Endris and O'Bannon had cleared the dining room table of entomology texts, placed the big pot in the middle of the table with a loaf of Italian bread and bowls of chopped onions and grated cheese, and they were already going at it. Cassidy put one six-pack on the table where it was quickly pounced on, and put the other in the freezer.

"Thanks for waiting," he said, sliding into his chair.

"Mmmm," said the other two simultaneously, nodding but not slowing at all.

And they ate like shipwreck survivors, communicating with grunts and sighs, still in their training togs, scratchy with dried sweat-salt. They ate and drank with such gusto at times they had to stop to catch their breath.

Cassidy had forgotten this.

34
Company

T HE RAINS CAME in February and soggy training shoes
stacked up on the porch and around the little potbellied
stove, often not drying before their turn in the rotation came up
again. This was always a hard time for him here. He was moody
anyway and the swollen clouds closed in on his horizons and
soaked his landscape.

In his college days it was an in-between time in the athletic
year, with the indoor season wrapping up and months before
the first outdoor meets. It was basketball time and he wasn't a
basketball player anymore.

Cassidy sent Bruce copies of his training logs every week,
and they talked often on the phone. Denton was not shy about
bringing up anything that was on his mind.

"What did you do when you came in from that ten-mile
tempo run?" Denton asked once.

"What do you mean?" A week earlier, per instructions, he
had run a measured ten-mile course in fifty-one minutes flat in
a downpour.

"You know, for dinner, later that evening, whatever."

"I think that was the night I went into town and met Endris and O'Bannon at the Pizza Inn. They have an all-you-can-eat deal on Tuesdays and Thursdays. Three different kinds of pizza. Salad bar too."

"I'm sure they're always happy to see the three of you. How about after?"

"We went to the Red Lion and played bumper pool. At least Endris and I did. O'Bannon had some stuff to do at the lab with his nematodes. He came later."

"How long did you stay?"

"Is this a bed-check deal? I don't know, Bruce, we split a pitcher and ate a couple baskets of popcorn, played six or seven games. I'm pretty sure I was home by ten, ten-thirty. Why?"

"Just curious."

Cassidy was halfway through a stack of student briefs when he heard Denton's Saab pull up.

"Hey, you're early!" he called out happily as Denton struggled through the door with an equipment bag on each shoulder.

"No thanks, don't get up, I've got it," Denton said, tossing the bags into a corner.

"I was going to clear out of the bedroom."

"No way. I'll take the loft. Last thing I want to do is interrupt your routine. Whatcha got there?"

"Briefs. I got so bored I went by the law school and got Steve Atkinson to give me a legal writing section. If you have any interest at all in the concepts of estoppel or laches, I've got some fascinating bedtime reading for you."

"Thanks. Maybe after I finish reading all the pill labels in the medicine cabinet." He flopped down on the couch, pointing to Cassidy's training calendar on the coffee table between them. "How'd your long one go Sunday?"

"Fourteen miles isn't exactly an ultra. It went okay. I thought I'd be doing twenty-milers by now."

"Hmmm. Well, that's pretty much the party line, I guess. Some people are starting to rethink it though, and I think they're on to something," Denton said, now leafing back through the pages of Cassidy's well-tended training records.

"Yeah?"

"Uh-huh. There's some question as to whether the training value is worth the wear and tear. And I've actually begun wondering if the whole approach isn't fundamentally flawed."

"How so?" Cassidy finished writing a note in the back of a brief, closed it, and placed it in the larger stack on the coffee table, pushing his reading glasses up on his forehead.

"Well, I just don't think it's possible to *practice* for an event like the marathon. In point of fact, we don't *practice* when we train for the middle distances either. We do exactly what athletes do in almost every type of sport: we isolate certain functions and do overloading kind of work on each, one at a time. Then at some point we do a limited amount of integration work, blending everything back together."

"Like when a weight lifter isolates one muscle group for the whole workout."

"Right. He'll spend much more time doing that, breaking things down into components, than he will just practicing a clean and jerk or a military press. Same thing even in ball sports. Linemen spend much more of their lives pushing a sled around than they do actually chasing quarterbacks. A basketball player will spend ten hours shooting from one spot for every fifteen minutes he spends scrimmaging."

"So you think just about every expert in the sport is wrong about the necessity for weekly twenty-milers?"

"Well, first of all, there just about aren't any experts in this sport yet. And think about it for a minute. If you're averaging a hundred miles a week and you do a Sunday twenty-miler, you're probably taking an easy day before and a recovery day after. That means nearly half of your training week is more or less pointed to one workout. If you go really hard, it may take two or three days to recover, and that just puts more emphasis on that one long run."

"But if it works . . . ?"

"Lots of things *work*. The question is, What's the most practical and efficient way to train for a certain task? We know that in every other running contest, the key is isolation and overload. In middle distances we run longer and slower to build up aerobic base, and we run shorter and faster to build up anaerobic capacity. Then we do fartlek, tempo runs, interval ladders . . . what else? Time trials, I guess, things like that, to integrate, to blend the systems and groove the metabolic pathways so they work seamlessly together."

"Makes sense, I guess."

"I think so. I also think it's even more true in an event like the marathon. Extrapolate it out to events like ultras and it becomes even more obvious. There is simply no way to *practice* running a hundred-mile race. Your goal in training has to be to simply prepare your body as efficiently as you can for a really rare but pretty daunting physical ordeal."

"Well, I have to say, I'm a little disappointed. I was sort of looking forward to seeing how a broken-down miler would hold up to the thing," Cassidy said.

"Yep. And that's why we'll be doing some longer runs later on. First, because it's part of that integration process we were talking about, and secondly for the psychological boost of knowing you can handle it. See? I've thought of everything."

"I hope you thought to bring your mountain bike, because I'm tired of covering twenty-three miles a day talking to myself."

"What happened to Endris and O'Bannon?"

"That's once or twice a week. They don't like to drive out here to run, although at first they said they were going to. I don't blame them, they've got a lot going on. Hell, O'Bannon still has course work to finish."

"Yeah, well, give me a hand tossing this stuff up in the loft and let's hit the trail. The two gentlemen in question are meeting us in town at the barbecue place for dinner. If we're late they'll start—and possibly finish—without us."

35

Wild Kingdom

DENTON WAS UP early Saturday morning and kept puttering noisily around in the kitchen until he woke Cassidy, who stumbled in wrecked from sleep, dressed in the faded blue and orange cotton team sweat suit he slept in all winter. He tried to give Denton an annoyed look.

"Morning, princess!" said Denton.

"Good morning, I guess, Bruce. Jeezus."

"Oatmeal?"

"Yuck. At this hour?"

"When do *you* prefer oatmeal?"

"Never."

"All right then."

"Okay, yeah, I guess. I probably need something in my gut if we're really going to do this."

"That would be my recommendation. Twenty miles is a long way to go on a cup of coffee and a bunch of happy thoughts."

It had stopped raining during the night and the sun shone

brightly as they started down the driveway, avoiding puddles by keeping to the wet grass on either side.

"Man," said Denton, "February and we're out here in T-shirts. That's one of the things I miss about this place. They say it will get to seventy-five today."

"If it's warm you want, you could head on down to West Palm. And you might get eighty-five."

"No thanks. Too many old people trying to kill you with their Chrysler Imperials. Besides, there's nowhere to run. Nowhere like this, anyway." He was gesturing generally at the countryside around them, which at the moment included the old Doobey pecan grove. Random groups of trees magically jumped into momentary perfect alignment as they passed.

"Hey," said Cassidy, "did you ever hear the story about Sidecar Doobey and the pink squirrels?"

"Pink squirrels? Like the drink? No, but nothing would surprise me. On the other hand I thought I had heard *all* the Sidecar Doobey stories in my six years in Kernsville," said Denton.

"Me too. But the guy at the hardware store told me this one. This was years ago; right after Sidecar retired as mayor, he moved back out here to tend his farm. One year the squirrels were about to drive him crazy with his pecan grove, as you can well imagine, and he called in the ag extension guys from school. He says, 'Fellas, I got a million 'a these bushy-tailed rodents out here. I don't want to harm them but how can I make them go away?' The ag guys said it was mostly pretty hopeless, but if he wanted, he could try trapping them and hauling them out to the countryside."

"Talk about your myth of Sisyphus . . ."

"Exactly. Anyway, the ag guys tell him he's got to haul them at least twenty miles away or they'd be able to find their way back. So Sidecar says, 'How would I be able to tell if they were coming back,' and the ag guys just shrug and unload a bunch of traps and leave. So Sidecar gets this brilliant idea of spray-painting the squirrels' tails pink before he hauls them off, so that if any of them showed back up he'd know."

Denton was bent over the handlebars, struggling to keep up his cadence: "And this is supposedly a true story . . ."

"Guy at the hardware store swears. Says he personally sold the spray paint to Doobey's foreman. Says a couple days later, Doobey himself is back in the store wanting more paint. Hardware guy says, 'You must be catching a whale of a lot of squirrels, Mr. Doobey,' and Doobey says, 'Naw, it's not that so much as the squirrels are not cooperating at painting time.' He says, 'You'd be amazed at how uninterested a squirrel is in having his tail painted pink.'

"They just wouldn't hold still, so Doobey's men ended up pretty much painting the entire beast, plus the cage, plus anything or anybody else nearby or downwind."

Cassidy was having a hard time now himself. They had turned off the highway onto the trail, which was single file, so Denton went ahead on the bike, and Cassidy followed, speaking loudly enough for Denton to hear.

"So this goes on for a while, and pretty soon everybody out here knows all about it. Everyone who worked out at Sidecar's place was showing up in town with pink forearms, and the back end of all their trucks are pink, the cages are all pink, there's pink everywhere."

"So, did the squirrels find their way back?" said Denton.

"Wait. Here's where it gets good. So, they're having one of their painting sessions out there, and it's like branding time at the OK Corral and there's squirrels running around like crazy in the cages and farmhands spraying pink all over hell's half acre and here's Sidecar's daughter, Cheryl Ann, remember, the good-looking one?"

"Oh yeah, you bet. How's she doing?"

"A little hefty, but okay. She lives in Kernsville, does something in administration at the school. Anyway, so she's out visiting and she's an animal person and she gets all upset and threatens Sidecar that she's gonna turn him in to the Humane Society. So they have this big fight and she leaves in a huff. Later, Sidecar's sitting around thinking about it and he gets this idea. He calls up Cheryl Ann and apologizes and tells her she's right and they're going to stop painting squirrels and how could he have been so insensitive and so on."

"Uh-oh."

"Right. So she's a little suspicious because this is not at all like Sidecar, but then she figures maybe he's mellowing and she starts feeling pretty righteous about the whole thing. After a few weeks she's about forgotten all about it. So one morning she's looking out her kitchen window into her backyard and she sees a squirrel sitting there on her lawn and it's as pink as an Easter egg. She calls up Sidecar and says, Daddy, your eradication program is having an impact on the squirrel population for miles around. I've got one in my own yard right this minute. Sidecar acts all concerned and says he doesn't see how it's possible, how they've been turning the squirrels loose twenty miles into the countryside, and besides, they hadn't been painting any for weeks."

They were at the bottom of Blackberry Hill and Denton had pulled the bike over and was just lying over the handlebars, making little squeaking noises.

"Stop, stop," he said. "Let me make this hill." He got into his granny gear and slowly powered up the grade, struggling for breath, but at least able to function. "Okay," he said, as the trail leveled off again.

"Sidecar tells her whatever she does, don't feed the thing. She says why? Says she feels sorry for it 'cause it's probably being ostracized by the nonpainted squirrels. Sidecar says, 'Okay, but don't say I didn't warn you.' Naturally she puts a bowl of nuts out, and of course when she comes home from work that day, there're *two* pink squirrels in her backyard. And so she's happy the first one has a companion and she puts out more food, and the next day there are *six*. And yadda yadda.

Pretty soon, she's thinking of herself as the Mother Teresa of pink squirrels and she's buying squirrel food in fifty-pound bags and she's basically got hot and cold running pink squirrels around the place."

"Stop," Denton protested weakly. He was wobbling again.

"Almost done now. So, care to venture a guess as to what happens now?"

"No. Tell it."

"Well, the first orange one shows up."

Denton's guffawing was so rigorous that he really did have to concentrate on keeping his eyes open so as not to leave the trail. Cassidy slowed down a little for him.

"And of course pretty soon the oranges are holding their own with the pinks and Cheryl Ann is pretty much in a tizzy. She calls up the *Kernsville Sun* and tells them that she has incontrovertible proof that there's some kind of nationwide squirrel-painting conspiracy going on and that somehow the squirrels were using her place as a refuge. The *Sun* does a little human interest story, kind of tongue-in-cheek, and they put in a photo showing a couple of painted squirrels munching away at the feeder. Pretty soon there's all these letters to the editor all pro and con on squirrel painting and several from some wags saying stuff like, 'It's an outrage to have all these painted squirrels running around when we have an entire countryside of unpainted badgers out there and if we're going to start color-coding Mother Nature by God we ought to start with the badgers.'"

Denton had to slow down again to keep his balance.

"And then some guy from Alachua wrote in and said that he didn't have an opinion about what they ought to paint first, but if anyone out there was fixin' to paint a lynx or a bobcat, he would sure appreciate knowing about it so he could come watch. The guy at the hardware store was pretty sure it was Sidecar who wrote that one under an assumed name, but he couldn't prove it."

Tired of jogging so slowly, Cassidy gestured to the teary-eyed Denton to keep up.

"So it got to be such a big deal," Cassidy continued, "that the *Sun* put a crack investigative feature writer on the case and she took a photographer out and they staked out Cheryl Ann's house for a couple of days."

"They catch them in the act?"

"Oh, it was priceless. Guy at the hardware store still had the issue. Lots of people saved it. Telephoto shot of old Sidecar himself, grinning like a leprechaun, all hunched over this cage, about to lift the door and unleash a batch of squirrels."

"Perfect!"

"But that's not all."

"Yeah?"

"This batch was purple."

Cassidy watched as Denton wobbled off the trail and failed to avoid a painful-looking palmetto.

36

Otter Springs

THE REST OF the twenty-miler went by uneventfully and they were sitting on the screened-in porch, still sweating profusely and thinking about showering, when Cassidy hopped up suddenly and tossed Denton a fresh towel from a stack in the corner.

"Come on," he said, shoving the screen door open and prancing on bare feet toward his sports car. The top was already off, as usual. "Got an idea!"

"Uh-oh," said Denton.

They drove to Otter Springs and raced each other into the water. It was a constant seventy-two and a half degrees and it wasn't long before they raced each other right back out. The sun was as directly overhead as it would get this time of year so they just flopped in the warm sand at the water's edge.

"You seem none the worse for wear," Denton said. He kept his heels in the cool water and let sunshine and warm sand work on the goose bumps on the rest of him.

"I told you, I'm in decent shape."

"I know."

"Better shape than I've ever been in for anything over three miles probably." Cassidy was on his stomach, face in his folded arms, quaking still with cold.

"Hmmm."

"I don't think I could break 4:10 for a mile for all the . . . if you offered me a . . . say, a hot fudge sundae though," said Cassidy.

Denton studied the stretched-out figure quivering beside him. He knew that most people would see a wiry, perhaps undernourished young man instead of the perfectly trained endurance athlete he saw. There wasn't an ounce of fat anywhere. The tight brown skin covered a sleek musculature that spoke only of motion and efficiency. Individual muscles pushed themselves into clear definition against the skin when he moved or when they jumped involuntarily. A vein in his neck broadcast the laughably slow pulse.

Denton knew that Cassidy was still within that special physical trajectory, the place where you can still call up the powers of youth, can still aspire to impossible physical tasks. He knew, as he suspected Cassidy knew, that it wouldn't last very much longer, but that for now it was still there.

For Denton, it was years in his past now. Even so, he was far more of a physical specimen than all but a handful of the twenty-year-olds on the campus where he taught. But for his tormented heels and hips he could probably still outrun all but one or two members of the school's track team. But this was something else entirely. Cassidy was physically now in a place that for Denton existed only in memory. He studied the skinny brown frame quaking with cold and couldn't help feeling a pang of envy.

It would always be the best of times, he thought. That's what we are condemned to know. And it's not just the youth. Everybody gets that. It's youth blazing along on some kind of spectacularly high octane. It's like having a benign fever all the time. It's like being in love.

No one around us could possibly have understood, but we did. We must have known. We must have drunk it up as best we could. But could we really understand how fleeting it all would be? Could we be sure we were squeezing every drop out of it? Could we understand that it would not, could not, last? That nothing burning that hot ever does?

A great blue heron came gliding in low at the far end of the springs, flared wings briefly, and stuck out comically long legs to peg a perfect landing in the shallow water.

You don't even get to play unless you have already won the genetic lottery. Then you have to win the nurture lottery, then the happenstance lottery, and then just in general be incredibly lucky in every conceivable way, and then you will have earned the right to work your ass off like most civilians could never possibly imagine. Then you might—*might*—get to stand up there like a dodo all teary-eyed pretending you know the words to your anthem.

Well, by God I did that. I stood up there. That is all that anyone could ever ask of a runner. You should be able to walk in grace all your days after that. Nothing else you ever do will be as difficult or frightening or as wonderful. Your life after that will be an epilogue.

Denton sat up for a moment with his chin on his knees, watching three small children in droopy underwear playing in the shallow water with plastic buckets. He looked over at Cassidy again.

He's not ready for an epilogue. He thought he was but he had a taste of the afterward and he knows there's all the time in the world for that. Now he wants to squeeze a few more drops out of it and goddamn if I can blame him.

At that moment Cassidy resembled a hunk of quivering wild game, dressed out, all sand-coated skinless muscles: ready for transport.

I would trade places with him in a hummingbird's heartbeat, Denton thought. It's the fever you live in that's the thing.

The hot pulse of it all. The rest is just knickknacks and souvenirs. What you miss is the dizzy crazy lactic-acid storm of training, racing. The ten-milers laughing the whole way with guys who are your brothers in ways beyond genetics. The thousand quarter-mile intervals in the hot sun, grabbing your knees for balance afterward and rasping for air. Consuming huge mounds of fried anything-at-all and laughing at each other because you know not a molecule of it can stick to your slippery bones. And knowing nothing in your life will ever be that wild and alive again. No quest ever again as honorable or as noble.

But it's the fever. That's the thing. The fever that connects you to lovers and poets and rare-air mountain climbers and madmen and lost tribes.

At the time it's happening you think you could never lose such a thing. But you can.

Still. It's just the best of times.

"Bruce," Cassidy said, voice muffled in the sand.

"Uh-huh."

"What are you pondering?"

"I was thinking how nobody realizes how much there is to this part of it."

"What part of it?"

"Training. Hanging around. Travel someplace to race, someplace to train. More hanging around. Eating stuff, get a degree. Hang around some more."

"That's the life all right."

"What I mean is that someone sees a race, and they think that's what you do. They sort of know you had to train, but they weren't watching then, so they don't understand how incredibly much of it there is. But to us, it's almost the whole thing. Racing is just this little tiny ritual we go through after everything else has been done. It's a hood ornament."

Cassidy was silent for a time and Denton assumed he had gone to sleep.

"Bruce," Cassidy said.

"Yes."

"You told me once not to worry, that things would work out."

"Uh-huh."

Cassidy turned his head, opened one eye.

"It's okay, Bruce."

"Hmmm?"

"You don't have to worry about this on my account. I don't have anything to prove."

"Yeah?"

"I just want to make it back on the bus one more time."

"Right."

"Everything else is icing now. It'll be okay. *I'll* be okay."

Cassidy turned his head down and, finally over his shivers, lay perfectly still in the warm sand.

The children had been summoned to lunch and it was suddenly so peaceful that Denton dozed off for just an instant until his chin slipped off his knee and he jumped. He looked over at the still-snoozing runner.

"Yes," Denton said, out loud but to himself. "I can see that's mostly true."

Pause . . .

ONE YEAR LATER, Denton sat with Dick Endris on the front porch steps of the A-frame, Endris sipping at a longneck, Denton a liter of Evian. Cassidy and O'Bannon were bustling around the charcoal grill on the rear deck and laughing about something. The sun was on the horizon, darkening the forest floor but painting the tops of the taller pines orange.

Cassidy had been back in the Carolina mountains all that summer and fall, and back to Kernsville for another winter. He was now four pounds lighter than he had been as a twenty-two-year-old college miler. He had averaged 122 miles a week over the winter, and the undergraduates on the track team still talked about an interval workout they saw him do one rainy Thursday afternoon, twelve times a half mile, all close to two minutes, the last one in 1:56.

"You think he can do it?" Endris said, carefully peeling the label off his beer bottle.

"It's still a stretch," Denton said. "Hard to say."

"He's too much for us, I can tell you that. Has been all winter. He doesn't even know it. He just grinds us up, carrying on a conversation the whole way."

"Yeah, I've been seeing that too. Even on the bike this afternoon there were stretches he had me working," Denton said.

"Still, the race is not the same as it used to be, Shorter and Rodgers out there all alone and pulling away. Now there're so many guys under 2:20 you can't count 'em. And there are guys under 2:15 who can't even get free gear."

"I know."

"Has anyone else ever done it?"

"I always go back to my magic trio. Rod Dixon, world-class in the mile *and* the marathon. And both Ken Martin and Geoff Smith were sub-four and sub-2:10. There were others close. Shorter could have gone under four in the mile if he'd tried. Hell, he ran 4:05 in college. Cassidy thinks pretty soon all the events will be dominated by miler types. He says a marathon will be won by someone capable of an 800 in 1:47 or 1:46."

Endris snorted.

"I'm not so sure he's off base," said Denton.

"How do you get that?"

"Well, just look at what's happened historically in the other events. Typically an athlete coming into the sport will settle on the shortest distance at which he can be successful. If you can beat everybody at 100 meters, you might run 200 on occasion, but you're sure not going to hurt yourself by running the 400 much. Same thing with the distances. A guy who cleans up in the half mile might get interested in the mile as he gets older, but that's about it. Peter Snell comes to mind."

"True enough, I guess."

"The marathon didn't get hot until the track guys started moving up in the late sixties. Before, you had all these plodder types who thought there was something mystical and unfathomable about the distance. Breaking 2:30 was a huge deal. They considered themselves a completely different breed. Then the track guys show up and pretty soon they're clipping off five-minute miles till the cows come home. The mystical guys were devastated."

"And they started running fifty-milers."

"And hundred-milers. The new mystical frontier. But what Cassidy is saying is similar to the axiom in ball sports: the good big man beats the good little man. In running it's, The fast guy with endurance beats the slow guy with endurance. The red fast-twitch muscle guy—the miler type—when he moves up to longer events and trains properly, wins."

"Well, it has certainly happened with every distance event on the track."

"Right. So, that's the theory, anyway . . ." Denton said.

"But?"

"He was away from it a long time. Things change. I hope he's not building it up too much in his own head."

"He seems content with his lot. I don't know. If you had a realistic shot, wouldn't you go for it?" asked Endris.

Denton drained the rest of the water, put his hands behind his head, and leaned back against the steps, looking through the tops of the darkening pines to the pale blue beyond.

"On the bus, always," he said quietly.

Neither spoke for several minutes. There was hubbub from inside the cabin, and through the screen door came Cassidy, a KISS THE COOK apron around his waist. He was still wearing running shorts and a T-shirt from the afternoon workout and the effect was ridiculous.

"Hey," he said, holding up a pair of barbecue tongs, "O'Bannon just told me that he wasn't an entomologist."

"He's not," said Endris.

"He isn't? I thought you were both bug guys."

"John's a *nematologist*. Nematodes aren't insects."

"I told you!" O'Bannon called out from inside.

"Oh, I get it. It's a *trick question*," Cassidy said, turning. "Five minutes to medium rare, boys."

"You just got my attention," said Endris, gripping the rail

and pulling himself up stiffly. "Entomologist, nematologist, call me anything but late for dinner."

Cassidy cradled a miniature snifter of tawny port and swung his legs gently back and forth like a six-year-old off the edge of the deck. Denton reclined in the wrought-iron chaise lounge with the last of his dinner cabernet, studying the full moon suspended between two towering pines.

"So, you taking off early?"

"Yep. Try to beat the noon traffic through Atlanta."

"It's been great, Bruce. I can't imagine that it was much fun for you but it was like a vacation for me."

"It's been fine. I love it here."

"Maybe it's the getting older, but I can't seem to just veg out like I used to. Until I took on that legal writing section, I was going stir-crazy."

"Herb Elliott talked about that, the lack of mental stimulation. As he got older, it didn't make much sense to him anymore, hanging out with a bunch of guys by the ocean in the middle of nowhere, running fifteen miles through the tea trees, racing up and down the sand dunes, eating boiled oats, going to bed at eight," said Denton.

"Add to that the fact that he was ten yards ahead of the next fastest miler in the world," said Cassidy.

"Yeah, it would be hard to sustain. And he was a pretty smart guy. Funny too. I met him in Melbourne once. I don't blame him for going stir-crazy. Hell, the whole time I was running hard I was working on my degree and starting a family. If anything, I was overbooked."

"But when he left, it pretty much started the breakup of Cerutty's little gang at Portsea. Too bad."

"But then Lydiard's group was getting cranked up on the south island and it was a whole new era," said Denton.

"It seems to go like that, doesn't it? You had that little group around Bannister and Stampfl. You had Igloi and his interval nuts on the West Coast. Then Eugene, of course, with Bowerman and Dellinger."

"And Grelle and Pre," said Denton.

"Yep, you get a barnacle on a rock and pretty soon there's a coral reef."

They were quiet for long enough that each suspected the other might beg off to bed. Finally, Cassidy cleared his throat.

"Bruce, you've been all through the workout logs . . ."

"Yep. I've got a pretty good grasp on things. This interval session on Wednesday should tell me a lot, so I want you to be pretty fresh for it."

"Sure, sure. We talked about it. I've got it worked out."

"But everything looks okay to me, Cass. What can I tell you? I have no idea how everyone else is doing, but there are some tough guys out there now. I'll make some calls. Hell, half the people you spend a year worrying about won't even be on the starting line. You just—"

"Don't know which half," said Cassidy.

"That's it. But you can pretty well count on it. Barney Klecker had it right. About all you can do is make sure that you're as ready as you can possibly be the morning you stand on the line in Buffalo. Top three guys make it. That simple. Everything else is just frittering."

"But shouldn't I do one all-out just to see? I mean, I've done a jillion miles in training but I still don't know what this thing feels like when you take it to the edge."

"That's true, you don't really know what it feels like to run out of glycogen in the middle of a race. That's what hitting the wall is. A lot different from the Bear, that's lactic acid. *That* you know a lot about. But you know what it feels like to run out in the middle of a training week. You've been through breakdown training, and that's essentially what it is. It's a system that has used up all of its higher-octane fuel, which makes burning the lower-octane stuff almost impossible. In the marathon the goal is just to put off that happening until as late in the race as you can. Hopefully, the last yard of the last mile of the race."

"But without doing it at least once . . ."

"Oh, you'll do one all right. Just not where anyone will know about it. I've petitioned to get you in with your half-marathon time, but we won't take any chances. You'll get to go the distance, but still not all-out. That way you'll get the confidence boost and you'll keep your powder dry."

Cassidy was quiet. Denton finished his wine, set the glass down, and looked at Cassidy.

"You okay?" he said.

"Sure. You know what you're doing," said Cassidy.

"No," said Denton, "no, I don't."

38

Spring

C ASSIDY CRUISED SHIRTLESS down Blackberry Hill on the last run of the last week of February, going over in his head the mileage figures for the month. For more than a year now he had been on the two-up, one-down weekly cycle that Denton had settled on after much discussion with coaches from all over the country.

"I talked to Pete Peterson, Joe Vigil, Vinnie Lananna, a whole bunch of them," he told Cassidy. "They all said different things but one thing they all said and that was that just making it to the starting line is half the battle. It was Vinnie who'd been the most convincing about the cycle, arguing that it was the best insurance policy, that it was more important to consolidate improvements and avoid injuries than to simply amass mileage."

The previous month Cassidy had gone 120, 123, 95, 126. February, despite the rain, had been 130, 105, 137, 142. It was a mild revelation that a hundred-plus-mile week had become his "down" week. Now, as he headed home at the end of a twenty-five-mile day, he was aware mostly of being hungry. He had gone ten easy that morning, puttered around the house, graded some papers, taken a short nap, then did a three-mile warm-up and a twelve-mile run with five miles of fartlek pickups in the middle. And he felt great.

The next week would be shorter in terms of mileage, but he was looking forward to it because on Wednesday he was scheduled to drive in to the campus for an interval workout on the track, his first in more than a month. Bruce had arranged it. Three varsity runners would take turns pacing, and Endris would supervise. It was supposed to be fast, but not all-out. No spikes.

Cassidy couldn't wait. He felt itchy.

As he trotted up the driveway he saw the blue Volvo in front of the cabin and for a moment couldn't for the life of him place it. Then he saw her sitting on the steps, smiling, a blade of grass in her mouth.

"I've been trying to make that noise, you know, where you make the grass blade into a reed." She held either end of the blade in her hands and blew, getting a brief, high-pitched scream from it, then nothing but a buzzing sound.

Cassidy lifted her up, removed the blade of grass, and kissed her really hard.

She looked at him with a sad little half-smile set on her face, her eyes glossy.

"Andrea?"

"Quenton, it's Joe. You have to go now."

39

Old Business

THE HOSPITAL ROOM was dim and Cassidy was relieved to see there weren't a lot of depressing flower arrangements or get-well balloons.

"I told Roland to tell you not to come," Joe said, eyes still closed, but smiling, barely.

"I thought you were asleep."

"You didn't need to be interrupting what you're doing up there."

"I thought I did."

"Well."

He scooched himself up on his pillow a bit and opened his eyes and Cassidy was happy to see in them the dancing light, muted but still there.

"Come on over here, I won't bite," Joe said.

"That's not true," sang the nurse gaily, politely edging past Cassidy to wrap a blood pressure cuff around Joe's bicep. She smiled sweetly at Joe and started pumping the bulb, alternating her attention between the dials on the device and glances at Joe that Cassidy could only surmise were warm and fuzzy.

"Present company excepted," Joe said. "Nurse DeAngelis, may I present my friend and colleague, Mr. Cassidy."

"We've had the pleasure," she said happily.

Cassidy studied her, smiling blankly.

"A few years back. I was in the OR then. The Beshakis case?"

"I'm sorry," Cassidy said, shaking his head. "I probably deposed you?"

"Seventeen-year-old soccer player in for minor surgery dead on the table?"

"Oh," said Cassidy.

He was completely unable to read the situation. This kind of thing happened with some frequency around town after he had been in practice for a while.

He remembered her now, and he remembered that her testimony had been straightforward, unadorned, and seemingly objective. It was also extremely helpful testimony to him, to his clients, the parents of the dead boy. Cassidy glanced at Joe, who looked merely amused. For the first time Cassidy noticed that his smile seemed droopy on the left side.

"Oh, don't get your undies in a knot, Mr. Cassidy," she said. "It was the most obvious malpractice case I've seen in all my years, that poor kid dying right there while the anesthesiologist wandered around somewhere, probably talking to his broker."

"Oh."

"He might have been in the doctor's lounge, smoking, if you can believe that for someone who makes a living monitoring the amount of oxygen in your blood."

She bustled around the bed, checked the IV, the various monitors, entered notes in the aluminum-clad chart under her arm, then stood there finally, hands on hips, giving her patient the once-over.

"You need anything at all, Joe?"

"You better believe it, Angie," Joe said, and Cassidy detected something more than patient-nurse bonhomie.

"Keep dreamin', darlin'!" she sang and was gone.

Cassidy stood looking at his senior partner, dumbfounded.

"Don't be such a little old lady!" Joe said, propping himself up into full sitting position. Cassidy moved quickly to help and found himself brushed aside.

"We went to the senior prom separately together," Joe said, smiling at Cassidy's wrinkled brow. He turned his bad side away from Cassidy to look out the window. They were only on the third floor and the wind from the Intracoastal was blowing fronds from a towering palm across the glass with a sound like a muted snare drum.

"That sounds like a story," Cassidy said, moving a chair close to the bed.

"Everything's a story. Dumb stuff happens in your life and you think it's just dumb stuff, and then it turns out that it was your history, your life happening."

"I can relate to *that*."

"I know you can. Angie and I could have . . ." He smiled in such a way that Cassidy could only smile back, feeling somehow connected to someone else's long-ago happiness. "Well, she was the only Italian girl in school, she was hot as a two-dollar pistol and could dance all night with a grin on her face. And I was—"

"You were a stud with a two-handed set shot from darned near half-court," Cassidy said.

"Well . . ."

"Your picture was still up in the training table at Yon Hall when I was there," said Cassidy.

"Well, I scored twenty-eight against LSU my junior year. That kind of thing was a pretty big deal back then."

"No kidding!"

"Quenton, you wouldn't get your picture up in Yon Hall these days for scoring *forty-eight* against LSU."

"Maybe. But I'm still a believer. Don't forget I have been humiliated by that shot myself in exciting league action."

"So you have. Okay, so I was team captain and she was head

cheerleader and Palm Beach was a fishing village. Things were different. Your dad must have told you."

"A little. He wasn't exactly a chatterbox. So what happened?"

"Ah." He held an arm up like an auctioneer, gesturing at the room, outside the window to the city, and to the Intracoastal beyond. "She went to the prom with my best friend, your dad. I went with her best friend."

"My mom?"

"No." Joe laughed. "Life's hardly ever that symmetrical. But in those days you made prom dates months in advance and by the time the event rolled around everyone was in love with somebody else. So you'd just go and try to make the best of it. Your dad was great. He brought her over to me and absconded for most of the night. I don't know if he was with my date or not. It didn't matter. We couldn't see anything but each other that night, Angie and me."

"So what happened?"

"Life happened, I guess. The two-handed set shot got me a scholarship to Kernsville back when the basketball coach was also a football assistant. Angie went off to nursing school in Orlando. We saw each other on weekends for a while." He was looking out the window again, and Cassidy heard what he took for a sigh.

"Anyway, I met Alice my senior year, this gorgeous Tri-Delt with a daddy on the state supreme court. Before you knew it I was at Duke Law and had a young son on the way. Next thing I heard, Angie had settled down with a pool guy in Sanford. Then we got a little Sunday-afternoon radio announcement about something going on in a place called Pearl Harbor. And so on and so forth. Suddenly captain of the basketball team and head cheerleader and Tri-Delt doings didn't seem to be very important at all. At all. In short, that's what happened: life."

"Pool guy? What, like billiards?"

"Swimming pools. There was a time in Florida when that

was just an outstanding business to be in. He was 4-F. Also was in the concrete business. Made blocks. Poured also. Made a fortune. Lost it in real estate in Kissimmee. Died of a massive coronary a few years back at forty-nine."

"And now here you are."

"Yep. Here we *both* are, back where we started. And the only thing that happened in between was life."

They were quiet for a while.

"So, speaking of which, how are you doing with all this anyway? Not to change the subject," Cassidy said. "You seem to be doing okay, right?"

Joe smiled at him until Cassidy started to fidget.

"I feel okay, Quenton," he said, finally. "But I can't walk right and I'm having trouble with my left hand. They say I was lucky. I'm going to be taking some serious medicine for the rest of my life." He made a dismissive gesture. "I don't know. It's a lot of bother."

"Joe. You're still the best damn litigator in south Florida."

"Not hardly. Good enough, I guess. But Quenton, I'm done with it. It's good-bye to all that for me."

Cassidy sat in silence. He shouldn't have been surprised, but he was. And he wondered what his attitude was supposed to be. Good-natured contrarian? Encouragement?

"Joe. Are you sure?" he said finally.

"I'm not one of these guys who wants to be carried out of Tom Sholt's courtroom on a litter halfway through some damn condemnation action. I've done it, Quenton, I don't have to anymore. When I die I want it to be with the sun on my shoulders and a sailfish on the line. Let the fish win for once."

"How is that different from most weekends?"

Joe laughed. "I want it to be on a Wednesday morning."

"Hey," said Cassidy, jumping up. "Do you remember that time in the middle of the week you came into my office and closed the door and whispered, 'Let's bust outta here,' and we gathered up a bunch of books and files and stuff and went rushing out the door telling everybody we had an emergency federal injunction hearing in Miami?"

Joe's eyes were squeezing shut the way they did right before he laughed really hard. "And we thought we were so damned clever until the next morning when they all looked at us like we were dog-doo on the bottom of their shoes. Who was it turned us in?"

"It was Lavinia, the one we called Lynn, the secretary I had back then. She went to law school later. She just gave me this dead-eye look and says, 'Look, you—and Joe too—obviously can do whatever the hell you want to, but if you really want to get away with your cock-and-bull stories, you ought to at least conceal your faces *when you're cruising underneath the Flagler Bridge on your way out fishing.*' "

Joe couldn't catch his breath for a minute and one of his monitors was going crazy enough that Angie put in another, much less playful visit, fixing Cassidy at the end of a red-tipped finger and cocking her head to one side.

"Sorry," Cassidy said.

"Okay, mister, that's your warning," she said, backing out of the room still pointing at him.

Cassidy shook his head slowly: "I *like* that woman."

"I know. I *know*!" said Joe.

"That Lavinia," said Cassidy. "You know, she was always all business around the office and all. Wouldn't so much as do drinks at Taboo with us Fridays. Then after she had gone off to law school—"

"Where'd she end up?"

"Stetson."

"Good school."

"So she's off in St. Pete and then next spring she's back on break—her mom still lives in Lantana—and she comes by the house . . ." Cassidy was staring out the window down the Intracoastal.

"And . . . ?" Joe was leaning up, trying to get his pillows situated behind him.

"What?" Cassidy looked blank.

"She came by the house?"

"Who?"

"Lynn. *Lavinia. That incredible creature who was your secretary for five years and who you were only moments ago speaking of!*"

"Oh." Cassidy shook his head like a fighter clearing cobwebs after a hook to the temple. "Yes, sorry. She came by the house that time and we visited. She did great at Stetson and I think she's practicing in Jacksonville."

"Good for her. And good for . . . *visiting!*" Joe said. He was grinning his old way, the droop not even noticeable.

"Anyway, so you're putting out to pasture," said Cassidy. "You sure you don't want to wait until I get through goofing around with my midlife crisis here?"

"No, hell. Have at it. Wish I could join you. Wish I had done it myself when I still could."

"You're not done yet."

"No, I've got a little fight left."

"Darn right you do."

They were quiet again. Joe motioned to Cassidy to pull his chair closer.

"Quenton, something I've been wanting to talk to you about."

"Yeah? About Karl?"

"No, never mind Karl," Joe said with a smile. "I know you always thought your dad was strange about your sports."

"Well, it seemed strange to me. He didn't come to games, races. Never said much about it."

"That's what I wanted to tell you about. I swore a blood oath, but I don't think I'm bound by it anymore."

"Joe, what in the world . . ."

"You're wrong, Quenton. He did see you race. He saw you in the Southeast Conference indoor meet your junior year."

"What?"

"He was going to surprise you. He was at a seminar in Gulf-sport and he was going to drive to Montgomery and watch you run, surprise you, take you to dinner."

"Joe, that is just, I don't know, kind of stunning."

"His rental car got a flat. It was pouring rain, cold as hell. He tried to fix it but something was wrong with the jack. He got soaked. Finally a trucker gave him a ride close enough to town he was able to get a cab. He got there just in time to see the race."

"I remember that year. The two Tennessee guys went out hard."

"Yes. He said that. He said he hadn't known what to expect, but when he was actually there watching, he said he was surprised at himself. Here he is, standing there in the aisle, shivering, dripping, still greasy."

"But why in the world . . ."

"He was embarrassed, Quenton. When you passed those guys in the last lap and won the race, he just broke down completely. Lot of stuff came to a head for him, I guess, and he just lost his composure. He couldn't face you like that because he didn't understand it himself. Except that he was ashamed, and he wasn't up to it. He got back to his seminar and he swore me to secrecy all these years. I told him he was crazy and I begged him to talk to you, but he was stubborn, your old man."

Cassidy was looking out the window, shaking his head.

"That is so . . . bizarre. Somehow it sounds just like him though. I just can't for the life of me—"

"Well, he was an unusual guy, no denying that, Quenton. He grew up hard, harder than most around here. And he had his own ideas about things, particularly about the emphasis on sports. We even argued about it some when we were kids, after I got involved in basketball. He started mellowing later after he saw how well things had turned out for me. And particularly after you got the scholarship to Southeastern. I think that's what that trip was all about. He thought it'd be this kind of lighthearted confession of error. He'd watch you run, congratulate you, and tell you how proud he was and that he'd been off base, something like that. But then there was all the turmoil with the storm and everything, and then when he got there, it just overwhelmed him. He was watching his boy coming from behind to win this race and . . . he just wasn't prepared for it, emotionally. He was embarrassed at himself."

"Joe, it was only the conference meet."

"Maybe to you, but you have to try to see it from his perspective. We were raised differently then. We weren't supposed to be emotional. Your dad landed soldiers at Iwo Jima, Quenton. His LCP took a direct mortar hit on his second run in. He had to swim through the soldiers' blood and . . . and worse."

"He would never talk about it."

"I'm not saying he was right, just that things were different. And you're not a father either, Quenton. It's not easy. I would ask you not to pass judgment."

Cassidy couldn't think of anything to say and Joe was lost in his own thoughts again, watching the fronds now thrashing wildly against the bottom of the window.

"Afternoon squall's coming in," Joe said quietly. "Lightning in it too."

Cassidy could see through the gap of the Palm Beach Inlet the gray smudge on the horizon, vertical rain lines chilling him from thirty miles away.

"We've been out in some of those, Joe."

"Yes, son, we have. Lost the left engine on the way back from Green Turtle that time. That was two boats ago. Raining so hard you had to breathe behind your hand. Those are the times you find out what people are made of. You remember that trip?"

"Of course I do. It was the first trip you and I took together after my dad—" He stopped, studied the squall line, now broken into two distinct storms.

"Do you remember late in the afternoon when I was completely done in and you were steering?" said Joe. "Jesus, you were steering through line after line of twenty-foot rollers. It was nerve-racking because you had to keep goosing it to climb the faces and not let them break on you, but still you had to crest them just right so you didn't go over the top and go airborne. It was relentless and I was just lolling back there, trying to rest as best I could, kind of half lying on the big cooler in the back. But there you were, hour after hour. I got fed up at feeling useless so I offered to get you a drink. You remember that?"

"No, I remember the rollers, but I don't remember that."

"You said you'd take a tot of rum, Cockspur, and I asked if you wanted ice."

Cassidy smiled, shrugged.

"And that's when I knew you were your daddy's boy, because you looked back at me between rollers and your face was white around the eyes, and your nostrils were flared, and do you remember what you said?"

Cassidy shook his head.

"You said, 'No, sir, I believe I am beyond ice.'"

It was strange, sleeping in his house again, but he and Winkler fell instantly into their old patterns and stayed up far too late jabbering like undergraduates.

It was also strange on his morning run to be cruising along the Intracoastal in the kind of shape he was in. He was accustomed to thinking of his seven-mile Palm Beach bike path loop as a major daily accomplishment, occasionally forgone for trivial reasons. Now that he was a seriously training athlete, it was a quick morning chore, a way to get the blood moving on a brisk winter morning.

The sun was showing fully round over the palmy vegetation of the island when on a lark he hopped up and ran along the top of the foot-wide seawall, something he had sometimes done as a cocky collegian home on break, but now giddily risky with the potential of a twenty-foot drop to the slashing barnacles and churning water below.

Ah, he thought, *When the wind blows the water white and black.*

It was akin to striding along a series of pommel horses set end to end, but with an occasional refreshing cloud of saltwater spray. It was actually easier to maintain his balance at a faster speed so he dropped down to near-five-minute pace, ignoring the startled looks of the seniors out strolling idly by or heading to fishing spots.

He was huffing pretty good by the time he jumped down to cross the bridge. He was about to ease back on the pace when he heard the horn and noticed the unmistakable gleaming white visage of Malcolm Forbes's yacht, the *Highlander,* bearing down from the north. Cassidy immediately picked up the pace again and held up a hand as he sprinted by the bridge tender's little shack.

"Thanks, Lester!" Cassidy called.

"Lester's retired!" called back the silhouette inside.

Cassidy gave a generic friendly "duly noted" wave and despite himself jumped when the first startling blast from the tender's warning horn sounded. He looked back and saw the black-and-white-striped crossbars already descending. The yacht was beautiful in the morning sun, all white and chrome, a twenty-four-foot speedboat toylike on davits in the back. Cassidy idly wondered if the gay old pederast himself was aboard, cruising down to the Keys for the several varieties of bonefishing he enjoyed.

When Cassidy got to the Palm Beach side and turned north toward the Sailfish Club the first person he encountered waddling along the bike path was a former governor, Claude Kirk, who managed to make the act of pushing a baby carriage look pompous.

"Morning, sir," Cassidy chirped. Kirk fish-eyed him. Chuckling, Cassidy picked it up as he passed the deserted old Flagler Hotel, thinking, *It is a morning for chance encounters with scions of the Republic. If we had drawn from such a gene pool for founding fathers we'd have been a banana republic three generations ago.*

Joe was finishing breakfast and chatting with a different nurse. Cassidy thought he detected more color in his face, that he looked more like his tanned, outdoorsy self, an attractive man, seniority notwithstanding.

Cassidy pulled a chair up and they talked quietly for a while about the law business.

"Joe, I'm sorry about all this flap with Karl. I know it's gotten worse. I'd hate to think my little adventure was going to hurt the firm. Or worse."

"Karl's going to do what he's going to do. His name's on the door and his dad was my partner and good friend. I hate that you and Roland have to bear the brunt of it, but there's not much I can do about it at this stage, and whatever you and Roland end up doing professionally, I'll understand. Just remember that no matter what anybody says, what you're doing up there now is important."

"You think?"

"They might claim otherwise, but most guys I know would jump at the chance. If they had even a remote shot, they would take it. Life is short, Quenton."

"I know."

"No you don't. You can't really know it in your bones like I do until you've lain in a place like this for a few days thinking about nothing else."

"Well . . ."

"Can you just imagine for instance how little I regret right now I didn't spend more time in that damn office?"

Cassidy chuckled.

"A couple thousand dusty files, Quenton. That's the sum and total of it. Disputes resolved or extended, property changing hands, wills and codicils drawn and amended, and sure, the occasional happy ending. But it's mostly people pissed at each other, either in love once or in hate now, husbands and wives, parents and kids, legatee siblings, feuding business partners, former best friends, gay lovers, coconspirators. Some were psychopaths, some were addled, many of them are dead and gone now, or staring at a wall somewhere and slobbering on their bathrobes. And what we did was, we helped facilitate or defend against whatever it was they were determined to do to each other. Sound and fury, Quenton, sound and fury signifying not much at all. And the actual physical residue is a tractor-trailer load of dusty file folders."

"Joe . . ."

"I'm okay, Quenton. I'll be fine. I'm rich and it looks like I'll have some good company."

Cassidy raised his eyebrows.

"Don't look shocked. I'm not dead yet," Joe said.

Cassidy picked up the limp hand off his sheeted chest and held it, looking at this man who had in some ways been more than a father to him.

"Stop that. Now, quit worrying about what's going on here. Go do what you need to do."

"Joe, I—"

"Get out of here."

"All right. But if anything—"

"Go."

"All right."

But when he reached the door, he heard his name.

"Yes, sir?"

"Remember one thing, Quenton."

"Yes, sir?"

"No matter how cool you think your generation is, fifty years from now when they show pictures of you all dancing, you're going to look just as ridiculous as those guys doing the Charleston."

40

Spring on Cedar Mountain

WHEN CASSIDY ARRIVED back at the Poutin' House in the middle of March for the second year in a row, he stood at the edge of the pasture and thought, My life is now a circuit of hermit dwellings.

But it was a crisp morning in the greening pasture and when he set foot on the rough board porch and breathed in the scent of hay and the awakening trees and plants in the meadow, he was grateful to have left the panhandle's oncoming heat and humidity far behind.

His first run to Thunder Lake that afternoon really made him happy to be back. Deer jumped across the trail, two eagles floated languidly over the lake, and he was fairly sure he saw a red fox scooting along on the Feedrock Trail a hundred yards in front of him.

He circled Thunder Lake twice and did several miles of fartlek on the way back, working the travel kinks out and enjoying his regained ability to select any pace he wanted for as long as he wanted.

When he got back to the top of the pasture he saw his uncle Neal's truck parked in front of the cabin.

"You didn't have to wait out here," Cassidy said, trotting up.

"It's a nice evening to set and rock a spell."

"Can I get you anything. Not sure what's here but I could make some tea."

"Nothing for me, thank you kindly. I just had a cold drink at the store."

"Okay, I'll just get some water."

Cassidy returned with a big plastic glass and a towel, plopping down in the other rocking chair.

"Nice refrigerator, by the way. You didn't have to do that on my account."

"Well, that little one wasn't much of an appliance, and this was an extra one Mary had setting in the basement."

"Speaking of which, how's she doing?"

"Fine and dandy," Neal said. "She and Dobie Kay have learned to weave baskets and we are currently up to our earlobes in several varieties. You don't need a basket, do you?"

"Not that I know of, but tell her I appreciate the fridge and I will think of her every time I put something in it that I didn't have to cut in half first. How's Leroy doing?"

"Good. He and James Gordon are at the coast now after stripers. They'll be back Monday week. If they do any good I'm sure they'll be by with a mess of fish, if you feel like cleaning them."

"If I can find a Rapala blade I'll do the whole batch for them. It'll be good to see them, even after they've been on the boat that long. How's everyone else getting along? I saw Grandma at the house before I came up."

"Everyone's doing. Not over Henry by a long shot, but gettin' along."

They sat watching the sun edge down into the tops of the hardwoods on Panther Mountain, Neal outlining the scant news from an uneventful winter. He wasn't as talkative as his younger

brother, but he told a good story. Cassidy also knew Leroy considered Neal to be about the cleverest fellow he'd ever known,
but also among the least demonstrative. "If he shows you how
to do something, and he comes back and sees you doing it different, he won't say a word. He'll just walk away," Lee had said.

"Why is that?" Cassidy asked.

"Don't know. Probably figures you're beyond help. It may
take a while but if you stay at it long enough you'll figure out
that what he told you was right all along."

Cassidy always paid close attention when Neal was talking
because he didn't waste many words. Tonight he was describing what various family members had been up to, but what he
was really doing was letting Cassidy know how they were coping
with tragedy, which ones were merely hurting, which ones truly
wounded. Cassidy asked a few questions but mostly listened.
Just as the sun was disappearing behind the mountains, Neal
stood.

"Well," he said, picking up his Ring Power cap and slapping
his denimed pants leg with it. "Come on up the road with me."

"Guess I'd better stay close by. Maybe light the fire. Looks
like it might be cool tonight."

"It might at that."

The hot weather came on slowly, always gentler in the mountains than down in the flatlands, and through the next few
weeks Cassidy carefully added the last miles that they dared
cram into his unrelenting schedule. He was now going ten
every morning instead of seven. On most interval days he
did half miles and miles on his flat stretch of trail, carefully
watching his feet on the tricky stretches for fear of some ankle-
breaking catastrophe. Once a week he went down into Brevard
and ran repeats on the college track. Occasionally one or two
of the undergraduates would hop in for a while but they usually
didn't last long.

His long runs were now twelve, fourteen, sixteen miles, and he no longer worried that he wasn't getting in twenty-milers every weekend. He was getting close to 150 miles a week on hilly terrain, sometimes more, and while he was generally handling it well, he couldn't imagine working much else into his routine. Denton had scheduled some long runs right at the end for mostly psychological reasons, and Cassidy had long since given up second-guessing his coach.

He ate down at his grandmother's several times a week, and still snuck into town for burgers, barbecue, ice cream, fried chicken. He sometimes hit the gourmet aisle at the Winn-Dixie in Brevard for what he called "pickled bees knees," the little odd cravings that came and went and made long-distance training seem gastronomically like nothing so much as an overlong pregnancy. His body had long since been burned away to basics again and his frame was so unadorned he sometimes felt translucent, as if he could feel the individual molecules of clean oxygen being taken up by his huge lungs and pumped through his system, combusting there in the mitochondrial barbecue pits with other individual molecules of fat, protein, and long branched-chain amino acids, producing a nearly endless supply of forward motion and little else save water vapor and carbon dioxide.

The big drawback about being back in the mountains was that it was too far for Andrea to drive up from central Florida for weekends, and not for the first time in all the years he had spent training, he had to occasionally deal with the kind of mind-numbing loneliness familiar to solo mariners and shipwreck survivors.

For a while he was reasonably content scribbling away in his so-called journal, keeping up his training records, reading and rereading the small library he had assembled. He even considered getting a television, but figured the reception would be problematic and the fare even emptier than his social calendar. He took to visiting cousins, making himself available for Ping-

Pong, pool parties, picnics. He couldn't participate in anything like waterskiing or volleyball, but he was an enthusiastic spectator and a truly world-class dinner guest.

Still, back in the cabin after a twenty-five-mile day, he would sometimes recline in the tiny living-dining-sleeping room, leafing through his training calendar, thinking, How did I ever do this all those years without going crazy? Or am I presuming too much?

Then it occurred to him that as solitary as the endeavor was, he hadn't really been alone much of the time. In his younger days there were Mizner, Atkinson, Nubbins, Hosford, and the rest of the guys; they were around all the time. On the runs, at the training table, next door in the dorm, or one floor down. Even this past winter in Kernsville, solitary though it was at times, it had also been leavened by runs with Endris and O'Bannon, sometimes with Liquori and Barry Brown. There were occasional track sessions with Sammy Bair, Byron Dyce, Juris Luzins, and even some of the undergraduates he had gotten to know. Of course, Denton came to visit several times at God knows what cost to his own domestic tranquillity.

But Cassidy remembered something Liquori once said as they were ambling along at the back of the pack on the Tobacco Road loop. He said: "If you want to train really well, you have to be a little bored."

"What on earth do you mean?" Cassidy said.

"Just that if you really want to be focused on training, those two runs every day need to be the most interesting things going on in your life."

And, thinking about his time at the cabin in Newberry, he knew that Liquori was right. All those months his afternoon workout was unquestionably the most interesting thing that happened to him all day. Everything else was padding, resting, waiting.

"It may be true," he told Liquori later, "but it's still a little frickin' sad, you have to admit." They were on the warm-up loop with a bunch of the cross-country guys and everyone in front of them turned around to see what was so funny.

As spring wore on, Cassidy bore down, resigned to the fact that his afternoon run would once again be the highlight of his day. He piled up miles, ran imaginary races against long-absent foes on interval days, did incredible tempo and fartlek runs in the forest. On longer days it was not unusual for him to run from one Carolina down into the other and back. He began noting animal sightings in his training log, and highlighted especially brisk days with exclamation marks, *honoris causa* once reserved for mind-boggling interval performances. Pathetically, he counted the days between life-giving visits from Bruce and, more rarely, from Andrea.

Through the spring he held on, kept his composure, trained with a discipline so honed it was simply a part of his personality once again. He ran, ate, ran, ate, slept, and arose to do it again. He did what it seemed he had been doing forever, what distance runners always do: he bided his time, he slept a really hard, really feverish sleep, and his escapist dreams were like those of a prisoner.

41

Raven Cliff Falls

H E KNEW HE was in trouble.

He tried to keep his fat furry tongue centered in his mouth, because it stuck when it touched anything. Sticking to the roof was the worst and made it hard to breathe.

They were having a warm spell in the mountains and it had been so mild all spring he really wasn't heat-acclimated. When he got to the shadeless stretch of gravel road around Thunder Lake he began to get prickly-heat goose bumps on his forearms. He was dehydrated despite the stashed water bottles along the way and he actually toyed for a moment with the idea of drinking from the lake. But a case of giardiasis didn't strike him as a suitable capstone to his running career. I guess I would if I had to, he thought, necessity being the mother . . . the phrase made him think of Mizner again and he could not imagine him dark in his grave at this very moment on a hot sandy hill in central Florida.

Shit, he thought, I've got my own problems. That's the way it is when running becomes in extremis, death comes rather easily to mind. The lake beckoned him all the way around, but he resisted until the very end, where the trail led up and away and he would no longer have the option. He stopped by a little area that was almost like a beach, toed off his trail shoes, and limped carefully into the water. The surface was warmish, but just a few inches down was cool water from the lake's spring sources, and when he got his throbbing head down deep enough, the relief was immediate. He knew it would take longer to get his core temperature down, so he sat on the mushy bottom with the water up to his shoulders and occasionally dunked his fevered head backward. Again he was tempted to drink but didn't.

Out of the water and moving again, slowly, he calculated that he had come about seventeen miles to this point, down to Raven Cliff Falls and back. He had always loved the idea of running to a place with a name like Raven Cliff Falls. Today there was nothing poetic about any of it. Five to go, he thought. And I'm behind schedule for my rendezvous with Bruce. If he gets antsy, he'll start back up the trail looking for me, which would be good. I need that water.

When he looked up and across the lake and saw Denton pedaling powerfully toward him Cassidy almost laughed with relief.

"You weren't worried, were you?" Cassidy slowed to a walk a few minutes later as he got to where the smiling, empathetic Denton was pulled over, holding one of the water bottles out.

"Nope. I figured you might go for a dip. Good idea, day like this." Denton was drenched in sweat too, his T-shirt hanging limply, dripping onto the bike frame.

"I did."

"I know, I saw you. I was doing a little wading of my own. I looked across the lake and saw you blowing bubbles."

Cassidy handed the empty bottle back and they started back up the trail.

"I didn't see you."

"You get tunnel-visioned. So how bad is it? You're beet red," Denton said.

"Okay, I guess. Humidity's a killer, I'm nowhere close to acclimated. I'm way off pace."

"Don't worry about that. Just concentrate on holding form and getting through it. If you hit the wall, the last couple of miles can seem like a hundred."

Cassidy tried, he really did. He concentrated and Denton watched him closely, talking to him in soothing tones as they made their way off the mountain. It was when they reached the scree on the Feedrock Trail that Cassidy said several things that didn't make any sense to Denton. Something about wallpaper. Something about dogs or wolves drinking from the toilet, an abandoned staircase with an ornate frame holding no picture but the fading paint behind it seeming to form a mountain scene. Denton was puzzling through all this when Cassidy looked over at him, his brow wrinkled.

"With this lightning, we need to get off the mountain," Cassidy said.

Denton glanced up at the clear blue sky, the pitiless sun.

"What lightning?"

When he looked back, Cassidy had disappeared over the side of the trail and Denton could hear him crashing through a thicket of mountain laurel. He slammed on the rear brake and brought the bike around, nearly falling himself as he hopped off and ran back up the trail, then down the slope where he had last seen the runner.

The room slowly came into focus and though it seemed familiar he did not know where he was. Come to think of it, he didn't know *who* he was. He had been dropped on earth as a brand-new fully functioning adult with no memory, no identity; a grown-up fetus.

The Swiss cotton bedspread tucked up around his chin triggered an orientation process and in rapid stages he assimilated his fetal, memoryless self into Quenton Cassidy, his surroundings into his grandmother's house, and the forms huddled around his supine self into that same grandmother, his uncle Lee, Bruce Denton, and Andrea.

Andrea!

"Hey, what's . . . ah, what's going on, y'all? Did I have a wreck?"

They eyed one another, chuckling nervously.

"You might say that," Denton said.

Andrea stepped over and began shining a light into his eyeballs in what seemed to Cassidy a very professional manner.

"We've already told you several dozen times," she said. "That's why we're laughing. You're like a broken record. We thought of just typing it up on a three-by-five card and pinning it upside down on your pajamas. Open wide . . ."

She poked around with a tongue depressor. What the hell were they looking for when they did that? Cassidy wondered, but said nothing. He did go "ah" when instructed to do so. She removed the depressor and held his chin gently in her fingertips, turning his head first one way, then the other, as if admiring his ragged profile.

"The card would say," she continued, still swiveling his noggin, " 'My name is Quenton Cassidy and I had an accident when I was running two days ago—' "

"Two days!"

" '—two days ago, and though I have been at times conscious and apparently lucid—' "

"Two days I've been unconscious!"

"You're not paying attention. That's why we're apparently going to have to do this three-by-five deal," said Denton. Grandma was seen scampering from the room, torturing her apron as she went.

"You've been in and out, but you never remember anything from one session to the next. You may not remember *this*. This is not uncommon with trauma victims. I just didn't know it also applied to knucklehead runners," Andrea said.

"Oh." Cassidy put his hand over his eyes, beginning to remember in bits and pieces. He got flashes of an inverted forest, sunlight coming down to him through the canopy, thick waxy leaves all around his face, Denton looking down, worried. Denton *slapping* him . . .

"Wait a minute! How did I get down from the Feedrock? How did I get *here*?" They looked at one another again.

"No, actually this is a good sign," said Andrea, staring at the wall, trying to remember something from her emergency medicine rotation long ago. "You've never remembered *anything* before."

"You got down yourself," said Denton. "I would have tried to carry you, but you insisted you were fine. You wanted to start *running* again. I made you walk. Even then you staggered a few times and you fell down again. I got you down to the bottom and parked your butt in the stream and took a chance on you drowning yourself while I went to get Lee. We loaded you in the pickup and brought you here. By then you were completely out of it and we had the pleasure of carting your inert carcass up the back stairs."

"He still looks peaked to me," said Lee, looking into Cassidy's drained face.

"He'll be okay," Denton said. "Salazar was given last rites that really hot year at Falmouth. An hour later I was drinking beer with him at the postrace party."

Andrea fixed him with a look.

"Yeah, you guys are bulletproof, all right," she said.

Denton shuffled his feet.

"Okay," she said. "I need to get back to the motel and do some phoning." Andrea packed doctor things into an incongruent red canvas satchel with some drug company four-color logo expensively embroidered on the side. "Needless to say, keep him as quiet as you can and keep pushing fluids. I'm going to keep the IV in for a while yet. He's probably fine now but tomorrow we need to get him into Asheville and let them do a workup just to rule out some things. This isn't really my line and I want an internist and a neurologist."

She had her jacket on now, but stopped again at the side of the bed, taking his chin in her fingers again, but differently this time.

"Okay, mister? You are to remain still. You are to meditate. You are to admire the cherry blossoms just now a-budding on yon tree. But that's the extent of it, hear me? One reason I'm leaving the IV in, so I don't come back to find you jacklegs playing handball against the side of the barn."

"Yes'm," said Cassidy groggily, and was asleep before she reached the door.

But then he awoke briefly an hour later in the darkened room and thought: Andrea!

42

Tryst

S HE WAS BREATHING hard as she climbed the last grade to the cabin. She had kept up a good pace and even her weak leg felt perfectly fine. At least the heat had broken and it was a pristine morning in the mountains. At first she had questioned her decision to wear shorts, but the cotton vest felt good and she had long since walked off the early chill. Her hair was pulled back in her usual workout ponytail and she thought she had looked quite girlish in the motel mirror.

The cabin wasn't as bad as she'd expected. Uncle Lee had been mostly kidding. She poked around the kitchen cabinet and found a cup, then worked the old pump handle and drank cold mountain water until she got an ice-cream headache. God, she thought, I didn't know water could be that good.

Looking around she recognized it as exactly the kind of place where he would live. There were fifteen pairs of running shoes, some lined neatly in the windowsills drying, some scattered around the floor, all in varying levels of dilapidation from almost new to thoroughly ratty. There was nothing on the walls except a faded poster of a shaggy-haired, mustachioed, not unattractive young runner she didn't recognize. His shirt read OREGON.

There was a small stack of books by the quilted hay-bale bed, including the second volume of the *Norton Anthology of English Literature,* a paperback novel called *The Gospel Singer,* and a big heavy blue textbook-looking thing called *Prosser on Torts,* whatever that was. His training log, a calendar, was at the end of the neatly made bed, and she plopped herself down on the tight surface of the quilt and picked it up.

She remembered seeing these before, each block of the calendar filled with numbers and abbreviations, with one number in the lower right corner of each square, segregated from the rest by a slash. This, she remembered, was the total mileage for the day. The previous week's totals had read 25, 23, 19, 24, 23, 15. The next square, Monday, was the day he had run himself unconscious, the day Denton had called her in a panic. The mileage total for that day was 20. The notation said: "10 AM / Planned 22 / 91° & hum. / crashed."

Stacked neatly on the lower shelf of the little bedside table were several numbered composition books. She picked the top one up, seeing he had written VI on the front in Magic Marker. It would probably be a journal of some kind and she would have liked to open it to a random page, but her conscience wouldn't allow it.

Where the hell was he anyway? He had said ten and it was a quarter after. She yawned, realized how tired she was. They had been out the night before, and it was after one when he left her room. Then she hadn't slept well. If she hadn't been so tired right now she would have been either elated or scared to death or both.

She gave in to some deep urge and flopped down on the bed, curling up contentedly with her hands between her drawn-up knees, placing her head into his feather pillow. Her senses were immediately awash in the smell of him, a deep earthiness that had struck her the first time years ago when she put her cheek against his bony chest. Almost dizzy, she felt that old something deep in her genetic code that responded to his complicated pheromones, essence of forest and wood, something leathery, horsey, reminding her of saddles and tack, but with undertones of unknown herbs or spices, something from cooking that she could never place, at once familiar and mysterious.

Christ, she thought, rising, I've got to get a grip. Her eyes were foggy and she was suddenly desperate to get outside, to clear her head.

She went back to the porch and sat on the edge, holding her legs out to catch the sunshine. It was then that she noticed the movement between the trees way up in the hill that flanked the cabin. She knew right away that it was him, coming fast down through the switchbacks, visible for stretches and then hidden briefly by patches of forest. It was quite a ways down—she remembered from hiking it on her last trip—and she watched fascinated as he flowed down it like some fleet predator accustomed to moving fast through the trees. She knew how rough the trail was up there, but the only sign he gave of it was the enormous concentration he focused on the ground in front of him. Watching him move like that down the hillside gave her a strange feeling beneath her sternum and her eyes went suddenly out of focus. She had to turn, to look away then, trying to compose herself. She thought, What I never really understood before was that he was willing to die, that he would run himself right to death if that's what it took. I just never understood that.

She got up and walked around to the back of the house to see him finally emerge from the forest and enter the upper end of the pasture. He ran along the dirt path that the Harmony Farm riders used to reach the highway. They had set up a series of three steeplechase barriers made of undressed logs alongside the path as an amusement for bored or daring riders and she was amazed to see Cassidy veer off toward them. He took them efficiently, one after the other, with a quick hurdler's stride clearing each with his back knee by inches, before he veered back onto the path for the last quarter mile down. Finally he looked up and saw her, quickening his pace over the last two hundred yards.

He was grinning, breathing hard, slightly red of face as he trotted up, taking her by both hands and swinging her around.

"Hey!" she said, thinking to object.

"That's it," he said. "Finished it!"

"Eh?" she said. He stopped twirling her, let one hand go, and led her around to the front of the cabin.

"Wait here," he said, disappearing into the cabin. He emerged seconds later with a zinc bucket of well water, stood out away from the porch, held it over his head, and upended it with a shudder over his head.

Andrea couldn't help laughing as he shivered and did a little goose-bump dance, shaking water off like a dog but less effectively. There was a not-too-clean-looking towel hanging over the hitching post, and he used that to dry his ragged hair.

"Quenton," she said, "I've got to pack, I've got to . . ."

"I know," he said, tossing the towel back over the rail. He came to her, put his arms around her and interlocked them in the small of her back, disregarding her aversion to his appalling condition. Then he lifted her up and placed her on the first step to the porch, where she was now only a few inches shorter than he. He kissed her really hard then with the kind of joy that took in the sunshine and the mountain and all the cold clear water running through and around it, all the trees and creatures upon it, the breeze now gentle across it. He kissed her with a zeal she remembered from the first time he had kissed her back when he had been not much more than a boy and she not much more than a girl.

"Oh," she said and put her face next to his steamy neck and smelled again the leather-horsey-herb-spice thing and thought that if you could die this way if your heart could explode from this if it were possible to expire from the joy-pain of holding on to something so quiveringly alive that you don't think you can make yourself let go then yes, she, Andrea Cleland, would be no more.

She whispered, "If you tell me anything now, I would believe it."

"You almost had the accent."

"I wasn't trying for the accent."

"Okay," he whispered. "You. Tell me something that's impossible but still true."

"I love you."

"I know. But that's not impossible."

"I don't care, I don't care."

He kissed her again, more gently this time, holding her face in both hands as if he were drinking from a brook.

When she opened her eyes finally, he was smiling at her again.

"You're supposed to say you too," she said, frowning.

"Me too."

"I'm not supposed to have to prompt."

He held her slightly away from him and smiled at her and she couldn't help smiling back.

"And I don't know why it was so important for me to hike up here—"

"I wanted you to know, that's all. I'm fine. I'm not going to die or anything."

"Quenton . . ."

"I did the whole twenty-two-miler this morning, down to Raven Cliff Falls and back. It was no problem. It was just the heat before. I'm fine. I don't want you to worry about me."

He let go of her face and stepped up onto the same step with her, and before she could object he picked her up and took her into the cabin, placed her carefully on the hay-bale bed, her blond head sinking into the familiar pillow. He slipped off his running shorts and stood before her with just training shoes on, no socks, his body an assemblage of fluted parts, pulsing veins, thin ridges, muscles the shape of elongated teardrops, sun-browned everywhere except the ghostly white band where the shorts had been.

"I'm kinda gross," he said, looking down at his still-glistening chest.

Little wincing sounds came from her throat as she extended her arms toward him, her waggling fingers making that little desperate come-here gesture.

43

The Trials

THE ATRIUM OF the Buffalo Adam's Mark Hotel was designed to send a message to Mother Nature. It said, *Hey, we can live in here if we have to.* Cassidy thought that was a very good idea for a place like this, but with winter long gone so much enclosed space seemed extravagant.

He sat dutifully in a corner of the lounge area, watching the glass elevators going up and down busily, and wondered if they had their own weather in here too, like the Vertical Assembly Building at the cape.

It was the first time he had been out in modern American culture for so long now that he felt very much the rube, all entranced by the gleaming brass, the indoor pool and tropical forest, all this wretched excess of *wattage* everywhere. What would future archaeologists make of such a dig? Would they posit a religious structure of some kind? A monument to a great warlord, with living quarters for his many retainers? How to interpret the video game room, the air hockey table, the StairMaster?

Denton had gone to check them in and pick up Cassidy's

race packet in the competitors' hospitality suite. Like a child, he had been instructed not to wander off. There were a number of runners in the lobby, easily spotted even in street clothes. Cassidy eyed the wiry, zero-fat bodies, most of them much shorter than he, efficient, five-minute-a-mile-forever bodies. Tapered for this race and unused to the excess energy, many of them had trouble keeping still, and even as they stood in loose groups of two or three, greeting one another, casually chatting, they bounced lightly on their toes, rocked gently sideways, flexed and rotated bony hips and shoulders. Cassidy didn't recognize many of them. He was several years and many specialties removed from these athletes.

Let's see, he thought, between milers and these guys you have the five, the ten, the steeple, cross-country, and nearly every road race, 5K, five-mile, 8K, 10K, 15K, ten-mile, and half-marathon, and every oddball distance in between. Was this the marathoner's version of What Am I Doing Here?

To his delight he spotted a familiar figure in another corner of the lounge area, obscured by a giant plastic replica of a date palm. He was blue-jeaned, sweatshirted, and a dead ringer for the cartoon character Zonker in *Doonesbury*. Cassidy hopped up and all but trotted over. What he thought was a paperback turned out to be a handheld video game.

"Benji!" Cassidy said, plopping down beside him.

"Hmmm? Oh, drat. Seventeenth level. There's a key behind a brick over the doorway."

"I bet there is. And a machine-pistol in the wicker basket in the room with the skeletons."

"No, that's *Castle Wolfenstein*."

"I'm amazed it's anything. I just made it up."

"Well, it's actually an Uzi and it's more of an amphora than a basket and the skeletons are one floor down."

"I'll take your word for it. So how the hell are you? Are you still in Stone Mountain? Still doing the sweat suits? And that breathing thing?"

"Yes, yes, and pretty much yes, although I'm not using the PO$_2$ as much as I used to. The cops finally got so they weren't stopping me all the time, but the idiots in cars never got tired of yelling stuff at me."

"I don't doubt it. What'd they say?"

"Oh, like, hey, moon man, you don't need that to breathe our air, that kind of stuff. Or they made the obvious scuba connection and they'd say, Hey, Lloyd Bridges, the ocean's that way. All very amusing the first few thousand times."

"Nothing that Edison didn't go through. Or Madame Curie."

"Edison was something of a kook and the Curies both died of radiation poisoning, but I appreciate the sentiment," said Durden, putting the game away in a denim backpack.

"So you're running well? I guess so or you wouldn't be here," said Cassidy.

"Pretty well, I guess. I've been hitting it pretty hard since New York. Skipped Boston last year. Only sick twice, which is a good winter for me. Anything timed I've done compares well to past years." He shrugged, smiled his Zonker smile. "You never know what's gonna happen in these things. In a marathon there's lots of time for weird stuff to go wrong. A blister can do you in. Took a shoe off once and poured blood out. It's not like the mile."

"No, it's not."

"So it's true? You're actually doing this?" asked Durden.

"I guess. I wanted a last fling and I couldn't see going back to the track."

Benji nodded, stroking his goatee thoughtfully. "Well, Dixon did it. Some other guys. But most of them had done some fives and tens."

"I know. It's a stretch. But the way I look at it, it's great to be back in shape again, and I don't have a thing in the world to lose."

"Guess not. Hey, speaking of track, I've been meaning to tell you something. Did you know we ran against each other in college?"

Cassidy was perplexed.

"When I was at Georgia, before I quit track," Durden said, "Spec had me running the mile and the three-mile, so I was one of the galloping horde behind you at the SEC outdoor meet your junior year."

"Benj, it's strange to say but I just . . ."

"Oh, don't fret. There's no reason in the world you would remember a guy back in the pack running a 4:15. I just thought you'd appreciate knowing an odd factoid."

"I do. And I suspect you're in an excellent position to wreak some long-simmering revenge."

"Hadn't thought of it that way, but okay." He smiled.

Denton walked over, dumped an armload of manila envelopes and plastic bags in a chair opposite them, then plopped down.

"Whew! Can you believe this crap? Hey, Benji," he said.

"You guys must be getting here just now," Durden said. "A lot of us have been here all week. They put us up in dorms at the college. I checked in at the dorm and the first thing they handed me was a Dixie cup."

"Yeah?" said Cassidy.

"I heard," said Denton. "We didn't get picked."

"What's this?" Cassidy asked.

"Doping. Article in the *Times* a week ago accused Magruder of either being out of touch or of turning a blind eye. So now he's all like, *Not on my watch* kind of thing," said Durden.

"What kind of drugs?" Cassidy asked. Denton and Durden looked at him.

"Steroids, mostly," said Durden. "Where have you been?"

"He's been underwater for the past few years," said Denton. "Literally, on occasion."

"I know all about steroids," said Cassidy. "I thought they were for weight men. What good would bulging muscles be for a distance runner?"

"I used to think the same thing," said Durden. "With us

they work differently. You don't get bigger, you recover faster. The 'roids help rebuild damaged muscle tissue, so with us they repair the fiber faster, so you can handle more of a workload. Instead of 130-mile weeks, you can do 150. Or more. You bounce back from intervals faster, so you can sometimes go two, three days in a row before backing off. It's a definite advantage. Or that's what I hear anyway."

"Christ, is this documented?"

"They've hardly caught any distance guys yet. Rumor is that some top sprinters have been caught red-handed, but they've mostly just been warned. They'd love to get their hands on a distance guy to make an example of. There are lots of Iron Curtain guys supposedly using the stuff. That Cierpinski guy who beat Shorter in Montreal? He's a suspect. Guy goes from being a mediocre steepler one year to a marathon gold medalist the next. Not quite as obvious as a nearly retired sprinter dropping half a second in the hundred, but it's close," Durden said.

"Anybody with half a brain won't get caught," said Denton. "They quit long enough before competition so that their systems are clear. But you don't really need it to race, just to train. Testing at competitions just catches the stupid and the careless. They got one idiot only because he was *also* blood doping, and when they reinfused his own blood, it was full of the steroids he had been taking months earlier. Brilliant."

"Where do they get the stuff?" Cassidy asked. Again Durden and Denton looked at each other.

"Hey, Mary Poppins," said Denton, "you should hang out in a high school football weight room sometime. There are dozens of jock-sniffing body chemists out there."

"I can't remember when I've felt so old or out of it," said Cassidy miserably.

"Welcome to twenty-first-century sports," said Durden. "Pretty soon it's going to be all My Chemist Can Beat Your Chemist kind of thing. Well, they won't nail me for anything more serious than Sugar Pops and vitamin C. And they're obviously not too worried about you. At least they didn't make you pee in a cup just to get your race number."

"No," said Cassidy. "I'm sure they looked at my credentials and decided not to waste a Dixie cup."

In the early afternoon Cassidy went out to jog a few miles of the course with Durden, Frank Shorter, and a few of the other marathoners.

When he got back to the room, he stood fiddling with the entry card until Denton finally opened the door for him, and Cassidy entered, chuckling, following him back into the room. Denton was carrying a yellow sheet of paper, holding it daintily by one corner.

"Did you know Frank was here?" asked Cassidy. "He's doing TV . . ." He stopped, seeing for the first time the grim look on Denton's face.

"What's going on?"

"Just got this ten minutes ago," Denton said, holding out the paper, which turned out to be a telegram.

"Eh?" Cassidy took it and read it once quickly, then started again at the top.

"Quenton, look at me. You've got to tell me straight up now. Is there any possibility whatsoever that there is anything to this?" said Denton.

Cassidy looked at him. Denton was deadly serious. No doubt about it.

"Bruce. You *know* me. Until this morning I didn't even—"

"Just yes or no, Cass."

"*No*, Bruce, goddammit! *Hell* no, in fact. No, no no!"

"Okay." Denton sat back, apparently relieved. "Do you have any idea what this is all about?"

"Not the foggiest. It doesn't make any sense. If they suspected me of anything, why didn't they test me when we checked in, like they did with Benji?"

"I don't know. They seem to be indicating they've got some other kind of evidence on you. And apparently they're confident enough about it they think you'll withdraw when you're confronted with it. That's why they set up this so-called *informal meeting* and not some kind of an official proceeding. Christ, what in the hell is going on? If you have any idea whatsoever, Quenton, now is the time. If I had any idea what we were up against, I could make some calls, get some help. Hell, Shorter's a lawyer—"

"Bruce, *I'm* a lawyer."

"Yes, but—"

"And I can tell you that this doesn't make sense to me on any level whatsoever. Why don't we just offer to voluntarily give them a urine or blood sample, whatever they want, clear it up right away."

"I thought of that and I called Magruder's assistant and suggested it."

"And . . . ?"

"He said just to be at the meeting. Wouldn't discuss anything else."

"That just doesn't make any sense."

"It does if they've got some kind of evidence unrelated to your current chemical status. They clearly don't think you'd flunk a drug test, or else they'd have asked for a sample when you checked in. I asked around, and they got samples from just about everyone who has a chance to make this team. That means that either they don't think you have a chance for the top three, or that they don't think they need a positive test result to nail you."

Cassidy groaned, pushed the hassock away from his chair, and draped himself over it facedown, stretching his back.

"Which do you think?" Cassidy asked.

"I think it's both," said Denton.

44

JJ Magruder

JEBEDIAH JACKSON MAGRUDER thought of himself as the most powerful man in amateur sports in America. He was fairly certain that when people recognized his gnomelike visage in hotel lobbies, they were saying that very thing to each other: there goes JJ Magruder, the most powerful man in amateur sports in America. What they were actually saying was, There goes the Angry Duck.

He'd picked that up during his athletic days shortly after World War II when a stroke of fantastic luck found him mustering out of the service many months before most of the other athletes in uniform, and thus on a hot dusty day in Bakersfield he was able to make his first and only international team in the intermediate hurdles despite the fact that he was, one, very short, and two, very slow.

The top three made the team and there were only five people in the race. One of them, the odds-on favorite from Villanova, pulled a hamstring on the first hurdle and another, Emilio Vasquez, unattached, had never run the hurdles in his life and was only doing so because of a bar bet he had made the night before with his brother-in-law, whom he despised.

"Do you have a qualifying time, Mr. Vasquez?" asked the gray-haired lady at the registration table.

"Jez," smiled Emilio.

"And what is that time, Mr. Vasquez?"

"Jez," smiled Emilio.

Since the race was nowhere close to full, she gave him a number and wished him good luck. He turned from the registration table, held up the number to show to his dubious-looking brother-in-law, spat once in the bone-dry dirt, and went to find a public restroom to change into the bright green Bermuda shorts and black high-top basketball shoes he carried in a grocery sack.

Emilio cleared every hurdle both feet at a time in a kind of sideways hop and took so long to get to the last one that the bored grounds crew were almost able to remove the hurdles before he got to them. Loitering proudly with his two teammates on the infield, JJ Magruder clucked his tongue unattractively as Emilio, to much good-natured applause, scooted across the finish line with a grin on his face and an upended finger aimed at his scowling brother-in-law. The brother-in-law was clapping too, but inwardly he was ruing the loss of the sawbuck, no small sum in those days, particularly to an undocumented tile layer.

JJ knew he wasn't the most graceful hurdler in the world, but he was way better than *that guy*. His physique was one thing, but it was his tender toes and penchant for choosing shoes two sizes too large that eventually earned him the hated sobriquet that no one ever used in his presence. He was on the Southeastern University track team in the early 1950s when the young assistant trainer, Brady Grapehouse, made him stop as he was clack-clacking his way out of the field house in long spikes.

"Stand still," said Brady, leaning his squatty body over to

feel the ends of JJ's shoes. "Hell, man, your shoes turn up at the toes. Your feet end way up *here*. You've got space you could sublet in there. No wonder you hurdle like an angry duck."

There was always a small crowd of sprinters and weight men around the whirlpool and when they heard this they completely fell over. The beet-faced Magruder was tagged forever. Fortunately he had already parlayed his questionable athletic prowess into a bid from the Alpha Tau Omegas, one of the "Big Four" houses on campus, and then he had parlayed *that* into several dates with Susan Farrior Lykes, a large-boned but harmless Tri-Delt whose Tampa-based family had made a gazillion dollars turning big friendly herbivores into sausages.

Susan's three brothers didn't need any help making sausages so they actively encouraged their pesky brother-in-law's interest in the politics of amateur athletics. It brought a modicum of prestige to the family name, involved a good deal of national and international travel, and was a simple job that mostly involved hounding a handful of poverty-stricken amateur athletes who had developed a troubling addiction to food. *No sausages for them!*

JJ had been several generations of athletes ahead of Cassidy at Southeastern, but there had been a large black-and-white poster-sized photograph of the hurdler on the wall at the training table in Doobey Hall. It showed a diminutive athlete in strange elfin spikes with his arm resting on a hurdle.

For several years at mealtimes Cassidy had stared at that round, smiling face and wondered what the deal was. The other athletes adorning the walls had been All-Americans or Olympians. This guy's time for the 330-yard intermediate hurdles, an event no longer run, seemed to Cassidy more befitting a decent high schooler.

It was simple, really: the framed photograph had been a gift to the athletic department from the Lykes family and might not have even been hung had it not been for the fact that it came with a much-needed ice machine for the Doobey Hall kitchen.

Cassidy didn't know that and he also had no idea just how much Jebediah Jackson Magruder hated his guts until he walked into the Fountain Conference Room of the Adam's Mark Hotel in Buffalo and saw the look in that familiar face: it was the look of animal loathing that the talentless have for the otherwise.

45

A Conference of Wallabies

A W JEEZ, HE flew in Sooz and the twins for this," said Denton. There were a pair of slightly miniaturized JJs sitting in the second row with a blond woman Cassidy judged to be a petit four shy of three hundred pounds. The twins, dressed in the all-black faux-ghetto white-guy style, along with barely visible attempts at mustaches, appeared to have been hitting the weight room and were both mouth-breathers. They were seventeen and college-bound if you counted Bob Jones University.

The huge room was set up for maximum intimidation value. The three athletic officials sat at a long table on the dais, with a smaller table and two chairs facing them out in the middle of a lonely expanse of carpeting.

Some functionary with an ALL-AREAS pass on a long chain around his neck escorted them to the little table. This was beginning to remind Cassidy of moot court in law school. Magruder was in the middle of the panel with a gavel in front of him. On his left was the wiry figure of Bob Giegengach, the Yale track coach and longtime AAC official. On his right was an athletic-looking woman whom Cassidy had never seen before.

"You know these guys?" Cassidy whispered as they sat down.

"Couple of run-ins over the years with JJ. Total A-hole. Swamp Dawg in the fifties, you remember."

"You know Giegengach through Frank, right?"

"Good man. The woman I don't have a clue."

"Gentlemen, if we could come to order, please," said Magruder, eyeing them over his half-glasses.

Cassidy noticed a studious-looking young man in the front row in a tie and corduroy jacket, writing into a long, skinny notebook.

"Don't look now," Cassidy whispered, "but the press is here."

"JJ's idea, I bet," said Denton.

There were several dozen other spectators scattered around the large empty seating area, including some coaches and a few athletes. A lanky-looking man in vaguely western attire slouched against the wall by the door in a decidedly relaxed manner. His beautifully waxed handlebar mustache must have taken thirty minutes every morning to sculpt correctly and Cassidy couldn't help but admire it. He might have been a sergeant-at-arms or some such official except for his indolent slouch. Something about the way his jacket fit suggested he was packing. He looked familiar but Cassidy couldn't quite place him.

Cassidy suddenly had the uneasy feeling he should have been paying attention. Magruder was clearing his throat, staring daggers at him.

"I said, is that right, Mr. Cassidy?" said Magruder.

Bruce whispered: "Wants to know if you're here voluntarily."

Cassidy stood up.

"Let's just say I'm here and leave it at that."

Magruder scowled over his glasses at Cassidy. "What is that supposed to mean?"

"For the record, I'm here with my personal representative and coach, Mr. Denton, pursuant to a telegram we received this

morning requesting our presence at an informal meeting. Neither Mr. Denton nor myself has been given any notice whatsoever as to the purpose of this, uh, *gathering,* and . . ."

He reached around to his back pocket, retrieved a folded
blue booklet, and tossed it on the table.

". . . since I find no grounds whatsoever in the bylaws of the
Amateur Athletics Congress for such an informal, uh, *assemblage,* I have to assume it has no official status and that anything
decided here can have no import. So, in essence, I'm willing to
say that I'm here, and I'm perfectly amenable to chatting. But
I am not willing to say formally that I'm making any sort of voluntary appearance."

Magruder's face darkened as a few spectators chuckled. Cassidy thought he saw Giegengach mutter something out of the
side of his mouth that only Magruder could hear. The woman
official looked blandly at Cassidy.

"Mr. Cassidy, there is no need for legalistic mumbo jumbo
here," Magruder said with a kindly smile. "We know you're
an attorney. This, however, is not a trial, sir. This is a *voluntary*
meeting that we hope will help us settle a very troubling issue
of the utmost importance to both the Athletics Congress and to
you personally."

"Under the terms outlined previously, I'm here," said Cassidy, sitting down.

"And you, Mr. Denton?"

"Under the same terms," said Denton, staring hard at
Magruder.

"All right, let us—"

"But before we begin"—Cassidy rose again—"I'd like to say
something for the record—"

"What record! There is no record!" said Magruder rather
too loudly.

"That lady at the end of the table is taking notes of some
kind, is she not?"

"That is our secretary, Miss Hennessy. She is making informal notes regarding this voluntary meeting, Mr. Cassidy," said Magruder.

"Well, then, she won't mind making an informal note regarding my objections to these proceedings—"

"These aren't proceedings, sir!"

"Well, whatever they are. Conference, get-together, *shindig*. I know, let's call it a chautauqua. I object to the extra-legal form of this chautauqua and its lack of basis in the bylaws of the Amateur Athletics Congress. I object to the complete and utter lack of adequate notice—or any sort of notice for that matter—regarding the purpose and basis for this chautauqua. I object to the public nature of this chautauqua and the presence of the media," said Cassidy. The scant crowd was mumbling again. Magruder had a rare, queasy sensation that he was losing a certain amount of control.

"Mr. Cassidy, I don't know what a chautauqua is and—"

"An informal gabfest, I believe," said Cassidy, seating himself.

"I don't care what it is. And I don't care what we call this meeting. I just—"

"Then you won't mind if Miss Hennessy"—Cassidy looked her way, and she looked up from her steno pad and smiled at him—"if Miss Hennessy takes a note or two about my objections." Miss Hennessy nodded and pointed at her pad, indicating, with a certain amount of goodwill, that she already had.

Magruder took a deep breath. He noticed that his spouse and their matched offspring were distinctly restless.

"Fine," he said. "Do you mind if we get to the matter at hand, Mr. Cassidy? Mr. Denton?"

"I guess," said Denton. Cassidy shrugged. He was tapered perfectly for this race and despite his five-mile trot that morning had far more energy than he was used to. He was remaining calm by main force of will.

"Mr. Cassidy," said Magruder, fetching a sheaf of legal-sized pages from his briefcase. "We are hopeful that at the end of this, uh, chautauqua, you will voluntarily remove yourself from the starting field for the United States Olympic Marathon Trials tomorrow morning."

Cassidy and Denton eyed the three officials stonily. Only Giegengach looked uneasy.

"This governing body has come into possession of extremely persuasive evidence that you have been a long-term, habitual, and willful user of performance-enhancing substances proscribed by this organization, whose function it is to govern amateur sports in this country. You are therefore in direct contravention of the bylaws and regulations of this governing body, not to mention various applicable state and federal statutes. The affidavit that Jerry there is handing you is quite complete, and you'll notice that it is duly sworn and notarized."

After getting his copy, Cassidy saw out of the corner of his eye that the official was handing out copies to the reporter and other members of the audience. The western-looking gent by the door gestured he didn't want one.

Cassidy was racing through the four-page document, wondering, What the hell, as Magruder droned on.

The thing was official-looking enough. Speed-reading, he picked up: "Affiant has on numerous occasions . . . the aforementioned subject openly admitted to affiant . . . Affiant witnessed and personally participated in an athletic event with said subject in which . . ."

"What the bejeebers?" said Denton, who was leafing furiously through the pages.

Cassidy had turned so quickly to the principal allegations in the document that he hadn't noticed the name on the title line, so now he quickly flipped to the last page and saw, with his heart turning cold in his chest, the ridiculously ostentatious signature of his very own colleague and law partner, Karl Farkus.

Cassidy sat, stunned, as Magruder's droning voice slowly made its way back into his head.

". . . unless of course you do not wish to do so. In that case, only the Infractions Committee has the authority to . . ."

"I get it now," said Denton quietly, putting down the copy of the bylaws he had been scanning.

"Eh?" Magruder looked up from his own booklet, from which he was preparing to read.

"That's why she's here"—Denton gestured at the silent woman on the panel—"and Coach Giegengach. You need one representative from women's sports and one from the college coaches to form an Infractions Committee. That's what this is all about. If you can't bully him into dropping out on his own, you're all ready to convene a session of the Infractions Committee on the spot. If we walk out, we look guilty as sin and you can probably talk at least one of the other two into voting with you."

Cassidy drew some consolation from the fact that Giegengach looked particularly miserable. He thought he detected the slightest nod from him as Denton was speaking.

"And if we stay," Cassidy interjected, "then we've effectively waived all our rights to notice and due process, and so on and so forth." He looked at Magruder anew. "Pretty good," Cassidy said, scratching his chin.

"You haven't even tested him!" Denton said. He was growing more agitated even as Cassidy grew calmer.

"Well . . ." said Magruder.

"They don't want to," said Cassidy quietly.

"What?" said Denton.

"They know it would probably come back negative. It would hurt their case. They want to keep it simple," said Cassidy. "They just want to mau-mau me out of the race."

"Mr. Cassidy," said Magruder, "everyone is aware that an intelligent athlete such as yourself . . ."

"Thanks."

". . . such as yourself would know enough to abstain from banned substances for at least fifty days before a competition.

That wouldn't change the fact that the rules had been violated and that sanctions must be—"

"Just out of curiosity," said Cassidy, "what would you have done if we had been able to get you into court? An affidavit wouldn't do it. You don't have a drug test. You'd need live testimony or some other form of hard evidence to make all this work somehow."

"The inner workings of this body is no concern of yours, Mr. Cassidy," said Magruder, obviously savoring the return of the whip hand. "What we have here is a completely credible, sworn statement by your own friend and business partner, Mr. Farkus, someone obviously in a position to know whereof he speaks. If it were necessary to have live testimony, why then—"

"Oh my God," said Cassidy.

"What?" said Denton.

"*He's here.* They flew the son of a bitch up here. They must have been working night and day on this thing."

"Mr. Cassidy!" said Magruder. "Are you or are you not willing to spare us all a great deal of anguish and humiliation by voluntarily withdrawing from these trials, sir?"

"Not on your life," said Cassidy, grinning, turning in his chair to scan the sparse audience again. "I wouldn't miss this. Where is he? Where've you got the bugger?"

"All right, Mr. Cassidy." Magruder sighed. "As president of the American Athletics Congress as well as chairman of the Infractions Committee, I hereby—"

"He was loitering in the coffee shop downstairs," said a voice from the doorway. With the impetus of just a tiny shove, the balding, sheepish figure of Karl Farkus lurched into the room, incongruous in his seersucker suit and wingtips.

Behind him, massively resplendent in tailored summer-weight gray wool with just the hint of a chalky pink pinstripe, was the fabulous figure of Roland Menduni, sporting a soft calfskin portfolio under one arm and a tiny red-haired woman on the other. His brilliantly hand-painted tie featured an extinct breed of parrot, possibly a Cuban macaw, thought Cassidy.

Menduni ushered the woman politely into the room and walked her to a seat in the front row, where she immediately sat down and began to open her oddly shaped satchel.

"Who the hell *are* you, sir?" roared Magruder, rising from his chair.

"Not yet," Roland whispered, holding one finger to his lips, gesturing toward the small woman who was still quickly and skillfully setting up her steno machine.

Amazingly, to Cassidy's thinking, Magruder hushed and sat back down, joining everyone else in watching with interest as the woman snapped the tripod legs onto the bottom of her contraption with a flourish, placed a stack of thin folding paper in the tray, threaded it through the mechanism, drew the machine between her knees and began working the silent keys, the paper now inching up over the platten and down into the empty receiving tray. She looked over to Roland with a smile and nodded once.

"Ah," said Roland, walking over and standing by Cassidy's table. Farkus was slouched forlornly in the front row.

"Let the record reflect that I am Roland Menduni of the law firm of Kern, Farkus, Greenbriar, and Shipley, 1408 Royal Poinciana Way, Palm Beach, Florida. I am appearing today on behalf of my client, Mr. Quenton Cassidy, who is a member of the same firm. This young lady here"—he gestured toward the court reporter, who smiled sweetly and nodded as she typed away—"is Miss Glenda Woods, a court reporter for the Erie County court system, duly licensed in the county, state, and federal courts in this jurisdiction—"

"We have our secretary here," sputtered Magruder. "We don't need any—"

"Glenda works for me, Mr. Magruder, not you. And what happens is that she keeps typing until I tell her to stop. You can say anything you want to, but all that's going to happen is that she is going to key it into that little machine there and then later type it up on regular paper and then sign it."

Magruder shut right up. Denton leaned over and whispered, "What the hell is going on?"

Cassidy smiled and raised his eyebrows.

"That gentleman by the door there is United States Marshal Raymond Gibbings—Ray, you want to do your thing now?—and what he is handing the three of you is a temporary restraining order without notice and a rule to show cause signed by Federal District Court Judge Jerome J. Stern of the Western District of New York. It essentially enjoins you from preventing Mr. Cassidy from participating in the Olympic Marathon Trials tomorrow morning and orders you to appear before the court at four-thirty tomorrow afternoon to show cause why you should not be held in contempt of court should you violate the said restraining order."

"You goddamn lawyers are pork-and-beaners every one of you," said Magruder evenly. "It has been noted before and it is as true today as it ever was. And you can take your temporary restraining malarkey—"

"Be sure to enunciate clearly," said Roland jauntily. "Glenda is very good but it's all done phonetically and we don't want her to misinterpret anything."

Magruder stared malevolently at him.

"Now," said Roland, taking a deep breath and buttoning the middle button of his huge jacket, "having said all that, since nothing that happens here this afternoon can prevent Mr. Cassidy's participation tomorrow, we would more than welcome a continuation of this, uh, *inquiry,* I guess."

"To what end, Mr. Menduni?" asked the woman official. It was the first time she had spoken.

"To the end of getting to the bottom of this goat rodeo," Roland said.

He waited a moment, eyeing the silent Magruder.

"Okay, I can see we're in a deliberative mode here, so while you all are gathering your thoughts, perhaps we'll just proceed," Roland said.

He walked back and picked up a folding chair from the front row and sat it squarely in the middle of the floor in front of the three officials.

"I call my first and only witness, Mr. Karl Farkus." The balding attorney rose shakily, walked over, and plopped down in the chair. He avoided looking any of the athletic officials in the eye. Magruder studied him intently.

"Glenda there will swear you in, Karl," said Roland gently.

"Sir . . ." said Magruder, attempting a small rally.

"I know, this isn't an official proceeding, there's no need for oath taking, blah blah, duly noted and all that. Just bear with me, okay? Glenda?"

She had Farkus raise his right hand and swore him in.

"Now, Karl, I'm sure Mr. Magruder and the others won't mind if I lead you a bit here for efficiency's sake. You are, are you not, Karl Farkus, Esquire, a partner with Mr. Cassidy and myself in the aforementioned law firm in Palm Beach, Florida?"

"Yes." The chin was out and up a bit, the old Karl coming out.

"And you are the affiant in this affidavit, which you recently furnished to these gentlemen, regarding Mr. Cassidy's alleged use of banned performance-enhancing substances? Glenda, mark as exhibit A and attach, please. Mr. Farkus?"

"Yes, I am."

"And would you tell this, uh, I forget . . . are we an Infractions Committee yet or not?"

"Mr. Menduni, the bylaws of our organization specify that we—" Magruder was desperate to get back into this thing.

"Okay, stipulated. We're an Infractions Committee. Karl, please tell this duly empaneled Infractions Committee of the U.S. Amateur Athletics Congress on what basis you made these allegations against Mr. Cassidy."

"All right. Two separate bases, in fact. One, I myself was an eyewitness and a participant in an athletic event in which his resort to illegal substances was obvious to everyone. And two, he has admitted as much to me on more than one occasion."

Denton looked at Cassidy, who was merely shaking his head.

"Can you describe this athletic event for the committee?"

"It was a mile relay."

"Was this a sanctioned event?"

"I don't know what that means."

"Was this part of a track competition under the auspices of any state or national amateur athletic governing body?"

"No, no. It was at a high school track in Palm Beach. It was like, I don't know, a challenge match."

Magruder sat back in his chair. Giegengach was muttering to himself.

"Who were the participants?"

"Mr. Cassidy, myself, and three other lawyers."

"I thought you said it was a mile relay."

"It was. Mr. Cassidy ran against the four of us. We did a lap each, he ran the whole thing."

There was a general hubbub going on in the room now and Cassidy noticed that the woman coach on the panel wore a tiny smile.

"And what was the outcome?"

"Uh, Mr. Cassidy won."

"And on what basis did you conclude there were drugs involved?"

"Well, it was just obvious, wasn't it? He trained for a maximum of two, maybe three weeks. Our guys were out there for more than two months, good athletes, all of us!"

"Mr. Farkus, how fast did Mr. Cassidy have to run to win?"

"I don't know, it was abnormal, is all. Just over four minutes, I think. Like four minutes and ten seconds, something like that. We did 4:22 or so. We weren't even in the same race. It was ridiculous!"

"Actually, 4:09.8," Cassidy whispered to Denton.

Giegengach was in his chair sideways, looking at Magruder.

"Deesus Kweist, Day-day!" he said. Magruder appeared to be hyperventilating. The woman coach was grinning broadly.

"Karl," said Roland, "do you know Mr. Cassidy's best time for the mile?"

Farkus, who had been slumping a bit, jerked up straight in his chair.

"Oh, I know he's run faster than that! I'm just saying, my God, man! Look at the circumstances. He hadn't competed in years! And don't forget, he admitted everything to me."

"Tell us how that came about."

"We were having a few beers after the race. That was what the bet was. Loser had to buy a pitcher at the Greenhouse."

More murmuring from the crowd. Denton looked over at Cassidy, who was smiling now.

"Go on."

"I got his confidence. I said, 'So what would a guy take if he really wanted to build up? I'd like to get my tennis game to the next level. Between me and you, what do you use?' "

"What did he say?"

"He hemmed and hawed around, said he didn't think I really wanted to get mixed up in anything like that. Said it could be dangerous, make you sterile, stuff like that."

"And?"

"I persisted. Said it was worth the risk to me and I would take it as a personal favor if he'd tell me. He said it was against his better judgment and that he doubted if I could find a supplier, but that he used the same stuff that Finnish guy used, the one who won all the gold medals."

"Deesus Kweist!" said Giegengach.

"Do you know to whom he was referring?" asked Roland.

"That Finnish guy, Viros, Veerus, who won all the different events. It was common knowledge! Cassidy said he went public and admitted everything!"

This drew the first actual laugh from the audience. Confused by the mirth, Farkus looked around anxiously.

"The gentleman in question, I believe, is named Lasse Viren," said Roland.

"That's it!"

"And Karl, do you know what substance Mr. Viren admitted using to achieve his remarkable victories?"

Karl looked perplexed.

"I'm not sure. I know there are a lot of different . . ."

The woman coach was packing her stuff up, not paying attention. Soozie and the twins had already absconded. Giegengach was again sideways in his chair, staring at the dejected JJ Magruder.

"*Waindeer milk!*" Giegengach shouted at Magruder. "This is all about waindeer milk! Viwin's damn joke!"

Karl Farkus had sweated through his seersucker jacket. He was trying unsuccessfully to get Magruder's attention.

"Move to adjourn," said Giegengach.

"Second," said the woman.

"All in favor?" said Giegengach, reaching over in front of Magruder to snatch up and bang his gavel down with a great *thwack*. He got up and headed for the door, rolling his eyes theatrically at Cassidy. Cassidy winked at him.

Roland, one moist curl now adorning his shiny forehead, turned to Cassidy with his best Fat Italian Kid grin and looked him in the eye for the first time all day.

"Why, hello there, Quenton," he said. "What's shakin'?"

46

The Race

CASSIDY WENT THROUGH the first mile in 4:55, his winning time years before in his first track race as a high school sophomore.

Back then he found himself on the infield of the Twin Lakes High School track, bent over at the waist, leaning heavily against the sturdy legs of his amazed coach, Don Blackwelder, throwing up on the man's ripple-soled coaching shoes.

Now, though, his breath would hardly trouble a birthday candle and he was grateful that no one had gone out crazy-fast, allowing him to tuck in with a big pack and flow along like a leaf on a river, barely conscious of the effort.

Just past the timer's station he flashed by Denton, leaning against his mountain bike. "Right on five-minute pace! Just cruise!" he said.

Standing next to Denton, improbably, was Roland, who appeared to be dressed in old-fashioned tennis whites, topped by a crisp Panama hat with a madras hat band. His nose, Cassidy couldn't help noticing, wore a thick coat of zinc oxide. He had kept them up perhaps a tad late the night before, explaining with great gusto how Karl's inability to type had led to the secretarial gossip that eventually did him in.

On the grounds of the Albright-Knox Art Gallery earlier that morning, Denton had spoken briefly to Cassidy midway through his low-key warm-up.

"You know what you need to do," he said, more nervous than Cassidy. "We've talked about it enough already. Just stick with Benji. He's going to run a fast time but he's not going to get sucked into anything ridiculous. Be careful. It's not hot but it's humid, so keep hydrating even if you don't feel thirsty."

Jeez, Cassidy thought, he's all but hyperventilating.

When they came up on the second mile marker, the pack loosened up a little and Cassidy spotted Benji through a gap, striding effortlessly alongside possibly the skinniest runner Cassidy had ever seen. He recognized him from the picture in yesterday's *Buffalo News* as the prerace favorite, Tony Sandoval. He reminded Cassidy of one of those "Visible Man" models kids use to learn anatomy: you could see every muscle and sinew moving beneath the cellophane-thin skin.

Everything felt fine except for warm spots on both insteps. He was wearing a feathery pair of Tiger prototype racing flats that were so new they didn't have a name yet. Denton had given them to Cassidy a month earlier with instructions to break them in carefully. Cassidy had, but now realized that he had not run a single step on pavement with them.

His feet were completely drenched already and of course he wore no socks, but the shoes fit snugly and other than the warmish sensation under both arches he was none the worse for wear.

Cassidy angled over and settled in next to Benji.

"What's the deal?" Cassidy gestured with his chin toward a tall runner leading them by twenty-five yards.

"Fanelli," said Benji, and after a few breaths: "Crazy."

"The Blues Brothers. Guy?"

"Yes but. He's good."

"No suit and sunglasses. Today though," said Cassidy.

Benji apparently considered Fanelli potentially dangerous, but more than likely to blow up. That's what everyone else thought too, because no one had left the safety of the pack to chase him. Benji went back to concentrating on his pace and Cassidy took the hint. The effort was so minimal at this point there was a temptation to chat or otherwise lose focus. Cassidy noticed that the runners spoke to one another rarely, and then in monosyllables. Otherwise they were locked in their own universes.

The sun had burned off the morning haze and it warmed rapidly as they made their way through pleasant residential sections of Buffalo, some of whose denizens were standing at the edge of the street, clapping and shouting encouragement, some offering Dixie cups of water, ignored by the runners. Though the pace felt easy, still Cassidy noticed drops of sweat coming off most of them.

When they came up on the first aid station right after the three-mile mark, Cassidy looked in vain for his blue and orange bottle of de-fizzed cola, and finally grabbed one of the generic Gatorade bottles. Out of his peripheral vision he thought he saw Denton over in a clump of attendants, bike at his feet, arguing. But it all flashed by and then they were back on their own, some of them still carrying bottles, sipping every few strides. Cassidy drank about half of his before tossing it aside. It went down okay, but he had trained by alternating with the flat Coke and water, and he was mildly irritated at the screwup.

In less than a quarter of a mile, Denton pedaled up. "I'm going on ahead to get across the bridge," he said. "Your bottles should be there from now on. Drink plenty; if this is any indication, it's going to be hot as hell before it's over."

After Denton left, Benji said: "It'll be cooler. In Canada."

Cassidy thought this an attempt at humor, like crossing a geopolitical boundary could affect the weather, but it turned out to be true.

They hit the next aid station at Prospect Park, just past the five-mile mark. They had heard 24:48 going by the timer, but Cassidy was far more concerned about his bottle, which he was relieved to see at the front of the first table. There was such a rush among the ten runners to get to them, however, that he almost lost it in the melee.

He sucked down as much as he could over the next several hundred yards then tossed the bottle just as they turned left off Niagara Street onto Massachusetts Avenue and saw the Peace Bridge looming ahead. He felt the cooling breeze from the snowmelt-chilled river all the way across the bridge and to Cassidy it was life-giving. Halfway across they passed some customs stations and found themselves in Ontario. Everyone in the race had been precleared the day before, and the Canadian customs and border patrol officials were on the sidelines with their families, cheering on their latest international visitors.

Cassidy felt better immediately, and apparently so did everyone else because the pace seemed to quicken noticeably. The downside was that as soon as they turned north on Niagara Boulevard they would be running directly into that same breeze, a small trade-off Cassidy didn't mind at all.

As the pack made its way north on the Canadian side, Cassidy noticed they had now picked up a press boat paralleling them from the river, to go along with the network helicopter, the two press trucks, and the various motorcycle-borne cameramen and photographers. At one point one of the press trucks seemed to break down and there was an amusing spectacle of several dozen notebook- and camera-toting journalists sprinting for the other truck. Cassidy would have chuckled but for the waste of energy.

Fanelli was now a good forty yards ahead, and as a track man Cassidy couldn't help feeling nervous. His focus in track races had been to never lose "contact" with his opponent. It was a psychological construct that runners understood intuitively. There was no set distance that constituted maintaining contact—it varied depending on circumstance—but everyone understood what it meant. If someone "got away" or if you had to "let him go," the race was usually over. On the track, that is.

But this was different. The race was so long that good runners simply didn't allow themselves to be drawn into the contact game. By the simple application of intellect, they determined in advance which runners were real threats and which could be dismissed. As decent a runner as Fanelli was—he had run 2:18:20—he would not be taken seriously unless he still looked dangerous much later on.

Cassidy knew all this intellectually, but he could not control his deeply ingrained racing instincts. He got Benji's attention again and gestured up at the bright orange shorts and white singlet of the fleeing Fanelli, his tall frame jauntily topped with an orange-brimmed bicycle cap. Cassidy arched his eyebrow, but Benji just shook his head.

Cassidy looked around the pack. Sandoval had finished a heartbreaking fourth at the last trials, losing his spot on the team to his friend Don Kardong, who went on to have the race of his life at the Olympics, finishing fourth and just a handful of seconds away from a bronze medal. Today Sandoval looked totally invincible, a creature not of flesh at all but of pure spirit, moving over the ground like a wisp of fog in the wind, with no discernible effort whatsoever. Unlike Cassidy and the rest, he did not even appear to be sweating.

Lee Fidler was now in the group, Benji's Atlanta Track Club teammate and training partner. Tall and bearded, he occasionally exchanged words with Benji; he also had no problems with the pace. The rest of the pack, with a few exceptions, was a Who's Who of American marathoning. Jeff Wells from Texas, Bostonian Randy Thomas, and Ron Tabb from the Nike group. Now at six miles, yet another Atlantan led the pack: lanky, good-natured Bob Varsha. Cassidy no longer saw Frank Shorter, who had been at the front of the group going across the bridge.

The breeze that flowed over the river was essentially providing an air-conditioned corridor, redolent of new leaves, chlorophyll, and ozone. The entire parkway was lined with emerald-leaved birch trees glistening in the spring sunshine, and Cassidy found himself gliding along with an incredible sense of well-being. There was still little sense of effort at all, as if he were watching the pleasantly passing scenery from some slow but comfortable vehicle.

Was this the Big Secret of the marathon? That once you got in really superb long-distance shape it was simply a Zen-like daydream of a race that went on until people started running out of gas?

It was certainly nothing like the rasping, pounding, lactic-acid storm of his earlier track racing, where one small error in strategy or pace judgment could cost him several tenths of a second and possibly the race. In that world the runners were all bound up in swirls and eddies of concentration and pain. And they were mute.

In this race people spoke. They weren't chatty, to be sure, but Cassidy had seen several exchanges since joining the pack. He had even heard one competitor politely thanking but declining an aid station worker proffering a water bottle.

Everything about this race was less intense. Because a marathon took hours, not minutes, to finish, almost any kind of error or mishap could conceivably be remedied in time. But there was nothing casual about the runners' concentration. Despite his current ease and the sudden bliss brought on by the cooling spring breeze, Cassidy was constantly monitoring every parameter of his effort. Like most of the others, he ran with a machinelike precision, like a watch movement, with legs and arms the moving parts, everything else still. His head bobbed not a millimeter, moving on an invisible horizontal plane like a glass on a waiter's tray.

Every so often some part of his body would send in a signal: a shoulder muscle tightening, a hint of a stitch starting in the side, a wad of saliva turning to gauze in his cheek. The corresponding roll of the shoulder, shifting of body position, quick expectoration would provide relief.

Other than that they rolled along monotonously, appearing to the casual observer to be merely a group of whippet-thin joggers on a spring morning. The speed with which they were covering ground could only be appreciated by paying close attention to how fast the background was slipping by. When a cyclist or aid station worker came alongside for a few strides to pass a word or deliver a bottle, the speed of the runners also became obvious for a moment or two. They were in fact traveling faster than twelve miles an hour, on foot.

Cassidy was trying to buy into his current contentedness.

"Don't get too up or too down about how you feel at any given time," Denton had told him. "This race is long enough for you to go through a bunch of different phases. Shorter told me he went through bad patches in every single race—and he ended up winning most of them."

They passed ten thousand meters in a little under thirty-one minutes, faster than he had run in his first attempt at that distance in a road race.

Fanelli now had a garish hundred-yard lead and appeared to be making a mockery of the race, yet everyone in the pack seemed oblivious. In the chase pack the Bostonian Thomas traded the lead back and forth with Ron Tabb and a runner Cassidy didn't know. When Cassidy nudged Durden and gestured at the mystery man, leading the pack with easy, ground-eating strides, Benji said, "Terry Heath. Idaho."

When Cassidy's face remained puzzled, Benji gave him a *damned if I know* shrug and went back to work. Varsha had now dropped back and was content to let the others manage the pace as he ran beside Sandoval, Varsha's six-three frame making Sandoval appear even tinier.

Cassidy was thinking that marathoners generally don't race as often as other runners, and consequently some obscure competitor would occasionally emerge from his hideaway and surprise everyone. Cassidy himself was a case in point, though an odd one. There were other examples around. Occasionally a late bloomer would appear out of the blue, like forty-year-old Kiwi Olympian Jack Foster, a former cyclist who ran 2:11:19 in winning the Commonwealth Marathon, or his countryman, John Campbell, who came out of a long retirement to break Foster's master's record.

But longtime champions also tended to fade only slowly, and it was obvious today that the old guard was changing. The past Olympiad's U.S. contingent was still active but wouldn't be a factor today. Shorter had wilted early in the race; Kardong's training had been sabotaged for months by the volcanic eruption of Mount St. Helens. Rodgers had battled injuries and he too was sitting out the trials.

As they passed fifteen kilometers Cassidy saw Durden chopping his stride a little, as if in distress. Cassidy moved closer to the bearded runner.

"You okay?" he said.

"Cramp. Hamstring. Be okay. Gotta talk. Myself out of it."

They ran on in silence, Cassidy empathizing, unable to help. He remembered Denton's lecture: "In the marathon you can get cramps almost anytime. They're not like the ones we used to get toward the end of hot-weather workouts, not based on electrolyte depletion. I got them halfway through my 2:15 when I picked up the pace suddenly. They're usually in the hamstrings, sometimes the calves or quads. You're over your anaerobic threshold, but just barely. You start generating ketones from burning fat without enough oxygen, the ketones start circulating, confusing your synapses, causing them to misfire. You cramp. Joe Vigil laid it out for me. The thing is not to panic. They feel pretty bad for a while, and you may think you're done for, but they'll go away if you back off a bit and run them out."

But Benji wasn't backing off. He was holding pace, now sharing the lead with Sandoval, behind only Fanelli and his scary 150-yard lead.

They reached the halfway point in just over sixty-five minutes, faster by far than Cassidy had run a half-marathon. There
was a water station several hundred yards ahead and Cassidy
was angling over to the right side of the road when he saw Denton, sans bike, running at race pace on the shoulder of the road.
Cassidy pulled over next to him.

"Don't get flustered," said Denton, "but your bottles are
missing again. I don't know what's going on. Just take the Gatorade and don't worry about it. How's it going?"

"So far. So good. Feels. Easy so far."

"Okay, that will go on for a few more miles. Then it'll start
to get tough. Be ready."

"Hey! What's this?" Cassidy gestured up ahead of Durden
and Sandoval. Fanelli's lead had shrunk in half.

"He's cooked. Yelled to the press truck a while back that he
had a blister on his left foot."

Cassidy smiled. "Me too. Both arches. But not. Blisters anymore."

Denton looked down and saw red splotches on the insteps of
both Tiger racing flats.

"Jesus, Quenton!"

"S'okay. Too late. Now."

"All right. I'm going back for the bike. Get ready for your
bottle. And for God's sake don't run up Fanelli's ass."

"Check," said Cassidy as he angled toward the table. Denton was right: there was no orange and blue bottle. He grabbed
for one of the green Gatorade bottles, missed, waited for the
last table and finally snagged one.

Durden and Sandoval had already gone by Fanelli and Cassidy was closing in on him when Denton flew by on the bike.

"I'll see you around seventeen or eighteen," he called. "Hang
in there."

Cassidy, back in his dream world, gave a little wave.

Two miles later Cassidy was consciously sequestering the
pain. The scarlet blooms on the insides of his racing shoes now

looked like part of the design of the shoes and he left a quarter-sized dab of red with every step.

As they approached the next aid station he tucked in behind Sandoval, with Durden and someone else just to his outside.

Cassidy was way beyond analyzing or even thinking about his bottle situation now. The day was warming up some and the sun was definitely hot on their shoulders, but it seemed the cool river breeze would keep the heat from becoming a factor. Benji probably hates that, Cassidy thought. He was fairly notorious for training in sweat suits in Atlanta's hot and humid summers and had once registered a fifteen-pound weight loss during a single workout.

The little knot of runners loosened quickly as they approached the aid station. Because the workers were in contact with the press truck, they knew who the leaders were and had carefully arranged their bottles at spaced intervals on the first table. Cassidy glanced quickly and wasn't surprised to see no orange and blue bottle for him. He snatched a Gatorade from the next table and almost chuckled to himself. He had been among the first guinea-pig athletes to try the drink years earlier when Dr. Cade was developing an electrolyte-replacement drink for sports. It tasted like salty dishwater and Cassidy and his teammates pronounced the invention dead on arrival.

Cassidy had his head tilted back, trying to squeeze as much of the liquid into his beak as he could between breaths. Out of the corner of his eye he noticed first one, then a second worker, carrying green bottles, step from around the table.

They weren't supposed to be doing that. They were supposed to stay behind the tables, away from the runners. Cassidy angled away from the table, holding his bottle out in front of him like a talisman, showing he had no need for assistance.

To his alarm they quickly responded to his new path and now dropped all pretense of trying to offer assistance. One moved outside his path and the other came right at him as it dawned on Cassidy that they weren't aid station workers at all but the demented spawn of JJ Magruder, each dressed in black, wearing engineer's boots and some kind of metallic emblem swinging from heavy chains around their necks. Cassidy looked into the eyes of the one coming from his outside and saw only stupid hatred.

Cassidy couldn't for the life of him figure out what they were up to. At the speed he was going he had very little room to maneuver now. He gave the outer one a quick little head fake, which caused him to pause for several beats, which was almost enough time for Cassidy to speed up a bit and thread the needle between them.

Almost. When they saw that he was about to escape their trap, both thrust shoulders and elbows in toward him and the one on the inside caught him with a glancing blow in the rib cage and Cassidy quickly bounced back and forth between them like a pinball going between rubber bumpers.

And that would have been that too, except his feet got tangled up in each other and in short order the pavement was closing in on his face in horrifying slow motion. He hit hard on his hands and knees and the twelve-mile-an-hour speed propelled him forward to his chest, which hit the asphalt hard and actually skidded. He let out an involuntary "Oooph!" and briefly entertained the amusing notion that he probably looked something like a hapless cartoon mouse scooting along the ground, his useless feet flipped back up over his head. He was also idly wondering how bad the road rash would be.

But even as he was trying to assimilate what happened he was thinking about Lasse Viren's fall and recovery in the '72 Olympic 10,000 finals, the one he had tried to replicate when he tripped and fell on his trail on Cedar Mountain. That same helpless feeling came back to him as the numbness and stiffness bound his body like a cocoon of ropes.

He was painfully conscious of every passing second and every foot and yard now growing between him and the leaders as he struggled just to raise himself back to his hands and knees. He was vaguely aware that some security people had his assailants occupied for the time being, and several others were approaching but warning one another not to actually touch him, for fear of causing a disqualification.

He also noticed that his vision was fogged, like in the last stages of a mile race, when the world seemed to be passing outside a dirty window. He tried to straighten up from his knees and found he couldn't. Some of the aid workers came closer, but were warned back by the security people. They had to get back behind the tables anyway, because the other runners were beginning to stream by now and Cassidy alone was more than enough of a hazard in the roadway.

Still in something very like shock, Cassidy again struggled to straighten up from his knees, when he felt a friendly hand on his elbow and he was propelled not only to his feet but back to a stiff-legged jog. As he ambled along for the first few strides, trying to limber up, he heard a familiar voice say, "Come on, Captain! You're not done yet!"

Cassidy looked over in amazement to see the red, beaming face of Jack Nubbins, his old nemesis and teammate at Southeastern.

"Jack!" Cassidy croaked, still jogging stiffly. "I didn't know you were in this thing."

"Well, Captain, there's a lot you don't know! But right now you need to concentrate on those guys."

Cassidy looked up and sure enough, Durden, Sandoval, and another runner were about sixty yards ahead, with a scattering of others who had just passed Cassidy while he'd been indisposed. Durden kept looking back to see what had happened.

The whole thing had taken just a few seconds.

Cassidy was stumbling along stiff-legged, but getting more flexibility back second by second, and within another hundred yards his pace was almost back to normal. His comfort level was something else. He hurt all over, but most of it was superficial, he told himself, nothing that would interfere with his biomechanics much.

Once he was running more or less smoothly again he looked around for Nubbins to thank his old teammate but didn't see him. He must have gone on ahead. There were a number of runners around him as he began to ease his way back through the group that had passed him. Both his hands and knees were bleeding, but not badly, and his feet still hurt though it seemed they were possibly starting to get numb.

After a mile he was back to his previous pace, and though he was sure he looked like hell, he was now in front of the chase pack and beginning to get some ground back on the leaders. He passed the fifteen-mile marker but was unsure of the time he heard because of some noisy spectators, and concluded that he probably couldn't have done the math anyway.

He slowly began to realize that the lead group in front of him was the Olympic team. If one of them fell back and he was able to go around, Cassidy could still make it, but not otherwise.

He began to really focus on the backs of the three fleeing figures, ignoring the pain in his hands and feet and knees. He began to get back into the zone where his pace became second nature, a part of him. And right now it needed to be just slightly faster than the runners in front. He needed to catch up to them, but as efficiently as possible, so that if he were able to get back to them the cost of doing so wouldn't leave him helpless over the last few miles.

By mile seventeen he had made up half the distance. But now he was suspended midway between the leaders and the chase pack and he ran utterly alone. There were stretches along the raceway that were lined with spectators and there were stretches where his only company was the distant roar of the TV helicopter hovering over the leaders. Nor was he bothered by the press boat on the river, or the truck full of damp journalists scribbling away at their notepads. Good, he thought. As far as they're all concerned, I'm out of this thing.

But he was beginning to notice that he was actually feeling this race for the first time. There were three miles yet before the fabled twenty-mile mark, the place where, Shorter had famously once said, the race really began. And yet though the pace still felt quite manageable for a miler, he could almost feel his body ransacking itself, seeking into the liver, pancreas, and other exotic and improbable sources of energy and succor. His body had begun to eat itself.

Whatever he was feeling, however surreal and faded the reality he perceived through his pain and concentration, there was no question the others were feeling it too, for the leaders were definitely coming back to him. Once the helicopter even paused overhead to allow him to run underneath, giving the cameraman a chance to get a close-up of the curiously persistent interloper, the former Olympian trying to steal a bit of his youth back.

At some point before the eighteen-mile mark he felt a stitch coming in his right side. Over the years he had learned that it was sometimes possible to reach deeply into his innards and get his fingertips on the psoas muscle, a strip of beef that ran deep in the body cavity on either side of the spine. Medical science knew next to nothing about stitches, but runners knew them well and knew they could become so painful as to force a runner out of a race. Cassidy now ran slightly bent to his right, his hand dug up deep into his side, and—maintaining pace—touched an incredibly angry spot deep inside himself, a squalling infant of a pain that insisted on not only his attention but his ambition, his spirit, his life. He touched it, pressed it, and held it through a more intense version of itself, squeezed the life and evil out of it, squeezed and made it hurt until it could hurt him no more, and finally released his grip on it, returning to his normal stride with the stitch miraculously dissolved and replaced by his own gruesome bloody handprint on the side of his wet singlet.

The stitch had all but destroyed his concentration for several minutes, but when he turned it back to the lead runners they had about the same margin on him. Now that the stitch had dissipated and his feet were nearly numb, he concentrated on closing the remaining thirty yards.

At mile eighteen just past Netherby, the river bent to the right and the breeze now came across dry land and lost most of its cooling effect. In no time at all he was wringing wet and with each stride he flung a frothy pink rain of blood, sweat, and saliva. Slowly, painfully, he shortened the imaginary rope he had strung between himself and the last of the three runners in front of him. His feet were starting to come alive again, losing the blessed numbness that had helped him get this far. He began working his mental games, corralling the pain and containing it, giving it its due, but keeping it from getting loose and blotting out everything else.

The raw parts of his feet weren't coming into contact with the ground, they just rubbed painfully against the inside of the shoes on every foot strike. This was what everyone had said about the marathon: it was long enough for lots of things to go wrong. But Denton had said there would be good patches too, and Cassidy was amazed to find he was sort of having one. His knees had limbered up again and he couldn't feel his scraped hands at all.

Maybe he was in sensory overload with regard to the pain. There was so much of it that his brain simply couldn't deal with it.

But there was no denying that he was once again all right, at least from a running perspective. He knew it couldn't last for long, as they were nearing the twenty-mile mark and the dregs of the glycogen stores in his system began to run out. Yet he found himself again running with almost no perceivable effort. He was even able to lock onto Benji's stride and match his own to it. Then he concentrated on getting ahead of it, a little at a time, until he had picked up a full cycle and was again back in sync. Then he repeated the process, pulling on that rope, drawing them in a little at a time.

As he gave little tugs on the rope and felt Benji come back a foot or two at a time, he told himself, Just don't try to do it too fast. You can't afford a mistake like that at this point. It has to be efficient. Smooth and efficient. Tug on the rope, get another foot, tug again, another foot.

He knew very well that it was a mental trick. All that was really happening was that the runners in front were running 4:55 pace and he was running 4:53. If he did it correctly he would be back up with them in a mile or so. That was the way the brain understood it and that was fine. But as they neared the twenty-mile mark, his brain was growing hazy, less sure of itself. His heart understood that rope, the pain of it, the labor, the longing. His heart had been pulling on that rope for a very long time and knew how to do it.

He was concentrating on the rope so hard that he occasionally forgot where he was in the race. In most races it felt like a computer in his head kept track of all that. He always knew precisely where he was, what his effort was, how long he would need to endure.

He knew that no matter how good or bad a runner looks toward the end of a race, the thing he wants most in the world is to stop.

The computer in his head was now clearly unreliable. With effort, he recalled the last mile marker had been eighteen and that a while back they had passed Sherk Street and were thus more than halfway to the next marker. All this figuring took mental effort and when he again turned his attention to the rope, he was surprised to see that Benji was only ten yards in front and Cassidy now had contact again. In fact, he could have easily surged up to him with a few strides, and it took great effort not to give in to this extravagant gesture. Instead he went to work on the rope and slowly reeled in the bearded runner.

When, a quarter mile before the nineteen-mile marker, he pulled even, Durden did not even look over.

"Guess. Who's back," Cassidy said.

"Nice friends. You've got," said Durden. "I tried. To give. One an elbow. For you."

"Thanks."

They ran in silence for several hundred yards. Cassidy looked ahead at Sandoval, striding with the same ease, directly in front. Nubbins must have been directly in front of him because Cassidy could not see him at all. Something didn't seem right, but he couldn't make his mind work on it.

"Are you. Hurt? You're a. Mess," Durden said.

"Just scraped. Thank God. For Nubbins though."

Durden gave him a strange look. "What did you do. To your head?"

Cassidy felt his forehead, withdrew bloody fingertips. "I'm okay. I think I just. Wiped it there."

Because he was now part of the lead group, Cassidy got a full helping of the noise and downdraft from the network helicopter, which now angled down annoyingly close to get a better shot of them as they approached the nineteen-mile marker.

The machine was close enough for him to see the pilot's face clearly and Cassidy was surprised to see that the pilot was Jerry Mizner. Something was not right about that either, but he could not keep his brain on it long enough to work it out.

Cassidy reached up with his left hand and squeezed the sweat out of his eye sockets, then focused on the asphalt twenty feet in front of him.

When they hit nineteen, for some reason the timer was standing on a folding chair beside the big mile marker sign, as if the runners might not see him otherwise.

"One thir . . ." he began to read, the rest drowned out by the roar of the helicopter.

"Dammit!" said Durden, who looked up angrily at the helicopter. He surged suddenly, leaving Cassidy running by himself, ten yards behind Sandoval, who watched Durden go by him with no apparent interest. He still looked like he was out for a Sunday canter. Where Nubbins was now, Cassidy had no idea.

But he noticed that his thinking was increasingly muddled. Mizner wasn't piloting the helicopter, Mizner was dead. At least he was fairly certain of that. When they were approaching the nineteen-mile marker, he had tried to calculate what the elapsed time should be if they were still on five-minute pace. He was unable to do so. His vision was becoming even foggier, and at times he thought he saw big balloons or clouds looming at the edge of his peripheral vision, only to vanish when he tried to look at them.

After Benji had taken off, Cassidy looked up ahead of Sandoval and finally spotted Nubbins, leading them by more than a hundred yards. He figured that was why Benji had taken off in pursuit. But the next time Cassidy looked over Sandoval's head, he saw only Benji pulling away, and Nubbins nowhere in sight at all.

In their undergraduate days at Southeastern, Nubbins had been something of an antagonist, and Cassidy had predicted that he was simply too much of a raconteur and scatterbrain to amount to much. But he had to hand it to old Jack. He was really taking the race to them. And doing so after stopping to lend his old captain a helping hand! He had always been a tough little competitor, but Cassidy never in his wildest imagination thought he would get to this level.

Sandoval, meanwhile, was unperturbed as Cassidy pulled up next to him, grateful for company after Durden's sudden departure. Sandoval looked over at him, glanced once over his shoulder, then gave Cassidy a quick high sign, along with a grin.

What the hell does that mean? Cassidy thought. Here it looks like we'll be battling it out for the last spot on the team, and he's acting all gentlemanly and good-sporty about it all. Cassidy then looked down at himself.

I don't know why he'd bother to try a psych job on me, he thought. Blood from his scraped hands and knees streaked down his legs. His left side was still blotched with bloody handprints from his efforts to crush the stitch out of his psoas muscle. His destroyed feet now sent stabs of pain with every foot strike and left crimson smudges on the pavement.

At the aid station Cassidy didn't even look for his bottle. He snagged a Gatorade without slowing and pulled the top open with his front teeth. He noticed that Sandoval carried his along for quite a ways, drinking small sips every few strides, so Cassidy did the same. Sandoval was as sweat drenched as Cassidy by this point, with his dark hair plastered thinly to his skull, his black-and-white Athletics West singlet clinging to his slight frame like a layer of new paint.

Sandoval's stride was much shorter than Cassidy's but it was depressing how easily he seemed to handle the pace, so Cassidy focused instead on Durden's orange-and-white singlet not thirty yards ahead. He looked again in vain for Nubbins, who he figured was directly in front of Durden.

But Cassidy was already getting the gloomy depression of unavoidable defeat. Durden had taken off with great energy, apparently in pursuit of Nubbins, and that left Cassidy sadly pondering his chances against this wisp gliding along beside him. In track races Cassidy had always had great confidence in his kick, particularly in longer events. If he could survive the pace he always thought he could race with anyone over the final furlongs. Even the great John Walton had felt the sting of Cassidy's closing kick.

But Sandoval was a 1:49 half-miler, Denton had warned him. Cassidy had run 1:45, but that meant next to nothing now. Sandoval was a true marathoner, with a 2:10 already to his credit. Cassidy had only run the distance twice, and never all-out. He was a journeyman, if not an outright poseur. He was also, he realized, pretty much doomed.

And now he was beginning to get bizarre intimations that his body was disintegrating at the seams. He was still running just under five minutes per mile right off Sandoval's childlike left shoulder. He was becoming increasingly aware, however, of just how much more effort it was requiring to maintain that pace. This was what Denton had hammered him on from day one. "Frank says, 'The marathon is a race of attrition.' You've got to understand that. You've got to come to grips with that, Quenton. No one really wins a marathon. You just survive it better."

But it was hard to change his head around so completely. In his mind the only way he could imagine salvaging this race was simply to hang on to this elfin Sandoval and try to outkick him. Cassidy didn't really know him, other than that he was a friend and teammate of Kardong's, that he was a medical doctor, and that he appeared to be a perfectly designed long-distance racing machine. Cassidy, at six two and even at less than 160 pounds, felt like a giant next to the 115-pound runner. Cassidy had been amazed before the race to see Sandoval chatting with Shorter and making even Shorter look like he'd been bulking up.

Somewhere after the twenty-two-mile mark, Cassidy was relieved to find the parkway again turning back toward the river so the breeze now came directly over the water again. Despite his efforts to down as much liquid as he could, he was finding his saliva thickening and he knew there were wads of the stuff dried to the sides of his face where he hadn't been efficient enough at expelling it.

His feet were now on fire and he prepared himself mentally for every foot strike. He didn't think he was wincing audibly when his ravaged feet touched the ground, but he really couldn't be sure. Denton rode by very briefly and seemed to Cassidy to be in way too good a mood.

"Okay, Quenton. Great work! Just hang in there now and you're set. They're going to throw me off the course anytime now, so I'll see you at the finish. Don't try to talk, just concentrate."

Cassidy gave him a little flip of his left hand, which he hoped would register as a wave. As for talking, Denton was crazy as hell if he thought Cassidy had the energy for conversation.

And why in the world was he so damn confident? Did he just

assume that Cassidy would be able to outkick Sandoval? Why in the world would he assume that? Four miles could be an eternity, particularly the last four miles of a marathon. He didn't know if he could even keep Sandoval in sight, much less outkick him.

And that was the revelation his mind picked up and bobbled around like a beach ball over the next several miles, surely the most painful and most dreadful and most revealing of any he had ever run.

He began to get a stitch in his other side, which didn't surprise him at all. He reached a bloody hand in to squeeze it out. He now hurt in so many places that the stitch didn't feel any more or any less painful than the rest of him. He was able to ease it somewhat over the next hundred yards, and afterward was even able to focus on his pace again.

But just as he was beginning to do so, he looked up and felt sick at heart. Tony Sandoval, at long last, was running away from him.

And this really is it, he thought, as he tried to pick up his pace at least a little, to give some semblance of a fight, some gesture of defiance.

But it was completely, utterly, depressingly hopeless, and he knew it.

He knew it because ever since the twenty-mile mark when he had first felt himself beginning to come apart at the seams, he had realized something so fundamental, so surprising, so profoundly simple, that he knew he would never be the same again.

He had finally found the ultimate limits to himself, the final boundary of his being that he had never before come near enough to truly contemplate, despite a lifetime of trying.

It was there he found it, just past the twenty-mile mark of this too-long race at the top of the hemisphere as he watched a far better runner easily disappear ahead into the cooling mists now drifting down over them from the massive falls. It was there that Quenton Cassidy finally relinquished the last of his dream and the last of his youth and the last of the road all runners come. It was there that he finally accepted his fate and the fate of his kind.

It was there that Quenton Cassidy, an Olympian who had once run at sundown from the dusty plaka up to the steps of the Parthenon to commune with the spirits of his forebears, there that Quenton Cassidy understood in a most visceral and personal way that he, like all runners, would die.

47

The End

NOW HE WAS so alone.

He turned and could barely perceive the following runner in the hazy distance. His highest ambition now was to disintegrate as little as possible, to give up as little as absolutely necessary to the hounds behind.

Time had slowed to the point that every mile marker was a small eternity in coming. In the early going they had flipped over like a time-passing calendar in a 1940s movie. The hardest part now was keeping his concentration. It wasn't the pain, whose signals so bombarded his weary brain from all quarters that they nearly canceled themselves out.

Almost every trace of glycogen was gone from his muscles and bloodstream, the sweetbreads had given up their last grains of sugar, his brain itself was stumbling along on fumes.

He dimly perceived that this was why he couldn't make his head work, why his thoughts went off on tangents, as if in a fever dream. Several times he caught himself coming to, as though he had been unconscious.

When he could summon the will, he squinted at the road ahead to see where the others were, to hope against hope that through some awful miscalculation one more would be coming back to him.

Sandoval, Durden, Nubbins, he could no longer tell who was leading and who following, but it no longer mattered. None dropped back to him. They were in a contest he was not privy to.

They would be the anointed and he the first of many losers. His speed had now slipped, he knew, to many seconds over five-minute pace, and though surely the same thing was happening to the others, they were all now fixed in their positions on the escalator, riding it slowly together to the end.

He hadn't realized how bad he must have looked until the aid station past the twenty-four-mile mark. A middle-aged woman in a visor stood just past the last table and he watched as her cheery expression turned to one of abject pity as he approached. He slowed to grab one of the bottles, and as he passed she put her hand out and very gently and briefly touched his elbow. It was the touch a nurse might confer on a wounded soldier. Cassidy started to say something to her but stopped when he saw that she was crying.

He had but two miles to go and he was still moving and he was grateful. He could now feel his feet moving around in the bloody mush inside his shoes, but it didn't matter. The stitches were threatening to come back, but they didn't matter. He had two miles to go.

And as short as two miles had come to seem to him over the course of his running career, it occurred to him now that two miles was an insurmountable distance to an infant, or a legless man, or a human cadaver for that matter. Einstein was right, he decided. It is all relative.

But he was still moving and moving and moving, and no cadaver could ever be moving so, or feeling so much anguish at the same time. Or worrying about losing another place, losing another second in a footrace.

With alarm he began to hear the foot strikes of a runner behind him. With massive concentration he tried to increase his pace but it was no good. He had immediately begun to get the queasy feeling in both his calves and quadriceps that he knew meant they were right on the edge of convulsive cramps. That would bring him to the horror of a complete stop, and if that happened, the last mile and a half might as well be ten, or a hundred, and he might as well be legless or a toddler or a corpse.

He concentrated on both sets of muscles and by main force of will brought them under control, but it took every ounce of attention he could muster. If he let his mind wander for a second, the queasy, crampy feelings came right back.

The footsteps behind him grew louder but now he knew he could do nothing about them. He kept his focus on his rebelling muscles. Have at it, fellow, whoever you are, one more place for you for the taking. A tad more glory in the losing, and you're welcome to the title of first loser if you want it so badly.

After another hundred yards the runner still hadn't gone by, so he finally turned his head to see who his tormentor was and was amazed to see there was no one there at all. He had been listening to, *fearing*, his own footsteps.

He found this amusing and he would have to remember to laugh about it. Later, of course, when he was able to. But time had now slowed so that it seemed not to move at all. And he realized that he had been hearing music, for quite a while actually. But from where?

It was haunting, angelic, deeply resonant, a Gregorian chant of some kind that filled him—despite his distress—with something like bliss. *Hallelujah, hallelujah*, went the chorus, *I used to live alone before I knew you.*

Just before the twenty-five-mile marker, he felt a stricken, horrible feeling in his abdomen, and immediately a bolt of chartreuse liquid shot from his mouth and splashed in front of him. It was still cold as he expelled it, as if his body were rejecting it so utterly it wasn't worth warming. He wasn't surprised by this. And he didn't slow down at all. In his mind things like this happened all the time. The few spectators standing nearby looked horrified, but Cassidy couldn't understand why, so natural a function did it seem.

He realized that he should have stopped trying to drink miles ago. All his systems had shut down save those necessary for placing one foot in front of the other.

He felt as if he had been running since the beginning of time. And his chorus had been, *Hallelujah, hallelujah.*

Another bolt of green liquid and he knew that was all there would be. A round of dry heaves produced nothing and finally they went away too.

He had passed the twenty-five-mile marker without realizing it and now he could make out just ahead the 25.2 marker, where an elderly gentleman Cassidy recognized as Walter Welch was calling the time out from a stopwatch. He had been the starter for every Southeastern University meet Cassidy had run in, and he was the starter the night Cassidy ran the race against John Walton that changed his life. Now he was reading the time with one mile to go. He smiled at Cassidy but kept reading: "Two oh four fifty-*four* . . . fifty-*five* . . . fifty-*six* . . ."

hallelujah hallelujah

One last mile, he thought, the road all runners come. His vision was now reduced to a small goofy circle and he could no longer make out even the blur of a runner in front of him.

In his jangled mind he could now envision, as if in the twilight before sleep, those squiggly lines of his life all over a multidimensional map of the world, his jaggy trail going everywhere from Florida to North Carolina, to Portland and Mexico City, Alaska and Nova Scotia, to Key West and Grand Bahama Island, to Norway and Athens, Greece. It went round and round myriad running tracks that dotted the landscape and up and down basketball courts and cross-country trails, and road race courses, all of it leading eventually up to the top of the continent and across a bridge into Canada and up to where he now put down his sad little red smudgy footprints, one by one.

I've seen your flag on the marble arch
Love is not a victory march
It's a sad and it's a broken hallelujah
hallelujah hallelujah

And in this infinitely expandable imagining, it seemed to him he could also see the squiggly lifelines of anyone else he wanted to. Bruce Denton's all over Michigan and then Ohio, and round and round the cinder tracks of the Midwest, then Florida's panhandle, then crossing the ocean to one last track and eleven and a half more circles to immortality.

hallelujah hallelujah

But he could see others too, Mizner's like his all over the place, ending abruptly in the jungles of Southeast Asia. And he could see the lines of the half-miler Benny Vaughn, and Hosford and Atkinson, the whole team, all the lifelines going off in all directions, most of them still moving like his, putting down little tracks toward some unseen goal, some moving target of achievement, some semblance of wealth, some jot of immortality, or perhaps just some measure of repose.

hallelujah hallelujah

He could see the moving lifelines of his uncles Lee and Neal, and his aunts and cousins in Cedar Mountain, and before them all the Pegrams from old George in Colonial Williamsburg through Daniel and William, then through all the Sarahs and Edwards, the Jameses and Marys, their tracks moving slowly down into the Carolinas, then to Tennessee and points beyond, all feisty and redheaded, full of energy and fretting to *get on with it*; all hell-bent for some promised land, some finish line beyond the horizon.

hallelujah hallelujah

He was now shrouded in the heavy mists of the Falls, and

he could not distinguish the roar of the falling waters from the roar in his head.

hallelujah hallelujah

He was dimly aware of people now, and aware that they seemed happy, excited. Aware that their happiness seemed to turn to alarm as he came closer.

It's a sad and it's a broken hallelujah

He didn't fully comprehend that he had crossed the finish line. There was no sense of finality. No sense of accomplishment or joy as he had experienced in other races. He was only aware that he had stopped, and that therefore it must be over.

hallelujah hallelujah

Someone was trying to make him move, but he could not. He looked down to see that he had stopped just beyond the finish line. Officials were tugging gently at his elbows to get him to walk forward so as not to block the next finishers.

He jerked his elbows violently away from them. "Stop!" he tried to scream, but it came out more like a croak.

"Please," one of them said, "the medical tent . . ."

Then Denton was there, holding him up bodily, the way he had done all those years ago.

"Easy, easy," he said, gently dragging him back from the finish line.

"Bruce," he said, trying to unstick his tongue from the roof of his mouth. "Bruce."

"It's okay. You're okay," Denton said. But Cassidy looked at him and saw he was crying. He thought to cry himself but there was no wet in him.

"I'm sorry, Bruce. I'm sorry," he whispered, unable to make real words yet. "They just pulled away. I tried. I really tried."

"Don't," Denton said. Others were coming around now and one official tried to separate them, but Denton pulled Cassidy away again and continued to hold him up.

"I tried to go with Benji," Cassidy whispered. "Then Tony too."

"I know."

"There was nothing I could do."

"You did great, Quenton. Nobody ever ran harder. Ever."

"At least Nubbins made it," Cassidy said. He pulled back, tried to stand on his own, wobbled, then threw an arm around Denton's shoulders and started to walk. They moved a few steps toward the medical tent, but had to stop again.

"Quenton . . ."

"Guy helps me off the ground . . ."

"Quenton . . ."

"And then runs on off to make the damn Olympic team. How do you like that?"

They finally got inside the tent and Denton got him to an open cot.

"Here, just lie down here and let them look at you." Denton left him with a group of trainers and doctors. Two strong hands gripped his shoulders and guided him to the cot. Cassidy turned around and looked down to see the cigar stub going round and round and the familiar grinning face. The patch on his windbreaker read: USOT HEAD TRAINER.

"Brady!" Cassidy croaked.

"Okay, sport," said Brady Grapehouse, "easy does it."

"Ahh," said Cassidy, easing himself down onto the canvas. His knees had stiffened up again and he still had to concentrate to keep his quadriceps from cramping. Two doctors began working on his various scrapes and wounds. Someone near his feet said "Jesus Christ," and began cutting off his shoes with surgical scissors. Denton came back.

"Quenton, did you hit your head when you fell?"

"Yeah, right."

"Seriously. Your head's bloody."

"No, Bruce, I didn't hit my head. Didn't I do enough damage for you?" He held out his hands, gestured with them at his knees.

"Quenton, don't you know what you've done?"

Cassidy looked at him warily, then looked away, wincing as someone poured disinfectant on his feet.

"I have failed to make the Olympic team in the last race of my career," he said softly.

"Stop it, Quenton. If you're kidding, stop it."

Cassidy lay back down, groaning, put his forearm over his eyes. The stuff they were cleaning his knees with stung like hell.

"Cass, don't you know? Really?"

Cassidy looked at him from under his forearm.

"You ran 2:10:54, Quenton," said Denton. "You were third. You made the Olympic team."

Cassidy lay on his back in the darkened hotel room. It was the only position he could get in that wasn't excruciating. He had pillows under his knees to keep his legs from straightening, which would cause his thighs to cramp even now. He had ice-packs on both knees and strapped to the bottoms of his feet. The curtains were tightly drawn and the room was nearly dark despite the bright edges of spring sunshine. The TV was on but the sound was off, some golf match.

Denton was trying to open the door quietly when Cassidy told him to just come in.

"Good! Get any sleep?"

"Hard to say. I think so. I keep having these dreams."

"I don't doubt it. But listen, considering everything, how do you feel?"

"I hurt all over, Bruce. That's just about how I feel. I didn't even know I landed on my hips, but I guess I did because they hurt too."

"Okay. To be expected, I guess. Take it easy."

Cassidy propped himself up so he could see Denton better.

"What I don't get and maybe you can help me with it," Cassidy said, "is why you won't talk to me. I don't get why I have to go back to my room and rest before the press conference. I don't know why nobody will tell me how I could have come in third with three guys clearly in front of me."

Denton grimaced.

"Well, Quenton, that's just it," he said. "Sandoval won, and Benji was second. You were third."

"So what happened to Nubbins? He bailed? Within sight of the finish?"

"I wanted to check something before I talked to you. I thought I knew but I wanted to be sure."

"So now you're sure. What the hell happened?"

"Jack Nubbins went to work for Coach Cornwall after school. Coach owned some trailer parks outside Kernsville, you know, as investments. Rented them cheap to grad students kind of thing. Jack was his manager slash handyman . . ."

"Bruce . . ."

"Yeah, well, old Jack didn't run much after school. He was still around Kernsville and all, but he basically—"

"Bruce," Cassidy was getting frustrated. "This isn't making any—"

"Quenton, Jack Nubbins died of a massive aneurysm two years ago."

48

Once . . .

C ASSIDY WATCHED ANDREA working hard up Blackberry Hill and it occurred to him that she was possibly more beautiful than she had been as a girl the first time he saw her on the warm-up loop in Kernsville.

"Ah," she said, standing before him with hands on hips, breathing hard, beads of perspiration glistening around the pink of her mouth. "Here is something I never thought I'd see in a million years."

Cassidy leaned back against the trunk of a mammoth live oak. "What's that?"

"Quenton Cassidy sitting under a tree."

"Sitting under a tree and eating an apple." He held out a green fruit the size of a golf ball, a small bite missing.

She gathered some pine needles and made a little place beside him.

"You know," Cassidy said, "back when I was in school, undergraduate, I was walking across the Plaza of the Americas after an economics class in Peabody and I was hotfooting it to the track to meet the guys for the Wednesday twelve-miler. I only had fifteen minutes to get there and get changed and it's a pretty good ways, if you remember, like at least a mile or so."

She reached over and touched him gently on the side of the face. "My poor bedraggled overachiever."

"Uh-huh. So I'm really walking fast by the bell tower and I look over and see this kid in the plaza, sitting under a tree reading a book and eating an apple."

"Yes?"

"That's it."

"What's it?"

"I saw this kid and he just looked so contented sitting there, and here I was, late as usual, a million things on my mind, and about seventeen miles to put in before the sun went down. It struck me that it would be the most wonderful thing in the world to just plop down under a tree with a book and an apple and do nothing. So I made a resolution that I would do that someday."

"And here you are."

"Here I am."

"It's taken you all this time . . ."

"We don't do those kinds of things because we're just so sure that there'll always be time later."

"Time and time."

"For decisions and revisions," he said, sitting up straight. "So this morning for the first time in my life I'm in the middle of a training run and I can't for the life of me figure out why. I'm training for a race that I'm never going to run."

"Oh," she said, looking down. "You know."

"Sure I know. They were talking about it even at the trials. Don't cry, sweetie. We've known all along it might happen."

"Bruce called me and asked me to drive up. He didn't know if you had heard or not and he wanted me to be here. He didn't know if—"

"I'd go crazy? Or *more* crazy? No, the coaches started calling the athletes days ago. They wanted us to know before the little peanut farmer went on television to retaliate against *American athletes* for what the *Russians* did to *Afghanistan! Christalmighty!*" He whipped the little apple about two hundred feet down into the valley where it bounced along, disintegrating along the way.

"I know."

"You know what it reminded me of? It reminded me of that scene in that Mel Brooks comedy where the black cowboy takes himself hostage. Grabs himself around the throat and points a gun at his own head and says, 'Next man makes a move and the nigger gets it!'"

"It's awful what they're doing. It doesn't make any sense at all."

"It's pretty bad. Almost three thousand years ago King Iphitos issued a quoit so all the soldiers could lay down their bronze swords and travel to Olympus to hold the games in peace."

"Quenton . . ."

"A thousand generations later and we're stupider than people who thought the sun was a chariot wheel and that stomach cancer was caused by swamp gas."

"I hate to see you like this but I know you're not mad at me."

He smiled, put his hand behind her neck and drew her closer.

"No," he said. "My whole life I figured that if I went to school and studied hard and got older and read a lot of things, sooner or later I would figure out where the grown-ups were. I realized during Vietnam that the leader of the free world and his toadies were the same student council dickheads you knew in high school, but I thought that was an aberration. I really thought that sooner or later if I kept looking I would figure out where the grown-ups were."

"Oh, sweetie."

"I guess we shouldn't dwell on the comings and goings of people in suits."

"No, we shouldn't. They'll break your heart just about every time," she said.

"To be honest, after Munich, the Olympics never meant the same to me as they did when I was growing up."

"You're not serious. It's all you used to talk about."

"I know. I still wanted to be a believer. It's taken a while for things to really sink in. And now the drug thing is coming on, and it's only going to get worse, athletes selling their souls for a headline and a few bucks. The corporations are sniffing around, trying to figure a way to associate themselves with anything the public thinks has some integrity left. You mix in serious money and global politics and you've got the old witches' brew all over again. When I was a kid I used to think the Olympics were the essence of sports, but I know now they're not. They're not anymore."

"Okay, so what is?"

"Doing something that's impossible to do. That's it. Nobody will ever run a four-minute mile. Physically can't be done. You can't drive a golf ball three hundred yards. Never happen. No one can throw a hundred-mile-an-hour fastball and no one can hit it out of a stadium. All of it is beyond human capacity. But athletes do these things all the time. They're still just as impossible, but we do them every day. Everyone scoffs at us right up to the time we do them, and then they slap us on the butts and want to know what we eat for breakfast."

"Oh, Quenton . . ."

"Don't get me wrong. I'm deliriously happy I made the team again. That was completely impossible too. Everyone said so. But I did it anyway. And I'm truly happy that I started the whole thing. These past two years have been wonderful, a rare and unexpected gift, and even if I hadn't made it, I would be glad I tried. So now we'll have a great time on our consolation trip to Fukuoka and we won't go to Moscow. Big deal. I'll come back and enjoy playing out what's left of my second childhood. Who knows? They say you can actually make money running road races these days. But missing the Olympics won't kill me, believe me."

"I believe you," she said, laughing.

"Oh yeah?"

She touched his neck again, leaned over and kissed him. "I believe everything you tell me," she said.

"*That's* not a good policy. Come on, let's jog back. I want to show you something."

The heat of the day was coming on as they lazily braked their way down Blackberry Hill. At the bottom was a thicket of Carolina jasmine humming with bumblebees. The combination of scent and sound made them both half close their eyes and go *mmmmmmm.*

It was mostly cool in the shaded parts of the trail and a pleasant breeze was blowing through Sidecar Doobey's pecan grove. It felt almost chilly on their glistening skin. They ran in silence most of the way.

When they got to the red-clay driveway, he made her stop, drew her close, and kissed her really hard.

"Hey," she said.

"Thank you," he said, "for everything. All of it."

"Couldn't have done it without me?"

"No, I could have. But I wouldn't have had much of a reason to."

"Quenton . . ."

She was having a hard time with this.

"That's sweet. I . . ." She looked up into his face and thought that he looked happy. Happier than she could remember seeing him look. It occurred to her that in all his moments of glad grace she had seen satisfaction, perhaps, and she had seen contentment or relief, but she had rarely seen what she would call happiness. Now she saw it in him and felt somewhere within the crystal matrix of her being that perhaps she did have something to do with it after all.

"Come on," he said, taking her hand and leading her down the driveway to the little cabin.

Inside, he gestured to the stack of composition books on the coffee table. She had seen these before, but now each one bore a circled number in the upper right corner of the cover. There were sixteen in all.

"Your journals?" She picked up the top one. "You've always been weird about these. You're saying I can read them?"

"No, I'm saying you *have* to read them. And it isn't a journal. It's more of a story."

"A story. Fiction? What's it called?"

"I don't know. I just wanted to get all this down somehow, to capture it all in one place. I wanted to have something like this so one day when I'm old and creaking around with a cane I could pick this up and remember what it was like to be young and strong and fast again. I wanted to be able to remember what it was like when I was once a runner."

She leaned back in the easy chair and opened the cover of the first very worn book and began reading: *The night joggers were out as usual* . . .

Acknowledgments

MY BROTHER JERRY rushed to my hospital bedside and helped bring me back to life, and he and my sister-in-law Annie offered both loving encouragement and a winter redoubt during this prolonged campaign. Lieutenant Colonel David Gould, USAF (ret.), an old family friend, neighbor, and all-around good guy, gave me timely technical help on the Spectre gunship. My old and good friend Tom Raynor was there before, during, after, and then some. Thanks again, Coach. Old friend and sometimes racing competitor Benji Durden, who appears as a character in this story, helped tremendously with his detailed recollections of the amazing 1980 U.S. Olympic Marathon Trials. My old friend and colleague Ron Wiggins, as he did with *Once a Runner*, offered invaluable editorial suggestions. Caldwell and Alice Smith were spiritual and intellectual lighthouse beacons during my seasonal migrations. Nola Pegram Duffy at patch.net was and is a wonderful storehouse of Pegram family lore. My long-suffering and ever-patient publisher and sounding board, Garth Battista, and my current editor at Scribner, Brant Rumble, both helped shepherd this book into print. And finally, my brother Jim, to whom this book is dedicated, offered up his heart-stopping experiences in Vietnam, a place I've never been. Thanks, y'all, and I love you each and every one.

A SCRIBNER READING GROUP GUIDE

Again to Carthage
John L. Parker, Jr.

Description

Quenton Cassidy returns in John L. Parker Jr.'s *Again to Carthage,* the sequel to *Once a Runner*. Having won a silver medal at the Olympics, Quenton attempts to settle into a normal life: attending law school and then working for a firm, living the good life in Florida with friends, running only casually. But there is something missing, and he knows it. After the deaths of two men close to him leave him shaken, Quenton decides that with the help of friend and coach Bruce Denton he will train for the Olympics again, but this time for the marathon. As he trains and pushes himself to the brink of human endurance, Quenton struggles to decide who he is and what his life can and should be.

Questions and Topics for Discussion

1. What do you believe is the primary motivation for Quenton's decision to try for another Olympic medal: Coming in second? Dissatisfaction and boredom with everyday life? Depression? Something else?

2. Quenton takes a dim view of post-Olympic life for medalists. Think about athletes you watched place in past Olympics. Do you know where they are now? What kind of lives are they leading?

3. *Again to Carthage* is told primarily from Quenton Cassidy's point of view, with brief interludes following pivotal characters such as Mizner, Henry, and Andrea. Why do you think the author chose to tell the story this way? How do these interludes affect the reading experience?

4. Parker includes a lot of running terminology—*fartleks*, for example. Were you already familiar with the vocabulary of running, or did you learn it along the way?

5. Quenton's drive to train as a marathoner is partly informed by the deaths of his relative Henry and friend Mizner, and he comes face-to-face with his own mortality as he struggles to finish the qualifying run. How does this paradox of extreme fitness accompanied by extreme physical trauma help Quenton deal with his losses?

6. Parker writes lovingly of the South, particularly Florida and North Carolina. How does geography play a role in the plot's development? Do the vividly described settings enhance the story, or are they background? Can you imagine living and/or training at the Poutin' House?

7. The sabotage attempt on Quenton during the trials may seem extreme, but in the 2004 Olympic men's marathon, a disturbed Greek religious agitator shoved Olympic men's marathon lead runner Vanderlei de Lima off the course, costing him the lead. While this real-life interference wasn't a personal attack, it does highlight the

delicate nature of the trials and events, in which the slightest unplanned incident can cost an athlete a chance for glory. Should judges take these kinds of incidents into account? What is the fairest way to deal with interference?

8. On page 179, Roland and Quenton discuss the theory that there are really only two sports: ball and chase. Do you agree? Which do you prefer? Which category does your favorite sport fall into? Can you think of sports that don't seem to fit this theory?

9. It would seem that sports in general, and particularly the Olympics, should rely entirely on the skill of the athletes. Quenton's unofficial "trial" for drug use points out the political side of athletics. How much have the politics of judging tainted the Olympics? How much do you trust the scoring and judging systems to be free of personal bias? Can you think of any examples of biased or faulty officiating or judging that affected the outcome of an event?

10. Quenton and his friends are constantly telling each other stories, both true and apocryphal. How does the author use these internal stories to shape the narrative? Are they merely entertaining anecdotes or do they connect to the plot in a more profound way?

11. Over the course of his training, Quenton frequently experiences the euphoria some call "runner's high" (although he dismisses it at one point). Have you ever experienced this high in running or another sport or activity? Would you agree that it can be, as Bruce suggests, a form of self-medication?

12. The novel ends before Quenton ever reaches the Olympics and Quenton tells Andrea that it doesn't matter. Do you believe him when he says it? Is it enough for him to know that he could have gone? How have his goals changed from those of his youth

13. If you are already a runner, how does Quenton's story resonate with your own experiences? If you are not, how does it shape your ideas about running and athletics? Does it inspire you in any way?

14. If you have read *Once a Runner*: Which characters were you happy to see return, and which did you miss? If you have not: Which characters do you wish you knew more about? Were there passages that you felt you didn't fully understand because you were missing backstory?

Tips to Enhance Your Book Club

Further reading on running:
- Haruki Murakami, *What I Talk About When I Talk About Running*
- Christopher McDougall, *Born to Run*
- Danny Dreyer, *Chi Running*
- Alan Sillitoe, *The Loneliness of the Long-Distance Runner*

On page 224, the fictional Quenton runs alongside real-life runner and Olympic medalist Frank Shorter. Shorter has been described by many as a driving force in bringing running to public attention, and is still active. Check out an interview with Shorter from the 2009 Bolder Boulder 10K on how running has evolved at http://www.youtube.com/watch?v=J1q5j_VxoU4.

It may be too soon to cheer on Team USA at the 2012 Summer Olympics, but the USA Track & Field website calendar lists championship races and qualifying meets for the next several years: http://www.usatf.org/calendars/teamUSA .aspx.